Praise for The Br

M000308964

THE BREAKU

"A heartwarming and funny story about friendship, romance, and the heart-wrenching reality of breakups—while busting out some spot-on dating advice along the way."

— Liz Tuccillo,
Bestselling Co-Author of *He's Just Not That Into You* and
Executive Story Editor of HBO's Emmy Award-Winning Series
Sex and the City

"Warm, charming, and flat-out funny—a delightful debut!"

— Sarah Bird,
Bestselling Author of *The Boyfriend School* and *The Gap Year*

"A pleasure from beginning to end. The Breakup Doctor is as wise as it is funny."

— Sherry Thomas,
New York Times Bestselling Author of
The Luckiest Lady in London and *My Beautiful Enemy*

"I was expecting a cute quick read, what I got was much more. Brook's character is great. She is well-rounded and her path to self-discovery through her break-up was realistic and at times heart-warming."

— *Chick Lit Books*

"If I didn't know better I'd say Brook was based on me; her story certainly parallels my life. Hitting rock bottom is the best thing that can happen to anyone (in hindsight) and laughter is the best medicine. The Breakup Doctor is packed with entertaining, good advice."

— Donna Barnes,
Relationship Coach, Author of *Giving Up Junk-food Relationships*,
and Founder of the Date Better Online Dating Network

the
breakup
doctor

The Breakup Doctor Series
by Phoebe Fox

THE BREAKUP DOCTOR (#1)
BEDSIDE MANNERS (#2)
(*March 2015*)

the breakup doctor

phoebe fox

HENERY PRESS

THE BREAKUP DOCTOR
The Breakup Doctor Series
Part of the Henery Press Chick Lit Collection

First Edition
Trade paperback edition | June 2014

Henery Press
www.henerypress.com

ISBN-13: 978-1-940976-15-0

Printed in the United States of America

I'm not usually much on book dedications, but I offer this one wholeheartedly to Liz Tuccillo and Greg Behrendt, the wise, loving, protective older siblings every woman should have. I also dedicate it to my husband, who was so, so worth waiting—and wading—through every other relationship to find. To my mom, who is not Viv. And I dedicate it to women. Because you are beautiful, and strong, and smart, and worthy. And if you're not quite ready to believe that yet, then until you are, along with Brook, I will believe it for you.

ACKNOWLEDGMENTS

Writing can be such a solitary pursuit, but the process of creating a novel—at least for me—is a cumulative effort of people without whom this story would not exist. I offer each of them my heartfelt, grateful thanks:

First, the knowledgeable, accommodating, indispensable team at Henery Press: my keen-eyed and constructive editor, Kendel Flaum; the savvy and always-available Art Molinares; Chloe Harper, and all the in-house chickens. Without fail, the Hen House team has gone beyond my every expectation of what a publisher does, and I consider it a privilege to be among their authors. Their unflagging enthusiasm for *The Breakup Doctor* has been immensely gratifying.

I would never have reached this point without the unswerving support and encouragement of my agent, Courtney Miller-Callihan at Sanford J. Greenberger. Not only did she love this story from the beginning, but she stuck by it with endless patience, diligence, and conviction until we found the perfect home for it. I am a lucky writer to have someone like her in my corner.

Laura Wright, PhD, a counseling psychologist at Florida Gulf Coast University who specializes in college student mental health and training and supervision of new psychologists, was generous with her time and professional expertise, so that I wasn't entirely shooting my mouth off in ignorance. Any instances of bad advice on Brook's part are my own fault; Laura was a wealth of information and excellent input, and I would never hesitate to entrust her with my mental well-being.

Dear friends had the fortitude and tolerance to read early drafts of this story and offer me their feedback, which was invaluable if I was successful in "leaving out the parts that people skip," as Elmore Leonard says. I owe a great debt of gratitude to Kathryn Haydn Hays, for her lightning-fast emergency read and brilliant comments that focused as always on what was best for the book, not my delicate ego; to Stephanie Davis, for helping me laugh at our dating sagas that helped form the idea; Marcie and Doug Walter, Jenny Smith, Richard LeMay, Merritt Graham, and Jan Davis, for being early readers and well-loved friends. A shout-out to English teacher extraordinaire Connie Corley, for nurturing the seed.

Thanks to Leah Loftin of LL Kent and Paige Throckmorton, as well as Lori Virdure and Amy Ewing of Langford Market, for their enthusiasm for this book. These generous women went well above and beyond the call of duty and helped me feel part of a team in bringing The Breakup Doctor to life.

Author, producer, and dating savant Liz Tuccillo has long influenced my writing and my life through her work. How lucky I was to discover she's as gracious and generous as her work suggests. My bottomless thanks to her for her kindness and support.

Authors Sarah Bird and Sherry Thomas have influenced me in ways they may not even be aware of. Their writing has nourished my imagination; their generosity and support have nourished my heart. Donna Barnes, relationship expert and founder of the terrific online dating site Date Better, is as kind and generous as she is wise in the ways of dating.

Kelly Harrell, Amber Novak, and John J. Asher, gifted writers in their own right, are the reason this book is in your hands right now. My Pennies, you allow me to learn and grow by working with all of you. Even as a writer, I can't find enough words to thank you: For your insightful, generous, and enlightening critiques of my manuscript in drafts ad nauseam. For delicious dinners and brain-sparking, wine-fueled discussions on writing. For limitless friendship, support, and commiseration. You three are almost entirely to credit for anything good in my writing. Your friendship is every bit as intrinsic. The multitalented Amber Novak also made me look better in photographs than I had any natural right to.

My mother, Carole Hlavin Burns, has ever been my first and most constant fan in any of my pursuits, and her admittedly biased belief in me has never faltered. Mom, in Brook's words, "You are amazing."

As I did in life, I have saved my husband for last. Joel, we met farther down the road than we wanted to, but I will be forever grateful for every single delay, because the journey ultimately led to you.

one

It was Sasha who gave me the idea. The day my life was literally reduced to rubble by a wrecking ball, my best friend called at six a.m., while I was still lying in Kendall's king-size bed at his condo, our legs entwined and sleep crusted in our eyes.

I answered my cell groggily and heard Sasha's voice. "Can you come over?" There was a familiar hint of distress in her tone.

I was used to these odd-hour phone calls from my best friend, but Kendall was not, and he grumbled as I slipped from bed. I leaned over to kiss him. "Go back to sleep."

She was waiting in the driveway when I pulled up. Her long blond hair was perfect, even at this hour, her body tanned and toned in an adorable Victoria's Secret short set I couldn't have pulled off even prior to the freshman fifteen I still wore fourteen years later, and looking gorgeous without a scrap of makeup on. She started talking as soon as I opened my door.

"It's Peter. He's cheating."

"Is that the guy you met at the speed-dating thing?" I'd long since stopped trying to keep names straight with Sasha's dates. It wasn't like they lasted long enough for me to worry about it.

"God, he's such an asshole! How could I not see it? If he'll cheat *with* you, he'll cheat *on* you. You taught me that."

"Sasha..." I searched for the gentlest way to phrase my question. "Didn't you guys only go out on the one date?"

She rolled her eyes. "Oh, come on, Brook. I told you how well we clicked. I wasn't the only one who sensed the connection—he was feeling it too. I can't believe he'd go behind my back with someone else."

There was no point trying to rationalize with Sasha at times like this. Rationality played little part in these proceedings. But I also had to tread carefully. She hated it when she thought I was "therapizing" her.

"Forget him," I said firmly, wrapping one arm around her and walking us into her apartment. "He wears his sunglasses around his neck, for God's sake."

"A Type Four? You think?"

Sasha and I had categorized the small pool of available men in the dating wasteland of Fort Myers, Florida. Type Fours—slick, self-satisfied playboys who dated way under their age range—displayed an overzealous use of hair product, all-designer-brand outfits, and inappropriate accessorizing: i.e., an abundance of jewelry, or sunglasses worn anywhere but over the eyes.

"Textbook. And he's a *chef!*" I didn't want to lose momentum, so I led her to the living room and sat her down on the sofa, still talking. "It's a known fact that all chefs are alcoholics. Or recovering alcoholics, which is no fun either, because then you can't drink around him, even though you're not the one with the problem, and you know you're going to lose at least one or two date nights a week while he goes to AA meetings. Where statistically most recovering substance abusers hook up, because they have the twelve-step thing in common."

Sasha laughed—and that was my goal. "That's not true. AA bylaws prohibit fraternization among twelve-steppers."

I forgot—last year she'd tried pretending she was in the program. She thought it would be a great way to meet new men.

"Whatever, Sash. Peter wasn't the one. You're going to find the right guy."

"I don't know," she said dispiritedly, fingering her red velvet sofa. "How much longer do I have to wait? I swear, Brook, I don't know how you pulled through when Michael—"

"Don't." Suddenly my throat felt choked with the sickly sweet taste of buttercream and the gluey thickness of fondant, the flavors that coated my tongue the last day I'd seen my former fiancé.

"Brook, there's no reason to be embarrassed—"

"I'm not. I'm just done with that. I've moved past it. It's history."

Sasha stared, then sighed, then heaved herself back against the cushions. "Sometimes I think you're the only thing that keeps me sane in the dating world."

Her basic premise of sanity could be debated. But now wasn't the time to point that out.

I squeezed her arm where it rested on the cushion between us. "Hang in there, Sash. There really is someone out there who'll want to be with you more than anyone else. Who'll always be there for you."

She sniffled and let out a shaky chuckle. "Yeah. That's you, Brook."

I gave my best friend a hug—that was what she always needed most after one of her relationship crises anyway. The talking was just what got us there.

After a few moments she sat back and wiped her non-red, un-swollen eyes—Sasha even cried prettily. "You're a genius at this stuff," she said. "I swear, you ought to go into business giving relationship advice."

I left Sasha to get ready for an interview she had been assigned and rushed off to take a shower at my own house, a fixer-upper I'd bought in the wrong state of mind last year, blithely congratulating myself for averting today's major catastrophe.

Her words didn't sink in until later.

Running late, I screeched into the parking lot of my McGregor Boulevard office—and saw a chunk of the building missing, a wrecking ball dangling in midair above it from a crane.

I left the car running and leaped out the driver's side, racing toward the building, past a bulldozer and a man in a yellow plastic suit spraying the wreckage with a fire hose, till I was yanked to a halt by thick arms wrapping around me from behind.

I wriggled to get free. "What the—Let go! I have to get in there!"

"Ma'am, you can't go inside."

I twisted to face my captor, a burly man in a shiny black protective suit and dark goggles that made it look like I was being restrained by a six-foot cockroach. I took a breath, willing myself to calm down.

"You don't understand." I spoke quickly. "That's my office. People may be inside. Other tenants. My patients."

A crash behind me had me whirling back around to see the wrecking ball rise up from the destruction, then drop back down like a lead tea bag.

The arms still restraining me tightened. "No, ma'am," the man said. "The building was cleared this morning."

I tried fruitlessly once again to shake off his iron hold on me. "What about my things! I have to get—"

"I can't let you go in, ma'am. All the tenants were notified to be out by last week."

"What?" I turned back to look at him, and his hold loosened as I finally stopped struggling. "Notified...? We weren't—"

"Brook!"

The voice came from the back of the parking lot, and I looked over to see my colleagues Tom and Uta standing near their cars, gesturing me over. The man let me go and I hurried over. They looked grim, Uta's face carved into an angry, forbidding expression. I think. Uta is German, and her face often looks like that.

"Thank god you're both okay. What the hell is going on?" I said.

"Ahzbuhztuz," Uta barked at me.

I cocked my head, not sure if I was meant to understand her or if she was clearing her throat of dust. "What?"

"Asbestos," Tom clarified, running a weary hand across his thinning blond hair. "They found asbestos."

"The building is condemned. It's all over. We're finished." This from Uta, who, in true Teutonic fashion, could always be called upon to put the best spin on a situation. Tom nodded morosely. "This is crazy," I said angrily. "They didn't even notify us!" Tom and Uta exchanged a look, and my stomach sank. "Tom... Guys, *did* they notify us?"

Tom coughed and looked over my head toward the destruction of our offices, and Uta gave an existential shrug. "Who can say what was in all the letters?" she intoned. "Americans hide their meanings in bureaucratic jargon."

I stared at her, then at Tom. This time the sudden crash behind me didn't even make me jump.

Unlike me, a licensed mental health counselor, my partners were *"real* doctors," as my mom was always quick to point out: Tom a psychologist, and Uta a psychiatrist. But for all their education and training, the practicalities of running a business often seemed beyond them.

"Jesus," I said slowly. "Jesus. Okay. We have to tell our patients...we'll have to look for new office space. We can start today."

Tom looked away. Uta looked like a shaken soufflé.

"I don't know," she said, her tone flat as the northern plains of the Fatherland. "Maybe this is the sign."

"What *sign?*"

"*The* sign. The signal. The reason I am waiting for to make changes." Uta nodded once, firmly, as though something had been made clear. "I think maybe it's time I go back home, to Germany. Be with family."

In all the years we'd been working together, not once had Uta ever mentioned any personal life at all. She didn't even have pictures in her office. I had begun to suspect she might be a highly efficient German Borg.

At her offended expression I covered my disbelieving laugh with a cough. "Back to Germany? But what about your patients?" I asked. "They need you, Uta." The thought of Hauptsturmführer Uta stirring around in someone's subconscious was a terrifying one, but her patients kept coming back. "*We* need you."

"Your emotional blackmail isn't a compelling argument, Ms. Ogden," she barked. "And therapists should be above it."

Now I remembered why we'd never gotten close.

"Maybe she's right," Tom said, shoulders sagging. "Maybe it's just time."

"Oh, come on now. You're just feeling discouraged. I'll take care of everything. Give me till the end of the week and I'll have us something even better than this place." The thought weighed like cement on my chest, but I remained jolly as Santa Claus.

Tom looked everywhere but at me, like a dog following the progress of a fly. "Yeah, Brook...the thing is..." He glanced over at Uta, who gave him a look of either encouragement or intestinal distress. "I'm going over to the Centeredness Center."

His announcement was punctuated with another sickening crash behind me, and the cracks and thuds of concrete raining to the ground.

I gaped. Tom stood there with an apologetic expression, staring over my shoulder.

Like a cut-rate retail massage business, the brand-new Centeredness Center offered counseling packages to "members" and kept a stable of therapists in house. Its plush Naples offices, about thirty minutes south of Fort Myers, were designed to impress, with attractive women in tight-fitting saffron robes behind the front desk, a smoothie bar in the lobby, and themed "meditation areas" throughout its five thousand bamboo-floored square feet. It was slick, streamlined, soulless...and had been the butt of most of our office jokes ever since it had opened.

I knew better than to laugh now, though. Tom looked too embarrassed.

"Oh," I said, at a loss. "Oh...well, okay. Wow. Congratulations. To you both, I guess. That... Those seem like...like really positive choices. And forward movement, great..." Psychobabble—literally.

Concrete crashed behind me. I read an article once about how a building is demolished. If you remove its support structure at a certain precise point, everything above it will simply collapse. The wrecking ball is just the trigger for the demolition. It's gravity that brings the building down.

"Thanks for understanding, Brook," Tom said, and now the apology in his tone was earnest. "I've been talking to them for a while—they're really taking off down there—and—"

"No worries, Tom. This could be a great opportunity for you. For both of you." I made myself look happy for the two of them.

But Tom didn't seem to notice; a relieved smile came over his face. "You're always solid as a rock, Brook. Nothing fazes you."

"Yes. You are tough." Uta nodded, startling me with her approval. "What is the expression? Stone-cold?"

I would have corrected the idiom, but at that point, fiercely maintaining the smile that now felt frozen and carved into my face as my professional life literally crumbled behind me, I wasn't sure that Uta hadn't said exactly what she meant.

two

I'd spent six years building a practice with Tom and Uta. Struggled to build a client list, a reputation. Worked ridiculous hours and invested untold amounts of energy into helping the people who came to me understand and solve the problems that were keeping them stalled in their lives. Now, in a morning, all of it was gone.

I went home and made pages of notes for my options: rents at various buildings around town (which I couldn't afford), names of existing practices (that weren't hiring), and lists of every therapist I knew to see whether anyone was looking to start a new practice with a partner (they weren't).

When I finally came to a dead end, I called all of my patients, reluctantly making referrals for those who felt they couldn't hang around waiting until I found an option for my practice.

I even, to my shame, pulled up the Web site for the Centeredness Center to see if they were still hiring. "The Centeredness Center openheartedly welcomes mental health practitioners from all disciplines and schools of thought," the Staff page said. "PhDs only, please."

No matter how long I looked at the information in front of me, it continued to tell me the same thing: Unless I could come up with a big chunk of money—fast—I was temporarily out of business.

I scoured my brain for more ideas while I drove to Kendall's condo and started dinner. Since we'd started dating, I hadn't spent a single night at my own dilapidated house, and he'd recently suggested we make it official and I move in.

I'd asked for some time to think it over, and I hadn't given him my answer yet. I knew he wasn't Michael—was nothing at all like Michael. Kendall was stable and solid—a hardworking, successful investment broker on the way up, not a flighty musician chasing fame and glory. But we'd only been together a few months, and I'd learned my lesson the hard way about rushing into commitment.

By the time I heard his key in the door it was almost nine o'clock. The chicken was like rubber, the tomatoes deflated into wrinkled red lumps, the asparagus soggy and limp. He appeared in the kitchen doorway as I was shoveling the mess onto two plates, the tired circles under his blue eyes giving his sheepish expression a mournful Basset hound look.

"Sorry."

I shrugged. "It's okay."

"I should have called."

"You were busy." I tried to let it go, and set our plates on the breakfast bar. "It's not as good as when it was fresh."

Kendall glanced at it apologetically. "I already ate with a client."

"Oh." I picked up the plates and whisked their contents into the stainless-steel trash can beside the counter.

"Hey!"

"It's too overcooked to reheat." I clattered the plates to the granite countertop.

"Brook..." He moved closer to me, so close I could feel his body heat radiating against me. He put his broad hands on my shoulders and turned me around, looking into my eyes. "What's wrong?"

Recrimination flooded me. I was pouting. That wasn't a healthy or adult way to handle my feelings. I took a breath.

"I'm sorry. I'm frustrated and annoyed because I had a terrible day at work today, and I wanted to talk about it with you, and you weren't here. And then you didn't call, and I felt unimportant. And throwing away dinner was a childish way of demonstrating my anger and hurt."

Kendall grinned, and then he started to laugh. I glared at him until he said, "Every man in the world ought to date a psychologist. They're the only women who actually tell you what's on their mind."

The grin, the laugh bubbling up from his chest and vibrating against me as he held me, and the sheer relief of telling him what I felt all combined to let my stomach finally unclench, and I relaxed against him and let myself smile.

"I'm not a psychologist," I said out of habit.

Kendall pulled away and kissed the tip of my nose. "Close enough." He led me to the sofa and pulled me down beside him, and the empty feeling in my chest bloomed into warmth as I told him about my day.

It wasn't until he asked about Sasha's emergency this morning—it felt like days ago now—that I realized my answer had been staring me in the face all along.

I was up so early the next morning I even beat Kendall out of bed, jittery with anticipation, and sharply at eight thirty I pulled through the chain-link gate at Sasha's office and into a visitor's space. The *Tropic Times* building was located just outside of downtown Fort Myers, on MLK Boulevard in an area of town a few blocks off the river dotted with run-down little apartment buildings, hotels that were two-star in their heyday forty years ago, and one of the highest crime rates in the city.

Sasha came out to the lobby when the receptionist called her to announce me, but the expression she wore didn't match her initial excitement when I'd run my idea by her.

"I'm not sure this is going to work out today," she said in a low tone, confirming my suspicions.

"What's the matter?"

She just shook her head and motioned for me to follow her into the inner sanctum.

Like every newspaper office I'd ever seen in the movies, the news area was a bleak, cheerless mélange of messy desks clustered together without even the courtesy of cubicles in most places. People were hunched ferret-like over keyboards, their faces washed sickly white from the overhead fluorescents and necrotic blue from the light reflecting from their monitors.

"Head down. Head *down*," Sasha hissed as we made our way through the chaos, and she pushed me toward the stairwell in the back corner.

"What was that about?" I asked when the door shut behind us.

She shook her head. "Manny Erwin. Sports editor. You don't want to know."

"Sash!" I gave a long-suffering sigh as I followed her up the stairs. "You know better than to date at work."

She shot me a withering glare over her shoulder. "I didn't 'date him at work,' Brook. Don't jump to conclusions."

Guilt plucked at me. "Sorry."

"I dated him when he was at the Cape Coral office. How was I supposed to know he'd get transferred?" She shoved open the door on the second floor and we emerged from the bowels of hell. It was quiet enough to hear soft classical music piped soothingly throughout the floor, with polite cubicles offering employees at least the illusion of privacy and giving the impression that the floor was nearly unoccupied.

"Wow," I said.

"Yeah. Features department. Much more civilized." She pointed us over to a corner, where behind a partition her desk nestled fairly removed from the others. I took the burnt-orange upholstered chair wedged into the narrow space in front of her metal desk, and Sasha plopped onto the desk instead of into the swivel chair behind it.

"So what about this not working out?" I asked again.

Sasha sighed. "This may be the wrong day to do this," she said in a low tone.

"What's the matter?"

"Shhh!" Sasha glanced around like Maxwell Smart on a caper.

"It's Lisa, my editor. I don't think this is a good day to pitch your idea. This morning she—"

"I've only got a minute," a female voice barked out. "What is it?"

Sasha jumped to her feet and stretched her face into a toothy smile at the woman who'd just appeared at the opening of her cubicle. The woman was short and almost skeletally thin, with glasses too blocky for her face and hair of an indeterminate not-quite-blond shade hanging limply on either side of her cheeks. Most startling were her eyes, the color of her irises lost amid the bright red sclera surrounding them. Unlike Sasha, this poor woman apparently did *not* cry prettily.

"Oh, Lisa," Sasha said. "I meant to call you. The timing is all off. Let's reschedule for—"

"What are you talking about?" Lisa asked impatiently, flopping into the chair behind Sasha's desk. "You wanted a meeting. I'm here. She's here. I've got five minutes. Go." She fixed her swollen, reddened eyes on her watch, and then on me.

Lisa looked like a taxidermist's experiment in capturing human grief, her face frozen into stiff lines of pain and her eyes blank and far away. I found myself wholeheartedly agreeing with Sasha that this was *not* the day to pitch her the idea I'd come up with yesterday—writing a few advice articles in the paper for singles—and wishing I'd made a quiet escape before Lisa had shown up. I wondered if she would notice—or move—if I gathered my things and slipped out past where she was slumped in Sasha's chair.

I couldn't say what was natural: *Woman, what on earth is troubling you?* I had just met Lisa Albrecht, and she was Sasha's boss, not a client or a friend. But I couldn't ignore that she was sitting there clearly in pain, either.

"I'm sorry," I said, leaning forward. "It looks like you might be having a really tough day. Are you okay?"

No sooner had the words left my lips than Lisa's eyes spilled over and a choked-off, animal sound came out of her mouth. And then the dam burst and she was sobbing, but in a silent way that was horrible to watch, her face growing dark with the effort she was making to hold it in. She straightened and rose from the chair and made a vague wave in our direction, turning to leave. Her shoulders were heaving, and inhuman noises were coming from her, and she was heading back out to the main floor—where anyone encountering her would think she was either having a seizure or needed the Heimlich.

Sasha's eyes were like ping-pong balls, but she seemed frozen in place, so I rushed to Lisa's side, putting a restraining, supportive arm around her. "Okay, Lisa. Okay."

"I'm fine," she said, but she stopped walking, just standing there, stalled, at the entrance to the cubicle.

"Of course you are," I said, keeping my voice calm and relaxed, as though I expected this were something that happened daily at the *Tropic Times* offices.

Lisa pulled halfheartedly away, her words coming out jerky. "I need...to get...work."

"Yes, I know you do." I was all business, a matter-of-fact Mary Poppins with an unusually wayward ward. "But why don't you sit back down for a minute and we'll get you some water?"

"No, I... No water—" Another of those helpless strangling sounds came out of her throat. "I'm... This isn't... I..." Lisa again tried to push past me, but I tightened my hold on her shoulders.

"Lisa, you're the boss," I said firmly. "You can't go out there like this."

Lisa stared straight ahead for a long, long moment, and then tears started spilling again from her eyes like a silent Niagara, and she collapsed against me as if I had stuck a pin in her. "I can't... I just... He—ggghhh." The end of whatever she was trying to say was lost in another choked sound from her throat.

I guided her back to Sasha's chair. Sasha gesticulated ferociously at me, but I couldn't tear my eyes off of Lisa long enough to make out whatever she was trying to convey. I made a sideways C of my hand and mimed pouring something down my throat, and Sasha rolled her eyes and made a clear "duh" expression that told me that was what she'd been trying to get across. She darted out of the office while I knelt in front of Lisa and patted her hands in her lap.

"I'm not... I don't usually... This is mortifying," Lisa said, sniffling.

I reached over and plucked a handful of tissues from a box on Sasha's desk. "Please don't be embarrassed. People tend to do this in front of me at least once or twice a day. I'm a therapist."

"Oh." She took the tissues I handed her and swiped at her red nose. "You are?"

I nodded. "I'm in practice here in town." *Or will be again. Soon. If you put me on the payroll.*

Lisa gave up on stanching the flow from her nose and blew loudly into the tissue. "A therapist. God, isn't that just what I need." I couldn't tell if the comment was meant rhetorically.

"You're doing great, Lisa." This from Sasha as she came back into the cubicle with a paper cone of water in each hand.

Lisa looked flatly at my friend with a quelling expression. "Really? This is 'great'?" She turned her eyes back to me. "My husband. He..." She took in a long, shaky breath. "He walked out on me."

This is one of the odd side effects of my career. The same way people will confide their medical complaints to someone as soon as they find out she's a doctor, or spill their personal gripes to an acquaintance when they learn he's a lawyer, I am often gifted with the most intimate revelations in casual conversation as soon as someone learns I'm in the mental health field. I've had complete strangers come out of the closet to me within fifteen minutes of meeting them, or confess to having been abused, or tell me they secretly cross-dress, or—more often than you might think—break down into sobs, as Lisa Albrecht had. When I'd assured her this was nothing new for me, I wasn't just being polite.

"I'm sorry. What a fool he is." I said it to cheer her, to bolster her confidence, even though at the moment, with her eyes swollen almost shut and red as raw steak, mucus streaming from her nose, she didn't exactly look like the one that got away. I took one of the paper cones of water from Sasha and held it out to Lisa.

"Out of nowhere..." Lisa said. "I had no idea."

I nodded, trying to look sage while discreetly remaining silent. This was Sasha's boss, after all. And, the practical part of my mind insisted, hopefully mine soon.

"This is sort of Brook's specialty," Sasha piped up.

Lisa turned those throbbing eyes on me. "Really? What do you mean?"

I pushed the paper cone toward Lisa again, though she didn't seem to see it. "She means relationships are one of the areas I work a lot with in my practice," I said, with a downward inflection I hoped gave the sentence an air of finality. I did not want Sasha launching into a résumé of the times I'd talked her down from this same ledge. Not in front of her boss.

Sasha made a scoffing noise. "Please. You're a savant with this kind of thing."

I tried through best friend telepathy to send her a message: *Don't say any more, Sash. You work for her. When things settle down she will hate that you know all her personal info, that you saw her like this. And you don't want her knowing your deepest-darkest either. Don't mix your work and personal lives*, I told her with my mind.

But Sasha blithely trotted on as though she could not, in fact, read my thoughts. "I can't tell you how many times I've gone through something just like this. All our friends come to Brook for help with breakups. She's brilliant at it—she's like a breakup guru."

Lisa's gaze shot to me. "A breakup guru?"

I rose from my crouch and turned to snatch the other paper cone from Sasha's hand, using the opportunity to glare her into silence. "Well, that's not the kind of—"

"What do you charge?" Lisa barked.

"I'm...sorry?" I had mulled over on the drive to the *Tropic Times* building what I might net as a freelance writer, but I wasn't sure when we'd skipped from whether I'd be doing it at all to how much I would get for it.

Lisa made a rolling motion with her hand. "Your services. The breakup guru thing. I need it. How much?"

"Oh...well, that's not exactly—"

"And I need you to start today. Can you do that?"

I felt as if I were caught in the wake of a speedboat that had cruised too close, leaving my mind bobbing out of control. She wanted me to what...coach her through her fight with her husband? Like a spot-trainer who targeted the heart, instead of the thighs? That wasn't the way therapy worked.

"Lisa..." I downed the cup of water I held that she had been studiously ignoring, dropping the cone into Sasha's trash bin. "I completely understand what you're feeling right now. If you're looking to talk to a professional about it—"

"Then you've come to the right person!" Sasha caroled.

I swiveled my disbelieving gaze over to my chirpy friend, who wore a toothy simian grin. I blazed over another telepathic message to her to shut up, but all I said aloud was, "Sash, let's not—"

Apparently our Wonder Twin powers were deactivated. "Her hourly rate's pretty high. But since you're a friend, I bet Brook will give you a discount." She fixed her aqua eyes on me and sent a little mind message of her own that I heard as clearly as if she'd shouted it at me: *Go with it.* "Won't you, Brook?"

"The money's not a problem," I heard Lisa say. "Whatever it costs is fine. I just need to fix this. Now."

"Hear that, Brook?" Sasha said with wide, meaningful eyes. "It's not about the money for Lisa. She is happy to pay for your help. Immediately."

I wasn't an idiot—I got it. I was desperate for money, fast. Lisa Albrecht's unfortunate marriage woes seemed to be the universe's strange answer to my prayer.

But it didn't feel right. Lisa was vulnerable. She was simply looking to deal with the pain of her troubled marriage, not start a formal course of counseling. Agreeing to work with her this way would be like...

I paused. Like helping Sasha through one of her many devastating breakups. How was this any different from what I already did for my friend?

Well, in one very important way: Lisa Albrecht was apparently willing and very able to pay me for my services.

And what was wrong with that?

I dragged my gaze away from Sasha's bulgy-eyed jump-on-this-already expression and looked at Lisa, schooling my features into a look of soothing sagacity. "Then we should get started," I said with calm authority. "How soon can we meet—somewhere besides here?"

Hard determination filled Lisa's swollen, tear-tracked face as she reached out a hand and pumped my entire arm. "We can start right after work. Seven o'clock?"

We arranged to meet at a nearby café later that evening, and Sasha tossed out an hourly rate that was a lot closer to Uta's and Tom's than it was to my lowly LMHC scale. Lisa nodded as if she'd quoted her the cost of a movie ticket.

"That's fine. I'll see you at seven." She started to leave the cubicle, and I was just about to open my mouth to Sasha when Lisa popped her head back around the partition. "Oh, and can you get me the first column this week?"

"First... What?"

"Of course she can," Sasha fired back.

"Start with fifteen inches—we'll run it this Friday. If it tracks well we'll run it weekly and bump it up—maybe twenty-five or -six inches."

I nodded knowledgeably, wondering what she was talking about.

"And come up with a title for it," Lisa said. "Something catchy." Her head disappeared, and we heard the loud snuffling of her blowing her nose again as she retreated.

I turned to Sasha, to see her looking smug and delighted with herself. She slapped her hands together as if she'd just finished tidying a room. "You're welcome."

"What was *that*?"

She gave a self-satisfied grin. "*That* was Sasha to the rescue. I knew we could convince her to try you with a weekly. And the consulting? Bonus!"

"What happened to 'this isn't a good day for this'? I thought we were going to wait?"

Sasha's perfectly groomed eyebrows shot up. "Who cares what the tactics were if you won the battle?"

I shook my head and lowered myself to Sasha's chair. "I don't know, Sash. It feels a little weird. Like ambulance chasing."

Sasha crossed her legs like a Buddha. "Brook, how is it weird? You work with people having issues; Lisa is *clearly* having issues. You are amazing at counseling people post-messy-breakup; Lisa is *experiencing* a messy breakup. You are desperate for money; Lisa has some she wants to give you. Problem? Solved. Who loses here?"

I shook my head, thinking hard. She made sense, but something still seemed off about it. It felt like taking advantage of someone in a tough situation. After all, usually when I did this, it was for free, because I cared about my friends and what they were going through. I said as much to her.

She shook her head, intractable. "Totally different. Lisa is not your friend. She is, in fact, now your client. Just like all the other clients who come into your office and need your help, and whose money you have no qualms about accepting."

"But that's different. That's therapy."

"And this isn't?"

"Well, yes, of course it is. But it's...it's not like I'm doing anything special with the breakup thing, Sash. It's easy—it's just common sense."

Sasha made a scoffing noise. "Huh. For you, maybe. You don't really get affected by things like most people do. You're so logical and matter-of-fact. Even after...well, after last summer, when no one would have blamed you for—"

"Sasha." My voice was flat and hard.

"What? Brook, you never even broke your stride after Mi— after he called things off. You just went ahead and closed on the house and moved on like he was a blip on your radar. Most people can't handle things that calmly. You're cool as a popsicle about breakups."

She was trying to bolster me up, but I bristled at her implication. It reminded me of Uta's words about me being stone-cold. She and Sasha made me sound like some unemotional ice princess.

"What do you mean?" I bit out. "I get affected by things. It's not like I'm a robot or something."

"Really? Name one time you've shredded all the clothing a guy had at your house with a box cutter. Or keyed his car, or had revenge sex with his best friend, or broke into his house and peed in his shampoo."

"Oh, come on, that's not fair. That's just not how I deal with things. My way of coping is to remind myself to hold on to the most important thing I have left after a breakup."

She raised her eyebrows. "All his good DVDs?"

"Ha, ha. No...my dignity," I said, trying not to sound too pointed.

Sasha waved away my words like a swarm of no-see-'ums. "Oh, *that*." I'd already lost her attention. She was looking down at her computer screen, not at me, her body blocking me from seeing whatever she was so intent on. "If Lisa wants to run this thing Friday, you're going to need to turn the column in to her by Thursday morning. Plus you have to meet with her tonight and get started with her on the counseling. And how many patients do you have left between now and then—any? Wow, you'd better get busy."

My little mental rowboat was bobbing crazily again. I'd gone from idle to overbooked in minutes.

"What do you think of this as a column intro?" Sasha pulled back so I could see her monitor, where she'd typed a few sentences:

Health troubles require a doctor. Car troubles require a mechanic. And dating troubles require Brook Lyn Ogden, LMHC, relationship expert.

I read through it, then looked over at my best friend.

She flashed me that smug grin again. "You're back in business, baby."

three

I was beginning to think working with Lisa Albrecht couldn't possibly be worth the money.

We were sitting at one of the outside tables at the McGregor Bistro, a row of purple bougainvillea blocking the sight of traffic on McGregor Avenue. Foxtail palms rustled in the breeze over our heads, casting spiny shadows in the moonlight as the patio slowly emptied out.

I began with the careful, objective listening approach I used with my patients, letting Lisa tell me—repeatedly, in great detail—the whole story of her husband's departure from their home. All while she never met my eyes once. Instead she stared fixedly down at her iPhone, texting expertly with her right hand while taking occasional bites of her sandwich with her left.

They'd been college sweethearts and had their two sons young, the year after they both graduated. Lisa was hired by the *Boston Globe* right out of school, and since Theodore was still looking for a job when she got pregnant with twins, it made more sense for him to stay home with the babies at first, until he could find a position that paid enough to make day care worthwhile.

"But that's not how it worked, was it?" she asked me the third time we got to this point in the tale as her fingers continued flying over her keypad. I assumed the question was rhetorical, but wondered for a fleeting moment if it was a test to see if one of us, at least, was paying attention.

No, that was *not* how it had worked, as I thoroughly knew by now. Instead Lisa did very well in her job, and her career began to take off. She liked being the breadwinner, and Theodore liked being a full-time dad. They agreed he should stay home permanently and raise the boys.

When Lisa was offered a plum position as features editor for the Fort Myers paper, the family pulled up stakes and moved to Florida. They'd both grown tired of harsh Boston winters, and they were worried about the high school in their rough neighborhood. Theodore started working on cars in their garage, and eventually they invested in a small mechanic's shop for him to run. He spent his days there until the boys got out of school, and everyone, Lisa kept repeating, was happy.

Then, two mornings ago, as Lisa stared sleepily out the kitchen window, she saw her husband hurling suitcases into the trunk of his car. She'd dropped her coffee to the counter so hard it sloshed everywhere, and ran outside.

Theodore had looked at her as coldly as if she were a stranger. "The boys graduate in a few months," he'd said. "I did my job. I'm out of here."

"He tore off while I stood there watching him," she said to her iPhone screen, her jaw set and her teeth gritted. "Like he'd just told a nasty boss off and clocked out for the last time."

"That must have been hurtful." I was trying not to repeat myself, but I was running out of neutral observations.

Lisa looked up at me as if I had picked up my sandwich and begun enthusiastically French-kissing it. "My husband walked out on me with no reason and no notice after almost twenty years of marriage. This afternoon you watched me have a quasi–nervous breakdown in my office in front of you, a complete stranger. 'That must have been *hurtful*'?"

I took a steadying breath. "Clearly Theodore has been feeling some things he neglected to share with you," I forced past a clot of annoyance. She was in pain, and, as some patients did, was simply taking it out on the person available. "What does that make you feel?"

Lisa threw her sandwich back down on her plate and regarded me incredulously. "*This* is the expert relationship advice I'm paying you for? I've got an absentee husband and two devastated children, and you want to know how that makes me *feel*? Jesus, I could buy a mood ring a hell of a lot cheaper." She dismissed me from her attention as if I were an annoying fly she'd finally flattened.

I watched for a moment, disconcerted, as she resumed working the keypad. Usually even someone as difficult as Lisa wasn't hard for me to handle. I wanted to help people, and if someone was willing to open themselves up enough to come to me, I'd stick by them even when their emotions sometimes made them prickly and defensive.

But Lisa wasn't my usual client. She hadn't sought me out on her own. She didn't seem to really want my help; she'd just been railroaded into it by the Sasha Express in a uniquely vulnerable moment. I wondered if I should just quietly pay the bill and leave. As engrossed as she was in her phone, would Lisa even notice? My stomach felt tight. I hadn't been able to help her at all. I'd failed.

"Lisa," I began, but she never took her eyes off her screen. I cleared my throat. "*Lisa.*"

"I heard you the first time."

"Look, this doesn't seem to be what you... I don't think I..." I was talking to the top of her head. She really ought to color all that gray. "I'm just going to take care of the bill and go, okay?"

"The hour's not up."

"I... What?"

"I'm paying you by the hour. You've been here for forty-two minutes. The hour's not up yet."

It was just as well that she wasn't looking at me, so she didn't see me gaping at her like a fish. There wasn't one moment in the evening so far when I'd felt as though Lisa had any particular desire for my presence. Did she just want me to sit here and watch her work her iPhone nonstop?

"Who are you texting?" My voice shot out like a whiplash before I could assume the measured, sympathetic therapist tone I'd been maintaining.

Lisa never even looked up. "Who do you think? We have things to discuss."

"Would you please put the phone down so we can talk?"

"What? No. We *are* talking."

I had been forming some theories about Lisa Albrecht over the course of the evening. She was a successful businesswoman who was the provider for her family and de facto head of the household. She was probably good at her job and felt her most comfortable and confident there—clearly she derived a lot of her self-image from her career and position.

Maybe because she was in a position of power and authority, she had developed a no-nonsense, cocksure demeanor that allowed for no admission of personal culpability or weakness. You would do it Lisa's way or you wouldn't do it at all. This mind-set was evident in the way she was acting with me tonight.

With one of the patients in my practice, this would be a long-term, gradual process where, over months or years of therapy, we'd gently begin to question the tenets that had allowed the client to develop these unhealthy thought patterns.

But Lisa Albrecht wasn't a normal patient. She was someone who was paying me to "fix" her as quickly as possible, but then sat there making it almost impossible for me to do so. She was acting like a spoiled, self-centered child who expected the universe to revolve around her and was used to getting her own way in everything. She didn't need counseling so much as parenting. And suddenly I understood the vast benefits of working outside the confines of the traditional therapist/patient relationship.

I reached over and snatched the phone out of her hands.

"What are you doing?" she said, startled.

"You're paying me to help you. Not watch you stalk your husband."

"I'm not stalking him. We're communicating. Isn't that what you therapists like for us to do...*communicate*? Give me my phone."

Her sarcasm and imperious order snapped the last thread of

therapeutic objectivity I had been clinging to. I popped the phone into my purse and leaned back in my wrought-iron chair.

"Since you know the price I quoted you for my services, you know my time is valuable. If you want me to work with you, don't waste it." I worried Lisa's scalp would shoot off from the top of her head like a bottle rocket, but now that the tide was rolling I couldn't stop it. "Texting isn't communicating, and most people over the age of eighteen know it. If you have things to talk about with your husband, you *talk* to him. But you're not ready to do that until you can take a step back and approach him as an adult."

Lisa's glare shot flames hot enough to ignite me where I sat, and my stomach curdled. What was I doing? I had just blown my own plans sky-high: I had forgotten professional boundaries and begun treating her as if she were Sasha, someone I could say anything to, could freely speak my mind with. Lisa had every right to get up and walk out—and I fully expected her to—to demand her phone, her money, and the column assignment back, leaving me mired smack in the financial morass I was in twenty-four hours ago.

"Fine," she gritted out through a tight jaw. "What is it I'm supposed to do now?"

My heart started beating again. It had *worked*? I hid my relief by pulling her iPhone back out of my purse and working the keypad.

"What are you doing?"

I didn't look up—if Lisa saw uncertainty she'd pounce. "Changing Theodore's name in your address book. It's best not to pick up the phone right now if he calls." I held the phone out so she could read the screen, where I'd changed her husband's name to DON'T ANSWER.

"That's crazy. I have to answer." She reached for the phone again, but I held it just out of her grasp. If stripping off my kid gloves was the only way to reach her, I was keeping them off.

"No, you don't. But he won't be calling. Not for a while, anyway."

"What are you talking about?"

"Lisa, he's looking for some space, obviously. Or else he wouldn't have left. By texting him constantly for the last several hours—and I'm assuming for the two days before that since he left—you've given him exactly the opposite. You are now the enemy, keeping him from getting what he wants. And he will avoid you."

Her face crumpled like a sinkhole. I'd stepped too far over the line, and was losing her again. I backpedaled fast, softening my tone. "You'll get to talk to him—eventually. But you have to make it a good thing in his mind—something he wants. And that means giving him room when he needs it. How can he miss you if you won't leave him alone?"

"I... He..." She swallowed again, clenched her jaw. "Okay."

"Good girl!" I burst out before I could censor myself. But Lisa didn't take offense. Instead, she preened. I made a mental note: *Responds to praise.*

It was going to be a later night than I expected. I leaned across the table.

"Let's talk about what you're going to do next."

Once I'd broken past Lisa's hard outer shell, she was insatiable for advice. It was nearly eleven o'clock by the time I wrapped up our session and headed out to my car.

I found Kendall sound asleep in bed when I crawled in beside him twenty minutes later. I didn't want to disturb him—this was his firm's busy season, and I knew he was exhausted with the long hours he'd been working. I hovered over his face, propped on one elbow for a few moments, hoping he'd rouse enough to kiss me good night. He didn't even stir. I gave up and lay back, snuggling up to his side and whispering, "I'm home."

Kendall slumbered on, blissfully unaware, in the mummy pose he always slept in—on his back, arms crossed over his chest—while the word *home* echoed strangely in my head. Was this my home? Nothing of mine was here except for some clothes and a few toiletries. My own run-down, neglected house had never felt like home either, though—just a storage unit for my things. And I'd long since moved out of my parents' house.

What was "home"?

I studied Kendall's face, soft and untroubled in sleep, and gently touched his warm arm where it rested over his chest, but still he didn't stir. The neediness that washed over me left an unpleasant feeling in my belly. I was styling myself as a confident, knowledgeable relationship expert, and here I was craving reassurance like a child.

"I'm home," I tried the word out again, more softly.

Kendall just slept on.

four

My first article for the column was much harder to write than I expected.

Fifteen or sixteen inches, Sasha calculated for me, was about six hundred words. So far I had three of them on the page.

Dating is hard.

Oh, that was excellent. Wonderful insight from a professional therapist. When I was a kid, chewing the end of my pencil always helped me think when I was stuck, but the blinking cursor just laughed at my frustration. I couldn't gnaw on my keyboard. I started over.

In the wild, wide world of dating, it's hard to navigate the ups and downs.

Eh. I couldn't even have the satisfaction of crumpling up the page and throwing it away. Computers sucked. Deadlines sucked. My writing sucked.

There's no such thing as a how-to manual for dating. Anyone who tells you different is probably—literally—selling you something, like one of hundreds of self-help books sitting in bookstores—and probably on your shelves at home.

Hmmm. That wasn't too bad. Kind of negated my setting myself up as yet another expert, though. Still, I kept writing.

The truth is, no one knows the rules for dating. That's because there are no rules—every situation is different. Every person is different.

So wouldn't you love to have your own personal dating guru to help you navigate the bumpy road to love?

"He didn't call when he said he would—what does it mean?" Ask...

I stopped and leaned back. *Think of a title*, Lisa had told me. *Something catchy.*

Sasha had called me a breakup savant, but that brought to mind a stammering Rain Man—not the best image for a relationship guru. "Ask the Relationship Guru"? No. I got a mental picture of a swami sitting cross-legged on a mountaintop. "Ask... Madame Mojo"? Sounded like a dominatrix. Dr. Love? That just sounded like a bad seventies porn film. The Love Doctor?

"I love her but hate her kids...can it work?" Ask the Love Doctor...

It wasn't bad.

I leaned forward again, my fingers tapping on the keys.

I ran the finished product by Sasha Wednesday night before I turned it in to Lisa.

"What do you think?"

She frowned into the screen, chewing her bottom lip. "I like it. It's good."

"But...?"

"What? I like it."

I sighed and flopped down onto her plush red couch, where

she sat with my laptop balanced on her knees.

"Sash, you never just 'like' anything. You love it or you hate it. What did I do wrong?"

She drew her eyebrows together, staring at the screen. "That's the thing. I don't know. It's good—really," she insisted at my rolled eyes. "It's just not...special. It's nothing I haven't seen before." She gestured absently behind her, where her bookshelves spilled with titles like *How to Find Him, Hook Him, and Reel Him In*; *Dating: A Survival Guide*; *How to Be Married in a Year*; *Get Him to the Altar*.

I flopped over so I was lying on my stomach, my legs bent up. "But readers can write in about their *personal* dating situation. I can answer *specific* questions."

"Yeah."

"It's like having your very own self-help book, personalized just for you."

"Mmmmmm." She nodded slowly, still eyeballing the screen.

"So what do you think? Is it ready? Should I turn it in? Is this what Lisa was looking for?"

Sasha stared intently into my laptop as if it were trying to teach her calculus. "Well...yeah. I like it. It's good."

It needed work.

I took another stab at it...and then another stab...and then another, until I had taken so many stabs I felt like a serial killer. Finally I wound up with something pretty close to what I originally shown Sasha, and I sent it in.

Thursday afternoon, my cell phone rang with an unfamiliar number.

"Is this the Love Doctor?"

For a second I stared dumbly at the phone before I realized it wasn't a prank call. "Um...yes," I stammered.

"My name is Tabitha Washington. I work at the *Tropic Times*? I just saw your first article, and...and I..." She faltered to a stop.

"You had some questions?" I'd figured there'd be some rewrites called for. Even after all my efforts, I wasn't completely happy with the final result.

A brief pause. "Uh-huh. I was wondering..."

"Yes?"

"Could you, um..."

Tabitha Washington was pussyfooting around as if my ego were fragile as glass. "Whatever it is, you can just tell me," I told her. "I'm sure I can fix it."

"Oh, thank God!" And for the second time that week a strange woman burst into sobs as I listened in bewilderment. "My boyfriend...his wife...*here*...!" I made out between her ragged gasps. "I think she wants to get back together. Maybe he does too. Should I ask him? That looks too needy, doesn't it? Am I overreacting?"

"Hang on, Tabitha. Breathe." In the momentary silence broken only by Tabitha's sniffles and the distinct sound of her blowing her nose, my mind raced. Here was another woman asking me what to do—*desperate* for me to tell her what to do—when she didn't know the first thing about me—not even my real name.

Was it possible that a *lot* of people were this hungry for direct, one-on-one help in the face of relationship problems?

Tabitha was still making wet noises on her end of the line, and I realized she was waiting for me to say something. "What do you need me to do for you, Tabitha?" I asked slowly. "How can I help?"

"I want to hire you."

And just like that I had my second client.

I got the gist of the story in between hitching breaths: Tabitha had started dating her boyfriend, Cooper, five months ago, very shortly after his wife had an affair and then moved away. Now the wife was back in town, and Tabitha was nervous.

She was at work and didn't have time for us to go much further into it. And my mind was suddenly bubbling with an idea I couldn't wait to act on. So after I quoted Tabitha the hourly rate for my breakup doctoring services that Sasha had come up with—without even a warble of hesitation in my voice—and we agreed on a time for our first consultation early next week, I got to snap out something I'd always wanted to say:

"Stop the presses."

"Um...what?" Tabitha said blankly.

Apparently I was the only Howard Hawks fan between us. I rephrased, asking her to hold off on printing the article I had sent her—I'd be sending in a new one in a couple of hours. And then I hung up the phone and let my fingers fly over the keyboard.

I finished the article in half the time I'd promised, checked it once more to make sure it said what I wanted it to, and pressed send.

five

My first column ran the next morning.

My father called at seven a.m., as soon as his paper was delivered, full of congratulations. "Wonderful job, doll."

"Thanks, Dad. Mom likes it too?" I asked.

"Oh...sure, sweetheart. We both love it." But I knew from his tone that he was speaking only for himself. I suppose it was expecting too much for my mom to call and tell me she was proud of me.

Sasha showed up at Kendall's condo at seven thirty—right after he hustled out the door for work with a promise to read the column that night—balancing an armful of newspapers and two big Dunkin' Donuts coffees.

"It's too early for champagne," she said, her smile stretching her face. "I thought you'd want extra hard copies. Rockin' it old-school."

"It's just a silly little article," I said, but I reached for the papers in her arm and eagerly opened the top one to locate my column.

There it was, with the big, splashy headline, "Ask the Breakup Doctor."

Sasha tore her eyes from the article and looked over at me. "You changed it!"

I nodded as Sasha and I read it together, bent over the kitchen table shoulder-to-shoulder with the paper spread out below us like an offering.

A broken leg requires an orthopedist. A broken car requires a mechanic. And a broken heart requires a spe-

cialist too. *Every week in this column I'll be helping you navigate the rough waters of dating and the stormy seas of rejection: The Breakup Doctor is now in.*

So you got dumped. We've all been there, and it stinks. But what defines us is what we do next, in the relationship's postmortem: how we handle ourselves, how we recover, how we move on and find someone new—and bring ourselves that much closer to finding the right one.

Handling a breakup gracefully and in a healthy way is a learned skill, like playing the violin or being good at tennis. And as with musical talent or sports, some people are more inherently gifted at it than others.

But it's a skill everyone can learn—if they are willing. And until our school system realizes that teaching Conflict Resolution or Coping with Rejection might be as useful as calculus or physics—maybe more so—there's me.

Send me your questions, your worries, your deepest, darkest fears and angriest revenge fantasies, and I'll help you through it all. I'll walk you through every aspect of a breakup—what to do, what not to do, and how to carry the whole thing off with style and panache, no matter how messy, ugly, or nasty your breakup is. In this situation more than any other, the old adage is true: The best revenge is living well.

You can *get through it, and I'll show you how. And believe it or not, when it's over you'll be grateful you got out of a bad relationship (because if it were a good one, you would still be in it, right?), and ready to find a good, healthy, positive one.*

At the end of it I had written a thumbnail bio that stated that I was a mental health professional who ran a private consulting service for "the recently and reluctantly single."

"This isn't the article you showed me," Sasha accused when she'd finished reading.

I looked at her, my best and truest audience, and chewed my bottom lip. "Yeah. I got to thinking about Lisa...and what you said about me and breakups, and making the article more original, more personal, and... What do you think?"

"Brook." She shook her head, and my heart plummeted. "It's fantastic! It's perfect."

"Really?"

She grinned at me and grabbed me into a hug. "It's so *you!* This is what you're great at! Anyone can offer relationship advice, but you're the best at breakups of anyone I know. I *love* it, Brookie. I love it."

In a spill, I told her about Tabitha, and how her phone call— and Sasha's encouragement—had sparked the impulse to make the column more specialized.

"I'm helping her, Sash. And your editor too—already I can see that they're feeling better about themselves, stronger. It's like an immediate gratification I never really get in my practice. Not like this."

She was beaming. "This is your calling, Brook. You were born to be the Breakup Doctor."

"Well, for now, it's great. I've got some money coming in, I'm still able to help people until I figure out how to get my practice back on track...and it's all thanks to you."

She waved me off halfheartedly. "Oh, now...it's not all due to me. Maybe *mostly.*"

I grinned and pulled her to me for another hug. "Thanks, Sash. You're the best friend on earth."

She left for work a few minutes later, promising to call when she heard the reaction at the paper.

At ten o'clock Stu called to offer his two cents: "Nice job, sis. And thanks for reminding me why I don't get into relationships."

I laughed. "Grow up, little brother. I can't wait until the right girl knocks all your bachelor BS flat on its ass."

"Good idea—a dominatrix. I haven't tried one of those yet."

And Kendall read the article that night after work, sitting on the sofa with a bowl of ice cream and the paper spread out over his knees while I chewed my thumbnail and paced the living room floor behind him.

He sat quietly for a moment after he read it, and then shook his head and found my gaze.

"Amazing. It's so hard to get my mind around the fact that people will look for advice on their most intimate issues from a stranger in a public forum. But it sounds good to me. Great job." He folded the paper carefully along its creases and set it down beside him.

Kendall wasn't much of a reader. If it wasn't the *Wall Street Journal* or *SmartMoney* magazine or *Golf Digest*, he never cracked a spine except his own. So I tried to be happy with his compliment.

But his reaction stirred something unpleasant in the region of my gut usually reserved for my mother's cutting remarks.

"Well, you know," I sallied, loitering near him against the arm of the sofa, "therapy in general is basically telling your most personal issues to an objective, uninvolved listener."

He looked up from his ice cream. "Oh, absolutely. I know it works for some people." He put down his bowl and flicked on the TV.

I leaned over to take his empty dish and carried it into the kitchen.

"A lot of people, actually," I called over the breakfast bar as I rinsed it in the sink. "I think I've helped a lot of people in my practice."

"I know, babe," he said, not taking his eyes off of *Kudlow and Company*. "For people who need that kind of thing I bet you're great."

I turned off the water and regarded the back of Kendall's carefully combed head. He'd promised to come home early tonight to celebrate my first column. I had dinner ready and on the table at six o'clock. At six thirty-three he'd swept in with a bouquet of carnations, full of apologies, plopped the flowers and his briefcase down on the breakfast bar, and sat across the table from me to wolf down cold salmon and braised broccoli with slivered almonds. At six fifty-four he'd made an occasion of unfolding the paper and sitting on the sofa to read my article, but I could see his eyes flicking to the clock on the DVD player to make sure he didn't miss the beginning of his show.

A surge of irritation swelled up in me. I wiped my wet hands in jerky movements on the kitchen towel, then walked back into the living area, still clutching the towel in taut fingers. I planted myself right between Kendall and Kudlow.

"What 'kind of thing' are you talking about?" I asked testily.

I was sure I saw him visibly swallow the urge to shoo me out of the way like a gnat, but he met my eyes with an apologetic smile. "I didn't mean anything by it, Brook. I wasn't belittling what you do."

"Okay."

"I wasn't, Brook. I'm sorry—I'm an insensitive ass."

"Sometimes." I wasn't ready to be mollified. "You could at least take ten minutes to be happy for me. To pay a little attention to *me*, instead of"—I gestured behind me at the TV—"some old balding banker."

"He's not a banker."

"That's not my point."

Kendall sighed and looked down into his lap as if he wished he had a manual lying open on it entitled, "How to Handle Your Girlfriend." When he looked back up, though, his expression was clear and conciliatory.

"Brook, I'm sorry. I had a crazy day, and one hell of a long week. I took off as early as I could. I'm sitting right here. I guess I'm not sure what you're looking for from me."

What *was* I looking for? He did come home early. He read the article. He complimented it—sort of. He was here, with me, instead of at the office.

So why did I feel...incidental? Invisible? As though I hadn't had his full, involved focus on me for weeks. Not since he'd asked me to move in.

As soon as the thought occurred to me, the lurch in my chest told me that was it: This thing was hanging between us, unspoken, leaving me stuck in limbo, mentally checked out of my own house, but not really sure I belonged here yet either.

Not talking about things didn't mean they weren't there, swelling up and waiting to explode. I couldn't keep letting his suggestion sit on the back burner of my mind, unresolved because of my own relationship baggage. Kendall and I needed to clear the air.

"Can we talk for a few minutes? About us?"

"Come here," Kendall said. He leaned forward and snagged one end of the damp towel, pulling me toward him on the sofa until I stood touching his knees. He gave a tug on the towel, but I didn't move.

"No, seriously," I said. "I just want to talk."

He pulled again on the towel, but I met him with just as much resistance. He started to grin, yanking harder, and I felt a reluctant smile creep across my face too. Our tug-of-war continued, more playfully now, until I abruptly dropped my end of the towel and Kendall smacked himself in the face with his own arm. I couldn't help laughing.

"Ow! Minx." He looped his arm around my knees and swept them out from beneath me, sending me landing hard on his lap. His arms came around me and he pulled me to him for a kiss.

I lost myself in it for just a moment, the softness of his mouth, the warmth, the closeness with him that made something relax in my belly. I was overthinking. Not for the first time (not for the hundredth, if I were honest), I cursed Michael. He'd left me suspicious and mistrustful. Closed off to someone who'd never given me any reason to doubt him. Who, in fact, wanted to move our relationship forward. My heart swelled at the thought.

I reached up a hand and touched Kendall's cheek. "I think I'm ready to talk about moving in together."

"Okay," he agreed. "But I'm going to use sign language." He

ran his hands down my sides, and lower, and it felt so good to have his touch on me, his gaze on me, to have a little bit of time with him when he wasn't rushed or exhausted.

"I miss you," I said softly, resting my forehead against his, looking directly at him.

"I'm right here." Kendall reached over to turn the TV off—although I couldn't miss his hitting the record button on the DVR first. And then, finally, he turned his attention completely on me, and talking didn't seem so important after all.

six

February is when southwest Florida flaunts everything it's got. It brings out the heavy artillery: bougainvillea so richly, luridly magenta it hurts your eyes; lush purple jacaranda blooms that war with the explosive red-orange of poinciana; yellow tabebuia playing a subtle counterpoint to all the blowsy color of the show-offs. Orange blossoms send their sweet perfume drifting into every secret crevice, and the sky is a blue so clear and vivid it makes your heart beat faster just to look at it.

I wasn't surprised to see Stu's Jeep sitting in my parents' driveway as Sasha and I pulled in that Sunday afternoon. My family—which had unofficially included Sasha since we'd met in third grade—had had Sunday dinner together for as long as I could remember, and when tourists and snowbirds clogged local traffic and crowded the beaches during season, we'd gotten into the habit of coming early enough to swim in my parents' blissfully uncrowded canal-front swimming pool.

Stu was rummaging around in the back of the vehicle when I pulled my car in next to his. He looked up and gave an upward jerk of his head in acknowledgment, then slammed his rear door shut and walked over to open mine for me, staring right past me and making a show of ogling Sasha's chest as she reached into the back for her beach bag. "Ladies...good to see you. Sash, hope you don't have the girls bound too tightly in that teeny-weeny bikini."

"Nope, letting them breathe, Stuvie. Thought I might grant them their freedom later on if we had the pool to ourselves. Whoops, too bad."

"Pretend I'm not even here..."

Stu and Sasha had had a relationship of mutual harmless sexual harassment practically ever since they met, when an eight-year-old Sasha gleefully pantsed the six-year-old Stu as he leaned over on the patio to put on his water wings. It was a sick thing, but it seemed to work for them.

"Sis, how's it shaking?"

"Mellow like Jell-O, my bro."

"Where's the Master of the Universe?" That was what he called Kendall.

"Working."

"On a Sunday?"

I shrugged. "Busy season."

Stu held out an arm toward Sasha as they both came around the front of the car. "It'd be my pleasure to escort inside a fine piece of tail such as yourself, little lady."

She tucked her arm in his. "How kind. Do try to keep it in your pants."

Stu shook his head mournfully. "Mind always in the gutter, this one."

My mother was waiting at the door when we rounded the corner, and Stu kissed her on the cheek before skirting by her and disappearing into the house. I joined Sasha in the doorway.

"Hi, Mrs. Ogden," Sasha said in the obsequious tone reserved for my parents alone.

Mom hugged her. "Hello, honey. Look how thin and toned you're looking! Brook Lyn, why don't you join Sasha's gym and have her show you some of her workout moves?"

"Are you kidding, Mom? She's had me pumping iron for months now—can't you tell?"

I kept walking into the house, past her baffled search for my fictional new muscles. There was no point answering the question seriously. No matter what I offered up, it was never enough. When I opened my counseling practice she'd reminded me how much more money I could command if I'd finished my graduate psych degree.

When I'd proudly brought her and Dad over to see my house the day I'd closed on it, she'd spent the whole tour pointing out everything that needed to be repaired, and not a conversation had gone by in the last year that she didn't ask about the money I still owed her and my dad from my forfeited wedding deposits.

Outside on the lanai Stu was already in the pool, the puddles of water sloshed over the sides attesting to a recent cannonball. My dad sat under the overhang at a patio table, a newspaper spread between his hands, and his glasses resting on his nose with the sunglass lenses flipped up like big plastic eyelashes. He looked up when he heard the slider open, and a smile branded his face.

"Hey, there's my girl!" He lifted the paper a few inches. "Not as good as Friday's edition," he said. "That article of yours was a humdinger."

"Thanks, Dad." I swung over for a kiss, then dropped into the chair opposite his, plunking my beach bag down on the concrete. "What's the news?"

He folded up the paper and set it on the table, jerking a thumb toward a headline. "Another six months on the new overpass. Your mother and I don't think they'll finish it before next season."

I made a sympathetic face. "That's a shame. We needed it *this* year."

"Don't I know it? I don't know what's worse—the seasonal traffic or the awful construction. Just a mess."

Even though my family had never lived anywhere else *but* Fort Myers, we discussed the traffic problems every season as though they were a fresh vexation.

"Bombs away!"

A shout at the sliding glass doors caught our attention, and Sasha barreled by in a streak of tan skin and yellow bikini, dropping her bags en route to leaping into the pool with all the grace of a bullfrog. She'd have landed right on Stu's head if he hadn't ducked under the water just before she hit the surface with a wince-inducing slap.

"Hey, you kids...take it easy," Dad called out mildly. "You

know your mother doesn't like water outside the pool, Stu."

"Sorry, Mr. Ogden," Sasha said primly as Stu surfaced, lifting her into his arms. "You got faster," she said to my brother.

"And you got fatter." He groaned as he picked her up higher and hurled her into the deep end.

"Stu!" My mother suddenly stood at the sliding glass doors like a Valkyrie. "You apologize to Sasha! And stop sloshing water over the edges—you know I hate that."

"Sorry, Sash."

"Sorry, Mrs. Ogden," put in my brown-nosing best friend.

And just that quickly we were all collectively twelve years old again.

After twenty minutes or so of our loud horseplay, my dad excused himself to his garage workshop to get back to his latest project—rebuilding the cabinetry he had ripped down in the kitchen, leaving a series of gaping maws lining its walls. Mom had disappeared after her last admonition from the sliders, and after a while I decided to go in and see if she needed help with dinner.

As I came into the ravaged kitchen my dad had been renovating for months, I found Mom standing at the makeshift plywood counter, rolling the last of a slaughterhouse's worth of lunch meat into a spiral and adding it to a platter already heaped with mountains of cubed cheese, cut-up carrots and radishes and broccoli, and an array of olives.

I carefully shut the slider behind me. "Geez, Mom, you go rob a tailgate party?"

She looked up at me, her eyebrows furrowing. "What? We're having casual dinner tonight."

"No, no, this looks great." I reached for a jar of pickles and started forking them onto the platter.

"How's that house of yours—have you gotten any work done on it?" she asked.

I was gratified for once to have the right answer: "Sasha came over a couple weeks ago and we peeled off the old paper in the dining room. I'm going to patch the walls and get it painted."

Mom's face brightened and she gave me a pleased smile that warmed me despite myself. "That Sasha! She's a good friend."

"The best," I said honestly.

Mom sighed as she rolled another piece of prosciutto into a neat, tight cylinder. "I wish that girl could find someone who appreciated her. Like your Kendall."

It took me a moment to realize that Mom wasn't suggesting I pass Kendall along to Sasha as more deserving of him. I wanted to blurt out that he had asked me to move in with him, that our relationship was getting serious, that the man she was talking about in such glowing terms had picked *me*.

But, "I don't think Kendall's her type," was all I said. "Too...traditional." By which I meant he didn't ride a motorcycle or own an arsenal of firearms or work in a job that started at ten p.m. and didn't finish until dawn. Sasha liked them edgy.

My column was the proverbial elephant in the room. I hadn't heard a word from my mother about it. I knew better than to ask, but some masochistic inner voice took control of my tongue.

"So," I said. "Did you read my article?"

My mom didn't look at me. "I did. After your father told me about it."

I heard the subtext: I should have told her myself. And probably she was right, but I'd long since stopped running to my mom for the approval I already knew wasn't coming.

And yet... "What did you think?"

She concentrated on the meat she was rolling, reaching for two more slices before speaking into the silence that had already told me the answer. "I just... I hate to see you publicize what happened to you."

"That's not what the column is about," I said tightly.

"Isn't it?"

I set the pickle jar back down on the plywood, the fork clattering beside it. "I'm going to get us some sodas."

"Don't be angry—I'm just worried about you. I don't want you to be defined by what that awful Michael did to you."

My chest grew tight, the way it always did at the simple mention of his name. Still. "Mom, please."

"What? He was a bad bet, and I told you that from the beginning."

"I know you did." Ad nauseam.

"Good riddance to bad rubbish. Look where you are now. I told you someone better would come along, and Kendall's nothing at all like Mich—"

"Can we not talk about it?"

My mother's lips tightened and she shoved a cylinder of ham into place with unnecessary vigor. "Brook, it's been nearly a year. At some point you have to stop wallowing in this dramatic grieving phase. You're not the only person who ever got left at the altar."

I gripped the plywood so hard I felt splinters pierce my palms. "I didn't get left at the altar," I forced out through a clenched jaw.

"Exactly. It could have been worse. So you lost a few deposits here and there. You'll pay them back. Move on."

That would certainly be a lot easier if she didn't constantly remind me about them. "I *have* moved on, Mom. I'm not 'wallowing' in anything. That's why I don't want to talk about this anymore. Okay?" It was all I could do to keep my tone level and my voice down, but I could still hear the fury in it.

So, apparently, could my mother. Her expression had gone wounded and hurt, and I felt a familiar mixture of guilt and remorse wash through me. "Fine. I won't take an interest in your life."

"Mom..." The expected words flew to my tongue from years of practice: *I'm sorry*. But for some reason I couldn't push them out. "Let's forget it, okay?"

She gave an exasperated sigh. "Fine. Bring out the drinks." She picked up the platter and left me in the kitchen. I pried my fingers off the plywood, surprised they weren't cramped permanently into claws.

Out in the garage, Dad stood at his worktable, a circular saw screaming and sawdust coating his sweaty skin like coconut sprinkles.

When he saw me he shut off the saw and lifted his safety goggles, their shape outlined on his face by the pale particles.

"Hey, beautiful. What's up?"

He looked so crazy and familiar and dear I had an urge to hug him, but instead I headed over to the garage fridge in the corner to get the drinks. "Dinner's ready. You want to take a break?"

He shook his head and indicated the piece of wood in front of him. "Nah. I'm gonna work on through. Your mother will divorce me if I don't get her some cabinets back up pretty soon." My dad's whole face crinkled up when he smiled. "How 'bout you bring me some leftovers later on."

"You got it, Dad." I blew him a kiss and went back out to the lanai, where Mom was already sitting down with Stu and Sasha, both of them wrapped in towels to keep the dreaded water from dripping onto Mom's patio. In the *pool* area.

"I was just telling the kids about my big news," Mom said as I sat down and distributed the drinks. "Your mom's going back into the theater!"

"No kidding," I said flatly. I was still smarting too much to work up the enthusiasm she wanted.

I knew my mom had acted—years ago, before I was born. It was *how* I was born, actually. She met my dad while she was doing an amateur local production called *A Sand Bar Named Desire*. Dad, a mechanical engineer, had been hired to create a moving onstage tour bus prop for the "I've Always Relied on the Kindness of Snowbirds" number.

Whenever Mom told the story of their backstage courtship— which she hadn't in years, thank God—she waggled her eyebrows and tacked on at the end: "But engineers do it in perpetual motion..." And she and Dad always used to laugh in a way that no child could ever be comfortable with.

Their "showmance" not only survived closing night; it survived my mom skipping her period the next month. Since she'd never made it to New York to pursue her "big dream," she named me for the prettiest-sounding place she found on a map of the area.

"Brook Lyn!" My wrist stung from her slap. "For goodness' sake, use a plate."

Mom was the only person in my life who always called me by my full given name.

"So," I said as I reached for a plate and started to load up, "what's the show—*One Flew Over the Seagull's Nest?*"

"Ha, ha—you're very funny, Miss Smarty-Pants. For your information it's a real play—a classic. *The Lion in Winter*. And you are looking at Queen Eleanor herself."

"Wow! Good for you, Mrs. Ogden," Sasha gushed.

"Mom spends the whole play imprisoned in her own castle," Stu put in.

She made a sound between a snort and a *hmpf.* "Yes, I was perfect for it."

"So when does it open? I bet you'll be great," said Sasha the suck-up.

Mom leaned back with a smile, enjoying the attention. "We had the first read-through last Wednesday. The cast is superb—top-notch, even though it's a non-Equity production"—translation: community theater—"and the gentleman who plays Henry has acted on Broadway!" She pronounced it with the accent on the second syllable—BroadWAY—like she was a 1940s film actress. "We open March fifteenth—the Ides."

My mother didn't always talk like this. She was in full theatrical mode. Over the years she'd told us about her acting days from time to time, and I could tell she missed it. I never saw her perform, because she quit when I was born. Dad always said she had been amazing—but Dad thought everything about Mom was amazing, and always had.

"Okay, Liz Taylor," my brother said, poking Mom playfully in the side, where he knew she was fiercely ticklish. "We're all coming on opening night, and we're sitting in the front row with enough flowers to make a float, and we're gonna hoot and holler and do the wave when you come onstage." He reached over and pawed up a handful of rolled salami.

Mom rapped his hand with the back of her fork.

"Ow!"

"Bedford Stuyvesant Ogden! Your manners."

"It's *finger* food, Ma!" But he picked up the tongs and gingerly transported the meat to his plate.

"And you will do no such thing. You children will dress nicely—no jeans—and behave yourselves, please."

I rolled my eyes. "Mom, we're adults. We understand how to comport ourselves in public places."

"It's the theater, and you have to show respect for the art form. Do you know I've actually seen Floridians attend the theater in *shorts*?" She made an expression as if she'd said "grilling and eating babies."

"Oh, I agree. My parents took us to shows in New York every year when our family would go up, and Mom always taught us to look nice and be respectful." Guess who said that?

"Whatever. We're coming, and we'll be good—I promise," Stu said. "We'll even make Dad wear a tie."

Mom cleared her throat and picked at something on her napkin. "Well...that's all right. I mean, I'm not sure if your father will be coming."

"What do you mean? He's your biggest fan." Too late, I covered my full mouth with a hand, but my mother didn't even notice my breach. She became very busy rearranging her silverware.

"I mean that your father and I may be taking a little break for a while," she said, her voice strained.

There was a moment of silence that her words dropped into like an anchor.

"Hang on," I said. "What do you mean, 'a break'?"

"A little time for ourselves," my mother said. She focused her gaze just over my shoulder toward the sliding doors. "Just...a *break*."

"What are you talking about?" I ground out. "You don't take 'breaks' from your family."

Stu looked bewildered, and Sasha's eyes had gone wide.

Mom thrust her cutlery back down to the table, but stopped herself just short of letting them slam.

"Keep your voice down, young lady!" she said in a harsh whisper. "Don't you dare broadcast our family issues to the neighborhood. I mean that I'm taking some time for *me*. I need some space. I'm going to be living down in Naples for a while, in theater housing. It's a long drive from here to there, and one of the patrons offered up her guesthouse, and...and I'm *sick* of feeling like the heroine of an Ibsen play. I'm going to go do what *I* want to do for a change, and if you kids can't support me in that, then I guess I'll just have to do it all on my own."

She took a shaky breath and then stood up. I didn't try to stop her when she brushed past me and went into the house.

"Jesus."

I looked over at Stu, whose voice was all but inaudible. His face was pale, and he reminded me of the little kid I'd grown up with. Sasha's mouth was open, and her eyes met mine as though looking for answers.

And all I could think about was my dad in the garage, skipping dinner so he could work on the cabinets he was making for my mother.

seven

We packed up and got out of there. Mom had disappeared into her bedroom after dropping her bombshell—somehow still managing to make me feel like the bad guy for yelling at her. I couldn't even say goodbye to my dad. I didn't know how to face him.

All I wanted was to drive straight over to Kendall's, wrap myself up in his arms, and pour out the whole story to someone who could give me the objective distance to process it. But Stu and Sasha had looked shell-shocked ever since the Mom Bomb. They couldn't be left alone. I told Stu to follow us to my house.

As soon as we made my front door, Sasha pushed my brother down onto my ratty yellow living room sofa and then plopped listlessly down beside him.

"What the *fuck* is up with your parents?" she said.

Stu didn't even react, just sat slumped, staring at his hands in his lap. I set my purse on the table by the door and came to sit on his other side, bookending him.

"Mom's not leaving him, is she?" he asked the room at large. "She can't be leaving him."

"They're the most solid couple I know," Sasha said. "If they get divorced, there's no hope for any of us."

Since her own parents had gotten divorced when we were in seventh grade, Sasha had adopted herself into ours. And we adopted her right back, as evidenced by the fact of my mom including an "outsider" in her casual announcement that she was leaving my dad. Sasha was family too.

I didn't answer her. I had no idea what to say. The two of them were upset enough for all of us—I didn't need to add to it. No one spoke for a long time. We sat together on my sofa leaning against one another, linked together like plastic barrel-of-monkeys.

Finally, Stu seemed to snap out of his stupor enough to look around for the first time.

"Damn, Brook. What ate your house?"

Sasha smacked his arm. "Not now, Stuvie."

But he worked himself free of our dogpile and stood up to get a better look at the walls. "Seriously, sis. What'd you use to get the paper off, a jackhammer? Ever hear of wallpaper remover?"

He was clearly recovered enough for smart-assery. I pushed up off the sofa. "I'm going to go wash the chlorine off me."

"Nice going, Stu," I heard Sasha snap behind me.

"What?"

Their bickering voices faded as I headed back toward my bathroom to take a shower. When I got out, towels wrapped around my head and body, Stu was sitting on my bed, leaning back against the pillows that were propped against the wall in lieu of a headboard.

"Geez, sicko," I said when I saw him. "You're lucky I didn't come out naked."

He made a face. "You walk around naked? Exhibitionist."

"In my *home*? Where I live *alone*? Yes, unbelievable as it may seem, sometimes I do come out of the shower naked." I was a little reassured that Stu was managing banter. A sarcastic Stu I knew how to handle; silent, devastated Stu worried me. "What did you do with Sasha?"

"She's in the other shower. Is this what you two do on girls' night? Kinky."

"Stu, I'm a mental health professional, so I want you to believe me when I tell you you're deeply sick."

Instead of lobbing back an insult, he fingered my beige comforter, looking down at it. "I like what you're doing in the house," he said after a moment. "I think it's going to look nice."

Weirdly, the unexpected compliment made my eyes prickle. I

sat down on the bed next to him, shoving at his legs with my butt to get him to scoot over.

"You don't have to say that. I know it looks condemned."

He looked over at me. "I'm not kidding. The way you're going at this is smart—starting with a clean slate before you start making improvements. It'll take some work, but this place isn't really in bad shape, structurally. I think you can make it look good. You know, with this floor plan you could actually use the other two bedrooms as a home office for your practice."

"I could if I had any money. Which I do not." I swung my legs up to lean back next to him against the pillows.

"Could you please go put some clothes on if you're going to sit so close? It's really kind of *Flowers in the Attic* for me."

I pushed his shoulder, laughing as I got up and headed for my walk-in closet. "That was such a chick book. You're really showing your feminine side," I called back to him as I grabbed jeans and a T-shirt and pulled them on out of his sight.

He said nothing, and I thought he might have left my room. But as I was sliding on a pair of flip-flops his voice came again.

"This thing with Mom is kind of freaking me out."

I leaned against the wall and shut my eyes. *You and me both,* I wanted to say.

But his dull tone told me how hard this was hitting Stu—nothing had ever been so grim before that he couldn't make a joke out of it.

So I rallied up my best big-sister, wise-therapist voice instead. "I know, babe," I said from inside the closet. "I'm sure this is just...just some phase or something. All couples have trouble from time to time. This is really the first time Mom and Dad have had anything big, so they're way overdue."

"You think? You've seen stuff like this before? You think they'll work through it?"

There was such naked pleading in his tone, I sagged lower against the wall. That singular vulnerability I could hear—that he'd let himself express only with me safely out of his eye line—made me take a breath and tell Stu the only big lie I'd ever told him.

"Yeah, little brother, I do. I think everything is going to be fine."

Later that night I snuggled into my queen-size bed, realizing as my legs curled into the cool sheets how long it had been since I'd gotten into bed alone. I wrapped myself around the phone receiver, instead of Kendall, and hoped he was still awake. I was glad Stu and Sasha had wound up staying so late—by the time we'd found *Meet the Fockers* on television and sprawled in my living room with a liter of white wine and every bag of cookies in my cupboard, they had both seemed to cheer up a little. But all I had wanted all night was to hear Kendall's voice and feel some reassurance myself.

"This is Kendall Pulver."

For one second I thought it was his voicemail, but the noise in the background and the pause after he spoke told me otherwise. I glanced at the clock. He was still with his clients after midnight?

"It's me. Where are you?"

"Brook? Hey! Hang on."

I heard the muffled sound of his voice talking to someone, and then the loud music and chatter abruptly torqued back as if he'd hit the volume button.

"Hey, babe. Had to go outside to hear you."

"Where are you?"

"Iniquity, can you believe."

"You're kidding." Iniquity was the kind of downtown nightclub you hated just to walk by, with the heavy bass leaking out and putting your heart into arrhythmia even out on the sidewalk, and a receiving line of freshly legal kids slouched against the front of the building smoking, sending their languid puffs of ennui wafting into your face. "With your clients?"

"No, I just felt like stopping in. Yeah, of course with my clients. Why else would I risk eardrum rupture and black lung? This guy's down here with his two sons, and I think they're determined to get in some pretty heavy-duty father-son bonding experiences."

"Oh."

"Hey, man, watch where you're going." Kendall's voice was sharp.

I heard a slight scuffling, male and female laughter, and a lackadaisical, "Chillax, dude."

Kendall muttered something under his breath. "Sorry, babe. It's a zoo down here."

"That's okay. We can talk later."

"No, no, come on. How was family dinner?"

I picked pills of fabric off the sheet. All I'd wanted all night was to talk to him about what had happened, but I didn't feel like shouting it into the receiver while Kendall strained to hear me between techno songs bleeding out onto a busy downtown street. "Fine."

"How's Sasha's nineteenth nervous breakdown?"

I'd told him about what's-his-name...the chef. I probably shouldn't have.

"She's fine. She and Stu and I ended up mostly hanging out."

"Those two ought to just date. Solve both their problems."

I wasn't sure what irritated me more—the implication that my brother and best friend were somehow defective, or the ridiculous suggestion that they date each other. "You don't know what you're talking about."

"Hey...don't be angry. I was just teasing."

"Sorry. I just... It was actually kind of a rough night."

I heard a flare-up of noise in the background—pounding bass under something that sounded tinny and shrill over the phone line, with a swell of chatter layered over all of it. Someone called out something I couldn't make out.

"Just stepped outside because I couldn't hear," Kendall said away from the receiver. "I'll be in in a few minutes." The voice called out something else, and then the sound was muffled once again.

"Go on," I said. "The client beckons."

"He's twenty-three, and it's his daddy's money he's investing. He can wait."

"What about Daddy?"

"Daddy's another story... But the last time I saw him was outside the bathrooms with two girls I'm pretty sure had to have sneaked in on fake IDs."

"Yuck."

"Hey, I just lead the horse to water. It's not my business what he drinks. So come on—tell me about it."

But I didn't want to anymore. Maybe I was tired of thinking about it, or just tired, but after waiting all night to talk things over with Kendall, now all I wanted was to put the phone down and go to sleep.

"I'll just see you tomorrow."

"What do you mean? Aren't you at the condo?"

"No, I'm at my house. We wound up here and... I'm pretty tired."

The sounds in the background faded and I knew he was walking farther away from the club.

"You won't be there waiting for me? How will I know I'm home?" Kendall's tone was teasing, and something loosened in my tight chest.

"It'll smell like boy. No girl cooties," I said.

"I like girl cooties... Your cooties anyway."

I smiled into the phone and we listened to each other breathe for a few seconds.

"I'd better get back inside," he said finally. "I'll give you a call as soon as I wake up."

"Okay."

We said good night and I leaned over to put the phone on my bedside table. I was so worn-out I thought I'd slip immediately into unconsciousness, but I lay on my back for a long time, blinking up at the ceiling in the dim blue light seeping in through the blinds, my eyes scratchy and wide-open.

eight

The newspaper assigned me an email address for reader mail, and when I checked on Monday morning to see whether anyone had written in, I had thirty-seven messages.

Seventeen were some variation on how happy readers were that our local paper finally had a relationship advice column. Eleven were questions from readers that I could use for future columns. Four were nasty diatribes against dating, the mental health profession, "ridiculous navel-gazing," and me. Three were requests for a date. One was the most pornographic come-on I had ever read, offering to erase the memory of every bad relationship I'd ever had with his "tumescent love wand."

And one was from a man calling himself "Duped and Dumped," wanting to hire me to help him through a breakup.

That made client number three, and it looked like Sasha was right—I might have found my calling.

"Duped and Dumped" turned out to be Richard O'Flaherty, a kind gentleman in his late sixties. Over cappuccino at Daily Beans off Gladiolus, he told me he'd met "the love of my life, my soul mate" on an online dating site, moved her and all her belongings to his waterfront home after a single face-to-face meeting in her Omaha, Nebraska, hometown, and was devastated when she disappeared a month later with his computer, his wallet, and ten thousand dollars she'd cleaned out of his checking account.

"Richard...you gave her your PIN numbers?" I asked gently.

"She was my soul mate!"

My initial step was to combat his naiveté so he didn't get taken advantage of again. We spent the first half of our session together going over the ins and outs of Internet dating, and what danger signs to look for. I created a list for him of potential big red flags in online dating profiles. ("An old-fashioned girl who likes a real man to take care of her" could mean "looking for a sugar daddy." A woman who made a point of saying she "believed in the institution of marriage" might be trying to put a good spin on the string of ex-husbands in her wake.) I made a mental note to devote a future column to the topic.

Then we finished out the hour talking about the woman who'd conned him, and the way it made him feel, and why he thought he might have been taken in by her. Richard seemed to be a good-hearted, sincere man who was looking so hard for love, he was seeing it even where it didn't exist. After he left I sat for a few more moments at our table, jotting down a game plan for our future sessions to help him slow down and wait for a relationship to develop, instead of trying to make it spring fully formed into life.

This was such a common relationship misstep that I wanted to write a column right then. Sasha did the same thing—had one or two dates with someone where she really connected, and then made the mistake of thinking she knew enough about the other person to be in a committed relationship. A *lot* of people did it, and while I understood the urge to connect and be known and loved, you had to travel the path of getting to know each other. There were no shortcuts to that destination. That was why I was taking my time to decide about moving in with Kendall.

I finally had to fold up my notebook to get to my next appointment—with Tabitha Washington, who'd asked whether we could meet at her house after work, instead of somewhere public. I realized why as soon as she opened the door to me: Her face was blotchy, her eyes swollen, her nostrils red and chapped. She wore a pair of stained drawstring sweatpants and a quilted housecoat that had to have belonged to her great-grandmother.

I schooled my features not to react as I introduced myself, and Tabitha invited me inside. She led me to a sitting area with chintz sofas facing each other across a Pottery Barn coffee table, and flopped onto one of them. I sat down across from her.

Lisa Albrecht had started spewing invective against her husband almost before we were seated. Richard O'Flaherty had wanted to ease into talking about his breakup slowly. Tabitha simply got right to the point.

"So where do you want me to start?"

"Well...how about with a little background on your relationship?" I suggested. And we were off.

She'd been dating Cooper for five months—beginning not long after his wife cheated on him and then moved out of town. He was smart; he was kind; he was handsome. An emergency room doctor, he worked unusual hours that made it hard for them to spend a lot of time together, but the connection was real, and the sex, Tabitha mentioned repeatedly, was phenomenal.

"But last week Maria showed up at Verdad, where I was meeting some girlfriends, and cornered me," Tabitha said.

I knew the place—a Mexican restaurant downtown. "The wife?"

"*Ex*-wife," she stressed, and then frowned. "Well...estranged, I guess."

"They're not divorced?" She shook her head. That was a red flag, but I didn't want to form an opinion till I knew more. "Okay. What did she say?"

Her toffee-colored eyes welled up again. "That she knew who I was. That I was a home wrecker. That she was back to reconcile with Cooper."

"I'm so sorry. That must have been awful to hear. Was it true?"

"Well, I asked him about it the next day—right after I talked to you, actually. He said they just had to work out the details of the divorce. We had a date Friday night, and I thought things were okay, but then Saturday he said he was busy, and I heard... Shit." She wiped at her cheeks and stood up abruptly. "Would you like something to drink? I need one."

I always advised against people using alcohol to cope with relationship troubles. It could so easily lead to the worst breakup behaviors—drunk dialing, rebound hookups—and it only helped make a depressed person feel more depressed. But I didn't know Tabitha well enough yet to comment. Instead I simply asked for a glass of water, and was relieved when she came back with the same for herself.

She sat back down and took a deep, shaky breath. "Okay. I've got a friend who's a waitress at the Gulf Grill down at the beach, and she said Saturday night Cooper and his ex had a really cozy candlelit dinner there. That's an awfully romantic setting to work out a divorce," she said bitterly, taking a big gulp of her ice water.

There are no secrets in small towns—everyone knows everyone, or knows someone who does, and Cooper had to realize that something like that would travel right back to Tabitha's ears. This was not looking good.

"What happened next?" I asked neutrally.

"Nothing!" she wailed. "That's the last I talked to him. I haven't heard from him since. I texted him when I went to bed last night—just a casual, 'Hey, just wanted to say good night.' Then I called again this morning. He didn't answer."

Tabitha looked miserably unhappy, and was staring at me as if I were the oracle at Delphi, waiting for me to dispense a magical solution for her. I leaned back on her sofa and thought.

When I was younger I used to love making drawings with colored pencil or Magic Marker, then covering the whole thing in a thick, waxy coating of black crayon. I always put the black pages aside in stacks, and later I'd pick one out at random and scrape away the crayon in various patterns, never knowing which bright-colored drawing I'd reveal underneath.

Helping someone dig down to the truth is like that. You can't see what's really there until you start scraping away slowly, carefully, so you make sure to remove all the waxy black overcoating, not just smear it around the page on top of what's underneath.

The situation Tabitha found herself in was rife with impending disaster—the affair and breakup had happened too recently and too suddenly, and Tabitha had fallen for Cooper too fast. He wasn't just on the rebound; he was freshly on the rebound. His wife's tire marks had barely faded from the driveway. Even if he had worked out all his feelings about her betrayal (which I strongly doubted), he probably wouldn't be in any hurry to jump back into another relationship.

But the sex between them was *phenomenal*, Tabby repeated when I carefully voiced the thought, and I began to suspect she was blinded by it. Too often I'd seen women take great sex as an indicator of great love, and read a lot more into a relationship than was actually there. As Sasha liked to say, the heart muscle is directly connected to the vagina muscle.

Still, they'd been dating five months. After five months, I felt she was entitled to at the very least a phone call. The fact that Cooper hadn't bothered spoke volumes about his feelings. I would bet he wasn't remotely ready for the kind of relationship Tabby was looking for. Even though he might like her and enjoy her company, he obviously had a lot of baggage he hadn't even begun to unpack when they started dating. Now that his wife was back, they were clearly addressing their unfinished business. And Tabitha wasn't a character in that play.

But I couldn't come right out and say all of that to her. She'd have to see the truth for herself, so little by little we scratched away what was covering up the real picture of their relationship together.

"So how often did you and Cooper see each other before this?" I asked her.

"Well, he usually makes a date with me one night a weekend. And then we hook up sometimes for happy hour, or a quick dinner during the week."

I nodded. "Okay. If you guys run into people he knows, how does he introduce you?"

She thought for a second. "'This is my good friend Tabby.'"

Even now, five months in. I tried not to wince.

"Any birthdays in these five months? Holidays? How did you guys celebrate; were there gifts or a card?"

Her expression clouded over. "We spent Christmas and New Year's apart, because Cooper said he needed to see his parents and sister in Michigan. I got him a set of Le Creuset cookware; he gave me a sweater." Tears formed in her eyes again, and this time spilled over. "On Valentine's Day he took me to brunch and gave me a single white rose and a card that said, 'Thanks for all your kindness, caring, and compassion.' And afterward he dropped me off at home—I spent that evening watching *Love, Actually* alone with a box of Norman Love chocolates I bought myself and a bottle of red wine."

She slumped back against the sofa cushions, her head tipped down, occasional sniffles piercing the silence I let fall. She was almost there, and needed to figure this out for herself. Finally she looked up and met my gaze. "He's going to get back together with Maria, isn't he?" she asked dully.

I raised my hands and shoulders in a "who can say" gesture.

"But he's not ready for someone new."

I didn't answer. It wasn't a question.

Tabitha made a noise between a groan and a scream and flopped back in the chair. "God, I'm such an idiot! How did I not see this?"

She drew her knees to her chest to form a tight ball with her body and buried her face in her hands—not crying, but obviously losing herself in self-recriminations. That was counterproductive—berating herself was only going to keep her mired in misery, and it wasn't going to help her see her relationship more clearly and figure out what to do next, how to honor her own needs. I made a few attempts to draw her out and get her talking again, but Tabitha was too far down the road of self-reproach to respond.

I stood, took her glass, and carried it to the kitchen in one flow of movement. "Come on," I instructed. Right now Tabitha desperately needed to feel better about herself.

So I took her shopping.

Sometimes it's the most basic solutions that are the most effective. And it's called "shop therapy" for a reason.

While Tabitha tried on designer outfits at Nordstrom and slipped on shoe after gorgeous impractical shoe, I kept her talking. Not about Cooper this time. We talked about her work—the time she'd gotten to interview Meryl Streep when she'd come to town for a benefit at the Harborside Convention Center. The articles she'd written about illegal immigrants in Laredo, Texas, for a series in her old paper in San Antonio—stories that had won her a Texas Press award. We talked about her family—her mom, struggling to get by with full-time care of Tabitha's autistic brother, whom Tabitha sent money back to help support. The advocating she and her mother and other two brothers had done for autism awareness and research. The feeling she got the few occasions her brother looked directly into her eyes.

I hoped she sounded as accomplished, capable, and kind to herself as she did to me.

She wore one of her new outfits home—a silvery gray pencil skirt with a ruffled teal sleeveless top that made her eyes glow like embers. The pretty, polished woman in front of me was a far cry from the bedraggled, beaten one who'd opened her front door a few hours earlier.

"You look amazing," I told her honestly.

Tabitha stopped and checked herself out in a mirrored column. "I do, don't I?" She straightened to stand taller, and made a quarter turn to check out her rear view. "I wish Coop—" She cut herself off. "I'm going to call him when I get home. I think it might be best if we spent a little time apart. For now, anyway."

I nodded and suppressed a smile. This was where I'd wanted

Tabitha to get to, but if she was going to stick by it, the resolution had to come from her, not me. "That's a smart idea. Are you okay?"

She shrugged. "Not yet, but maybe in a while. He's got to figure out things with his wife"—she grimaced at the word—"before he starts something new with me. Or...whoever."

"Call me later?"

"If I need to. Thanks a lot. For everything."

"Good luck."

I watched her walk away toward her car, a little sashay in her hips. I wished it were always so easy to help someone figure out how to do what was best for themselves—most of us fight harder against seeing the things we don't want to see.

nine

Lisa Albrecht paid me an actual compliment on my first Breakup Doctor article.

"It didn't suck. Let's see where it goes."

She bumped up my inches to twenty-five (nine hundred to one thousand words, using newspaper math) and gave me the go-ahead to make it a weekly feature. I started working on my second column, combining reader questions with my own thoughts from the two clients I'd met with that day. The Breakup Doctor was like another persona, all-knowing and wise, compassionate, straightforward, and no-nonsense. Sliding into her skin was freeing. Exhilarating. All the tough-love advice I'd ever wanted to shout at my more self-destructive patients, and couldn't, flew unchecked from my mind through my fingers onto the page.

The number one rule of breakups is that you can always see them coming—if you look. It's easy to cling to the happiness you felt early in, to be willfully blind to the signs that things aren't as rosy as they used to be, and that trouble is looming on the horizon.

But the signs are always there.

Maybe his voice completely changes tone when he talks to other people, flatlining into disinterest as soon as he's talking to you. Maybe she stops telling you things about her day, her life, how she's feeling, when she used to be a Chatty Cathy. Maybe he comes home later and later every night, swearing nothing is wrong, but the unsettled feeling in your belly makes you wonder.

Trust that feeling. Trust the little voice in your head—the one that is always there, the little lizard brain that picks up on all the subtextual meanings that your crazy-in-love brain is impervious to—that says something is wrong.

The best way to handle being dumped is to prevent it. That might mean fixing the problems before they become relationship breakers. Or it might mean jumping off a sinking ship yourself, before you're pushed off the plank. Either way, awareness is the first step.

If you can't shake that uneasy sensation in your gut lately, open your eyes and take a good, long look at your relationship, and see if your instincts are trying to tell you something.

Then check in with the Breakup Doctor to learn what to do next.

When the column ran on Friday, I had a fresh deluge of emails. My new client roster steadily expanded, and suddenly I was scrambling to keep up.

Izzy Truman had called things off with her boyfriend of two years when she realized the relationship wasn't going anywhere. Even though it had been eight months since she ended it, she was still in love with him, and having a hard time letting go. Rachel Moretti caught her boyfriend in flagrante with his ex—she'd dumped him on the spot, but now she wanted to know if she should try giving it another chance. I suspected my verdict would remain my knee-jerk "hell, no," but I tried to keep an open mind till I heard the full story. Timothy McGarrett walked out on his girlfriend when she started pushing for a ring—now three months had gone by, he was miserable, and she wouldn't take his calls.

Paul Simon seriously underestimated: There are so many more than fifty ways to leave your lover.

*   *   *

Since I had no office, I arranged to meet my new clients at restaurants, at coffee shops, in hotel lobby bars, and sidewalk cafés. With what I charged my clients, picking up the tab at the places I arranged to meet them wasn't a hardship, and it was far cheaper than renting office space. It wasn't ideal, but at least the public places kept most people from careening over the edge as they told me about their breakups—and often it was the only reason I found time to eat. I tried to keep my orders outside of regular meals down to a cup of black coffee or bottled water—otherwise my waistline would expand as fast as my bank account was.

As my inbox filled up day by day with readers writing in, it seemed logical to create some sort of materials I could easily send out to people inquiring about hiring the Breakup Doctor—starting with what I did, and my rates. I racked my brain for specific descriptions of the services I felt qualified to offer: relationship counseling, grief therapy, life coaching. Thinking of Tabitha Washington, I added *image consultation*, figuring that if a makeover project were too daunting for me to handle alone, I could always pull in Sasha.

I also thought it was a good idea to specify what I *didn't* do. Among the list I proscribed any interaction on my part with a client's ex; investigative services; and posing as a new girlfriend. I stipulated a set of parameters as I thought them up, like "initial consultations by appointment only" and "payment payable at the end of each session."

At the rates I was charging, eight consultations a month would pay my mortgage. Two more would take care of most of the utility bills. If I could add another handful of clients to my roster each week, then within six months or so I could pay back what I still owed to my parents, catch up on my student loan payments, and set aside enough to convert half of my house into an office for my own practice.

I felt a happy little glow at the thought.

*   *   *

As I was putting the final touches on my third column the following Monday, I got a call from a local radio station. Would I be interested in doing an on-air interview as the Breakup Doctor a week from tomorrow?

My heart jumped as I thought of the possibilities—the number of people I might reach on the air...the new clients it might bring me. Yes, of course I would, I told the pubescent-sounding girl on the other end of the line.

"We'll do it live," she told me, her words firing out at me like machine gun bullets. "You'll be on the Kelly Garrett Morning Drive Time show, and then we might take some callers on the air; that okay with you?"

"Kelly Garrett? Like the Charlie's Angel?"

"What?"

"Never mind. Are there a list of questions I should be looking over ahead of time?"

"Don't worry about it. It's all casual—Kelly will ask about what you do, the new column, that kind of thing—just bring your best advice, and get there a little early so we can take you back into the studio, okay?"

Naturally I called Sasha instantly once I hung up the phone, and Friday after work we met at her apartment so she could prep me for the interview—and help calm my nerves.

"Take deep breaths before you go on-air, but not too deep— you don't want to hyperventilate," she told me as we sat in her living room with glasses of wine and a plate of fruit—Sasha's idea of hors d'oeuvres. "Make sure you're speaking from your diaphragm."

"What does that even mean?"

There followed a ten-minute demonstration of diaphragmatic breathing, with me lying on Sasha's floor making humming sounds while she rested a hand over my abdomen.

"When you get in front of the mike, pretend you're talking to one person—someone close to you, like me," Sasha instructed. "And remember, even though they can't see you, if you're smiling, you sound more confident and approachable."

"How do you know all this stuff?"

She shot me a disbelieving look. "How do you *not*?"

Sometimes I think Sasha is one superpower away from taking over the world.

"What do you want to do tonight?" I pushed myself just far enough off the floor to flop over onto the sofa, idly brushing carpet lint off my jeans.

"Where's the master of the universe?"

"Ha, ha. You've been talking to Stu. He's working late. So, what? Movie? Go see a band? Hang out here and make fun of reality TV?"

Sasha's silky blond hair curtained her face as she brushed away my imaginary body indent on the carpet. "Can't tonight. I have plans."

"A date?"

She nodded. "Someone special, actually."

It was all I could do to hold back a sigh. Weren't they all?

"Okay." I leaned up and pushed off of the sofa. "Have fun. *Careful* fun."

"Why is Kendall working so late? On a weekend?" Sasha looked disapproving.

"'Tis the season," I said lightly, poking my feet back into the shoes I'd kicked off. "It's not forever. And I asked him to set aside the whole day for us tomorrow. Even God rested." This week I'd made sure to ask him in advance. I picked up my purse. "Hey, you have to promise you'll be listening on Tuesday."

"I promise. I've got an interview in Naples first thing that morning, and I'll have you on in the car as I drive down there."

"That's an early interview."

Sasha cleared her throat and avoided my eyes. "Actually, I sort of wanted to talk to you about this story I'm working on."

"Talk to *me*? Why?"

"Well...It kind of has to do with you, actually."

I grinned. "Me? You want to do a story on me? What do you mean, as the Breakup Doctor?"

"Not exactly." She blew out a big breath, her cheeks bubbling out. And even so, she managed to look pretty. "I'm doing a profile—a big feature, actually. Interviews with a number of people...background, that kind of thing. With a tie-in to the theater. And I was hoping you'd let me use you as one of the interviews."

Two things set me on the path down which Sasha was traveling: her guilty expression as she looked everywhere but at me, and her quick, throwaway use of the word *theater*.

"Sash, you're not talking about a feature about the Breakup Doctor."

She examined the ceiling and shook her head slightly.

"You're..." I took a deep breath and then forced it out, knowing that where Sasha had looked Kewpie doll doing it, I probably looked blowup doll. "Are you doing a feature on my *mother*?"

She carefully investigated one baby blue fingernail. "Oh, you know...yeah."

"Oh, my God! How the hell did they find out about that? Why would they care? She's a community theater actress! She's not even that, actually—at least not for the last thirty years."

"Yeah, that's part of the angle. A local performer's return to the stage, in such a huge role."

I *thunked* my purse back down on her sofa table, disgusted. "Sash, the last thing she needs is positive reinforcement. Can't you kill the piece? Or at least get out of doing it?"

"Um, no. Not really."

"You have to. My mother thinks you're perfect. She would eat it up if you interviewed her. She'd think this whole thing was all okay. Can't you tell the paper you can't do it? Make something up—get them to send some crappy freelancer, if they have to do it."

"Yeah. Thing is, Brook... I pitched the idea."

I stared stupidly at her for a moment, no words forming in my head. I finally summoned up: "Why?"

She shrugged. "We were low on stories and were all throwing

around ideas. It just popped out. Amid, like, five other pitches, but this was the one Lisa latched onto."

"But...why? How is my mother newsworthy? Who is she? Just some middle-aged housewife who thinks she's Blanche Dubois."

Sasha looked like I had slapped her. "That's what you think of her? Really?"

"I don't want to talk about it, Sash." I yanked up my purse and charged over to her front door.

"But, Brook, you don't think she—"

"I'm not kidding. I don't want to talk about it. You know how I feel about you doing the article. You want to do it anyway, I can't stop you. But don't expect me to give you some Norman Rockwell happy-family interview for it."

She was looking at me now with an expression I couldn't read. Which was weird—I could always read Sasha.

"Okay," she said after a few awkward beats. "Are you sure you're fine with it?"

I shot her a look.

"All righty, then. Break a leg on Tuesday."

"Right."

"I'll call you afterward to tell you how you sounded."

"Yeah."

"Brook..."

I turned around and faced her. She looked so forlorn it was all I could do not to rush over and hug her, tell her not to worry, that I wasn't that upset. Except that I was.

"It's rotten timing, Sash," was all I said.

"I know." It hung in the air like an apology.

Finally I heaved a great, long-suffering sigh. I couldn't stay mad at her. I never could. "Call me after the radio interview. I want to know what you think."

Her face brightened like sunshine after a storm, and I let myself out the front door.

ten

With Kendall at the office and Sasha on her date, I stopped at the grocery store and picked up a few things, then headed over to my father's house. Though I'd checked in on him with phone calls since Mom had moved out and he'd sounded okay, I felt guilty for not making time to go see him.

I was nervous about what I'd find—Dad sitting motionless in front of a blank television screen, maybe, gazing down at the remote in his hand as if he wasn't quite sure what it was. Or sifting through old photo albums and hurriedly wiping tears from his eyes when he saw me. Or sitting on their bed, clutching my mother's bathrobe to himself and staring slack-jawed into space.

But I found him at his workstation in the garage, just like he always was. As if today were any other day.

"Doll!" he said when he saw me, and put down the paintbrush he was using so he could hug me. He smelled like wood stain and sawdust and sweat.

"Hi, Dad. I thought we might have dinner together tonight."

My dad looked a little confused. "Oh, yeah? Well, that sounds great, sweetheart. Let me get cleaned up here and I'll take you somewhere..."

"It's okay. I brought groceries. We can eat in. Roast chicken and broccoli sound good?"

He beamed. "My favorite."

It wasn't—my mother's beef bourguignon was. But it was just

like Dad to say so. I settled onto a stool next to his work area. "How are you doing, Daddy?" I asked gently.

"Me? I'm fine, doll. Doin' fine. Watch you don't get your pretty blouse there into the stain."

"Have you heard from Mom?"

Dad's hand jigged to the side, just fractionally, enough to mar the almost perfectly straight line of stain he was applying.

"Well, you know, hon, rehearsals are so busy at the beginning of a show..."

"She hasn't called you at all, has she?"

"Brook, honey, she—"

"Geez, Dad! Don't make excuses for her she hasn't even had the decency to make for herself!"

"This is between your mother and me, sweetheart."

"But she—"

"That's enough, Brook. We're not going to talk about this anymore."

The hard tone of his voice made my mouth snap shut in surprise. My father never reprimanded me. Ever.

"Why don't you tell me what's going on with you?" he went on easily, as though I'd imagined his sharpness. "Those columns you're writing are really something. That gonna be your new job?"

His back was to me as he talked, a dark patch along his spine where he had sweated, the material of his shirt clinging and bagging, clinging and bagging as he moved his arms while he worked. The sight transported me back to my childhood, to a hundred other conversations just like this after school or before dinner or on a weekend morning. It was always easier to talk to my father than my mom. I watched every expression that flitted across my mother's face for a clue to her reaction, tailoring my conversation according to her frown, a nod, the light of approval in her eyes. With my father I simply sat and let my mouth follow wherever my mind wandered, talking to Daddy's back while he murmured just enough noises to let me know he was listening.

I found myself rattling off everything that had happened—the reaction to the column, my bulging roster of new clients, and the radio show. I even idly mentioned Stu's idea to create an office out of the guest areas of my house.

"Hey! I'm proud of you!" my dad jumped in. "I tell everyone my girl knows which end of a drill is up. How 'bout I come over there and lend a hand till we get the job done?"

I thought about it. Maybe Dad and I could do it on the cheap, and with an office in my home I'd be back in practice in no time. Plus I'd be able to keep an eye on Dad meanwhile. It was actually a really workable solution.

"Really? You wouldn't mind?" I ran my palm along a cabinet door awaiting staining. It was silky-smooth from hundreds of patient passes with a sander. "That would be fantastic, Dad. You just reignited my entire career."

He made a dismissive noise and gave a partial shrug without disturbing the geometric precision of his brush line. "It's nothing. My girl's an entrepreneur—a parent's proud of something like that."

The words hung in the air between us, and I wondered if my dad was thinking the same thing I was—that only one parent was around to be proud.

"I'm going to start cooking, Dad," I said, getting up off the stool. "I'll call you in time to wash up."

He'd tuned me out before I was even out of the garage, utterly absorbed again in his project for my mother.

As I started putting dinner together in their gutted wreck of a kitchen, for just a shiver of a second I sympathized with my mom. Dad was a craftsman—when he did a job, he not only did it right; he did it artistically. Like the butter-smooth cabinet I'd run my hand over in the garage, everything he ever did, he did meticulously. When he finished a job, it looked as though it had cost a fortune. But he'd been promising her the refinished cabinets for months, and meanwhile my mom had been living in a kitchen that looked like a hurricane had swirled through.

I stopped in the middle of rubbing fresh rosemary underneath the skin of the chicken, frozen with a thought. Did that have something to do with her departure? In every way Dad's philosophy was, "It takes as long as it takes to get it right." Mom was more of the "Get it done" school of thought. If Dad was a Renaissance man, Mom was the Industrial Revolution.

The thing was, while I could appreciate my dad's thoroughness and care with his projects, I was a lot more like my mom. Now that I lived in a half-finished renovation "before" of my own, I could understand how the disarray took a toll on your psyche. Living in a state of "almost there" and "not quite done" and "still in progress" made you feel like your whole life was on hold, waiting...always waiting to be "finished."

I pulled my hand out, realizing it was just resting between the clammy chicken meat and its pebbly skin. I grimaced and turned to the sink to wash the stickiness away, my momentary empathy for my mother swirling down the drain with the fatty bits of chicken.

Over dinner I worked hard to keep the conversation lively, but my mother was as fully present in her absence as she ever was sitting at her end of the table. My dad's eyes drifted to her empty chair too often despite his pasted-on smile, and looked like swallowing was an effort. I knew that my laughter was too sharp, too loud, like the barking of a maniacal seal. But at the end of the night, after we cleaned up the dishes and put them away, Dad gave me a massive hug in the foyer and repeated over and over how nice this had been, what a wonderful surprise. His cheerful smile lasted almost until the door closed behind me.

Almost.

The sky was clear and untroubled as a baby's conscience the next morning as I steered Dad's eighteen-foot runabout, the *Joie de Viv*—named after my mother—down the canal behind my parents' house.

Kendall sat in the chair next to me with his feet splayed and planted on the deck, one hand gripping the starboard gunwale and the other clenched around the seat cushion as though it could be used as a flotation device. I made a mental note to dig out the life jackets so he could see them. The cooler I'd packed last night was stowed under the bench seat in the bow, and I had an entire romantic day planned.

We bobbed out of the canal and into the Caloosahatchee, motoring mostly at idle through the manatee zones until I could pick up speed. Just before the river opened up into the gulf, I pulled the boat into a cove that formed an inverted comma on the northwest side of Picnic Island, a little mound of land in the channel. I knew it as well as I'd known our backyard growing up.

Normally in the winter months, locals stay far away from the beaches. Snowbirds clog the roads and the sand, rowdy spring breakers make relaxation impossible, and vacationing families line the shore with their umbrellas, coolers, and plastic children's toys. But Picnic Island is accessible only by boat, and it tended to be overlooked in the tourists' rush to tonier Sanibel and Captiva and Cabbage Key. There's nothing on the tiny island but mangrove and scrub pine—no restaurants, no souvenir shops, no palm trees, not even any bathrooms—and for that reason it tended to be a lot less popular with the weekend-boat-rental crowd.

"Just drop it straight down," I called to Kendall, who was standing in the bow struggling to twirl the anchor line like a lariat, rodeo style.

"I don't have to toss the rope way out there so this'll hook us?" Kendall frowned at the Danforth anchor dangling from his hands.

"It's line, not rope. And no—it's all soft sand here. The anchor will bite in as we drift with the current." I throttled into reverse to hold our position while he examined the line. I'd grown up here, and boating and the water were second nature to me. Kendall's landlocked Nevada upbringing hadn't prepared him for the life aquatic.

He dropped the anchor like a millstone into the placid gulf water, and after a moment I felt it catch. I cut the engine and came up

into the bow, where Kendall was leaning over the port-side gunwale, staring down into the clear water.

"How deep are we here?" he asked.

"Right now? About five feet or so. But at low water this'll be a
sand bar. I wouldn't anchor here in a bigger boat." I'd learned that
lesson as a teenager, after a couple of frantic missed curfews while
my friends and I waited for the tide to come back in.

He straightened to look at me, and I saw that already his nose
was turning ruddy. Kendall's skin was tender and pale as a nectar-
ine. I turned to the seat behind me and lifted the cushion to hand
him sunscreen from the storage compartment.

"So how do we get to shore?" he asked.

"Up to you. We can swim. Or wade. Or float. There's no standard technique."

As soon as my feet hit the sandy bottom and the warm water
wrapped around me like a hug, I felt all the stress and tension and
worry of the last weeks ebb away with the tide. The gulf always did
this for me—nothing was so bad that the sea didn't make it better.

Kendall stood in the boat watching me for a moment, and then
stepped awkwardly over the gunwale and *thunked* to his feet beside
me in the shallow cove.

"We couldn't just have driven to a beach the old-fashioned
way?" he asked, wrapping one long arm around me and pulling me
close.

I leaned in to kiss his soft, warm mouth, the taste of salt water
splashed on his lips mixing with the feel of his hand on my waist
and the sun on my shoulders. "You're a local now. Regular beaches
are for tourists."

We waded toward the shore hand in hand, the bottom sloping
almost imperceptibly up until we trailed out of the water and onto
the dry, sugary sand and crisp brown drifts of seaweed. A congrega-
tion of fluffy plovers scurried up the beach to avoid us, their match-
stick legs moving so fast they blurred, while colorless sand crabs
sidestepped into their holes, saved from being a meal by our intru-
sion. One lone great blue heron stood forty feet away, tall and stalky

and elegantly unconcerned with us. We were early enough that we had the beach to ourselves, but I knew it wouldn't last. I wasn't the only local who came here to escape the throng.

"You want to explore the island?" I asked, shoveling sand with my toe over a tiny deflated jellyfish.

Kendall hiked an eyebrow. "Barefoot?"

I pressed my lips to his shoulder, smelling coconut. "Pretend you're on *Lost*."

And then I showed him my world—the side he hadn't seen yet, the world of my childhood, where mangrove roots grasped at the water in a forest of tangles, slowly claiming land for itself from the surf; where roseate spoonbills flashed incongruously pink and cartoonish on a narrow strip of sand fingering out into the gulf; where frantic coquinas worked to rebury their sherbet-colored shells when a passing wave carved them out of the sand.

When Stu and Sasha and I were kids my family would come out here and build campfires and pitch tents and spend whole weekends on an island all our own. Dad and Stu caught snapper while Mom wrapped potatoes and corncobs in foil and buried them in red embers to roast. Sasha and I went down to the water with my little brother trailing behind us like a hopeful puppy, and gave each other sand scrubs and mud facials, and snapped off the stiff sea grasses that grew at the high-water mark and pretended we were smoking spindly cigarettes while Sasha threatened Stu with an ugly death if he told my parents.

In high school someone always had a runabout or a dinghy or a paddle boat, and there'd be ten or twenty kids from my school on the island on any given weekend night, standing too close to the fire, blaring music too loud, smoking things we weren't supposed to smoke, and making furtive, forbidden body contact. Sasha lost her virginity on one of those nights—to Tommy Housworth, after making me swear to keep watch for overcurious classmates outside the lean-to they'd created from a raft and two beach towels.

I closed my eyes, soaking in the smells of saltwater and sea life and rich, earthy decomposition. I hadn't come here in years, too busy with my practice and my house and everyday life to remember how basic the sea was to my makeup. Now I relaxed, feeling like me again.

I felt the jolt from Kendall's touch before I registered his hands trailing around my hips from behind and coming to rest on my belly, pulling me close against the heat of him. We were both damp from sweat and salt air, a fine coating of sand on our skin, and as he held me I felt his heart beating against my back, strong and steady.

"I love you, Brook," he said low into my ear. "I really do."

I pressed back against him and we stood there like that, twined together alone on an island in a perfect moment. It didn't matter that we'd been so busy at work lately that we'd hardly seen each other. It didn't matter that my house was a wreck, or that my career path was up in the air, or that my mother had turned her back on our family and I didn't know what would become of my dad. All that mattered was this moment by a gentle sea, the inviolate present, on an island rich with both my history and my future.

I had packed a feast too bountiful for two people to consume, and it took both of us to tote the cooler from the boat, buoying it on the water's surface as we glided it to shore. From the Italian deli I loved on McGregor I had fat olives in every shade of black and green and brown and yellow; strips of prosciutto and sopressata and pancetta so thin you could almost see through it; hunks of bread that warmed in the sun, golden crunchy on the outside and tenderly doughy inside; cheeses in buttery shades. From Fat Louie's, the gourmet shop, I brought containers of red pepper relish and wild berry spinach salad and Tuscan bean salad. For dessert there was key lime mousse and chocolate layer cake from a delectable bakery I'd discovered at one of my client meetings.

We ate on towels on the sand as we watched boats pull into our cove and anchor, until it looked like a regatta. Finally I set down my paper plate and leaned back.

"Ugh."

"Ugh," Kendall echoed, lying beside me and closing his eyes against the orange sun, holding his belly. "Good thing the water's shallow—I don't think I float anymore."

I turned my head and watched him as he lay on the beach. Kendall was so often contained, careful, perfectly groomed. Now his limbs were sprawled across the towel, legs bent up and arms splayed out to his sides. His short hair, usually parted on the side and combed down, stuck up in random directions from his head, giving him a boyish look. A fine sprinkling of sand coated his skin, clumped here and there where he'd rested a hand or a thigh on the beach. I loved him like this, and I wished I had a camera.

"Take a picture—it'll last longer." His eyes never even flickered.

I laughed and scooted closer to him, flipping onto my belly and resting my chin on my hands. "You read my mind. I was just thinking that I wish I had a picture of you like this—all beachy and disheveled and relaxed."

"Mmmm." His eyes were still closed, but his lips smiled. I watched him some more, inching my fingers closer to rest on top of his. He clasped them but otherwise didn't budge.

I turned back over and lay beside him, closing my eyes and letting the wash of red behind my eyelids and the warm blanket of sun lull me into a half-sleep to the sounds of the crying gulls and the gentle susurrations of the Gulf of Mexico and the distant snippets of a family's conversation that eddied over on the breeze.

"...needs to keep an eye on him."

"...enjoy herself...see them from here..."

"You...coddle her. When...learn responsibility?"

The voices were growing louder and I shifted position and opened my eyes, glancing to where they were coming from: a couple not much older than we were, lounging on their boat with their gazes trained on a little boy about five or six squatting on the shore with a garden trowel and a plastic bucket. A wiry, sun-browned teenage girl walked along the water forty or so yards away, studiously avoiding looking in her parents' direction.

That was my family when Stu and I were little—except that next to me as I pretended my parents didn't exist was Sasha, who could only ignore my brother for so long before sneaking up behind him and scaring him senseless, or plopping down on the sand beside him and drizzling baroque wet-sand designs on top of his sand castles from her fingers. I smiled at the parents on the boat, even knowing they couldn't see me. *They'll be okay,* I wanted to tell them. *One day they will like each other. And you'll have done okay.*

I pictured Kendall relaxing next to me on a boat like that, while the two of us watched our children play and argued harmlessly over our parenting styles. We still hadn't talked about his asking me to move in. It scared me to death to think about taking a plunge like that again. I'd been burned so badly the last time I'd thought I'd found forever. How could I trust in that again? How could I trust that forever even existed? If I'd ever thought any two people were indivisible, it was my mom and dad, and look where they'd ended up.

But Kendall wasn't Michael. I'd picked him specifically for that reason.

Laughter carried over on the wind and I saw the woman on the boat playfully shove her husband's arm. I felt the sun-stiffness on my face as I smiled.

Kendall had sat up and was watching the couple too, his face furrowed from sleep. He looked adorable—logy and rumpled and familiar.

I took a deep breath of the salt air. "Kendall."

"Mmmmm."

"Why don't we go get my things tonight and take them to your house?" My heart was thudding, but this time with excitement as much as nerves. I was ready. I'd said it.

"Oh...babe. I can't tonight."

"What?"

I'd been ready for a smile, for his face to light up. Instead he pushed up off the sand and busied himself organizing the cooler and our sunscreen and our discarded shorts. He pulled on the end of the towel we'd been lying on, so I rolled off of it and he yanked it up.

"Don't get mad. I just have to go into the office for a while." He started rolling the towel into a giant, sloppy doobie.

I stood up, trying to brush the sand from my thighs, but gave up when it felt like aggressive dermabrasion. "You have to be kidding. On a Saturday? Our first day off together in how long?"

"It's my busy season." He leaned over to lift one handle on the cooler and waited, but I made no move to grab the other.

"What are you doing?"

"Come on. Let's head back."

"No."

"*No*?" He almost spluttered it.

"It's our *life*, Kendall. I know you're crazy at work. So am I, but our relationship doesn't just go away." My voice broke on the last word, and I realized with horror that I was about to burst into tears.

He dropped the handle and rubbed his forehead with a single finger—hard, as though something were stabbing its way out from the inside. "Brook, please. I'm just... I'm trying to do the right thing here."

My heart was pounding—with fury...with fear. "I don't understand what that means. You have to be on call twenty-four-seven for every client you have? Their personal lackey?"

"That's not it. Look, you can't understand—"

"I can't *understand*? I have responsibilities too, Kendall. I've been running around for weeks trying to hold my career and my house and my family together. And I'm a psychologist! Understanding is my *job*!"

"You're not a real psychologist; you're just a counselor."

I had known the second the word had come out of my mouth that it was inaccurate, and I had no idea why it popped out. But Kendall's answer floored me. Half the time *he* called me a doctor, and I corrected him every time. Silence dropped between us like a sandbag. I wondered if the couple I had been watching a few moments ago was watching us argue now. This was when we needed to break the tension with laughter, the way they did. To defuse this potential bomb before it exploded.

But Kendall didn't crack a smile. "I'm sorry, Brook. That was uncalled-for."

I shrugged, not meeting his eyes. "It's the truth." It was the first time I'd gotten the not-quite-good-enough feeling from anyone except my mother.

He was the one who'd asked me to move in with him, but now I felt like a pathetic, needy girlfriend pushing for too much, too fast. I felt the way I had when Michael torched the future he'd promised me with a single phone call. I waited for Kendall to backtrack—the touch of his hand, reassurance, anything, but the only sound between us was the crying of seagulls.

"I'll get you back so you can get into the office." My voice was flat. *Say no. Change your mind.*

"Thanks."

eleven

I dropped Kendall off at his condo without another word after our fight, and stormed back to my own house. Furious at him, and needing to bleed off steam, I seized on a home improvement project: running my Dad's electric sander over the pitted living room walls where Sasha and I had ripped up the wallpaper. Flying dust made my chest ache from coughing, and the fine particles lodged into my sinuses, so I finally tied a pair of panty hose over my face as a filter. I couldn't find my safety goggles, so I wore an old snorkeling mask strapped over my head. It was not my best look.

My mind couldn't let go of the thick stew of anger and resentment I'd held on to ever since Kendall and I had wordlessly reloaded the cooler onto Dad's boat and I'd yanked up the anchor and thrown the boat into reverse.

How could he have planned to work *today*, the first day we'd spent together in weeks? How could he be so thoughtless?

Worse, why did he have to tell me right when I finally said I was ready to move in together? Didn't he know what it had cost me to finally say yes to him? How hard it had been for me to trust again, and take another leap of faith? What a big step this was for me?

Shame heated my face. No, actually, he didn't.

I'd never told Kendall about Michael.

I justified the omission: You didn't talk about previous relationships when you were starting to date someone—that was Dating

101, as I'd tried to tell Sasha a hundred times. And then, by the time things were starting to get serious between us, we'd been together for a couple of months, with me practically living at his house already. At that point it felt like it was too late to bring up something so huge.

So how could Kendall have had any idea how sensitive I was in that area? I'd never let him see it.

And that meant that our fight was really my fault.

I shut off the sander and stepped off the ladder, nearly setting my flip-flop down on a tack strip I'd exposed when I'd ripped out the old carpet. Its rusty nails bristled like burnt-orange fangs. *Slow down*, I admonished myself. There was no need to let my recriminations make me careless.

I fired the sander back up and started the same mindless process of smoothing it in gentle circles over and over small areas at a time, wishing I could smooth my agitated thoughts so easily.

Was this how I'd driven Michael off too—by not letting him see any vulnerabilities? By hiding how I felt, being too reserved, too careful? Maybe he never felt like I loved him enough?

What a hateful irony.

Kendall was a saner kind of love...solid and secure. Even though we'd moved fast, I'd been sure to be careful, to keep my head about me. Maybe he had taken my caution as a lack of interest—maybe I'd hurt *him* by not answering him right away when he asked me to move in?

I was so lost in my thoughts, I didn't realize I was pressing too hard on the sander until I saw I'd left messy circular gouges in the drywall. Dammit. I shut the machine off and set it on the bare concrete floor, then ran a hand over the wall to assess the damage.

It was damp.

What? I tore the snorkel mask off and pushed the panty hose down to rest on my neck as I poked at the wall.

My finger sank in as if it were made of softened butter.

I stood staring stupidly for a moment at the bizarre image of my finger embedded in my wall before I pulled it back out. Hunks of drywall crumbled around the hole it left like a malevolent black eye staring back at me.

I rested the flat of my hand against the wall and pushed. My arm disappeared into it as if I were a ghost.

I registered the wet-dough feel clumped on my fingers, and I knew before I fully yanked my hand out what the matter was.

A leak behind the wall, from the adjoining bathroom.

With a sickness in my stomach, I began pulling out chunks of soggy, crumbly wall until the hole was the size of a grapefruit...a cantaloupe...a watermelon...and then there was no fruit large enough to describe the gaping maw in my living room.

As I stared into the bowels of my house my vision literally went red, and rational thought vanished in an instant. Suddenly I was tearing at the walls, soggy drywall splatting everywhere.

And still it wasn't enough—I needed to destroy something. I reached for the closest weapon at hand and my fingers wrapped around the handle on Dad's sander, and before I could check the impulse, I swung back and smacked the heavy sander with all my strength into the wall.

Two things happened as I put the full force of my body behind the swing: The sander gave a disgusting wet-flesh thunk and then dropped from my hands to the concrete floor with some ominous rattling sounds. And my foot landed with all the weight of my body directly on the rusty exposed tack strip.

I let out a howl.

I grabbed my foot, hopping in place to keep my balance. Blood was dripping along the rubber of my flip-flop, but even after I tore it off I couldn't see how deep the wound was. I took a few deep breaths, coming back to myself, and hobbled into the master bathroom, leaning against the counter so I could draw my leg up yogi-style. The flesh around the punctures was white and shocky-looking where I wiped away the slow-welling blood. Did I need stitches? A tetanus shot?

My mom would know. I realized with a jolt of surprise that she was the person I wanted to talk to most. Because I had a boo-boo. I limped toward where I had left my cell, but four numbers into calling home I jabbed the "off" button. Mom didn't live at home anymore.

My foot continued seeping sinister dark, thick blood, so I hopped back toward my bathroom, still holding the phone, trying to keep from dripping all over the concrete slab. Then I looked down. What did it matter? I deliberately planted my foot, watching the dark stains it left on the bare gray cement.

I dialed again—this time Mom's cell—and she picked up after two rings, her "hello" so deliberately impersonal I knew she had seen the caller ID.

I didn't respond, abruptly feeling stupid.

"Brook Lyn?" my mother said.

"Yes?" I said, as though she were a telephone solicitor inquiring, "Is this the lady of the house?"

Another beat. "Brook Lyn, are you there? I can't hear you. I have plenty of bars, so I think it's your phone."

I sat on the bathroom counter and pulled my injured foot up across the other leg, wishing I had never picked up the phone. But it was too late to simply hang up. "I was calling to...to make sure that Stu and I know how to reach you."

"You can reach me on my cell phone, Brook Lyn. Obviously."

"*Obviously,*" I said sarcastically. "I was worried about emergencies." *Like what if I get gangrene and my foot falls off and I need a blood transfusion and you're the only donor match?*

"It's the Neapolitan Theatre. Your father has all of my contact information."

"Fine. Just making sure." My foot was throbbing, and I waited for my mother to fill the silence.

I heard a sigh. "All right, then. I'll talk to you later—"

"Do you know if I need a tetanus shot?" I blurted.

"A tetanus... For what? Are you hurt?"

"I cut my foot. Punctured it, actually. I stepped on a carpet tack strip."

"With nails?"

"Yes. Huge metal ones. Rusted."

"You stepped on a strip of rusty metal nails? Of course you need a tetanus shot, Brook Lyn. Don't be dense."

As a palliative, "don't be dense" wasn't really what I was hoping for. But that looked like the best I was going to get.

"Do you need someone to help you?" my mom asked.

She'd walked out on Dad. On our family. There was nothing I'd need from her.

"No."

Another sigh, and then my mom said, more gently, "Honey... I'm sorry. Are you okay?"

I didn't know if she was talking about my foot or everything else, but either way I'd give her the same answer. "I'm fine. Everything's fine. Thanks anyway."

I hung up the phone, hobbled over to my purse, and then headed for the emergency room.

twelve

The sun had sunk out of sight and dusk had set in by the time I limped into the ER. Only one other patient slouched against a chair in a corner of the quiet waiting area, a man reading the spread newspaper that rested on his lap. Behind the counter a blonde in scrubs chatted animatedly with someone out of my eyesight. I hobbled to the counter and stood in front of her for a minute or two, my wounded foot propped at an angle against my left leg, before finally clearing my throat.

"Can I help you?"

A curious greeting. *Yes, I have come to the emergency room of a hospital. Clearly you* can *help me.*

"I have an injury—I stepped on some metal nails. I think I need a tetanus shot."

"Insurance?"

"Yes, I do."

She finally looked up. "I need your *card*," she said in the tone you use with morons.

After I dug it from my wallet and placed it on the counter, she clattered a clipboard in front of me. "Fill out these forms, please, and have a seat. We'll call you in a few moments."

The guy in the waiting area was sitting next to the sole table provided, so I took a chair on the other side of it and started filling in the paperwork. A sour smell came off of him, like the weight room of a gym, and I breathed through my mouth.

By the time I had filled out the information form (front and back), my medical history, the release form, and the privacy policy—which I had actually had time to read—we were both still sitting in the teal-and-white waiting area. Molly Welcome Wagon was continuing her involved conversation with her unseen confidante.

"You have to wonder how long we'd have to sit here if it *wasn't* an emergency." The man's voice was strained, but amused.

I looked over. He was younger than I thought—maybe mid-thirties. He wore a plain T-shirt that had probably started as white, but was now smudged and sweat-stained. His jeans were faded and as dirty as his hands.

"How long have you been here?" I asked him.

He checked the watch on his left wrist, never moving the arm from where it rested across his lap. "Maybe an hour, hour and a half?"

I lifted my eyebrows. "Great. Well, I guess they have to prioritize." I slumped back against the chair.

He nodded to my bandaged foot in the sandal I'd stepped gingerly into as I left the house. "Cut your foot, huh?"

"I just need a tetanus shot."

"Ow. Step on a nail?"

"How did you know?"

"That's the only reason anyone ever gets a tetanus shot. That or opening beer cans with their teeth, and you don't seem the type."

I couldn't tell if he meant that as a compliment.

"How about you?" I asked politely.

He shrugged, right shoulder only. "Broken, maybe," he said, indicating his left arm with his chin. "Fell off a ladder onto a retaining wall."

"And they've left you sitting out here all this time? Doesn't it hurt?"

"Not as bad as it did when I fell. Maybe they've got someone else back there in worse shape than us," he said, again with the one-armed shrug.

We fell silent, having exhausted our conversational repartee.

I thought about calling Sasha, or Stu, or my dad, but I didn't want to worry them, and there was nothing they could do about it that I wasn't already taking care of myself.

I really wanted to call Kendall. But he was working, and until I could make things right after our argument, I didn't want to call him about something trivial.

More long minutes ticked by. It was awkward sitting so close to the man in the empty waiting room without talking, and I was grateful when the blonde at the counter called my name. I sneaked a glance over at him as I stood, his head bent a little and his mouth tight with pain. He still had the newspaper open on one knee, but clearly he wasn't seeing it.

"Excuse me," I said quietly when I reached the counter, "but you might want to see that gentleman before me."

"I can't hear you, ma'am."

I leaned over the counter close to her face and raised my voice not at all. "That man has a broken arm," I bit out. "My injury isn't that serious. I suggest you take him back first."

She pulled back, but her face stayed expressionless. Finally she snapped my insurance card down sharply on the counter in front of my chest. "We aren't ready yet," she said icily. "I was calling you to pick up your card."

I slid it toward me across the laminate counter as noisily as possible, glaring at her the entire time. She looked bored.

I went back to my seat, braving the man's sweat smell in a futile show of solidarity.

"Well, it was a nice try," he said as I flopped down angrily. "Thanks."

"You heard? She's horrible." I leaned back and grabbed a magazine off the table, tearing it as I yanked it open.

"So I'm gonna guess...up on a ladder painting, stepped down onto a two-by-four with a nail sticking out."

I looked over. I liked that story a lot better than the real one, in which I starred as the mentally unbalanced, dangerously violent destroyer of my own home. "Yup—you got it."

He winced. "That had to hurt. Major renovations, huh?"

"You have no idea."

There was an article in the magazine about Brad and Angelina having another child, or adopting another baby, or whelping puppies, for all I could tell. Mostly I was looking at the pictures, too unsettled to concentrate.

"I'm in home improvement myself."

"Oh, yeah?" I kept my eyes glued to the magazine.

"Yup. I build houses." I heard a slapping sound and glanced over to see him brushing at his muddy jeans leg. "But you probably guessed that already."

I thought it rude to tell him that no, I hadn't actually been speculating on him at all. "Oh. Well, tough time for it these days."

"You're not kidding. Market's dried up like crazy." He reached into a pocket with his right hand—carefully—and extracted a business card that had lost all its original crispness. "But we're looking to create a niche here—maybe you've heard of us?"

I took the crumpled card by a corner and glanced at it: *Millennium Homes—Conscious Building for a Greener World.*

"No, sorry, I guess not," I said, handing the card back.

He waved me off. "Keep it."

"I have a boyfriend," I blurted.

He looked amused. "That so? Congrats. I have a dog. Nice we could get to know each other a little better."

Heat flooded my face. Ridiculous. I was covered in particles and chunks of drywall, my hair flying in uncontrolled frizzies all around my head, and I still wore a pair of panty hose around my neck. He wasn't hitting on me. I yanked off the hose and shoved them into an outside pocket of my purse, tucked the weathered card in after it, then focused hard on my magazine.

The man went on as though I hadn't made an idiot of myself. "So what are you renovating?"

"My entire house," I said, and then muttered, "My entire life."

He whistled. "Whoa. Now that's an extreme makeover. So is that what you do—flip houses?"

I looked up and met his pale, drawn face. The man was only

trying to distract himself from the pain his arm was clearly causing him. I yanked myself out of my embarrassment and self-involvement. "No, I don't—that's just to keep the walls from literally crumbling around me. Actually I'm a counselor." I nodded down at the paper in his lap. "A relationship counselor. I write an article in the paper."

To my surprise a wide smile came over his face, straight white teeth against his sun-browned skin. He had a really nice smile, actually. "That's you? 'Ask the Breakup Doctor'? My mom showed me that article."

"Really? I just started writing it."

"She says you've got a good head on your shoulders. She loves reading about stuff like that, even though she... Well, it's been a hard time for her." He pressed his lips closed and stared back down at his paper.

"Divorce?"

"What? Oh—no! My dad passed away a few years ago. She just... Well, you know. Dating's tough at her age."

"Not in this town." Actually, his mother's demographic was probably the *only* age group for whom Fort Myers was a dating mecca. It might even be in the welcome materials for AARP.

He gave that one-armed shrug again. "Yeah, well...she's having a hard time letting go of my dad."

"Oh. I'm sorry." I didn't know what else to say. My mother didn't have a hard time letting go of *my* dad.

We both heard the blonde's tinny little voice drone out, "Benjamin Garrett?"

He stood up, but didn't walk toward the counter right away, standing in front of me as though he'd had something he wanted to say. The moment stretched out awkwardly until we heard the receptionist call out his name again, this time with a crisp edge of impatience.

"Hope that's not indicative of the bedside manners around here," he said finally.

I laughed. "Good luck."

"You too," Benjamin Garrett said. "With everything." He continued over to the counter and a moment later disappeared into the hospital's inner sanctum.

The receptionist called me back about twenty minutes after Benjamin Garrett went in, and I waited another forty-five minutes in an exam room until a male intern came in to take my blood pressure (which to my surprise was not 180 over 110). Then I waited another half hour before the doctor came in, glanced at the wound, gave me a tetanus shot, and advised me to be more careful.

When I left the hospital it was after eight o'clock. As I turned the car toward my house to face the mess I'd left and take a much-needed shower, I turned my phone back on—the snarky receptionist had informed me that all cell phones had to be turned off in the hospital, and then stood there in my exam room, arms folded, until I did it in front of her. I thumbed my call log. Nothing from Kendall.

I wasn't surprised, but I felt a pang in my stomach. It was our first argument, and I hated the unsettled feeling it had left me with. Now I wished I had called sooner to let him know about my accident, and that everything was okay with me. And with us.

I dialed his cell number. It rang four times before going to voicemail.

"Hi, it's me..." I started, then trailed off. I didn't want to apologize on voicemail, and I didn't want him listening to it while a client drummed impatient fingers if he was still at the office. I did the best I could in the meantime: "I hope... I hope you had a good day. I'll be over in little while—let me know when you'll be home." I held my finger over the "end" button, then changed my mind, brought the phone back to my ear, and hastily added, "Love you."

I pressed the phone off and let it flop onto the passenger seat. I knew he was busy—we both were. But it would have been nice to have someone there to talk to today at the emergency room, to wait with me, help me calm down, and keep me company.

Well, someone besides Benjamin Garrett.

As soon as I stepped in my front door I felt my eyes start to sting and my lungs contract from the acrid smell. My living room was a demolition zone. In the heat of my anger I hadn't fully taken in the damage I'd done to my wall, but after the pristine, clinical sterility of the hospital, it looked even worse to me. Most of the wall bordering my guest bath was gone, the edges deckled haphazardly around a gaping dark pit. Bits and clumps of sodden drywall were splattered on the walls and floor. A trail of dark red blood splotches stained the bare concrete slab leading across the floor. The house felt tired and empty and sad.

Wearily, I unplugged the sander from the wall, noticing as I picked it up to wind the cord that it rattled like a boxful of screws. I'd add buying Dad a replacement sander to my list of expenditures. Along with the cost of fixing my wall—and whatever plumbing catastrophe was happening inside it. And probably the cost of mold remediation. And my visit to the emergency room—since I was nowhere close to meeting the deductible on my health insurance coverage for the year, the entire visit would be out of pocket. On the plus side, if my home improvement efforts kept going the way they'd begun, I'd meet the deductible in no time, and then all my subsequent medical emergencies would be covered.

It felt hard to stay optimistic when my "bright side" scenarios were growing ever more feeble.

When I neatened up as much as possible, I went back to the bedroom and, with arms that felt heavy as lead, threw an armful of clothes into a suitcase. I drove to Kendall's town house and let myself in. I was too tired to even unpack my clothes, just wheeled the suitcase into the closet and dropped it onto the floor, shutting the door so he wouldn't have to see the mess.

In his expansive frameless slate-walled shower I let the hot water run over my shoulders and back for a long time, the high-pressure showerhead loosening up tight muscles.

When I came out there was still no sign of Kendall. I hoped he'd listened to the message I'd left him. If he was still angry or frustrated or annoyed, maybe he was working late to avoid me. Now I wished I'd called him at work and apologized directly. I picked up his house phone and tried him again.

After four rings it slipped into voicemail. "Kendall, it's me. I'm home—here, I mean, at your house. I hope you're not... I'm sorry about today. I know you're busy. So am I. I just get frustrated. I miss you. I miss spending more time with you. I wish our day hadn't ended on such an unpleasant note. I had a great time until then." I sighed, feeling stupid for pouring my heart out to a digital recorder. "We're okay. This is just...you know, one of those couple things. I miss you. Come on home, okay?" I pressed his phone off and set it on the sofa table behind the couch.

Then I lay down on the cream-colored leather and reached for the remote, letting the drone of CNBC bore me into an exhausted, restless sleep.

I woke up with a start, my heart racing, feeling disoriented in total darkness. Michael. Where was he?

I sat up, my fingers on the cool leather of the couch bringing me back to myself with a rush of shame. Kendall. I was at Kendall's house. What time was it? I blinked blearily at the DVR. Three in the morning? How had I slept so long?

I swung my feet off the couch and shook off the lingering dream I'd been having about my ex. I rubbed the back of my neck. It was stiff from being propped up against the armrest, and my shoulders had once again started to ache. I wished Kendall had woken me up when he got home, so I could have moved into the comfortable king-size bed.

I hauled myself to my feet and stumbled into the bedroom, focused on soft pillows and cool sheets and warm boyfriend.

Except that the bed was still perfectly made, and there was no lump in it where Kendall should have been.

I blinked again and tried to clear my head. I trudged over to his side of the bed and sat down, pulling the small alarm clock over closer in the darkness to peer at the numbers, wondering if I'd mis-read the other clock, or the power had gone out while I slept.

Two forty-nine.

A.M.

I reached to the nightstand for the phone and dialed Kendall's cell. Four rings, then voicemail. I hung up without leaving a message. Where was he?

I racked my brain. Had he told me he was taking clients out tonight? I couldn't remember. I didn't think so. Then again, if some visiting big shot had been in town looking for a good time, Kendall would of course have shown it to him.

My foot throbbed where I'd punctured it. My shoulders ached from wielding the heavy sander, and my eyes felt gritty from the Sheetrock particles. I knew this wasn't the way things would be forever—that I'd get the house into some kind of order, that Ken-dall's work would slow down. But right now I hated it. I might as well be single.

I scooted over to my own side of the bed and pulled the covers over me. Then I reached for Kendall's pillow and brought it over to my face, inhaling. It smelled like laundry detergent. I drew the pil-low all the way against my body and curled myself around it, and after a few more minutes of feeling sorry for myself, I finally man-aged to drift back into an uneasy sleep.

Bright, sharp sunlight woke me up shining directly into my eyes, because I'd neglected to draw the blackout curtains. The cheery daylight illuminated the entire room, including the other side of the mattress—where the undisturbed covers clearly showed that Ken-dall had never come to bed.

thirteen

No need to get upset. Nothing would be accomplished by storming into the other room to find out why Kendall had stayed out so late without calling, or didn't even let me know he was safely home before crashing on the couch. We were both adults. We could discuss this calmly.

I stood up, smoothed my hair, and even took a moment to brush my teeth and check for eye crust in the bathroom mirror. No sense coming at a "we need to talk" moment with sheet creases and bed head.

When I thought I was ready to approach him in a rational, calm way, I strolled into the living room.

Where Kendall was *not* lying on his cream leather sofa.

Of course. He didn't even like me to curl my feet up on it. I headed for the guest room, not even trying to tippytoe. If he wanted more sleep, he shouldn't have stayed out so late.

The navy-and-cream comforter was as pristine and undisturbed as it always was, thick pillows plump and perfectly creased at the tops.

Had he not come home at all?

I fumbled my cell out of my purse and checked the call log—nothing.

Dropping down onto the leather-backed stool at the breakfast bar, I forced my foggy brain to think. Granted, yesterday was the first fight we'd ever had. But how bad had it been, really? A little disagreement, some tense words, that was it—we'd barely even raised our voices. Was this how Kendall dealt with conflict? We hadn't dated long enough for me to know, but if it was, it wasn't a great sign.

Maybe he'd just been out with a client, and it had gone late. I tried to imagine what kind of client could convince even Kendall to do an all-nighter, and couldn't imagine anyone with enough money for that. Well, at least not any of his clients I knew about. If a high-roller had enough money to invest, I could see Kendall dancing nude in the middle of the Edison Bridge if the client wanted him to.

What if something had happened to him? My heart faltered and then started back up double time.

No point in panicking, I told myself firmly. It was only seven a.m. Kendall could come strolling in any second, looking rumpled and wrung-out and sheepish. If he'd taken his clients out too late—or had just decided to pout all night about our argument—maybe he stayed at his friend Ricky's house. Not calling was unacceptable, and we'd be having that conversation in no uncertain terms when he came home. But at least he'd had the sense not to make the long drive home if he'd over imbibed.

My phone vibrated in my fingers before the ring even started, and as I fumbled to answer, relief made my hands shake and my heart race.

"Where have you been?"

There was a beat of silence, and then, "Well, I've been to paradise—but I've never been to me."

"Oh. Sash."

"Wow, you know how to make a girl feel special."

I sighed and got up to go around the counter and into the kitchen. I didn't really need the caffeine after the jolt of adrenaline the phone had given me, but I started the coffee brewing for the comforting routine and smell of it. "Sorry. I thought you were Kendall."

"I can't imagine any way you might mistake me for him."

"He didn't come home last night."

"What?!"

I was instantly sorry I'd said it. "Don't get excited. He..." I didn't want to tell her about our stupid argument. Sasha had never warmed to Kendall, and she didn't need any fuel for that particular fire. "He was with clients, I'm sure, and probably just stayed with a friend once it got too late to drive home."

"Uh-huh. A 'friend.'" In case I missed her implication, she underscored it with a heavy tone of irony.

"Stop it, Sasha. That's not helpful."

"Did you call him?"

"Of course I did. It kept going to voicemail. He turns the ringer off if he's with anyone really important."

"Like you?"

I battled an urge to hang up on my best friend—the old-fashioned way, with a slam of the phone down onto something hard and unforgiving.

"Sasha, it's fine. Please don't worry." But she was right—I should have tried calling him already this morning. "Listen," I said, keeping my tone deliberately casual, "was this something important? Can I call you back in a minute?"

Sasha knew me too well. "Call me *right* back, whether you reach him or not. I mean it—immediately." She clicked off and I dialed Kendall's cell.

Voicemail. I waited through his outgoing message and then said, "Kendall, please call me as soon as you wake up." That was all. Simpler was better.

Despite my reassurances to Sasha, I actually was starting to get worried. Not that he was up to anything illicit—just that maybe I should seriously consider that something might have happened to him. Was I in his phone yet as his ICE? We'd never talked about it. Like a lot of things.

I didn't want to overreact. I forced myself to calmly pour my coffee and stir in sugar and milk, then coolly booted up my laptop and pulled up the numbers for the three hospitals between Fort Myers and Naples. A quick check, just to make sure, wasn't alarmist. Just cautious. Concerned.

Not one of them had a record of a Kendall Pulver being admitted, and I let myself take in a full breath. At least he wasn't hurt. He was fine. He'd be home any minute.

As if I'd summoned him, I heard a rattling at the front door, and I shot down the steps to open it wide.

Sasha stood there looking grim. She had to have left a *Smokey and the Bandit*-style caravan of cop cars piled up willy-nilly along the sides of every secondary road in her wake between here and her house. "You didn't call me back."

"Dammit, Sasha! I keep thinking you're Kendall."

"Seriously, you have to stop saying that. It gives me the willies."

I let go of the doorknob and turned to walk up the stairs. Sasha followed me up to the living room, hammering me with questions: "What time was he supposed to come home? When was the last call you had from him? Could you hear anything in the background? Did he sound different—funny? Who was he with? Did you call the hospitals?"

I answered only her last one. "Yes, I did. You want some coffee?" I shuffled back toward the kitchen.

"Why are you acting like this? How can you be so calm?"

I turned around with a clean mug in my hand to see her standing planted in the kitchen entrance, hands on hips, fixing me with an exasperated stare.

"Because," I said, in the unruffled, overenunciated tone you use with children, "he's not checked into any of the hospitals; ergo, he is fine. He'll be home when he gets home, and getting all stirred up about it isn't going to bring him back a second sooner. There's no sense being dramatic."

She continued staring at me for a few silent moments. Then she shook her head, threw up her hands, and walked out of the room.

"Sash?" I stopped midway through filling her cup. "Sasha? Where are you going?"

I found her in the master bathroom, wrist-deep in Kendall's

vanity drawers, pulling out the contents and lining them up on the counter.

"What are you doing?"

"Teeth whitener—I knew it—spare glasses...ew, nose hair clippers... Ha!" She held up a strip of condoms.

I snatched them out of her hand. "They're *ours*."

She raised an eyebrow. "Have you counted them?"

"No, I haven't counted them, freak show, but trust me—these are not exhibit A."

She yanked them back and gave me an arch look before throwing them into the drawer. "Trust *me—always* count the condoms."

"Sasha. Stop it. I mean it."

She paused in rifling the drawer and turned to face me, leaning against the marble countertop. "Okay, look," she said. "I'm not saying this is what happened. But being realistic for a moment, I do think you have to admit at least the possibility that he might be screwing around."

I braced myself in the doorway, curling my fingers tight around the frame, feeling my nails nearly dig crescents into the wood.

"No, actually, I don't think I do have to admit that possibility. Not everyone's relationship is a soap opera." I could hear the frost in my tone.

Sasha held up a hand. "All I'm saying is—"

"No. Stop saying it, because you're wrong, and I won't forgive you for saying it once you realize you're wrong."

"Yes, you would."

"Okay, I would, but seriously, Sasha, stop. That's not possible, okay?"

"Honey... I'm sorry—it's always possible. Men are men... You never thought Michael would—"

I slammed a hand against the doorframe so hard it made both of us jump. "That is so cynical. Has it ever occurred to you that maybe part of the reason you can't keep a relationship going is that shitty attitude?"

I'd gone too far, and I knew it even before I saw the look of hurt flash across Sasha's face.

I slapped a hand to my mouth and pulled it down across my lips as if I could wipe the words away, trying to calm myself down. "I'm sorry. That's just fear talking, and... I'm sorry, Sash—I really, really didn't mean that."

She nodded, even though I could see my comment still stung. Still, she didn't make any move to walk out.

There were a lot of times I thought I didn't deserve Sasha.

I reached over and squeezed her hand. She didn't return the pressure, but she didn't yank away. I pulled her with me out of the bathroom and over to the bed I still hadn't made, drawing her down to sit beside me, then took a couple of calming breaths.

"Okay, could Kendall be seeing someone else? Well, I suppose so, in that people are only human and they are capable of doing anything, given the right circumstances. But do I think he is? No. I don't."

Sasha looked like she'd swallowed a bee and it was buzzing to get out.

"Go ahead—it's okay," I said. "What?"

"Well...so would it hurt, then, just to take a quick look around the condo?"

I mulled that over for a second, and no sooner had I nodded my head than Sasha was up and off in a puff of dust like Road Runner. I stood to watch as she tossed the bedroom with a practiced efficiency: underneath the bed, underneath the *mattress*, in dresser drawers and beneath them, even knocking on the bottoms, presumably to see if they were hollow ("This isn't a Russian spy novel, Sash," I protested, but she was in the zone), and along every square inch of closet, including the pockets of each and every pair of pants, jeans, and shorts he owned. She was really alarmingly thorough, and I was beginning to think that maybe my dearest friend's issues ran just a little deeper than I had suspected.

Finally she leaned back against the bed (from where she had been sitting on the floor peering into all of his shoes) and gave a frustrated sigh. "Well. You may be right," she admitted.

My knees felt suddenly loose, and I sank back down onto the bed. I blinked fast, feeling helpless. The seed of doubt she'd planted was starting to send up ugly shoots. I didn't want to, but I was traveling back to last summer...when my fiancé told me over the phone as I drove down Gladiolus that he was sorry, but he just couldn't go through with our wedding.

After I'd calmly said goodbye and hung up, I'd found myself continuing on to the bakery where we were supposed to meet for our cake tasting. I knew even as I made the drive that it was crazy to go now—alone—but all I could think was that we'd had an appointment. I couldn't break it.

Michael was scared, I'd told myself as I forced my throat to swallow tender bites of expensive cake that might as well have been sponge. He needed some space. Some time. Everything would be fine.

But the space Michael needed turned out to be halfway across the country, and the time he needed was...forever. I ate the cake, along with seven thousand dollars in deposits—the money I still owed my parents—sold my wedding dress and cashed in our honeymoon tickets to Hawaii, and put that money down on the first house I found inside my price range, determined to move on and not get stuck in regrets for what might have been.

But that was the past. It was *not* now. Kendall wasn't Michael. I pushed away the panicky feeling that was threatening to engulf me and made myself focus on Sasha.

"See?" I said, my tone hollow even to me. "There's no one else."

Sasha levered herself up onto the bed beside me. "Well, if it were me, the next step would be the paper trail. Cell phone bills, credit card statements, that kind of thing. That'd tell you if there's some other woman."

I put a hand on her leg to try to soften my words. "Sash...that's kind of crazy. And it's also a big breach of trust."

She lifted an eyebrow and made an exaggerated show of checking her watch. "Huh. Well, here it is close to nine a.m., and there's still no sign of him. No call, no show...no explanation. From a guy you've spent every single night with since the day you met him." I thought I heard a little resentment bleed into her tone, but she kept talking. "The man you expected home last night, like always. Who, if he's not dead or in a coma—and, Brook, you're the one who taught me this: they're *never* dead or in a coma—has now broken a big, fat, foundational trust with you."

I thought for a moment, then shook my head. "I can't. It just isn't right. And I *know* he isn't seeing someone else," I tacked on, but even to my own ears it was starting to sound less forceful. Maybe I should tell her about our argument. But what would that accomplish? He still hadn't come home last night, and Sasha would only take that as further corroboration of her theories.

"Okay," she said, unfazed. "Then your other choice is to call his best friend—who's that tall guy he's always golfing with? Richie? Randy?"

Sasha was being a little bit disingenuous. She'd met Ricky after work at a happy hour with us once. She found out he was single and Googled him that night to pull up his address, voter registration, and the satellite image of his house, until I headed that potential landslide off at the pass. Having her potentially go Glenn Close on Kendall's best buddy was just a little too close to home.

"Ricky," was all I said.

"Right. Call Ricky and ask if he's heard from him. If anyone knows where he is, it'll be his closest friend." She looked thoughtful. "On the other hand, you run the risk of looking like a psycho to the guy. And he'll tell Kendall you called, which, if everything is actually okay and this is just a misunderstanding, might make *Kendall* also think you're a psycho."

I looked at her in amazement. I'd had no idea she was this self-aware.

I gave a sigh from the bottom of my soul. I was exhausted—adrenaline had left me feeling like a deflated balloon, and my defenses were down. I was pretty much out of other choices at this point anyway, so I found myself nodding and reaching for the cordless phone on Kendall's bedside table. Ricky was speed-dial number one.

I looked up at Sasha when I heard Ricky's recorded voice. "Voicemail."

"Don't leave a message." She plucked the phone out of my hand and disconnected, and then we sat there, both staring at the thing lying on the bed like a loaded weapon. I picked it up and dialed Kendall's cell one more time. I got his voicemail again and hung up.

"How many rings?" Sasha asked.

"What?"

She nodded toward the phone. "His voicemail. How many rings till it went into voicemail?"

"It didn't ring. Why?"

She frowned. "Huh. Well...that could go either way. Three or four would mean he just didn't answer. One or two means he looked, then declined—that would be bad."

I thought about the calls I'd made to Kendall last night and this morning. About the ringing and ringing until it finally slid into voicemail.

"And none means it's off, right?" I asked slowly.

I saw understanding creep over her face, and Sasha's eyes held a sympathy I didn't want to acknowledge. "At least that tells you he's okay, honey," she offered in a bright-side voice that made me feel pathetic.

I looked at her, a dark feeling growing in my chest. "It means he's turned it off."

fourteen

Over the years the Breakup Doctor has devised an informal handbook of breakup etiquette, based on information culled from hundreds of stories.

If he "needs some space," give it to him. It's usually code for "I want to see other people," and trying to cling to the relationship is only going to make you seem even less appealing.

"I'm confused" means "I don't want to dump you and be the bad guy, so I am hoping you will give up and break up with me and save me from having to do the deed."

If things are "moving too fast" for him and he wants to slow it down, bring them to a full stop yourself. A man who's crazy about you isn't going to risk letting you go, no matter how fast things are going.

"I lost your number" means "I lost interest." Move on.

If he says, "You need someone who can give you everything you deserve," he means he very much enjoys taking you out and having no-strings-attached sex, but he does not think of you as girlfriend material and never will. Get out quick.

"I just don't know if I still want to marry you" means...exactly that. That's one of the hardest ones, and there's nothing you can do but put it behind you and move past it.

*   *   *

"We're getting you out of this place," Sasha said, springing back to her feet after the briefest of consoling moments. "Toss out your toothbrush and whatever else you keep here, so he can see all of it in the trash, and let's go. Do you want to put Visine in his Gatorade before we leave? It'll give him wicked shits."

"What? No!" It was instantly clear to me that in her present state of mind, I should probably get Sasha out of Kendall's house as quickly as possible, before she could wreak any damage. Despite the suffocating feeling in my chest, I drew on every reserve of rationality I had, and invoked my Wise Therapist demeanor.

"Okay, hang on. We still don't know for a fact what's going on here."

"Brook—"

I held up a hand to stop her. "We don't. Okay, he's not dead or in a coma. But any number of other things could have happened."

"All of which involve him being a tool who hasn't bothered to call you and never showed up when he was expected."

"True," I conceded reluctantly. "But not necessarily a deal breaker yet, right? In a healthy relationship you talk about things, Sash, establish your rules and expectations."

Sasha narrowed her eyes. "You're the one who taught me to get out fast, as soon as you see the signs things are falling apart. Hello? This one's in neon."

She was right. I was the queen of cut-and-run as soon as I saw the writing on the wall. No sense dragging things out and humiliating yourself. But this time I couldn't, for some reason. Maybe the problem wasn't that I kept picking immature men who were afraid of commitment. Maybe the problem was me.

"Look, nothing's going to be accomplished by sitting here waiting to see what's going on," I said decisively. "Clearly Kendall and I are going to have to have a talk. Why don't you and I go get some breakfast while the dust settles?"

The last thing I wanted was to go make chit-chat over eggs

Benedict, or fend off Sasha's apocalypse predictions for my relationship. But I needed to get her out of Kendall's house. I needed to get out myself, or I was going to sit here tied up in knots until he walked in the door, and I'd be in no frame of mind to have a calm, mature discussion.

As I talked, I stood up, hoping that I could shepherd Sasha out the door if I moved in that direction myself.

"What happened to your foot?" Sasha said, noticing my bandage for the first time.

I was grateful for the chance to keep my mind occupied with embroidered stories about my injury and the hospital visit while I went into the bathroom and brushed my hair and swiped on some blush and lip gloss. Then I quickly threw on shorts and a T-shirt from the closet, slid into some sandals, grabbed my purse, and headed for the bedroom door.

Sasha wasn't following me, though. When I checked over my shoulder she was still sitting pensively on Kendall's bed.

"Brook, I don't think heading out for croissants like nothing's happened is healthy for you right now."

"Come on—I'm starving. I'll follow you in my own car so you don't have to bring me all the way back."

"Don't you think you should at least—"

"I'm fine." My tone was thin and brittle.

"Brookie—"

"Sash...please." My voice cracked a little, and that got Sasha moving.

I turned to pull the door shut behind me around as she headed down the curving sidewalk toward the parking lot. I took a long look back up the stairs, into Kendall's condo, not sure how soon I'd get back, or what would be waiting for me when I did.

Breakfast was an exhausting affair. Morning Glory was packed, reminding me why I hardly ever went out to brunch from Christmas through Memorial Day. We gave our names to the harried hostess and helped ourselves to coffee from the cart the owners wheeled outside to attempt to placate the hordes of tourists and snowbirds who spilled out onto the sidewalk.

Keeping Sasha off a topic she wanted to discuss was like juggling cats. Cats carrying chain saws. Which were on fire. I used the crush of people as an excuse to keep us away from any subjects but superficial ones for the nearly thirty minutes we waited.

Once we were seated, I asked her about her date Friday night.

A huge grin took over her face. "It was amazing."

Weren't they all? At first.

I wished Sasha would slow her roll with men. I tried not to encourage her when she got so carried away too early in, so instead I told her about my new clients, asking her advice about starting a Web site, and running by her some ideas for future columns. All the while I tried to sneak surreptitious looks into my bag to see if I'd somehow missed my phone ringing. By the time the check came and we headed back out to our cars, I felt drained.

I mustered one last hearty smile. "Thanks, Sasha. I feel so much better. I'll call you later and let you know how our little talk goes," I said, rolling my eyes with a shake of my head as though I were talking about Kendall leaving the toilet seat up.

She hesitated at the door of my Honda. "You sure? I can come back to your house with you if you—"

I waved her off. "Nah, I'll probably just lie down for a while. I'm feeling kind of tired."

"Didn't sleep much last night, huh?" she said sympathetically.

Worn out from my day yesterday, secure in the childish belief that everything was basically okay and safe and good, I'd slept like the proverbial baby, actually. But I didn't correct her.

"It wouldn't be any fun to watch me nap. I'll call you later on," I repeated. It was the only assurance that would get her to go.

She leaned forward and kissed my cheek. "You'd better. And be tough, Brookie. 'A man will treat you only as badly as you allow him to.' Another one I learned from you. See? I do listen." She gave me a smile that made my heart ache with its pure kindness and love before leaving me at my car to go home, alone.

But I didn't go home. Kendall's condo pulled me back to it as unerringly as if it had attached prongs into me.

I pulled into the parking lot and circled to the residents' spots, praying his car would be there. Not sure what it meant if it was.

His assigned space was empty. My heart plunged. Instead of heading back around to the visitors' area, where I usually left my car—why hadn't Kendall ever gotten me a permit for the other assigned residents' spot his condo entitled him to?—I continued around the lot to where it curved toward another block of units. It was a numbered spot—reserved for a resident—but no one was in it, and I didn't care anyway. It offered a direct line of sight across the little retention pond right outside Kendall's front door. I turned off the engine and sat for a moment, not sure what to do next.

I retrieved my phone from its side pocket in my purse to check it yet again for Kendall's missed call or a text message. Nothing.

What was I supposed to do now? Go inside and wait, drilling my fingers on the table like a wronged housewife? Start calling police stations, morgues, hospitals within LifeFlight distance of Fort Myers? Sit by the phone and wait for a ransom call to come in? Should I be panicking, or enraged? In the complete absence of any information, I didn't even know how I was supposed to react.

I called his cell phone again—desperately, hopelessly—and adrenaline jolted through me when it rang. After one ring I heard Kendall's voice, and I wanted to cry ridiculous tears of relief.

"This is Kendall Pulver. Your call is important to me. Please leave a message—"

I jammed my finger down on the end button. Sasha's voice replayed in my head: *One or two means he looked, then declined— that would be bad.* My chest tightened and my eyes grew hot and prickly.

Then my heart started to pound like an oil rig when I suddenly saw Kendall's black Mercedes nose around the corner from the back entrance to the complex and snuggle into its usual spot. Just as if it were any other day.

I ducked my head, praying Kendall wouldn't look in this direction.

His car had a dent in the side I had never noticed. I wondered if he knew it was there. Probably. He noticed everything about the car. I was surprised he hadn't had it fixed already.

Some part of me acknowledged that my mind was occupying itself with inanities. I told myself I was simply being very calm and very rational, and ignored Wise Therapist's voice that suggested my mind had chosen to cope by removing itself to a safe distance and observing what was going on in my life as though it were happening on a movie screen.

Kendall got out of his car and sauntered toward his building as though he'd been out for a morning constitutional. He had on shorts and a T-shirt—his usual workout wear—and a duffel bag over his shoulder. I watched him scan the visitors' parking area. For a second my heart plummeted as his eyes panned over to where my car sat on watchdog duty directly across from his condo, but his gaze didn't even falter, just swept smoothly right on past. Context was everything—he wouldn't have been expecting to see my car in a different area.

I watched him draw his cell phone from the side pocket of the bag—the cell phone that no doubt read 736 MISSED CALLS—and punch in a number.

Not mine, I was forced to assume when he started talking. He was too far away for me to hear anything. Or else the weird roaring sound in my ears was drowning out everything else. My heart was pounding and I felt sick to my stomach.

Kendall opened his front door still talking. I registered that I ought to pull out, or at least slouch down in the seat so I didn't look like I was doing exactly what I was doing—sitting in the parking lot stalking my...my...stalking Kendall. But I didn't do either of those things. My body felt heavy and hot and icy cold all at once, and I couldn't really move anything.

His eyes trolled the parking lot again, and this time I swore he saw me frozen in the driver's seat of my little blue Honda. He looked back down at his phone, and I watched him punch the keys. A few moments later, as if hearing it from underwater, I distantly registered the chiming tone on my cell phone that told me I had a text message.

Numbly I looked at the caller ID window and saw that it was from Kendall. As if in slow motion I pressed the button.

I'm sorry, Brook. I can't do it.

When I looked up Kendall was walking inside his condo, the door swinging shut behind him.

fifteen

Sasha called before I'd even made it back into my own driveway.

"How are you? What's going on? Where was he? Did you talk to him? Do you need me to come over again?"

"And the category is, 'Things you say to your best friend after a breakup,'" I said, my voice dull and flat.

"Oh, no. Oh, Brook. What happened?"

I told her, at least as much as I knew. I'd thought that between Sasha and me I knew every breakup strategy in the playbook, but a breakup by disappearance and text message was completely new to me.

"What do you need?" Sasha said briskly. "Recovery plan one, two, or three?"

Plan one was the tried-and-true self-indulgence approach. It involved large quantities of ice cream, breakup music (suicidal songs by Joni Mitchell and Ani DiFranco for Sasha; angry relationship rock like Alanis Morissette and Ben Folds and Maroon 5 for me), shopping, and ex-bashing. Plan two was purging and desensitization—throwing out all the old pictures and notes, deleting every email, erasing all his contact info, and creating long journal entries detailing every reason why he wasn't "the one," from a tendency to cheat to leaving pubic hairs on the soap.

Plan three was Sasha's province alone. It included coping mechanisms like staking out the ex's house, watching to see where he went and with whom; as well as some minor property damage:

letting the air out of his tires, or running over his mailbox, or TP'ing his lawn. I never selected plan three, but Sasha always asked with what I thought was slightly rapacious hope.

None of them felt right to me at the moment. Not even three.

"I don't know yet. I'm not sure I need a plan. I feel...fine."

"It hasn't sunk in. You're in shock."

I swung the car into my driveway and shut off the engine, but stayed sitting in the driver's seat. "'Shock' is a strong term..."

"No, think about it. It's like when you stub your toe really hard or accidentally set your hand down on a hot burner. You get one quick moment while your brain makes sense of what just happened before the pain actually sets in. You know it's coming, but for that one flash of a second you get a reprieve. I think it's your body's way of letting you get prepared for it."

"Yeah. Maybe. Or maybe I just wasn't as invested as I thought I was." I really did feel strangely indifferent, removed, as if I had watched Kendall's carefree walk to his town house like a scene from a movie.

"Well, then you're smart. He's just a self-important little wanker."

"Not ready for that, Sash."

"You're right, you're right—my bad. You can't force your strategy. We'll just wait for the numbness to wear off and then pick the recovery plan that feels right. I'm coming over."

"No!" I barked out, surprising myself as much as I probably did her. Right now I couldn't stomach the idea of hashing anything out with anyone. Even Sash. "No," I said again, softening my tone. "I've got some things I can get done. And I'm fine. Really. Okay?"

"I don't know." Sasha sounded skeptical. "You always tell me it's not healthy for me to be alone right after a breakup. You *always* come over."

"That's just to keep you from doing anything harmful or felonious."

Sasha laughed obligingly before trickling off into a silence. "Brookie, are you sure?"

"Hey, I'm the Breakup Doctor. You know the saying—'physician, heal thyself.'"

"I don't think this is what it means. But okay. If you're sure. But I'm checking in on you every hour on the half hour. You'd better answer."

"Sash, you don't have to—"

"That's the deal. Take it or leave it."

"Okay. Deal."

I meant to go inside after we hung up, but I sat in the car for a long time, overcome with inertia and unwilling to make any effort to put things in motion.

My cell phone vibrated in my hand, solving the problem for me. A shrill voice started in before I could manage a "hello."

"He's not...I'm *blocked*! And there's some woman posting things... And I can't even *check*!"

"Lisa," I said, incongruously grateful. My own personal issues cycloned down into a separate compartment when I was dealing with clients, giving me calm, clear focus on theirs. "I can't understand you. Take a breath and tell me what happened."

She did, haltingly and in between bouts of vitriolic ejaculations about Theodore, his anatomy, and his ancestry. Apparently she'd logged into his Facebook account and read a series of messages between him and some woman named Becky. He was having an affair, she moaned. There was another woman.

"I thought you were giving him some space," I said sternly.

"I am! I didn't contact him. You never said anything about checking his Facebook."

Social media was changing everything—even the way we broke up. I made a mental note to write a column about Facebook hacking as another postbreakup no-no.

"Okay." I took a breath, glad to have something to concentrate on. Despite my assurances to Sasha, I feared being alone would leave my mind free to wander to territory best left unexplored at the moment. "This isn't a disaster. It's just a stumble."

"Um...there's more. A lot more. It might be a disaster."

I reached over to where I still hadn't pulled the keys out of the ignition and turned the engine over. "Give me your address. I'm on my way."

Lisa Albrecht was standing in her driveway when I pulled up. I parked in the area under her basketball goal, beside a riot of vivid pink oleander, and started to step out of the Honda.

She was at the driver's side before I got both feet out. "Jesus. You look like I feel. What the hell happened to you?"

I dropped back into the seat and pulled down the visor mirror. She was right—I looked like roadkill: all the blood had drained from my face and relocated, apparently, to my eyes. *Twilight*-chic, thanks to Kendall Pulver. I'd been Pulverized. I snapped the mirror closed and shoved the visor back in place.

"Allergies," I said, thinking that Lisa Albrecht had a way of making it hard to want to help her. "What's going on?" Again I started to push out of the car, but Lisa took a step closer, blocking my exit.

"Not here. The boys are home." She cast a glance toward the house and rounded my car, pulling open the passenger door and flopping into the seat. "Come on! Go, go, go!"

I pulled my door shut and wordlessly backed out of the drive, Lisa's single-story tile-roofed stucco retreating behind us as I put the car in gear and drove us away. "Where are we going?"

She was leaning back against the headrest, her eyes closed, one hand rubbing her forehead. "Anywhere. Somewhere we can talk—privately. Where we won't be seen."

I drove down McGregor, the royal palms planted along both sides of the street ticking off our progress at intervals far less regular than they had when I was growing up, since so many of the ancient trees had died in the last string of hurricanes. Fort Myers had never been the same since then. What the hurricanes didn't destroy, the economic crash did, and the town was a pale facsimile of what it had been in its heyday.

Not unlike Lisa Albrecht, I supposed.

I sneaked a glance over at her and tried to imagine what she'd looked like when she was younger and carefree, before the newspaper business had hardened her and her husband's departure had finished the job. She had good bone structure—cheekbones high and sharp, deep-set eyes that might have looked exotic before overwork and worry made them hollow, a mouth that might have been full before she'd grown habituated to pulling it into a tight, disapproving line. In her youth her hair had probably been a sunny golden blond. Now her drugstore efforts to recapture that color left it a strange grayish-yellow, silver roots showing at her part.

"Didn't your mother teach you it's rude to stare? Take a picture; it'll last longer," she muttered without opening her eyes.

I was actually grateful for the rush of annoyance I felt as I snapped my eyes back to the road. It crowded out the reminder of yesterday on the sand with Kendall, when he'd told me the same thing as I gazed adoringly, pathetically at him.

"You seem drained," I said. "Are you okay?"

She opened her eyes and lifted her head, fixing a flat gaze on me. "Does this look like okay?" she asked, pointing a knobby finger at her face.

"You don't look good," I agreed.

I pulled onto Travers, a street of high-end but older homes that was my favorite biking route. The neighborhood bordered the Caloosahatchee, but only the residents seemed to know about the gorgeous, private views from the rear streets.

I parked alongside an overgrown line of areca palms that opened onto a tiny unpaved pull-in that was invisible until you were actually on it. The pathway was between two properties but seemed to belong to neither, and I often tucked my bike amid the arecas and sat on the sun-warmed rocks along the riverbank. Throwing another glance at Lisa, who was seemingly blind to our surroundings, I wished I hadn't brought her here.

But she was already getting out of the car, so I did the same, pulling off my sandals and dropping them into the footwell before closing the door.

"Come on," I said, making for the river.

Lisa followed, but left her shoes on. I settled onto a relatively flat rock and tucked my feet up under me, breathing in the musk of the river and hoping it would fill up my soul the same way it did my lungs.

Lisa stood somewhere behind me.

"You're the one who said you wanted to talk," I said without turning around. "Somewhere private." I wasn't in the mood for her attitude.

After a few moments I heard the swishing of her shoes across the stiff St. Augustine grass and then she picked her way onto a large rock near me with uncertain steps and lowered herself awkwardly to a tenuous perched position. Lisa Albrecht was not the outdoorsy type, I guessed.

"Okay, Lisa. What happened?"

It rushed out in a torrent, like water bursting into a foundering ship. She hadn't called Theodore—she'd done just what I'd instructed and left him alone. But he didn't call. He didn't try to get hold of her. What was she supposed to do, just sit idly by while their marriage swirled down the drain? So she checked his Facebook page—at first just a time or two a day, as a way to feel she was still having some contact with him. And then, when she saw a post from Becky Anastasi—a new "friend," someone Lisa had never heard of, whose page featured pictures of a tan, lissome blonde sailing and windsurfing and wakeboarding—posting, "Not bad, for an old man—you can really hang, Theo!" Lisa friended her. What wife wouldn't?

But Becky Anastasi ignored her friend request. And she ignored Lisa's second one…and her third. And then when Lisa tried to friend her a fourth time, Becky Anastasi's page had disappeared.

So she tried several of Theodore's usual passwords until she successfully logged into his Facebook account, and then she checked his message history. Becky Anastasi had quite an interactive relationship with Lisa's husband, cute, chatty little notes dating back a few weeks, and to each one Theodore had replied. Maybe just a few words, maybe only the pubescent "LOL." But he replied to every single inane, ridiculous thought coming out of Becky Anastasi's tiny bleached head...when he'd always told Lisa that not everybody worked with words for a living and was such a "compulsive communicator."

And what do you know, when she clicked on Becky Anastasi's name from Theodore's page, her page pulled right up, only this time with lots more info visible. Her age—twenty-eight. Her hobbies—rock climbing, Pilates, water sports, and "good friends and good times." Her favorite quotes: "I live for the nights I can't remember with the people I'll never forget" and "All the things I really like to do are either immoral, illegal, or fattening." Her relationship status: "It's complicated."

"'It's complicated,'" Lisa repeated, glaring holes through me. "Who even says that past high school? Unless your boyfriend happens to have a wife." She blinked hard a few times and transferred her glare out over the river. I was hoping its soft splashing sounds as it mazed through the rocks we were sitting on might soothe her, but Lisa did not look soothed.

I wondered if Kendall had a Facebook page. How strange that I didn't even know. Sasha had been trying to get me on Facebook for years, but I kept resisting. It risked blurring too many lines with my clients.

"Hey, are you even listening to me?" Lisa's acidic tone cut across my straying thoughts. "This morning he changed his password on Facebook and he *blocked* me. It's like he doesn't even *exist* to me on there—I'm *dead* to him. What am I supposed to do *now*, Dr. Phil?"

The sun's warmth sank into my scalp, my shoulders, my eyelids, and I realized my eyes were closed. I blinked them open and looked right at Lisa, just staring at her without a word as I wondered why on earth I had ever agreed to help this harpy of a woman. If she'd come to me as a regular patient I would have refused to take her on, made a polite excuse for why I wasn't the right doctor for her, and given her a referral elsewhere. A patient had to be open to self-investigation and change for me to make any progress with them. Lisa Albrecht was too hard, too closed off, too infallibly *right* in her own mind to do any real work on herself. All she wanted was a magic formula to keep her husband roped tightly to her side, no effort required on her part. I found myself cheering the guy on and hoping he kept running from this harridan far and fast.

My fingers clenched against the warm stone I was propping myself up on. Was that why Kendall had left me? Was I as bad as Lisa Albrecht, rabidly self-assured, blind to anyone else's needs, bossy and abrasive?

A clicking sound dragged my gaze back to Lisa, who was leaning forward, snapping her fingers as close to my face as she could reach. "Hey, snap out of it. You're on the clock. You know, I don't pay you just to hear myself talk. Where's the advice, *Doctor*? How about a game plan, here?"

I sat up straight, trying to focus on Lisa. "I'm not a doctor... I'm just an LMHC." For the first time I understood why my mother felt the title was so inadequate. Why Kendall apparently did too.

"You are a *professional*. You're supposed to be an expert. That's why I hired you to write a column for all of my readers, isn't it? Isn't that why I am paying you this exorbitant amount to tell me what the hell to do to get my husband back where he belongs? Come on, 'Breakup Doctor.' Doctor me."

I felt a surge of pure, absolute hatred. For mouthy, mean Lisa Albrecht. For Kendall. Even for my mom, though it was her voice that flared in my head, a firm, ineluctable, *Cowgirl up.*

I stood abruptly and started off the rocks.

"Hey! Where are you going?"

I didn't turn around. "Back home. We're done."

"Wait a minute. *I'm* not done. I'm paying you—get back here!"

I stopped and turned around, slowly, enjoying making Lisa Albrecht wait. A good therapist gently guides the patient toward understanding her own situation, rather than making a snap, blanket diagnosis and vomiting it up on her.

But I didn't feel like a good therapist at the moment.

"Lisa...you're so afraid to be vulnerable—to yourself or anyone else—that you've built a wall of rage around you. No one can hurt you, because no one can reach you past the unkind, angry, self-centered shell you've built up. I don't know if you were always like this or if it's just since your marriage troubles began, but that's not how a relationship works. You didn't hire me to help you figure out how to fix what went wrong in your marriage—you just want to know how to control your husband, and I won't help you do that. I'll send your check back tomorrow. Now get in the car. I'm leaving."

Power surged through me as I strode back to my car. I wondered what I would do if Lisa just refused to get in—could I really just leave her here?

I thought of her snarky little comments while I was sitting on a rock with her by the river trying to solve her problems—ignoring my own. The problems she had so clearly caused herself. Yes. I *could* leave her. I got in and started the engine, starting to back away.

Suddenly Lisa appeared out of the break in the areca palms, waving her arms and shouting. "Wait! Wait! Brook... Please."

From the look on her face I could tell that last word tasted like acid on her tongue. But I had figured Lisa Albrecht out: She needed a firm hand. She didn't respond well to the kind of gentle, unobtrusive therapy I was used to. Lisa Albrecht basically needed disciplining.

I kept creeping backward for a moment, letting her wonder if I would leave her here, in what was surely the wild to her.

"Brook...please stop. I... I could really use your help."

That was the closest I would ever get to an apology from this woman, I decided. Slowly, I pressed the brakes, stopped the car, and unlocked the passenger door.

sixteen

There wasn't a lot I could do for Lisa in the way of damage control—thanks to her compulsive phone calls and her hacking into his Facebook and email accounts, Theodore had simply excised her from his life like a malignant tumor. She couldn't undo the things she'd done to push him completely away from her.

What we *could* work on—and did, for the next two hours—was impulse control. Like an alcoholic, she had to battle her behavior with Theodore one compulsion at a time. I didn't kid her that there was any hope for reconciliation—not from what I'd seen and heard from her. But she had to get a handle on her behavior for the sake of her dignity—and her children.

I realized, viscerally, that part of the reason Lisa was acting crazy—besides the fact that she might, in fact, *be* a little mentally unstable—was not having any concrete answer from Theodore about what was going on in their marriage. For all that her behavior was off the deep end, he *had* walked out on her without any further explanation or clarification, leaving her in relationship limbo.

I could certainly sympathize with that.

"You don't have the right to terrorize Theodore—or his friends," I told Lisa once we got back to her house.

"'Friends?!'" she huffed. "You can't tell me for one second that little pinheaded blond bimbo is anything but—"

I gave her a warning look and she pressed her lips shut. I went on in the same calm tone of voice, as if she hadn't interrupted: "But you do have the right to know what's happening with your marriage. It isn't fair for Theodore to just walk away from the commitment he made to you without letting you know his intentions. You have a right to know if he's actually filing for divorce and what you need to do as far as getting an attorney to—"

Lisa shot to her feet. "Filing against *me* for divorce? When he's the one running around with some Malibu Barbie practically the same age as his *sons*? After I've supported him for the last twenty fucking years? Good luck taking that before a judge—I'll leave him living under a bridge in his underwear. Let's see how much his little *Baywatch* babe wants him then."

I crossed my arms and simply looked at her. Lisa Albrecht had sarcasm Tourette's, and I'd now learned that the key to managing her was threatening to take away what she wanted—which, even though she had a hard time saying it, was my help.

I watched as she painfully schooled her features into complaisance and settled meekly back down onto the sofa. She took a deep, shaky breath. "Okay. You're right... I need to... I need to..." She looked up at me and for the first time her face softened into a more open expression. I blinked in surprise. Lisa Albrecht was actually almost pretty. "I don't know, Brook. What do I need to do now?"

So together we drafted a letter she would send to Theodore at the friend's house where she'd found out from her sons he was staying.

"I don't see why I can't just email it," she grumbled as we sat side by side in front of her monitor, carefully composing what she would say. Or rather, as I made her delete most of the acerbic language she used and rephrase it into something concise, clear, and venom-free.

"Because he will delete it without opening it," I said matter-of-factly.

"Why don't I just drive it over to him myself?"

"No. That's just an excuse to stalk him."

"Then why don't I just give it to Jack and Michael to take to him on one of their visits?"

"Absolutely not. This is between you and Theodore. You don't stick your kids in the middle of it."

She sighed, exasperated, but fished an envelope out of her desk and started to address it. "Fine. But this is so medieval. And he won't read it."

"Then after a fair amount of time, if you haven't heard from him, you start divorce proceedings yourself. This is abandonment, and you can't live your life waiting for Theodore to let you know what's going on in your relationship." Suddenly it was hard to breathe. I leaned back, concentrated on slowing my racing heart, and gentled my tone. "You deserve better than that, Lisa. And it's time you took control of this situation."

Her eyes grew wet, but she simply blinked the tears away and gave a nod. She finished the letter and yielded the keyboard to me for final approval. I took out one last dig—*we both know split-ups are hardest on the children—by which I mean Jack and Michael, not your new girlfriend*—then we printed the letter and sealed it into the envelope, which I took with me to prevent any creative revisions on Lisa's part before it got mailed. It was a chastened and unusually quiescent Lisa Albrecht who waved me out of her driveway.

That's right, I congratulated myself as I pulled off down her street. I was a take-no-shit Breakup Doctor. If I could whip a client as difficult as Lisa Albrecht into shape, then getting over a cowardly little weasel like Kendall Pulver was going to be a snap.

I woke before dawn from an uneasy sleep and got up to work on my column. I had a full day of clients and a deadline. My topic was, "Red Flags: Early Signs of a Later Breakup."

> *From the very first date with someone new, although they're probably putting forth their best first impression, they're still telling you who they really are— even if they don't know they're doing it. Watch what they do, and listen to what they say.*

I remembered now: Kendall took two phone calls at dinner on our first date. They were business calls, he explained apologetically, holding up a finger and sliding out of his chair to step outside. He wasn't gone long either time, but I sat there during his absences feeling awkward and unimportant.

> *Does he give you his full attention? Does she listen when you talk? Does he ask questions about the things you say, showing interest in you? Sure, we're all trying to present ourselves at our very best, but a person who's fixated on him- or herself from the very beginning isn't going to magically become involved, engaged, and interested in* you *as the relationship goes on.*

It was an hour into our date before Kendall asked what I did for a living. And then he got engrossed in the dessert menu in the middle of my explanation.

> *And watch out for mentions of former lovers or spouses! Yes, that's information most of us will share with someone as we become closer. But if a date brings it up too soon—or too often, or in too much detail—chances are they're still emotionally hung up on whoever came before you.*

Kendall talked about his ex within fifteen minutes of sitting down to dinner. And not just a casual passing mention, but a lengthy recitation of how he'd been sure she was the one, moving across the country to be with her in Chicago, and the slow, painful, unavoidable realization once he'd settled in that she'd changed her mind.

He'd hung on for almost a year, but when he finally couldn't kid himself anymore that they were just going through a hard time of adjustment, he moved to Fort Myers for a clean start, to pursue his own career and interests and not make the mistake of planning his life around someone else.

Big Red Flag. Of all people, I should have known better.

And yet at the end of that date, Kendall pulled his car into my driveway, and said, "Wait here," before getting out of the car, walking around to my side, and opening my door with his palm held out to help me out of his black S550. He walked me all the way to my doorstep, then stopped me with a hand on my shoulder when I reached my key to the lock. I braced myself for the crown jewel of unfortunate dates: the awkward avoidance of an inappropriate kiss.

But all he did was say, "I had the best time tonight. Better than I've had in such a long time. Thank you."

There was such an unexpected, unguarded sweetness to his words and expression that they prompted a tiny, inconsequential lie, meant simply to make him feel better: "I'm glad. I did too."

A relieved smile had bloomed over his face. "I want to take you out again. Soon."

And right then...that was the moment when I'd overridden my instincts. Kendall Pulver wasn't relationship material—not yet, and not for me. But I told myself that just because there wasn't a possibility for anything serious didn't mean we couldn't enjoy each other's company casually for a while. I certainly wasn't ready for anything deep either. After what had happened with Michael I just wanted to feel attractive again. Wanted.

So I had started it—or allowed it to start. I opened a door I knew should have remained shut, thinking there was no harm. Thinking I'd know when to pull back. Feeling sorry for a broken man, knowing my own neediness at the time, and thinking we might simply offer each other a friendly hand to pull out of the swamp of our own despondency. And yes, I had to admit, lapping up the way he looked at me as if I were the sunrise after a long dark night.

The walking wounded often commit deeply, and quickly, to fill whatever void their ex has left behind. In no time at all they make you feel needed. They make you feel important and essential and desired—you have made this person happy; you've fixed them.

But you are not a savior. You can't build a relationship on rescuing, and if he or she needs help, let them get it from a professional. You're looking for a partner, not a project. And if you do succeed in "fixing" someone's problems for them, chances are they'll go find someone new who didn't know them when they were broken.

It was so easy to see in hindsight that I made some stupid mistakes early in with Kendall. I broke my own rules of relationships. If I'd been able to stay objective I would have seen the danger signs more clearly and avoided where I was right now—dumped by a man I hadn't even wanted to go out with in the first place.

Which made me wonder why.

I knew, viscerally and firsthand, the futility of trying to parse out a breakup—when did things go wrong, what changed, why did the person you loved fall out of enchantment with you? There are no answers to these questions—at least, none that are helpful to know.

But it didn't stop me from working it through over and over in my head.

Why did I chase Kendall for an opinion on my stupid column? Why did I need his validation? Why did I keep him from watching *Kudlow and Company?* I was a nag. I was insecure. I'd been too demanding.

Why did I have to get so upset about his going in to work on Saturday? He'd taken the morning to spend with me. I knew when I met him he was a workaholic. It was one of the things I liked about him—his strong work ethic, his commitment to doing his job as well as he could.

But even though we'd argued, it hadn't been that bad, had it? Bad enough to make him change his mind about us completely— after he was the one who'd asked me to move in? It was just one of those disagreements couples have—a minor blip on the radar. Did he not realize that all couples fought? Life wasn't a movie—in real life, couples argued and bickered and disagreed. Sustaining a successful, long-lasting relationship wasn't about avoiding altercations—that wasn't realistic—but about learning how to handle those moments in a positive, respectful, healthy way. Didn't he know that? Overall, he and I had been in great shape—healthy, stable.

The realization dawned on me: It was just like what happened to Lisa. Theodore had walked out when Lisa thought everything was just fine. And then she found out about his Facebook flirtation with someone else.

Suddenly my stomach felt queasy again. I leaned back in my office chair, where I was still parked in front of my computer, doing the final edit of my column. I remembered Sasha asking if I thought Kendall was screwing around. *That's not possible*, I'd told her.

It's always possible. Men are men.

Sasha was right about that, and I'd been too blindly naive to see it. Just like Lisa Albrecht, who didn't realize how her own behavior had driven her husband out of their house and straight into the social media of another woman.

I played back the last few weeks. He was always busy with work, but recently his hours had gotten ridiculous. I remembered the night he'd been out till the small hours with his "clients" from up north—when he'd gone to Iniquity, a club he hated. I thought of every missed meal, every late night, and finally the great unexplained absence when he simply hadn't come home.

Where had he been?

The answer was so obvious I felt like the world's biggest fool.

seventeen

I realized why they called it "saw palmetto" as I pushed my way through an overgrown tangle of the low-growing palm shrubs. The sharp blades of its fanlike leaves left slices all over my hands, as annoyingly painful as paper cuts, as I forged a path through the overgrowth and across a dried-up drainage ditch.

Except at the moment, I realized as my foot squelched into its moist, slippery bottom, it wasn't completely dried up. The sun had been swallowed by ominous-looking clouds when I left my house, and a spritzing mist had turned into a drizzle by the time I got to Kendall's. I pulled my foot out of the muck, nearly leaving behind my red canvas espadrille. It was ruined now anyway, its braided-rope heel smeared with thick dark Florida mud that looked like chocolate frosting.

I didn't know what I intended when I got up from the computer, grabbed my keys, and jumped in my car. I was headed to Kendall's, but for what? To catch him with someone?

It wasn't until I was halfway there that I realized it was Monday.

Well, in that case, I would gather all my things, I decided resolutely. I could empty everything out as though I had never been there, make the break clean and tie off all my loose ends so I could start getting over it. Over him.

And maybe I could do a little bit of looking around while I was there. Nothing too intrusive—nothing on a Sasha level. But it had been a day since she'd tossed his house with such alarming efficiency. Maybe now that I was officially out of his life, he'd have left some incriminating evidence lying around—a phone number, a note...a pair of panties lying forgotten on the bedroom floor.

I pulled into the subdivision's entrance and swung around toward residents' parking, and my heart slammed into my ribs as I saw Kendall's car.

Before I realized exactly what I was doing, I tore out of the parking lot, my tires slipping a little on the wet pavement. Why was he home from work so early? Had he seen me pull in? Was he looking out the window, noticing my car screeching past, shaking his head at his pathetic drive-by ex?

Or...was he in there with someone else?

That was when I'd yanked the wheel into the small, half-deserted strip mall behind his subdivision, left my Honda in the parking lot, and headed for the wall of greenery that bordered Kendall's complex.

I finally slashed my way through the last of the thick foliage and came into the complex toward the back, two squat white buildings behind Kendall's. I raced across the asphalt toward his unit, stopping occasionally to secret myself behind an oak tree or a wall of oleanders, like a bad private dick on a caper. It was hard to be stealthy in three-inch wedge heels, and for the first time ever, I wished I had some of Sasha's stalker skills.

I bent to catch my breath behind a Dumpster and looked down at what I was wearing—frayed cutoff shorts and a stained, oversize giveaway T-shirt from some radio event Sasha had covered, both sticking to my body in the rain, and the incongruous red espadrilles that had been the shoes closest to the front door. My hair was half twisted into a plastic claw and I could feel it drifting down in frizzy strands around my face, and I wasn't wearing a speck of makeup. I was violating one of the foremost rules of post-breakup behavior: Never go out looking anything less than fantastic. You never knew when or where you might encounter your ex—or someone who knew him, and the last thing you wanted was for him to hear about how awful you looked.

But if all went according to plan—which I'd hatched during my Crocodile Dundee safari through the tropical flora—Kendall wouldn't see me at all.

And neither would whoever was in there with him.

I took one last deep breath of the sour, dank air near the Dumpster, ducked my head against the drizzle, then made my final push, skidding to a halt behind the stucco wall at the corner of the unit of condos that faced Kendall's across the opaque beige retention pond. I checked his parking spot—his car was still in its usual spot. If I stuck my head out just a few inches, I could see his end unit: the facade, the front door, and the two windows in his living room.

I peered slowly around, my heart flipping in my chest. In the rainy gloom, golden light poured out of Kendall's windows, mocking my wet chill. Somewhere inside he was warm and cozy. Was he thinking about me? Did he wonder how I was feeling? Was he doing the same thing I was right now—trying desperately to picture what I might be doing, where I was? (He'd never guess this one, I thought, wiping away a stream of water that trickled down from my hairline.) Was he wondering, like I was, if I was alone or if I had already found someone new?

Of course he wasn't. It had been less than forty-eight hours—and *I* wasn't the one who'd bugged out of the relationship.

The more likely scenario filled my head. Kendall came home for a little "afternoon delight" with his new flame. He was probably lying on the sofa inside, bathed in that warm golden light I saw filtering out his window. His shoes would be off, neatly lined up beside the sofa, but his socks would still be on—he always wore them, even in the hottest weather, because he didn't want to ruin the cream carpet. ("Feet sweat, Brook," he would say, looking pointedly down at mine.)

Suddenly the comforting drone of *Taking Stock* or *Mad Money* or *Squawk Box* would be cut off, the picture snapping to gray, and Kendall would look up as a woman slinked up beside the sofa.

"I can think of more enjoyable things for you to watch," she'd purr, slipping one silken strap of her plum-colored lingerie off a tanned, smooth shoulder.

I could hear Kendall's throaty laugh as he reached for her, pulling her toward him, closer, down on top of his tall, muscled body. "You're right. This is better than any silly finance show. You're the only woman I've ever known who's more interesting than Jim Cramer."

The vibrating in my pocket snapped me out of the stockbroker porn in my head, and I reared back behind the building and fumbled for my phone, hating myself for wishing with all my heart it was Kendall. Then terrified that the woman I was imagining rubbing herself along Kendall's body upstairs had seen me out here and was somehow calling me.

I looked at the screen. Sasha. She'd stopped calling me every thirty minutes late last night when I blasted her that I wasn't on suicide watch and wouldn't get two seconds of the sleep I so desperately needed if she kept burning up the phone lines every time I started to drift off. She agreed to stop only if I checked in with her today every hour on the hour. I had to answer.

"Hey, Sash."

"You didn't check in with me last hour."

"Sorry. I'm... I was writing my column."

"What's the sitrep?" Sasha took breakups very, very seriously.

"Nothing. I'm fine. Same as yesterday. Nothing to report." I pushed my wet hair off my face and tried to scrape away mud from one shoe with the edge of the other.

"Are you sure this isn't denial? Or shock? Have you been drinking? Should I come over? Do you want me to go over to his house and get your things? You need a clean break. As long as his lock isn't a Schlage I can pick it and—"

"Sasha! Jesus, no! That's breaking and entering...or trespassing, or burglary or something—at any rate, a felony." My head suddenly cleared. What was I doing here? I wasn't Sasha. I was a therapist, for God's sake. I was the one who counseled people against behavior like this.

I wiped moisture off my streaming face and smoothed my crazy hair out of my eyes. "I just finished the column, actually," I told her—a white lie only, depending on how you defined "just." I told her about the hole in my living room wall and the unidentified leak that needed investigating. "That's what I'm planning to tackle next—don't worry; I'm keeping busy."

It took several more reassurances that I was fine, coping well, and didn't need anything at the moment to get Sasha to hang up. A case I somehow made to her even while standing with my feet half buried in sludgy Florida mud and with rain plastering my ratty clothes to my body. As soon as she ended the call I eked my phone back into my damp pocket and leaned around the corner again.

Kendall's apartment light was out, and his car was gone from his spot. Dammit. Had someone been with him?

There was one sure way to find out. Sasha herself had actually planted the seed. She might be an expert with lock picking, but I didn't need that kind of skill.

I still had a key.

eighteen

My hands shook as I fitted the key into the cobalt front door of Kendall's condo and turned the knob to the left.

The door swung open too easily, as if the house itself were inviting me in. It should have stuck, should have been hard to turn, so that I had a moment to stop and think about what I was doing—violating someone's personal space, breaching the bounds of propriety, shattering whatever trust still remained between Kendall and me.

But *he'd* done that, I reminded myself, firming my backbone. Not me. All I was doing was following his lead. I left my muddy shoes on the stoop and stepped inside.

I wasn't sure what I was expecting once I crested the top of the stairs and took in the open living space of the condo—maybe a trail of sexy, slinky underthings like the ones I never bothered with. Should I have? If I'd greeted Kendall at night wearing only a corset and thigh-high stockings with a pair of fierce and impractical spike heels, would I have been the one he skipped out on work for in the middle of the afternoon to come home to?

But there was nothing littering the off-white carpet of the living room. Of course. Sexy foreplay was one thing, but it was no excuse for Kendall to tolerate a mess.

I made a quick circuit of the living area, my chest constricted. It felt so odd to be scared of being caught roaming Kendall's home. How on earth could I no longer have the right to be here? Forty-eight hours ago this was on the verge of being my home, too. Now I was an intruder. My eyes felt hot and I blinked fast.

Nothing was out of place, everything just as it had been when I'd last seen it, as it had been every single day that I'd come home to this place exactly like this—except that then I was happily waiting for Kendall to come home, and now I was terrified of it. If he walked back in now—if he forgot something, if a neighbor had called to report that he'd better get back quickly, because his crazy ex had just let herself inside—there was nothing I could say to justify my presence. I was doing exactly what I counseled every client I worked with against—violating someone's privacy and engaging in borderline stalking behavior.

But I couldn't stop now. I was already in, after all. I might as well look around a little.

Sasha had tossed the place pretty thoroughly the other day, so I doubted there was anything I might find that she hadn't sniffed out. But if he *had* come home to meet someone... I headed down the hall toward his bedroom, the door of which was closed. My chest squeezed so tightly it was hard to breathe as I reached out, turned the knob, and pushed it open.

The bed was as neatly made as always, not the rumpled, twisted mess of sheets I'd expect from an afternoon quickie. But that didn't mean anything—Kendall was anal-retentive enough to ask the girl to help him make the bed after even the wildest session of lovemaking. There was only one real test. I flipped back the duvet, ripped the sheets down, and lowered my head, taking a deep, full sniff.

Nothing. Laundry detergent, and maybe a slight whiff of my own scented lotion. No musky, earthy smell of satisfied stranger. Not even the smell of Kendall's sweat. I hastily made the bed back up the way Kendall liked it—sheet folded down over the cotton blanket, comforter pulled up over it.

In the bathroom everything was in order—even my own toothbrush, still standing in its holder like a watchful soldier.

He wouldn't have left my toothbrush and toiletries out if he'd had another woman here already. Would he?

I reached down suddenly and snatched up the trash can, diving a hand into the wadded-up tissues and used Q-tips, looking for evidence I desperately didn't want to find—like a discarded condom I hadn't had anything to do with. There was nothing. I shoved the wastebasket back in place and washed my hands, grimacing.

I yanked open the bathroom drawer, remembering Sasha's advice—always count the condoms. Why hadn't I listened to her? There was still a string of them where they had been before, but who knew if any were unaccounted for?

I chewed my lip. Maybe no slinky, slutty stranger had been here—yet. But that didn't mean there was nothing to find. All my scruples when Sasha had wanted to probe into Kendall's personal business seemed distant and trivial now. *Now* I had reason. I headed down the hall to Kendall's office.

His computer was turned off, and without letting myself have time to talk myself out of it, I powered it up.

I waited, forgetting to breathe, until his wallpaper finally popped up—a background photo of the New York Stock Exchange. And then, fingers trembling, I hovered the cursor over his email icon.

What was I doing? How was this any different from what I'd just berated Lisa Albrecht for not twenty-four hours ago? I had no right to invade Kendall's privacy like this—no matter what he'd done.

But even as I gave myself that lecture, I clicked the icon. His password window popped up—with asterisks already in place in the password box. One click on the "enter" button and I was in.

Kendall's email inbox spread open in front of me like the pearly gates of heaven—or the seductive, beckoning gates to the Underworld. I jerked my eyes frenetically over the names in his inbox—Ricky...Kendall's mom...and a string of my own name. Nothing suspicious. I checked his sent mail, where there were more names—a lot I didn't recognize. I opened any of them addressed to what could be a woman's name—including Pat Evans and Alex Givens. But all of them appeared to be clients, the emails full of dry, mind-glazing financial information.

Frustrated, I checked his trash file, methodically opening every single deleted message, even the ones that looked like spam. Nothing. Not one email that even gave a hint as to why my boyfriend who wanted to move in with me a few weeks ago had suddenly backpedaled all the way out of my life. Irritated, I shut down the computer.

And opened the file drawer next to my knees.

Say what you want about someone who is compulsively neat—it sure makes following his paper trail a whole lot easier. I pulled out the files marked AMEX, CELL PHONE, and RECEIPTS, spreading them open one by one on the desk. I checked every single scrap of paper, looking for anything unusual: credit charges from a hotel, or a jeweler, or a florist, or a travel agency. Receipts for valet parking at a romantic restaurant, or from a lingerie store. Cell phone records to a woman's name on a regular basis, or even a 1-900 call line. I had no idea what I might find—I just desperately needed to find *something*.

But there was nothing.

I returned the last piece of paper to its correct spot and replaced the file folders in alphabetical order, sliding the drawer shut.

Goddammit, Kendall. What happened?

I realized when I finally looked up and took in my surroundings again that the light had changed color, turning an overcast gray that heralded the coming dusk. In the winter months the sun set early—it couldn't be much past five o'clock—but even though Kendall had never made it home earlier than six thirty most of the time we'd been dating, I couldn't take any chances. I needed to get out of here.

My lungs seemed to fill only partially, not enough for me to breathe easily. One word kept repeating over and over, plaintively, pathetically, in my head: *Why?*

Why didn't Kendall love me anymore? What had happened between one moment and the next to turn that off as if it had never existed? I pressed my eyes shut hard—I would not cry. There was one last thing I needed to do before I left.

I knew where to find Kendall's Visine—in the "eye drawer," of course, next to his saline, contact cases, and rewetting drops. Emptying it inside his orange Gatorade did give me a twinge of conscience for a moment, but Sasha was right—there was a lot of satisfaction in it.

As soon as I got in my car I started to shake and couldn't stop. What had I done? Who was the woman rifling through Kendall's private records and snooping into his correspondence? Let alone what I'd done to his digestive tract before I left—the memory made me cringe.

Worst of all, I'd had two Breakup Doctor clients scheduled for the day and I'd blown them off completely. I hadn't meant to—I just forgot. It wasn't just bad business to stand up a client—it was bad therapy. Really bad. I called each one and crossed my fingers as I made up a story about a family emergency and gushed apologies; their understanding responses made me feel even worse.

Then I called Sasha. I needed my best friend around to restore me to sanity, to remind me who I was.

"Are we in the sweatpants phase?" she said as I opened my front door, fresh from showering off the filthy feeling that was only partly due to the rain and mud. "Sweetie—you look like shit."

I was getting tired of hearing that. "No, no, the pleasure's all mine."

"Sorry, Brookie. Hey, I brought supplies." She hoisted the bags in her arms a little higher, then walked past me toward the kitchen. I followed behind her.

She set the groceries on the counter and started unloading them: bags of Doritos and Cheetos and—ugh—Combos, a hideously guilty pleasure. Two pints of Haagen-Dazs. Several boxes of chocolates, and a magnum of wine I eyeballed warily. "Phase one," she explained at my look. "So what's the latest? Any word from the douchebag?"

I shook my head despite the swell of guilt in my chest and reached for the Combos.

We sat on yoga mats in the devastated living room on my bare-concrete floor with junk food and the wine arrayed out before us like the Last Supper, and I popped *Sliding Doors* into the DVD player, a movie that never failed to make me feel hopeful.

Except this time. I couldn't even focus on it, instead seeing in my head a movie replay of me, soaking wet and covered in mud, lurking outside Kendall's apartment like a peeping Tom.

By the time Gwyneth Paltrow was flatlining in the ER, the wine was alarmingly low in the bottle and I was slumped back against my tattered floral sofa. John Hannah loved her *so much*, even though they'd just met. He held her hand while she died and he promised to make her happy. He wouldn't leave her, even when she was *dead*. But Kendall left me. And I was *alive*.

On some level I knew I was becoming maudlin, but my eyes prickled.

All my fault. I drove men away.

"I shouldn't have made him read my column," I said, aloud, forcing my suddenly fat tongue to make words.

Sasha didn't even need to ask where my mind had gone.

"You didn't make him, Brookie." She stared at me, hard, with an expression that made me feel worse, even though it was nothing but kind.

"Yeah." I leaned my head back onto the sofa seat and stared at the ceiling. "But he prob'ly felt like he had to. Then I *nagged* him for his opinion."

"You didn't nag him. You asked what he thought."

I refilled my empty wineglass just before Sasha reached over and plucked the bottle away.

"We were moving too fast. He got scared." I made an expansive gesture with my arm that would have ruined the carpet with my sloshing wine, if I had had any carpet. I reached behind me for the ancient yellowed sofa arm cover and tossed it carelessly over the spreading purple puddle on the bare concrete.

"Please!" she scoffed. "You were together four months. You were dating. You were exclusive. Big deal—that's normal. It's not like you ran to get pregnant or engaged or shack up or something."

"Yeah," I agreed weakly, my voice thin.

She stood up and walked toward the kitchen, removing the bottle from my reach. Her steadiness on her feet made me wonder if I'd had the lion's share of the wine.

For the millionth time I wished I had told Sasha earlier about Kendall's asking me to move in. But until I'd made up my mind I hadn't wanted to show her my uncertainty. Now I was trapped into pretending things had been casual and light, and unable to explore with my best friend my biggest fear about why he spooked and bugged out.

Sasha was back all of a sudden, standing there with her long thin legs right in front where I still sat on the floor. "Maybe he has herpes."

"What?" I peered up at her. "That doesn't even make *sense*."

"No, listen," she said, perching on the sofa and leaning toward me as she warmed to her topic. "I bet he was too much of a puss to tell you, and then he had an outbreak and instead of having the guts to come clean, he just ran."

Not that I found this theory viable for a second, but the grin spreading over my face felt too good for me to dismiss it. "Yeah! Or...syphilis, maybe. If he was cheating on me, he could have gotten syphilis and been too afraid to tell me."

"Yes!" She gently removed the wineglass from my fingers and set it on the floor at the end of the sofa, out of reach. "Or gonorrhea. I heard you can get brain damage from gonorrhea."

I laughed at the rapacious expression on her face, and then we fell silent, contentedly contemplating Kendall with gonorrhea-induced brain damage.

"I want to go over there, Brook," Sasha said finally. "I can find out what the hell is going on."

"No!" I barked. It came out more harshly than I intended.

"Shh-shh, honey. It's not like I'm going to go key his car or rototill his lawn. Not till you give me the go-ahead, anyway. I'm just going to take a look. He'll never even know I'm there."

Been there, done that.

"That is now how you handle this kind of thing," I said, enunciating carefully; then at Sasha's perplexed expression I realized what I'd said and giggled. "*Not.* That is *not* how you handle it."

"That's not how *you* handle it. That's exactly how I handle it."

I realized with a flare of shame that for all my superiority, I'd acted no saner than Sasha, and my giggles dried up.

"Brookie, are you okay?" Sasha asked. She looked concerned. Both of her.

"Fine. I'm fine." But I didn't feel fine. I felt sad. Lonely, ashamed, and sad.

Suddenly her face came into 3-D focus, and she was right in front of me. "Come on, honey. Let's get you into bed."

Then I was sitting on my bed, and my legs were cold. I looked down and saw Sasha yanking my jeans over my ankles. My eyes closed, then blinked back open when I felt something hard being pressed into my fingers. A cup. Oh—a cup of water, I realized when I sloshed a little onto my legs, raising goose bumps.

"Take them," Sasha said, and I realized she was pushing some little tablets into my other hand. Our old hangover-prevention formula: a vitamin B complex, two aspirin, and a full glass of water before going to sleep.

I smiled—"Good Sasha"—then there was a soft pillow under my head, and I was warm again. I felt something squishy on my forehead—Sasha's lips were really soft.

"I'll call you in the morning."

"Yes, you will. Because you love me."

"That's true, my little lush."

"You love me, and you are the *only* one." My words were fuzzy, and my eyes felt hot and wet. I blinked fast, but tears spilled over the corners and ran down my temples into my ears.

The bed sank a little, and warm hands wiped the moisture away. "Kendall Pulver is a douche."

I sniffled and nodded. "A douche with gonorrhea."

"That's right." She smoothed my hair off my face in gentle, soothing motions, and my eyes fluttered closed.

nineteen

I woke up with the kind of pounding dehydration headache that only red wine inflicts upon you. I lay as still as possible, knowing that as soon as I moved it would become excruciating and nothing would help but time.

It was early—the sun wasn't even up—and I felt as if I'd hardly rested at all in the fitful sleep of intoxication. What time had I gotten to bed? I peered blearily over at the clock, but the nightstand wasn't there.

As I sat up, disoriented, three awful things slammed into my head: the throbbing pain of a hangover; the realization that I was lying on my sofa, not in my bed; and the stark, sudden rush of memory that today was the day of my radio interview. I bolted into the bedroom—trying to hold my throbbing brains in with my hands—to find my clock: 5:33. I was supposed to be at the studio at six thirty.

How had I completely forgotten? In the middle of everything else it had utterly slipped my mind. I stumbled into my bathroom and frantically started brushing my teeth, wincing at the clamorous car-wash noises it made inside my head. What the hell had I been thinking, drinking almost a liter of wine on my own? I knew better than that—especially right after a breakup. That could have been bad. Thank god Sasha had put me safely to bed last night. Particularly in the state of mind I'd been in.

Except...I hadn't woken up in bed. I'd woken up on the sofa. The toothbrush stalled against my molars. If I'd had enough wine to wander out of the bedroom and into the living room without re-membering it, god knew what else I might have done.

Like call my ex in a drunken stupor, and say embarrassing, un-take-backable things. I stepped away from the counter, the tooth-brush still dangling from my mouth, and looked around the bed-room for my cell phone. *Please, no. Don't let me have done it.*

No phone. My heart somewhere down around my bare feet, I strode back into the living room. Nothing. Entertaining visions of me compulsively dialing Kendall all night, leaving God knew what messages until the phone dropped from my unconscious fingers, I clambered carefully to my knees and peered under the sofa—a mis-take, I realized as my brain tried to escape in angry throbs out of my forehead. But it wasn't there, and it wasn't on the kitchen coun-ter, or in my purse. I felt a little panicky—what had I done?—until I headed back into my bathroom to spit out the toothpaste I was about to gag on and from the corner of my eye saw a yellow Post-It note on the toilet lid: *Phone inside left black ankle boot in closet. Just in case. ;-)*

Sasha. I let out a long breath. Thank God. I retrieved the phone from where she'd hidden it and gratefully checked the call log—unchanged since I'd last used it. On many a post-breakup night I'd ruthlessly confiscated her phone, and I could have kissed Sasha for doing the same for me. It was too early to call her, so I texted a quick note of gratitude and hurried into the shower to get ready for my interview.

"Breakup Doctor?"

I looked up from the hard plastic chair where I'd been waiting when I heard the machine-gun voice, recognizing it as belonging to the woman who'd called me to set up the interview. The door to the reception area from the inner sanctum seemed to be excreting her head. In person, the girl looked roughly twelve years old, with blond hair parted in the middle and pushed behind her ears, and big owl glasses. She was chomping a piece of gum as if it had personally offended her and she was punishing it.

"That's me. Brook Ogden." I'd been moving slower than usual this morning, trying to nurture my screaming head, and I'd had to break some speed limits to get to the station by six thirty. Now it was three minutes to seven, and I'd been getting progressively more nervous.

I stood and held out a hand. The girl looked down at it perplexedly, then placed limp, perfunctory fingers in mine and sort of vibrated them.

"Come on back. Kelly's waiting."

I sprinted behind her to keep up as she charged back through a maze of hallways lined with pictures that blurred as we sped by. Then she came to an abrupt halt outside a door with an "on-air" light above it, just like in the movies. She held up a finger.

"Are we going to—"

She brandished the finger more sternly at me and I fell silent. After a moment the light went off, the girl opened the door, and her whole personality metamorphosed.

"Hey, Kelly! She's finally here. I prepped her, and we're all ready for you," she chirped, ushering me into the studio.

The brunette perched on a stool behind an incomprehensible bank of lit switches nodded in our direction but didn't get up. "Great. How ya doing? Kelly Garrett."

"Brook—"

"Get her cupped, Meg." Kelly was listening to something with one earphone held to her head, fiddling with the buttons at her fingertips. "Sorry," she said toward me. "Gotta throw to traffic."

Meg hustled me over to the only other seat—another stool— and handed me a set of headphones big and chunky as 1985. I slipped them over my ears, and listened to her muffled voice saying, "This one if you have a hairball or something—don't cough into the mike," as she pointed to one of a trio of buttons in front of me. "Don't touch anything else, an inch from the mike is best, and lose the necklace—I could hear it rattling all the way down the hall." She turned back to Kelly, who had apparently finished "throwing to traffic" and was setting her headphones on the desk. "All set, Kel! Have a great interview!" Meg stretched her face into a smile that looked like a workout and let herself back out the heavy sound-proofed door as I released the clasp on my beaded necklace and dropped it into my purse.

"Sorry about all this," Kelly said, reaching a hand over the low counter separating us. She had the shiniest sable hair I had ever seen, pretty coffee-colored eyes that squinted with her whole-face smile, and a good firm handshake. "Radio's generally nuts. I'm Kelly Garrett, and you're Brook, right?"

"That's right. Brook Ogden."

Kelly nodded. "Got it right here," she said, tapping a monitor in front of her. "Nothing to this—I'll ask a few softball questions; then we'll take a couple of calls, okay? Don't be nervous."

I exhaled my first full breath in the last half hour, my mouth arid as dryer lint. "Does it show?"

"Remember, no one can see you, and all you have to do is be yourself. This is great stuff, your column—the listeners are gonna eat it up, okay?" She nodded into a corner. "Bottled water over there. Crack it open before we go live."

"Okay."

"Hold tight." Kelly picked up her headphones and slid them on almost as soon as she started talking into the mike.

While she started a live testimonial about a local weight-loss center, I used the reprieve to fetch a water and quickly review all of Sasha's coaching.

As I took my deep breaths—"imagine you're breathing right from your uterus," she'd suggested—I pictured Sasha sitting in front of me, a look of support and rapt attention on her face. I wondered if she had told my mother about my radio interview, and if Mom would be listening too—and then choked the thought off when I felt my pulse start to pound in my ears again.

"All right, ladies, you're going to love my next guest—and you guys too!" On air, Kelly's voice was smooth and rich as a truffle. "If you read the paper, you probably already know her—Brook Ogden, a licensed mental health counselor, better known as the Breakup Doctor, is here to answer your rejection questions." I sent her silent gratitude for getting my job title right. "Brook, thanks for coming on the show today." She gave me a wink and I smiled in response despite my leaping heartbeat.

"Thanks, Kelly. My pleasure." My voice was close and intimate in my headphones, as if I were murmuring seductively into my own ear. It was disconcerting, but Kelly nodded encouragingly and I told myself to relax.

"Judging from the reader response on the *Tropic Times* Web site, and what I've been hearing around town, you've hit some kind of nerve with your column. Why do you think that is?"

"Well, um...everyone's gone through a breakup at some point or another. Often a nasty one."

She chuckled. "You sound like a woman who's been dumped."

For a moment I thought this was some kind of sick setup. My eyes shot to Kelly's face, but she was still smiling at me, calmly waiting for my response as if this were just a pleasant conversation. *Calm down, Brook. Cowgirl up.*

I cleared my throat, remembering to reach for the cough button just in time, and said, "Oh, sure. Like most of us, I've been down *that* road..." I gave an awkward chuckle.

She laughed. "Amen, sister."

She asked a few questions about my background as a therapist, and my one-on-one Breakup Doctor services. Kelly was right, I realized as we got going—there really was nothing to this if I just treated it like any other friendly chat.

But when she invited listeners to call in with any questions, suddenly I froze up again, wondering if Kendall could be listening, if he might phone the station, if I'd lose my just-discovered on-air cool and reveal myself as a complete sham of a Breakup Doctor.

I tried to concentrate on breathing from my uterus.

Of course he wouldn't call in. Kendall wouldn't even have the station tuned in—KXAR didn't have any financial programming.

The lines lit up almost at once, and Kelly clicked a button and said, "Good morning, caller—you're on the air with the Breakup Doctor."

"Oh..." I heard a woman's throat clearing. "Um. Do I have to say my name?"

Kelly shot me a glance, and I stared dumbly back for a moment before I realized she was waiting for an answer from me. I shook my head.

"Up to you, friend," Kelly said smoothly into her mike. "What's on your mind?"

"Okay, well. Um, it's my...my boyfriend. Ex. Or whatever." The woman's voice shook and it hit me that she was more nervous than I was.

My own anxiety was forgotten. I leaned forward and keyed my mike. "Sometimes those labels are a real bitch, aren't they?" As soon as the words were out of my mouth I felt heat flood my face. Could you say *bitch* on air?

Apparently so: Kelly simply looked amused, and my caller let out a chuckle that told me I'd managed to relax her at least a little.

"You're not kidding," the woman said. "Anyway...we broke up a while ago—like, months. And I should be over it now. I should be fine." Her voice wobbled. "But I'm not. We were in the same bowling league, and we have a lot of the same friends, and every time I see him it...it just kills me still."

I closed my eyes, the raw pain in the woman's voice touching a chord of empathy in me.

"So my question is...what's wrong with me?"

My eyes flew back open, my own situation spiraling away into its separate compartment while my focus was pulled squarely onto her.

"There is *nothing* wrong with you. Not one thing," I said forcefully. "How long were you with this man?"

"Not that long. Just a year and a half."

I shook my head. "Look...caller—"

"Mindy," she said softly. "My name's Mindy."

"Look, Mindy, a year and a half is plenty long enough to care about someone—deeply. And it sounds to me like maybe the breakup wasn't your idea, and it was pretty hard on you."

"Yeah. It was." Mindy's voice was almost a whisper.

"And you still see this guy in social situations, without ever having had a chance to get over him first? Who *wouldn't* have a hard time with that?"

I noticed I had Kelly's full attention now—she was looking at me, nodding.

"I don't know," Mindy said shakily.

"No one with a heart, who'd given it to that person, that's who. So go a little easy on yourself for having a tough time with this. It's totally normal."

"It is? Really?"

"Let's see if we can't help you through this rocky patch a little bit."

"Oh, God, that would be great." Her tone was thick with relief.

"First off, you're going to need to take a break from your bowling league for a while—not forever. Just till it's easier to see him. And for a little while, you've got to stay away from any outings with your mutual friends where you think you might see him."

"I do?"

"You have to. And if it's even too hard just to see those friends, with all the memories they might spark, then you need to take a short break from them too."

"But isn't that just...just avoiding my problems? Sticking my head in the sand?"

"Mindy, if you're out of ammunition, you don't hang around in the foxhole. It's time to retreat and reload. Hang out with friends who are only yours. Or make new ones. You have to start to create a life that's about you as an individual—not the two of you as a couple. After a while, you'll be strong enough to see your old friends again—I promise. Eventually you can go back to your old bowling league if you want to—although by that time, you might have found another league somewhere else, or another hobby you enjoy doing even more."

Kelly made wrap-it-up motions with a finger, and I gave Mindy a few last words of encouragement and wished her luck. I looked over at Kelly, who was grinning and shooting me a thumbs-up, and finally I relaxed. From Mindy's almost cheerful tone as she said goodbye, I knew I'd helped her.

For the next twenty minutes or so Kelly filtered calls over to me—relationship questions from both men and women, younger people and older ones, about everything from long-distance relationships to infidelity, from obsession to neglect. My comfort and confidence grew until, at the half hour, Kelly announced the end of our time.

"Can we convince you to come back sometime?" she asked on the air. "Maybe even as a regular feature—what do you think?"

"I'd love it," I said, meaning it. Not only had the appearance wound up being a blast, during which I felt I'd honestly done some good, but I could only imagine what the exposure might do for my client list.

For a moment, I let myself dream really big: clients would come pouring in from the column and this show and word of mouth, and I'd have more money than I knew what to do with. I would pay off all my debts, rent the most gorgeous office space in town, and turn my house into the showplace I'd once dreamed it could be when I signed my name to the stack of papers that made it mine.

The Breakup Doctor was turning into more than just a stopgap solution while I got my practice back together. Maybe it would wind up being the key to getting not just my career, but my whole life back on track.

Sasha called before I'd even made it into my car, bubbling words in my ear like "confident" and "professional" and "a natural."

Even the gaping wound in the living room wall that stared at me as I let myself in the front door didn't bring me down off the high I'd ridden since leaving the radio station. I hardly registered the hole, just floated right past it into the kitchen to start the coffee I desperately needed.

As I poured water into the back of the percolator, I glanced over to where my computer monitor rested on a corner desk in the adjacent den, surprised to see the shifting patterns of my screen saver. I remembered powering it down right after Sasha came over last night.

Dim memories started to seep in as I measured out scoops of coffee: Waking up suddenly in the darkness of my bedroom, Sasha gone. Unable to go back to sleep, I'd lain awake rehashing yet again what had gone wrong between Kendall and me. The thoughts chased around in my head pointless as rabbit racing until I made myself get up. And then...then there was a black hole in my memory.

I sent another foreboding look at the computer. I was so relieved I hadn't made any stupid calls to Kendall last night in my inebriated stupor, I hadn't stopped to think what else I might have done. Rambling, drunken emails were only marginally less awful than rambling, drunken phone calls. I felt sick in a way that had nothing to do with my hangover.

The walk to my desk felt like the Green Mile, and I jiggled the mouse with dread blooming in my stomach. My email account snapped up on the monitor—but it was the one the paper had given to me, I saw with a flood of relief.

I clicked on the inbox—forty-three new messages already just from this morning. I scrolled past the new ones and noticed another stack of messages that I didn't remember looking at, but which had been opened.

I clicked on Sent Mail. Apparently I'd made some replies too. That could be bad.

The subject line of one message caught my eye—Re: ASHAMED. My reply was sent at 3:21 a.m. My hands felt a little clammy. There was no telling what I might have said to people in the state I'd been in.

Dear Ashamed,

You should NOT feel embarrassed! What did YOU do wrong? You just came home and there was your boyfriend in the driveway, telling you he didn't love you anymore and kicking you out. Is that YOUR fault? No sirree it is not. You know whose fault that is? Your BOYFRIEND'S.

A little overly emphatic, maybe, but so far, not too damaging.

Don't you let that make you feel bad about yourself. His judgment is not YOURS, and don't you adopt it!!! This man decided to leave you, for probably NO GOOD REASON, and you know what that makes youuuuuuuuuuuuuuuuuu?

Little glitch there.

LUCKY! Yup. Think about THIS, Miss Ashamed— you could have ended up with that man, that man who looked into your pretty, pretty face (I know I don't know you but I KNOW you are pretty) and said I DON'T LOVE YOU ANYMORE. Phew! Close one—you escaped from winding up with a guy who didn't love you like you deserve to be loved. Be grateful you found out now. Now go find the man who will, because he's out there, and you WILL find him.

I signed it, *Good luck, and lots of love, your Breakup Doc.*

Well, it wasn't the careful verbiage I might have employed sober, but overall it wasn't bad advice. Good to know that even blind drunk my best instincts kicked in. I clicked on another of my replies, this one headed, *Re: Now What?*

Dear Left Behind in Lehigh,

First of all, I am very sorry. Having your husband leave you for someone else after thirteen years must be hurtful and confusing.

At least I'd adopted a professional tone in this one.

Seriously, that totally sucks.

Or not.

Because what is trust, then? What does a commitment mean? What is "marriage" if you can walk out the door as easily as you can leave a restaurant after you've finished your meal? I'm sure you're thinking, "None of it means a thing. None of it ever mattered. I don't matter."

I am tearing up, here, Left Behind. This is heartbreaking. And it SHOULD be—because it mattered to YOU. You came into the relationship believing in it, didn't you? Believing in forever. Giving your whole heart. And your husband took it and stomped all over it like a grape.

But remember this, Left Behind, my friend: stomped grapes make wine. And you know what's way better than a whole unbroken grape? A glass of wine.

I winced a little bit at how sozzled I sounded, but I was actually somewhat impressed with the metaphor.

I want you to remember this idea, okay? In the next few weeks and months, as things get a little tough, you remember you gotta crush some of those grapes to get the wine. And in time you are going to be a fine, fine wine, friend. I promise. I'm going to check on you, okay? You believe in yourself, and until you do, I will believe in you for you.

Again I signed off, *Much love, your Breakup Doctor*.

I sat back, blinking. For all their somewhat drunken tone, these weren't actually bad letters. Not that I could ever imagine saying these things to a patient sober, but...I'd say them to Sasha. And I'd do it because I knew that what she needed at times like that was lots of love and support and self-esteem building. I wouldn't worry about proper therapeutic conventions.

Rather than the disaster scenarios I'd feared, maybe a little too much to drink actually helped me figure out how to be a better Breakup Doctor.

Suddenly my eyes drifted to the bottom of my screen and I noticed that I'd had another window up last night. My personal email account.

My eyes flew wide open and my headache from the morning made itself screamingly known to me again. I sat straight up, fast—which hurt—and brought up my Outlook account. I skipped past the handful of new messages in my inbox—Sasha, a client from my practice, and Faryn Mitchell, an old friend from high school I heard from about once a year, for her annual Ragin' Pagans camping party. Then I clicked on SENT MAIL with every prayer, plea, and bargain with God running through my head.

And there it was. My masterpiece.

> *Kendall,*
> *Sasha says you're a douche with gonorrhea, but I say you have to sprinkle a lot of manure to get your garden to bloom. So I'm writing to tell you I'm grateful for all of your shit.*

I sank my head to my hands and rubbed my face as though I could erase myself. Dammit, I knew better: Don't drink and dial, and don't drink and email. More than anything I didn't want to continue reading, but I forced my eyes back to the monitor.

Looking back, I wonder how I overlooked for so long the fact that you were completely lacking ethics, morality, and a soul. I am a professional counselor! You'd think I'd be experienced at looking through fake people who put up walls to hide their deep inadequacies and insecurities.

But listen, I'm writing only for professional reasons. Because I always try to grow as a therapist—and, unlike some people, as a human being—it would be useful to me in my practice to help my patients understand their own dysfunctional relationships by figuring out what makes them fall apart. So strictly for research purposes, can you tell me why you are such a complete dick?

Thanks,

Brook

I felt a hot rush of mortification. Not just that I had sent this piece of garbage to my ex-boyfriend—which was humiliating enough. But also that I could name at least ten times that Sasha had composed similar emails in fits of hurt and anger and I had tried to rationally talk her off the ledge and convince her not to send them. She always did, though.

And now I was no better. I, who had always prided myself on my dignity and levelheadedness where relationships were concerned, had turned into...Sasha.

Say what you want to about technology—how it's improved our quality of life, allowed us to enjoy more leisure time, opened up the world to us right in our own living rooms—the computer revolution has its ugly downside. Back in the olden days a letter like this would have had time to simmer in my mailbox, perhaps mellowing like a fine wine overnight, when a girl might wake up in the sane and sober light of day, realize how over-the-top she had been, and thankfully, sheepishly retrieve the letter before the friendly postman took it away.

Now with the click of a button, all opportunity for second

thoughts vanished. There were no do-overs with email. Just like a mentally ill person in danger of harming herself or others, I was committed.

Contrary to what the movies would have you believe, it's not that easy to hack into someone else's email account.

I tried every password I could think of. Kendall's birthday. My birthday. His mom's name—no. Name of his childhood pet (which I knew only because we'd played the porn name game lying in bed one night: the name of our childhood pets and the streets we grew up on. I was Benji Bahama; Kendall, who'd lived for a time in Hawaii with his military family, was Poco Wiliwili, which made us laugh so hard I literally thought we would choke to death).

I was sure I had it with *stkbrkr*, but no. Clever Kendall didn't pick anything easy. Knowing him it was probably random letters and numbers, and he probably changed it every day. Like anyone cared about hacking into his personal business.

Well, except for me, at the moment.

I even entertained the thought of letting myself into his condo again to erase it before he read it. The only reason I didn't was because I wasn't sure I could sneak in and out quietly enough not to wake him up. Or whoever might be sprawled in bed with him.

That thought carved into my belly like a knife through rotten fruit: Kendall lying in his bed—the bed we'd shared, and might share forever, I had thought—with someone new.

No. I wasn't going down that mental path today. The damage was done, and now I had to face it like an adult and move on.

But first I wrote a quick letter and sent it:

Just a warning that my computer has been hacked or has a virus or something. If you get any emails from me with the subject line "Hey, ass face," DON'T open it!

Now I'd start being an adult.

twenty

My doorbell rang just past noon. My dad stood on the front porch, his face beaming with pride that brought a rush of tears to my eyes I had to blink back.

"Hey, there's my little radio star!" He held up a bakery bag shiny with oil that had seeped from whatever was inside. "There was a special at the bakery. I can't eat all this..."

While I forced down a few bites of the sticky pastry, he asked to see the leak in my guest bathroom. Once he'd seen the black fur behind the sodden drywall, and the corroded pipes, browned and lacy like a wedding dress stored in a musty basement, he went out to his truck and came back with a full complement of tools and armfuls of PVC pipe.

My first appointment of the day wasn't for a couple of hours, so I spent part of the afternoon helping him scrub and sand and spray bleach.

Mold, my dad told me, could cause everything from irritated eyes to skin rash to serious head and lung congestion. "You go stay with that boyfriend of yours while things clear up here," he said with a wink.

My stomach dropped at the word, but I couldn't tell my father what had happened. He had enough to worry about on his own. I just agreed with a smile like a rictus as he pushed his shirtsleeves up higher and settled in to remove the ruined pipe.

"Dad, you've done enough," I protested. "We can finish another day."

"Go on, sweetheart," he said, shooing me away. "I wanna go

ahead and get this done."

"But I'm leaving you with such a mess," I said, staring at the gaping cavity of my wall and the piles of sodden, blackened drywall we'd removed.

Dad reached out and awkwardly patted my shoulder. "Sometimes you can't avoid doing a little more damage before you can start fixing things, doll."

With my dad's insistence that I stay out of my home, I sought asylum with Sasha, but we didn't see much of each other over the next couple of days, between her work and my back-to-back consultations—including two cheating spouses, one floundering long-distance relationship, a porn addict, and one woman who claimed her husband was "emotionally dead inside."

But on Friday afternoon her car was in her spot when I parked in the apartment's visitor lot, and I found her in her bedroom getting ready for a date, contemplating herself critically in front of the cheval mirror in her bedroom in an outfit that looked tailored to her perfect body. And probably had been. I never knew how Sasha funded her clothing habit.

I lowered myself onto her bed, leaning against her headboard to watch the fashion parade. "So who is it tonight?"

Sasha eyed me in the reflection. "Does it matter? You don't usually care."

I sat up, stung. "I care. Why would you say that?"

Sasha turned to look at me. "No offense, Brookie. I just mean that you never seem to want to know much about anyone I go out with. Why now?"

I fingered the coverlet, uncomfortable. Sasha made me sound like a rotten friend. "I'm an asshole," I muttered. "No wonder Kendall left me."

Sash sighed and came over to sit next to me on the bed. "You're not an asshole, sweetie. Or at least, that's not why that asshole bailed on you."

"Ha, ha."

She patted my hand and stood, headed back to her closet. "Chin up, baby. You're going to get through this." Her voice grew muffled as she rummaged through her clothes.

"So tell me about him," I called out guiltily.

There was a beat of silence, and then, "No, you're right. Why bother till we know if he's just a sprinter or in for the marathon."

She stepped out in a little wrap dress that made her waist look twelve inches around before the skirt flared into a flippy little flya-way that ended just above her knees. The watercolor blend of blues and greens and teals made her light aqua eyes practically jump out of her face.

"Whoa," I said involuntarily.

"Good?"

"Gorgeous." Her expression cleared like the sun had come out, and I swung my legs over the edge of the bed and went over to where she stood. "You look beautiful, Sash," I said simply, reaching out to fine-tune the silky fringe of honey-colored hair skimming those amazing eyes. "He won't know what hit him."

"You think?" But she was over the hump—I could see the confidence come back to her face as she turned to look herself over.

"Mack truck. Have lots of conversation ready, because he'll be lucky to retain the power of speech." Sasha giggled, and I went back and sat down, perched on the bed with one leg drawn up under me. It reminded me of a hundred other times we'd gotten ready for dates together, and I was suddenly glad for the mold that had forced me to come spend a few days with her.

Sasha trotted into her closet and came out seconds later with two different shoes on—a beaded turquoise kitten-heeled sandal and a metallic gold peep-toe pump. "Which one?"

I pointed. "The pump. Look at your calves."

Sasha turned so she could see behind her in the mirror. "Oh. Yeah." She turned back around to face me. "Okay, I'm gone. Wish me luck."

"He isn't picking you up?"

Sasha looked uncertain. "Well..."

"Good girl!" I blurted in surprise. For years I'd tried to impress on Sasha a list of rules for her many first dates, hoping to force her to slow her pace: no getting into strangers' cars, new men didn't get to know where she lived, and no going anywhere except the designated meeting spot. Finally my admonitions had sunk in.

Sasha grabbed up her purse—a fringed gold clutch that matched her shoes—and then hesitated. "I feel bad leaving you. Are you going to be okay?"

"Of course."

She chewed her lip. "Yeah, but I know the whole breakup thing is pretty fresh. Listen, why don't I reschedule and we can—"

"Sash, *go*," I cut her off. "I'll be fine. When you get home we can sit and have ice cream and cookies."

She frowned into my face for a few moments, as though staring at a topographical map of some particularly rugged terrain she was preparing to traverse. "All right. Don't do anything I would do."

"*Wouldn't* do."

She shook her head. "No... I meant it the way I said it. Do I need to take your cell phone with me?"

"Sash, please. Go. Have fun," I said, waving her out, hoping against hope that she'd take my advice and *not* sleep with this guy on the first date.

Sasha didn't make it back by the time I'd created an improvised stir-fry out of the dozens of veggies I found in her fridge. She wasn't home by the time I finished eating, or cleaned up the kitchen, or sat and watched two *Sex and the City* reruns. I knew what that meant.

Same old Sasha. When was she going to grow up?

I was dangerously bored—Sasha may have had a point about not leaving me alone. Solitude gave my mind too much room to race, and my thoughts weren't healthy ones. Trying to distract myself, I browsed the titles on her bookshelves: *Snag that Man!*; *When Love Hurts*; *Turn Adieu into I Do*. I yanked the last one out.

Sometimes when he says, "Goodbye," what he's really saying is, "I'm scared." That's when it's up to you to hear the hidden fears and pain of the little boy inside him.

Blech. I snapped the book shut and threw it to the floor. What was Sasha doing with this kind of garbage? No wonder she had so much trouble with relationships.

I checked my cell phone—just to see if I'd somehow missed a text or call from her, I assured myself.

Nothing.

I tossed the phone down on the guest bed and it lay there, staring indifferently up at me with its blank LED eye. I gave it a prod to make it stop. And then another prod. And then some more prods until—miracle of miracles—all that prodding resulted in a text message: *We need to talk.*

Goodness, look at that. Like a Ouija board. Well, I couldn't mess with fate. Clearly the universe meant for me to send it, so I thumbed in Kendall's speed dial and hit send so quickly I didn't give myself time to remember I was strong and independent, and didn't want anyone who clearly didn't want me.

And then the phone and I faced off in a staring contest.

Beep or something, damn you.

Nothing.

There was every chance it didn't send correctly, I reasoned, so I sent the same message again and waited for the reply.

And waited.

Sometimes cell towers freaked out. Just to be safe, I hit send again.

Maybe twenty or thirty more times.

Nothing, nothing, *nothing.* I picked up the phone and started hitting the corner of it on Sasha's nightstand—*bam! bam! bam!*—until I heard an ominous crack.

The sound triggered a little sanity in me.

Stop this. Get ahold of yourself. This isn't who you are.

I threw on some flip-flops, snatched up my car keys, and headed out to the Honda.

* * *

Downtown is a grand word for the business area of Fort Myers. Originally built as a base of operations for the U.S. military to fight the pesky Seminole Indians who insisted on defending their ancestral lands, it was eventually abandoned and lay fallow for ten years before being settled as a residential community. It was another decade before Thomas Edison, our town's patron saint, discovered the sleepy tropical town of Fort Myers and built his sprawling white riverfront home and laboratory along the Caloosahatchee in 1887 just outside the confines of the downtown area.

I drove past the relentlessly white Edison home on my left, newly restored after damage from hurricanes and termites. Mercurial Florida carries devastating risks you can count on, yet they never seem to deter people from trying to thwart the certain and eventual wrath of nature.

But even Edison's august patronage couldn't turn the riverfront town into a metropolis. Despite grand plans over the years, including a recent face-lift and image makeover that renamed the area "the River District," a term I'd never heard cross the lips of any native of Lee County, the downtown area could only ever be described as "quaint."

Bricked streets gridded several blocks' worth of buildings, some of them dating back to the turn of the previous century. Only the old Arcade Theater building still fulfilled its original purpose, housing the Florida Repertory Theater. The rest of downtown's remaining historical buildings had been bastardized into kitschy boutique stores, restaurants, and lawyers' offices.

Though I was grateful to one such of the latter, as what Sasha and I called "the lawyer lot" provided one of the best parking areas in town after hours, a secret held by only a few natives that allowed us to find parking even during the most crowded events downtown. I'd shared the coveted secret of its existence with Kendall, and I knew that if he were prowling around downtown tonight, this was where I would find his car.

But there was no black Mercedes in the lot. I drove up and down the gridded streets, checking the street parking on either side, looking for it. Nothing. There were lots off Bay Street near the Harborside Convention Center, and scattered lots in the banking areas and city hall. But no Kendall there either.

Then I made the same circuit again, crawling so slowly past the entrances to every bar he usually frequented that cars behind me honked in irritated impatience. I shot a hand out my open window, my middle finger stabbing toward the sky.

Where was he?

A car in front of me suddenly peeled out of a street parking spot, and I whisked my car into it.

I sent another message. *Kendall, we need to talk. Where are you?*

I sat in the dark, waiting. After a while I turned off my engine and leaned my head back, lifting my phone in front of my eyes every so often to check the screen.

We need to talk! I punched in angrily. I sent it.

Still no response. This time I called. It went to voicemail after only a few rings, and a haze of red literally filled my vision. *Fuck* leaving a message. I hung up and called again. And again. And again. Finally the line stopped ringing and went straight to voicemail—Kendall had turned the damn thing off again to avoid me—and this time when his recorded message ended and I heard the beep, I screamed unintelligibly into the phone like zombies were tearing my flesh off.

A girl walking by my car on the sidewalk who barely looked legal jumped about a foot into the air before turning to cast me a nervous look and scurrying away.

I shut the phone off and threw it into the foot well, tipping my head forward over the steering wheel and trying to breathe. Minutes dragged by as I listened to the sounds of the downtown bar scene. Music seeped out of several bars on Hendry Street, bleeding together into a cacophonous noise. Bursts of laughter punctuated the drone of chatter from people passing by on the sidewalk.

What on earth was I thinking? Screaming into Kendall's voicemail like a crazy person? I needed to calm down. I was acting irrationally, erratic.

I was acting like Sasha.

That thought was all it took to throw me into action. I needed to get out of downtown—Kendall could be anywhere, and this was *not* how I wanted to run into him. And I needed to steady my fraying nerves. A drink would help take this frazzled edge off—but I'd learned my lesson about cracking open a bottle, so going back to Sasha's wasn't the best idea either.

I'd head up 41 toward her house—far from any of Kendall's usual haunts—and stop somewhere along the way to have a soothing glass of wine. Once I'd unwound from the tight coil my nerves were in, I'd go back to Sasha's and sleep off this terrible, unsettled mood.

Everything would be better in the rational light of day.

twenty-one

I woke up from a dream about Sasha. She was young, maybe twelve or thirteen, and sitting in an inner tube floating somewhere, while methodically applying colored Band-Aids over every exposed inch of skin until she looked like a human piñata. Then she was dancing on a stage, the bandages loosening and fluttering with every pirouette she made. Suddenly my mother was beside her doing a soft-shoe, the two of them falling into step as though they'd choreographed the dance, and my mother pulled off the bandages with each lunge and whirl and twist. I watched from the audience, wanting to get up, rush the stage, press the bandages back down and keep them from falling away, but my legs felt like sandbags and I couldn't move.

I blinked up at the unfamiliar ceiling. It took me a minute to realize where I was—not nestled in Kendall's plush Frette sheets. Not huddled in my own hand-me-down sheets on my secondhand mattress. But in the soft full-size bed in Sasha's guest room.

Oh, yeah. Memory rushed back: the mold, Sasha's date... My texts and crazy stalking and phone calls to Kendall. How mortifying.

I sat up and sandbags slammed into the inside of my skull. I groaned and rubbed my bleary eyes as the first streaks of sunlight purpled the sky outside the window. Out of habit I reached for my cell phone. Not even six a.m. What time did I get home last night?

Wait. For that matter...*how* did I get home?

I tried to swing my legs over the side of the bed, but something was wrong—they were trapped. I thrashed to get them to move, but they seemed tied together. Throwing the sheet back, I saw the problem—my jeans were bunched around my ankles. Lovely. Apparently I'd passed out mid-disrobing.

Was I drunk last night? I didn't even remember drinking.

Something neon green was on my top half. I pulled the unfamiliar T-shirt away from me in front to try to read the writing on it upside down.

I GOT TANKED AT FISHY BOB'S.

Fishy Bob's? Why—and when—had I been there, done that, and literally gotten the T-shirt? I let the shirt drop into place and stared unseeingly at the louvered closet doors in front of me as the slow pounding in my brain began to bring back memory with every throb.

I'd planned to track Kendall down, hadn't I? To confront him? No...no, that was lunacy—I'd had the good sense to realize that, and I'd decided to...what?

The pounding grew into a full-fledged splitting headache.

Oh, yes. Have a drink. Somewhere out of downtown, where I knew I wouldn't see Kendall. I remembered stopping somewhere—images flashed through my mind of a strip mall up Cleveland populated by seedy business like bail bonds and some kind of tattoo and piercing parlor that couldn't possibly have passed any health inspections.

Like a snapshot I saw in my mind a partially burned-out sign that hung crooked at the other end of the strip mall: SHY BOB'S. That hadn't sounded so bad. I'd gone inside.

Memory filtered back in snippets: a few sad-looking booths lining the walls, concrete floor, torn vinyl bar stools, and a weathered bar front-and-center with what looked like a moonlighting Hell's Angel behind it. I thought I'd started to turn back around to leave...until the big grizzly tending bar had called out something about "taking a load off, darlin'."

I could hear his voice in my head as clearly as if he sitting on the bed beside me: rough and gravelly, but his tone so kind it made me want to hug him. So I sat, and when the bartender put a shot glass on the bar and held up a bottle, I nodded and did the shot without even thinking twice.

I remembered nearly choking on the sickly flowery taste of it—gin. But I got it down and kept it there. There was no telling how many times that routine played out. I was so hungry for appreciation that I would have set myself on fire if it meant I kept getting the nods and grins and benedictions the burly bartender offered.

I got talky, I remembered now. I told him about Kendall after drink three, or four, and at the man's unexpected sympathy and compassion, I might have segued into telling him about Michael and our shattered engagement. And then...I struggled to recall what happened after that.

Nothing. Apparently at some point I'd blacked out.

Surely I hadn't driven home in that state?

The sick feeling in my stomach was becoming as familiar to me as the wash of self-loathing that came with it. Post-breakup drinking was one thing...but drinking and driving was dangerous...irresponsible...reprehensible.

I stood up—a mistake, as my head swam and suddenly I was pretty sure I was going to throw up. No, thank goodness, I was—

God. Luckily I made it into the guest bath in time to not be the absolute *worst* house guest alive. Sasha had a hair-trigger gag reflex; if she saw a puddle of the remnants of my evening, it would have created a really unfortunate chain reaction.

Sasha. Oh, god—was she home when I'd stumbled in last night, so drunk I had no recollection of it? She'd be so pissed at me... We'd promised when we were teenagers that if one of us was ever too drunk to drive, we'd call the other one to take care of us—or get hold of someone who could.

Wait...*had* I called Sasha?

I splashed my face and rinsed out my mouth, then stumbled out of the bathroom and into her room. Sasha was tucked safely in bed, sound asleep. No indication of whether she'd had to come get me from some dive bar last night and pour me into the house.

Desperate for clues, I walked into the living room and flicked the curtain aside to look outside, the sun now bright enough to feel like nails being driven into my eyeballs. Sasha's car was there—but so was mine.

Oh, god, I did drive home. I could see my keys on the table just inside Sasha's front door, along with my purse and...a crumpled sheet of paper? I walked over and saw that it was a note on Fishy Bob's letterhead—they had letterhead?—scrawled in Magic Marker: *Bernice and me drove you home. Hair of the dog'll fix you back up. Forget that asshole.* It was signed, *Stalker*.

Stalker. The Hell's Angel bartender.

And there was a P.S.: *The blood probly ruined your shirt.*

My heart froze. Blood? I could see the white fabric of my top shoved into one side of my purse and yanked it out, the stiff brown patch on one side in the back making my heartbeat resume with a thud. What had happened to me? I clapped my hand onto my shoulder and felt nothing, then did the same on the other one.

"Ow!" I nearly jumped out of my skin at the raw sting of it.

My heart dropped to my stomach as I raced back to Sasha's guest bath and carefully peeled the garish T-shirt over my head. Sure enough, my right scapula was covered in a wide gauze bandage. Breath held, I peeled up the tape on one side and gently pulled, the gauze sticking to whatever wound I'd sustained.

It was glossy with some kind of ointment, and reddish brown with dried blood. I pulled out some tissues and gingerly wiped at one edge—the sting needled through me, but I kept at it. Under the blood, something dark was embedded into my skin. *Crap*—had I ridden bitch on Stalker's bike and wiped out?

But the dark edges were too crisp for asphalt burn, and slowly a sinking feeling began in my belly. I kept dabbing, but I already knew what I was going to find.

I'd gotten a tattoo.

There on my shoulder were letters in bold, black ink. I prayed I was reading them wrong backward in the mirror, but I knew I wasn't.

"NO MORE JACKASSES."

Oh, no. No, no. Drinking and dialing was one thing—even stalking I could cope with. But there was no way I'd done something as ridiculous, as *permanent*, as tattooing myself with something so appalling. I'd thought I'd hit rock-bottom, but this was much, much worse.

And then, impossibly, it was even worse than that, I saw as I kept wiping. Below the letters was some kind of cartoon, and I leaned closer to the mirror to make it out.

It was a full-color drawing of a donkey with—oh, dear God—a very evident equine erection, a bright red circle over the whole thing with a line drawn through.

If I'd had anything left in my stomach, I'd have thrown up again.

Thank god Sasha was still sound asleep. I couldn't let her see this. As crazy as she ever got after a breakup, as far as I knew she'd never permanently defaced her body. She'd have shown me if she had—*shame* wasn't in her vocabulary.

Uselessly, I tried scrubbing at the thing with a washrag, praying that it was a temporary tattoo, or henna—but the first scrape of terry cloth against the raw skin felt like I was using the sander that had rubbed a hole into my moldy wall, and I had to bite my lips shut to hold back the scream that nearly resulted, for fear of waking Sasha.

It was real.

How the hell had I gotten a tattoo on my shoulder and had no recollection of it? Why had Stalker and the rest of my new BFFs let me do it? Or had they encouraged it? Guilt bit at my conscience at the thought—he'd had the kindness to drive me home when I was in no shape for it. But surely it was clear that I wasn't the tattoo type? And I certainly hadn't been in any state to make a decision about permanently inking donkey genitalia onto my body.

I found some antibiotic ointment in my purse, along with a re-

ceipt from the tattoo parlor—apparently I paid $250—and applied
it over the thing, then carefully placed the bandage back over the
evidence and taped it into place. Back in the guest room, I shoved
the Fishy Bob's shirt into a corner of Sasha's closet and pulled one
of my own T-shirts over my head. And not a second too soon—I
could hear Sasha's phone alarm chiming in the next room.

I stepped to her doorway and looked in—she was still sound
asleep despite the incessant alarm. For the first time I actually
hoped Sasha *had* gone home with her date last night. If she'd gotten
in after I did, she wouldn't ask any questions about my evening.

Watching her curled up, looking innocent and young with no
makeup and her mouth slightly open, I remembered the day she
wanted us to be blood sisters when we were in sixth grade—one of
the many days she rode home on the bus with me after school.
There were a lot of afternoons when she did that, that year her dad
started to come home less and less often, he and her mom arguing
all the time when he did.

Sasha had whipped out a safety pin the size of an ice pick and
said, "You and me. Sisters. I want it to be real. Family." We wound
up spilling rubbing alcohol all over my bedroom and almost being
caught by my mom, and in the end I'd chickened out.

I blinked, trying to clear my vision that had suddenly blurred
around the edges.

Longing stabbed me for the innocence and ease of those days
when we'd been kids together, our biggest concern whether the
alcohol would bleach the carpet, and how much trouble we would
be in if it did.

I tiptoed over to the other side of the bed and crawled in under
the covers, lying on my non-freshly-tattooed shoulder with my head
on the pillow facing Sasha, the way we'd fallen asleep together in
my bed on all the nights she'd stayed over at my family's house
instead of her own.

Her eyes flickered and then blinked open, and a sleepy smile
bloomed over her face when she saw me. "Are we thirteen again?"
she asked.

I smiled back at her echo of my thoughts. "Yes. There's been a time warp and it's 1992."

"This time don't let me get a perm."

We lay there in silence for a few minutes, listening to a persistent mourning dove making its cooing hoot. I wished with an aching in my throat that it *was* 1992. That we could go back to when we didn't know how much everything in the world could hurt us. When we didn't know we weren't the fearless heroes we thought we were.

"Remember the day you wanted us to be blood sisters?" I whispered.

"The alcohol all over the carpet."

"And my mom thinking we were drinking." We giggled together for a moment.

"We should have done it," I said quietly. "Become sisters."

Sasha reached over and twined her fingers through mine. "We did."

I wanted to tell her what I had done last night—what I had done over the last few days. I wanted her to laugh about it, to make *me* laugh about it, to lessen the sting of it with the soothing balm of normalcy. *Oh, God, who* hasn't *done that, Brookie?*

But I knew the answer. *I* hadn't. I wasn't the one who jumped off the deep end after a relationship ended. I was supposed to be more mature than that. More evolved. I was the Breakup Doctor, for God's sake.

But here I was, hungover and freshly tattooed, and too ashamed to tell the best friend I'd ever had anything about it.

I squeezed her fingers and we dropped back into silence, listening to the dove's sad little call.

All I wanted to do was find out how to get a tattoo removed, and start the process immediately. But I had a Breakup Doctor appointment first thing that morning, and somehow I had to figure out how to advise someone else on their own broken relationship when I was proving to be such a complete failure at handling my own.

A man I assumed was my client sat alone at a table by the edge of the outside dock when I walked into Ship to Shore down on Hurricane Bay, and he stood when he saw me. I guessed him to be in his mid-fifties, about five-eleven, with sandy hair graying attractively at the temples. He wore cream linen slacks, a silky baby blue short-sleeved button-down, and an ascot in a fresh cool lime green. I'd pulled myself together as best I could after a much-needed shower that didn't do anything to wash my self-loathing away, wearing tailored pants and a blouse, with a three-quarter-sleeve cardigan, despite the day's warmth, to help hide my badge of shame.

"Duncan O'Neill?" I asked, extending a hand.

"In the flesh."

"Brook Ogden."

"Yes. The Breakup Doctor."

I cringed at the title as we settled back down at the table and gave the waiter our orders. When the server left, Duncan leaned back in his chair and tented his fingers.

"I'm about to tell you all about my relationship woes, which are between me and my husband, Wagner, and I'm desperately hoping you're the sort who's as open-minded as you seem from your column." He'd put emphasis on the word *husband*, watching me closely as he said it.

I nodded. "Love can be complicated no matter who you're with. Ready when you are."

His expression cleared. "Wonderful. I had a feeling from your column. You just sounded...fair."

My juice came and I took a long sip, hoping it would revitalize my confidence.

Duncan waited until our waiter had finished warming his coffee and left. "Well. Wagner and I have been together for ten years," he began. "Which is like dog years in a gay relationship—each one counts for seven hetero years. We were married in Canada in 2007, and have been inordinately happy far more often than not. There's no one else I'd rather do things with, tell things to, or even argue with. He's more than my lover—he's my best friend, and I flatter myself that I'm his."

I felt an ache in the back of my throat. It sounded...lovely. I nodded for him to go on.

Duncan paused and looked out over the bay, where a midsize Regal was just puttering in alongside the restaurant's dock to tie off.

Then he gave a hard sigh and continued. "One of the things that makes us work so well, in my opinion, is that we have always had an understanding about extramarital relationships. Things...happen—but we both agree they must be strictly physical and are kept completely separate from our marriage."

He stopped talking to take a sip of his coffee but his eyes never left my face, and one corner of his mouth lifted into a smile.

"You're doing a lovely job of not reacting to that, dear, but I can feel your surprise from here."

Actually, I was thinking who in the hell was I to judge anyone else's choices?

Duncan put down his cup and leaned forward. "You're a mental health professional—how often do the studies say men think about sex?"

"Every seven seconds, according to the Kinsey report," I answered automatically.

Duncan nodded. "Well, that's a bit overstated. But I can tell you—it's pretty often. You get *two* men together, and it's a safe bet that most of the time, one of us is thinking about having sex. Wagner and I *are* in love. Deeply. But we're realistic, and we both know there's no sense throwing away something as solid and rare as what we have over the occasional insurmountable impulse."

A pelican lit on the wooden dock just underneath the patio where we sat, its scoopy beak bobbing up into the air as it swallowed whatever it had just plucked out of the water. I tried not to come to snap judgments about people in my practice, but I did pay attention to my instincts. I liked Duncan O'Neill. I wished I had his self-assurance.

"You two sound like you have a committed, healthy relationship," I said honestly, "on terms you both agree upon."

The cheerful, open expression abruptly left Duncan's face, and the downcast look that replaced it seemed out of place. "Yes, well, I thought so too. Until recently."

The waiter sidled back up to our table, delicately setting the plates in his hands down in front of us.

Steam was still rising off my omelet, along with a delicious, spicy scent, but I couldn't have forced a bite down.

Duncan unfolded his napkin and set it down in his lap, staring down at it for a moment. Perhaps he was reflecting on my complete inadequacy to help him, or anyone else. "I feel like such a pathetic fool," he muttered, so softly I almost missed it.

He felt like a fool? Before I thought about what I was doing, I reached under the table and gripped his thigh. Duncan looked up at me, startled. That made two of us. I retracted my hand. "You're not a fool, Duncan. Or stupid. You're just...trying to cope with your pain."

He smiled, a small one. "Thank you," he said quietly, and the constriction in my throat eased ever so slightly. When he picked up his fork and started to eat, so did I. Between bites Duncan started telling me the rest.

"Wagner drinks a bit. That's not an issue," he said, holding up a hand. "I drink a bit too—spirits can blunt life's harsher edges, as long as you don't use them as a crutch too often. But sometimes, well, he can...overdo it. As can we all," he hastened to add. "But when Wagner does it..." He trailed off and then stopped, and I waited, not wanting to interrupt. "When Wagner does it, sometimes he turns...he turns..."

My stomach sank. *Violent,* was what I feared Duncan was about to say, and no one should tolerate that.

Duncan seemed to be choking on his words. "He turns *straight!*"

I blinked. "What?"

"He flirts—outrageously!—with *women*." He looked so miserable and horrified that I wanted to get up and hug him.

"Is that part of your agreement?" I asked.

"Absolutely not!"

I clattered my fork down to my plate. "Then that is bullshit, my friend. Total unacceptable bullshit." Even as the words were leaving my mouth, I was horrified at myself. Where was Wise Therapist?

"I know!"

"Does he do more than flirt?"

"I don't know," he said sadly. "We've always kept that part separate from each other, out of respect. So I can't ask, can I, after we both agreed to those terms nearly a decade ago?"

"You most certainly *can* ask. In fact, you have an inalienable *right* to." Wise Therapist had apparently ceded the floor to righteous Founding Father. My usual careful phrasing was nowhere to be found, my tongue tripping along without any input at all from my brain. "So let me get it straight: It's not the idea that he's screwing around that's suddenly bothering you, right?"

"Of course not. A man has needs."

"It's that it might be with a woman sometimes?"

His face crumpled. "Yes! I just can't handle it, and I'm afraid we've come up against a brick wall. I don't see any alternative but to end it all."

My heart leaped in alarm. "Oh, Duncan, suicide is never—"

He cut me off with a dismissive snort. "Of course not suicide, dear. Not my style. I meant *us*...our marriage."

"Oh. Well, have you talked to Wagner about this?"

"No. One of the things that makes us work is that we don't indulge in petty jealousies."

"But this *isn't* petty to you!" I sputtered.

"I can't *say* anything," he wailed. "What if he...what if he thinks I'm insecure? It's so unattractive."

"But that's how you're feeling, isn't it?" His fingers curled around mine and I realized at some point I'd reached across the table to put my hand over his. Disconcerted, I gave an awkward squeeze before pulling my hand back. "You told me yourself Wagner's your best friend. If you can't tell your best friend when you're worried about something, or hurt, or yes, even insecure, something's a little off, isn't it?" Guilt flared inside me as I spoke the words. Wasn't that what I was doing with Sasha?

But this wasn't about me. This was about Duncan.

"At least *talk* to him," I said. "Tell him exactly how you feel—have an honest, straightforward discussion about it. You owe each other that much."

He frowned, but nodded.

I pulled a small notebook from my purse. "Look, I'm going to make a list of some specific questions you might ask him—and some you might ask yourself—to start to know exactly what you're dealing with." What was I doing? My job was simply to lead the horses to water, not shove their faces into the river and make them drink.

But Duncan had brightened at my words. "Oh, that's very helpful. It's hard to think straight sometimes when I'm so upset about it."

I looked up and gave him a real smile. "Of course it is. We're not wired to think calmly during a crisis—we're wired for fight or flight. Sitting and facing the tough stuff flies in the face of human nature."

"You're very kind, you know that? I expected your wisdom. But your warmth is a lovely bonus."

I felt myself flush. I wasn't at all acting like the kind of therapist I'd been trained to be. I'd cursed, initiated physical contact, and objectivity was out the window. I was acting like Duncan was a friend—like he was Sasha, rather than a professional client. And as for wisdom...clearly I was no expert on how to handle relationship issues. I didn't know what to say, so I just tore the page I was writing on from the notebook and handed it over.

When we finished eating I paid the bill and we stood to leave. Duncan reached out a hand to shake mine. I wasn't sure who was more surprised when I leaned forward instead and pulled him into a quick hug. Wise Therapist had now been taken over by a Care Bear.

"It's going to be okay, Duncan," I said when we broke apart, my hand still on his shoulder. "Whatever happens, you're going to be fine."

"I feel worlds better already," Duncan said. "Thank you. I'll start working on my homework right away, and I'll be in touch soon to get together again."

"Good. Don't you back down—you deserve to know what's going on."

Duncan was looking at me with a warm, genuine smile. "It must be lovely to always know the right thing to do. That kind of certainty is such a gift."

I pushed out a smile and said goodbye, hoping he couldn't read in my face what a fraud I actually was.

twenty-two

Tattoo in haste, repent at leisure. It turned out that removing a tattoo took a lot more time—and money—than getting one. The doctor estimated that mine would take nine to twelve treatments to fully remove, at $270 a pop, with seven to eight weeks of recovery time between each session—and we couldn't even start until the freshly tattooed skin had healed. That meant that one night's stupid, drunken decision would take me more than a year to undo. If I was lucky, the treatments wouldn't leave a visible scar—but they would likely do nothing to erase my invisible shame.

Between that, client meetings and keeping up with my column, and heading over to Dad's whenever I had any downtime to make sure he wasn't left alone too much and had food in his refrigerator, the next week passed by in a blur. I hardly saw Sasha. Partly I was avoiding her—I felt guilty at keeping so much from her. But she was out nearly every night anyway, and I feared she was back to her old relationship patterns.

But I was hardly in a position to judge.

At the end of the week my dad pronounced my house dry and mold-free.

"How's about Monday to start the work—good for you?" he asked as we dropped off his tools in my garage, along with the supplies we'd bought at Home Depot to fix the drywall. "Hate to interrupt your weekend with Kendall."

I flinched. I kept meaning to tell him, but every time I opened my mouth I thought about my dad all by himself in his house, lonely and miserable and missing my mom. I didn't want to give him one more thing to worry about. I was keeping an awful lot of things from an awful lot of people lately.

"Monday's fine, Daddy." Lately the childish nickname kept slipping out.

Dad wiped his hands on a rag he'd tucked into his belt. "Hey, you hear about your mom, gonna be in the paper?" He actually sounded proud.

"Did she call you?"

"Oh, well, you know, she's really immersing herself in the play. That's a hell of a role she's got there. Stu told me."

"Did *Stu* talk to her?"

"I wish you'd give her a ring, hon. Check on her. Let her know you're thinking of her."

I pressed my lips shut so I wouldn't spit out what popped to mind, which was, *But I'm* not *thinking of her.*

"I've been pretty busy myself, Dad," I hedged instead.

My father looked down at the towel clutched in his hands, his body seeming to sag. "She's still your mom, Brook."

Yeah. I wished *she'd* remember that.

After he left I drove back over to Sasha's to pick up my things. With the mold cleared up there was no reason for me not to be at my own house, but I wasn't in any hurry to leave. Maybe I'd stay one more night and move back home in the morning, and tonight we could have a silly, giggly slumber party together, like we used to when we were kids.

But Sasha was in her bathroom putting on fresh makeup when I let myself in at her apartment. She had on a fitted sleeveless black wraparound top, with a pair of flowing cream palazzo pants that would have looked overdone on anyone else, and I knew without her telling me that she already had plans.

"You look hot," I told her honestly. "Another date?"

She smiled. "Same one."

I sighed. "Oh, Sash. Don't you think it's a bit much, a bit fast?"

Sasha shrugged, her smile disappearing.

I felt bad. "Maybe we can do something tomorrow night?"

"We *are* doing something tomorrow night. Jan and Faryn's party."

"Oh, I forgot." I sagged against the jamb. "I hadn't planned on going to that this year, with...everything else."

"We always go. It's awesome."

"Sash, at last year's party you woke up in a clearing on Faryn's neighbor's property—three houses down. You threw up green for two days from Jell-O shots. I had skid marks on my elbows for a week and a half from where I took a facer after you convinced me to get on your shoulders and play chicken against Spencer Halloway and Hunt Jackson."

"Right? How fun was *that*!" Sasha dipped a fat, fluffy brush into a vat of loose powder and then tapped it on the side, most of the powder sprinkling off. "You *have* to go. We always have a blast there. It'll be good for you." She shrugged. "You never know—maybe you'll even meet someone."

"Among the same people from high school who've been coming every single year since we graduated? Doubtful."

Her forehead wrinkled up at my acidic tone. "Brook, I'm worried about you."

I moved my gaze from hers in the mirror. "Don't be. I'm fine."

She turned to face me directly. "You're *not* fine. How could you be?"

Her tone was the one you use with sick people who don't realize how ill they are, and she was regarding me with a concerned, pitying look I didn't like being on the receiving end of. At all.

"Really, Sash," I said, reaching down to the lipsticks lined up on the counter and making a show of investigating each color, "I'm totally okay. I've even kind of met someone."

I wanted to snatch back the words the second I'd uttered them. I'd only meant to deflect her—not tell an out-and-out lie. But her entire demeanor had changed as soon as she heard the words, and I knew a Gitmo-worthy interrogation was coming.

"You did! Who? Where?"

I yelped—loudly. Her playful slap wasn't that hard, but it landed right on my still-healing tattoo.

"Oh, don't be so dramatic," Sasha said, with a roll of her eyes. Then she turned thoughtful. "You know, maybe this *is* just what you need—a couple of dates with someone nice who can get your mind of off Ken"—she bit off the word—"things. Where'd you meet him?"

I racked my brain frantically. For a second I thought about using my new client Duncan as my fictional potential new boyfriend, but I didn't think I could sustain that with any believability if she asked too many questions. Before I thought it through, I blurted, "At the hospital. The night I got my tetanus shot."

Mistake.

"Brook!" Her arms were crossed and storm clouds knotted her brow. "That was two *weeks* ago! Why didn't you tell me!" Then her eyes got huge and she gasped. "That was even before you and K—" Again she caught herself. "Sneaky girl. You know what? Good for you. What's his name? What's he do?"

Mortifyingly, to save my life I couldn't pull up the name of the man I'd met in the emergency waiting room, so I focused on the second question. "Uh, he's in building. A...construction worker." I had no idea if that was exactly true, but it wasn't as though it mattered.

Sasha's forehead crinkled again, and then she shrugged. "Perfect. No possibility of commitment—the ideal rebound guy."

"There's no such thing as an 'ideal rebound guy,' Sash," I replied automatically. "Rebound guys are a bad idea."

"Are you kidding?" She pulled another brush from a leather case and turned back to the mirror to blend a light shadow along her brow bone. "They're part of the process. How else do you forget about your ex and feel good about yourself again?"

I watched her for a moment, struck dumb. How was it that after a lifetime of friendship with me, Sasha still hadn't absorbed *any* of the breakup rules? As the number one recipient of my post-dumping ministrations over the years, she was a terrible advertisement for my services.

"Sasha." I kept my tone level—a patient parent guiding her child. "Rebound guys are just a way of avoiding dealing with the pain of a broken relationship."

Sash stopped tapping her brush into a sparkly copper-colored eye shadow to give me a "well, duh" look. "That's the point."

"No. Completely against the point. You have to work through your feelings so you can move past them. And the way you feel good about yourself is from inside—not outside." I might not be walking the walk, but I could still talk the talk.

Sasha blew off her brush and set it into its space in the fancy leather case, retrieving a bigger one. "Blah blah blah. I've read all the self-help books. My way's quicker."

What did it matter, anyway? If Sasha hadn't altered her breakup MO in more than twenty-five years of friendship with me, she wasn't going to start now.

By the time I pulled into my driveway, I was wondering if Sasha was right. Maybe the best way to forget an old love really was in the arms of a new one. Or as she said...if not to forget, at least feel better about yourself. I could use a little of that right about now.

Inside I threw my suitcase into a closet and dug around in my purse until I found what I was looking for.

And then I made a phone call.

twenty-three

I was worried that I might not recognize Benjamin Garrett when I showed up at Andale's. But even without the dark blue sling holding his left arm across his abdomen against the brighter blue of his shirt, I would have remembered him. He was standing by the bar, looking like a lost kid in a busy department store, but in no particular hurry to be found. Brown hair, tall, in good shape; when he wasn't wearing a coating of grime and sweat, he was a nice-enough-looking man.

I'd been going about this all wrong, I had realized as I got ready for my impromptu date. I was chasing Kendall all over town, putting myself in the weaker position, the position of supplicant. What I needed to be doing was taking over the power position—making him realize what he'd lost, instead of crying after him.

I'd taken extra care getting ready with that in mind, wearing a white scoop-neck sundress with a big, bold fuchsia-and-orange flower print. The dress hugged my torso in ways that made the most of my God-given assets, cinched at the waist in a way that skimmed at least five pounds off my actual weight, and then flared into a feminine spill to my knees. Unfortunately, the effect I was going for—*Oops, I didn't mean to look so sexy when I threw on this old thing*—was mitigated by the sweater that was apparently going to be my uniform for the next year and a half, to hide my shoulder.

I'd carefully chosen Kendall's favorite restaurant downtown in the hopes that he would see me. Or at least maybe someone we knew would, and through the small-town grapevine he'd know about within twenty-four hours that I was out with someone else.

I deliberately kept my eyes only on Ben as I walked toward him across the crowded bar area, as if there were no one more important in the room. And then I was standing next to him, and he was smiling (nice smile, I remembered), and I had time to think, *Oh, God, this was a very big mistake*, before he said, "Hey, there! How's your wound?"

I blinked at him, then realized he was talking about my foot. "Better, thanks." Then, hoping someone Kendall and I knew was looking my way, I gave Ben a tight, warm hug. He stiffened a little in surprise, but put his good arm around me obligingly until I pulled back.

I nodded toward the sling. "How's the arm?"

"Oh—clean fracture. I just have to take it a little easier for a while. A few more weeks of this"—he lifted the arm—"and then business as usual."

"Good."

"Did you want a drink before we get a table?" Ben asked politely as I looked over his shoulder, trying to catch the bartender's eye. If Jabber Jeffrey saw me out on a date with someone new, word would get back to Kendall fast.

"Hmm? Oh..." Jeffrey was slammed—the other bartender, a girl I didn't know, was headed over our way. "No, that's okay. Let's just go sit down."

On the way to our table, Ben remarked on the décor—elegant and modern—and the architecture of the old building.

"Do you know what it used to be, before they made it into a restaurant?" he asked as we were seated at a small, intimate table in the corner. Low visibility, I fumed, but on the plus side, I had a panoramic view of the entire restaurant.

"Um, no. Drugstore, I think?"

"Huh. You wouldn't guess it."

In the awkward silence that followed that exhaustive conversation about everything we had in common, we perused our menus. Or at least Ben did. I'd spent enough time in Andale's to rattle off the ingredients of every dish they served. While Ben decided on his meal, I surreptitiously scanned the restaurant over my menu as intently as if trying to find Waldo.

"Nice article this morning."

I dragged my eyes back to Ben, trying to decipher his words. Oh—today was Friday. I racked my brain, trying to remember what I had written.

"I've had first dates like that too," Ben said, taking a sip of the water a waiter had brought over. "Where I felt like I was just there to be someone's audience."

Right. The article I'd written fresh from my hurt and anger about Kendall. I didn't want to talk about that. Certainly not with an all but total stranger. I floundered for something else to say. "So...what are you doing with your time while that arm heals?"

"I'm not really taking any time off. Can't afford to, with the economy like it is. The guys at work are helping pick up my slack."

Well, that didn't seem fair, but whatever. Band of brothers. The loud buzzing of the chattering crowd around us only punched up the silence that fell once again at our table. I took a sip of my drink and used the distraction to scan the patrons again.

"I didn't mean *this* date, just to clarify. About the feeling-like-an-audience thing."

I looked at Ben. What on earth was he talking about? Oh—his comment before about my column. Right. *Focus, Brook.* The last report I wanted getting back to Kendall—besides that I'd completely lost my marbles since he'd left me—was that I was out with someone and having a rotten time. I heaved out a gay, girlish laugh. "Of course not, silly! I didn't think that!"

He looked at me strangely—maybe my laugh was a *little* loud—but the arrival of our waiter saved me from manufacturing more such witty repartee. We placed our orders, and then once again I panicked. *Conversation, Brook. Look like you're having one.* I needed something we could talk about for longer than three lines of dialogue. What in the world did I have in common with someone who worked in construction?

Oh. Duh.

I projected what I hoped was a charming smile. "So, I guess I told you a little bit about my disastrous home renovation project when we met..."

Ta-da. We were off to the races. I started telling Ben all about my house—how I'd bought it with such big plans for it, all the problems I'd discovered since, the work I'd done so far. He was a good listener—that was a pleasant surprise. And he had nice eyes—chocolate brown and kind. I hadn't noticed in the emergency room.

"Have you ever heard of I can?" he asked when our food came and I paused in my litany of home ownership woes.

I frowned as I forked into my snapper. Was he giving me some kind of a pep talk? A lecture in get-it-done mentality? "What?"

"It's a local organization for people with HIV/AIDS."

As he unfolded his linen napkin and placed it in his lap, I stilled as if I'd been flash-frozen. I knew what he meant—ICAN, the Island Coast AIDS Network. I'd referred a patient or two there when necessary; they provided wonderful support and education for the HIV positive in the community.

But why was he telling me this? I shifted uncomfortably on my chair, rifling my brain for an appropriate thing to say. Oh, God, was he HIV-positive? Was he looking for serious counseling help—while I'd been sitting here chattering ad nauseam about my stupid house and trying to show up my ex-boyfriend like some ridiculous woman scorned?

What kind of person had I become?

"They run a thrift store in North Fort Myers where a lot of builders donate their surplus construction material, and it's sold to the public for a fraction of what you'd pay retail." Ben was sliding his fork into the purple-hulled peas on his plate and didn't seem to have noticed my reaction. "You been out there yet? ICAN Junction? That's a great place to go look for a lot of what you need for your renovation—new closet doors, cabinetry, appliances, light fixtures, windows—even art."

"Oh...no." I swallowed. "I didn't know about that."

"Our company donates all our surplus there. It'll save you a fortune, and a lot of it's pretty nice stuff—you wouldn't believe the way some of those condos were getting decked out during the real estate boom."

I flashed to Kendall's immaculate, state-of-the-art kitchen, with its gleaming granite and stainless and mahogany and porcelain tile. "Actually, I would," I said thinly. I dug my fork into the wilted greens on my plate, this time welcoming the silence that fell between us once again.

"You have to talk to her at some point."

"You know what? I don't, actually." What I'd meant to be a chuckle sounded alarmingly like a giggle. There was a chance I might have had a little too much wine.

Surprise.

When Sasha overimbibes, she gets charmingly sloppy, hilariously disjointed, and very, very affectionate. When I do it, I get diarrhea of the mouth. Ben's idea of ordering a bottle of wine had finally lubricated our stilted conversation, but now, with the bottle empty and most of it having gone into my glass, I somehow found myself telling Ben all about my mother and her defection to the stage.

A crash of glassware came from the bar area, and I glanced over in that direction. I'd forgotten for the last few minutes to do a regular scan of the place for Kendall. Still no sign of him.

"Don't you want to know what's going on?" Ben asked.

"Not really. Somebody probably just dropped a glass."

Ben was grinning when I looked back at him. "I meant with your mom."

"Oh." I picked up the bottle of wine to pour the rest into Ben's glass, but nothing came out. I frowned. "Do you mind if I change the subject?"

"Of course not. If you're not one of those women who thinks

there is no other dessert but chocolate, how do you feel about crème brulee?"

"Ben." I picked up my dessert fork and pointed it seriously at him. "I feel very, very good about crème brulee."

I liked how easygoing he was about shifting topics. Of course, it could just be that he was a guy, and bored to tears talking about my mama drama. But the evening had actually turned out to be...well, not a chore. Despite the fact that it didn't look like Kendall was going to show up, that I hadn't spotted anyone we knew in the crowd for the first time *ever* at Andale's, and that I hadn't been able to find an excuse to go get something from the bar so I could make Jeffrey undeniably aware of my presence here with another man, I was having a pretty good time. Sasha had had a point—it felt kind of good to have someone new paying attention to me, coddling me a little bit, making me feel attractive and interesting again.

After dessert, so creamy and warm and silky that our spoons clashed as we both scraped the dish of its last traces of custard, Ben insisted on paying despite my protests that I had asked *him* out. As we walked into the warm, breezy night, he said, "It's late and I go right by your area on the way home. How about I drop you off?"

It was a really polite way of suggesting I might be in no condition to drive. And he was right. That was one lesson, at least, that I had learned in the last two weeks.

I angled a teasing look at him from under my eyelashes. "Benjamin Garrett, are you trying to come home with me?"

He smiled, leading me across the street with a light hand on the small of my back. "I wouldn't do that. You told me you have a boyfriend, remember?"

We'd reached the opposite curb, and I stopped to face him. "No, I don't. Not anymore." It was the first time I'd said it out loud to anyone except Sasha, and I didn't know why I blurted it out to Ben.

He nodded and took my elbow to usher me on toward the parking lot. "Yeah. I figured." That was all he said about it, and I was grateful.

He let me erratically operate the radio on the way to my house, which I directed him to in between drunken exclamations of, "Oh, my God, I *love* this song!"

When we rolled into my driveway I invited him inside. "Only to show you the house, you understand," I said with a wagging finger.

He laughed. "Brook, that's all I'm interested in tonight."

I pondered that as I unlocked the front door. Did he mean he wasn't interested in me that way at all? Or that he didn't want to rush things? God...I forgot how hard dating was.

I gave him the ten-cent tour of the house, seeing all of it through fresh eyes as I did—the water-stained ceilings, bare concrete floors, sagging doors, and peeling cabinets. I showed him the two guest bedrooms where I hoped to put in my office, and the bathroom my dad and I had gutted and cleaned.

"It's got good bones," he said as we circled back into the living room.

"Thank you!" I said, as though he'd complimented my bone structure, rather than the house's. Then my face fell. "There's still a ton to be done, though. Most of which I can't afford to do at the moment."

"I can."

"What? No! That's not at all appropriate."

Even in the dim light from the single lamp in the living room I could see his amused expression. "Brook—ICAN. The builder-supply thrift store. You can get what you need pretty cheap."

"They really ought to rename that thing," I muttered. We were standing awkwardly at the front door.

"I'm glad you called tonight," he said. "I had fun."

"Me too." I wondered if he was going to try to kiss me. And whether I wanted him to. But then he reached for the doorknob.

"Hey, Ben," I blurted out, and he turned back to me. "Do you... Would you like to come to a party with me tomorrow night? It's kind of big—huge, actually. And it's an overnight party—camping outdoors. You won't really know anyone but me, and I don't even know if you like camping, or if you have a tent—I meant separate ones, of course. But—"

"Brook, you're really selling it," he said, cutting my rambling blessedly off. "I *would* like that, actually. And I do have a tent of my very own." He was giving me another one of those nice smiles of his. "But I can't tomorrow night. I'm sorry."

"Oh." I flushed. "Right—last-minute again. Sorry."

"It's no problem. I hate to miss it—it sounds like a fun time." He put his good hand in his pocket and jingled his keys in a way that reminded me of my dad. "Would you like me to come back tomorrow to take you to your car?"

I waved him off. "No, that's okay. My friend Sasha can take me on our way to the party." I wanted him to know I wasn't pathetically going alone. "Or my dad can take me to it—we might make another building-supply run tomorrow."

"Don't forget ICAN."

"I know, but I can too, and you don't know exactly what I need."

"I meant—"

I smiled and pointed at him. "I know. Gotcha."

Ben laughed out loud, and then I thought that maybe I did want him to kiss me after all. But he just thanked me again and let himself out the door, and I stood at the front window staring after him, wondering what would have happened if he weren't just a rebound date.

twenty-four

Faryn and Jan Mitchell's annual Ragin' Pagans party started as a birthday bash for Faryn, but had grown and expanded like an amoeba every year since.

Every third weekend in March literally since senior year of high school, they'd hosted an all-night, no-holds-barred, crazy throwdown of a party, each one more elaborate than the last. The previous year's party offered Jell-O shooters ringside of the huge Jell-O wrestling vat that partygoers could climb into with the opponent of their choosing, provided both parties were willing. So that combatants didn't have to retire to their tents afterward covered in sticky gelatin, there were huge metal tubs filled with soapy water for scrubbing, a Slip 'n' Slide for the rinse, and Jan and Faryn's oversize Jacuzzi tub bubbling in the gazebo on the deck for warming back up afterward.

The south-of-the-border-themed Pagans party the year before featured a margarita fountain big enough to swim in, circulating mariachi players, and Mexican appetizers served out of sombrero plates balanced on the heads of little-people entertainers. Every year everyone pitched tents overnight on the wooded fifteen-acre property in Bonita Springs Faryn had inherited from her parents, and there was always a live band, a drum circle late into the night, and a catered breakfast the next morning that rivaled the brunch buffet at a five-star hotel.

The last thing I wanted to do was have to put on a happy, confident face in a huge group of people. But Sasha showed up to pick me up at three o'clock on Saturday afternoon, her car stuffed with gear: the tent we'd share, four huge Rubbermaid containers I assumed held camping supplies, a giant duffel bag, and what appeared to be a bed frame.

I reluctantly slung my backpack and rolled-up sleeping bag on top of the pile. "Are you bringing enough gear for other people too? Like the cast of *Survivor*?"

"Hi!" Her face was covered with a grin when she jumped out of the car to hug me. "Wait till you see the stuff I have for our tent." She looked so excited I made myself pretend to feel the same.

I'd woken up that morning with a slight headache—not the full-blown hangover I probably deserved, and was getting uncomfortably used to—and a feeling of guilt. I shouldn't have called Ben Garrett. He seemed like a nice guy, and I'd treated him like every bad date I'd ever warned Sasha away from: calling him last-minute, using him as a prop to make Kendall jealous, and talking about myself most of the night.

At least I hadn't slept with him.

One good thing had come out of the evening, though. Dad came over just after ten a.m. and took me back to my car (no questions, happily), and then we went to check out ICAN. Ben was right—the prices were incredible. I loaded up: new closet doors and cabinetry; a door so I could block off the office rooms from the rest of the house; upscale light fixtures for both bathrooms and the front hall; some lamps and furniture; and even, literally, a kitchen sink. The whole pile cost me well under a thousand dollars, and I'd been delighted—until we unloaded everything into my garage and I realized the mountain of work that still lay in front of me.

As soon as Sasha and I pulled into Faryn and Jan's driveway and I saw the usual crowd of people milling around their yard— many of whom I had known since pre-K—I knew I'd made a huge mistake in coming. I said as much to Sasha as we started unloading her gear from the back of the Jetta onto the baggage trailer that Jan had hooked to his ATV for delivery to each guest's preassigned campsite.

"You can't think of it that way," Sasha said, straining under the weight of one of the Rubbermaids until I grabbed the other end.

"Jesus, Sash, seriously—what the hell is in here?"

She ignored my question. "If you try to chase a good time, you're never going to catch it. So don't even try. If you feel crappy, just feel crappy."

"Sounds like a great party."

We hefted the container onto the trailer and turned back to the car for the rest. "What I mean is, just relax and don't try so hard *not* to think about everything," Sasha said. She had opened one of the remaining Rubbermaids and was rummaging around in it. "You might end up really being able to have fun."

She pulled out a small battery-operated fan, replaced the top on the Rubbermaid, and set the fan on top of it. She flipped it on and stood in front of the whirring blades. "Whew. Eighty-eight degrees in March. Only in southwest Florida. How can you stand to wear that sweater?"

The lie that sprang to my lips was knocked out of me as a rock-solid something hit me from behind, and a vise clamped around my ribs.

"Brookadelic...Sashalicious. How are my two favorite backup plans?" a voice boomed in my ear.

Jan Mitchell would have taken a lot more teasing for his name if he hadn't been six-foot-three by the tenth grade, and built like a strip-club bouncer. Our gang just called him Man Jan, to differentiate him from Jan Seever, the class slut. (Who, unsurprisingly, was known as Slam Jan.)

He and Faryn were the first of our class to get married, right out of school, and they were as crazily in love now as they had been at the prom. It would be nauseating if they weren't so ridiculously good together.

Jan had one club-like arm wrapped around my waist, the other around Sasha's, and he lifted us both off the ground in an intestine-crushing hug. I wrestled one arm free to squeeze him back. It was impossible not to cheer up just a little in Jan's presence.

"You sick degenerate," I told him. "Does your wife know how you talk to other women?"

Faryn walked up behind her husband, her crinkly gauze skirt swinging, brown feet bare, curly hair wrapped up in a scarf. "Are you kidding? I count on you guys to give me a break from him." She put a hand on her husband's Popeye arm. "Jan, put the women down." Then she looked at Sasha and me. "We've got you two in your usual spot."

He smacked a noisy kiss on each of our cheeks before he lowered us back to the ground. "And wait till you see what we got in *our* spot for this year!" Jan said as he clean-and-jerked a Rubbermaid in each arm. "We just had it installed."

"A hot tub? A media room? A driving range?" Sasha hazarded as she followed our gear, holding the battery-powered fan in front of her and looking like the star of an eighties hair-band video. She was being only a little facetious—one year Jan had a pit dug outside his and Faryn's tent and filled it with water and clay for spa-style mud baths. Another time he'd brought out a full living room set and arranged it under an awning as a tent-front sitting room. He strove to outdo himself every year.

"Would you believe a yurt?" Faryn said dryly, shaking her head.

Jan tossed the keys to his wife as he gestured Sasha and me inside the ATV. "Hey, hon, pick me up at the parking field after you drop off the girls. I'm gonna put Sasha's fancy German station wagon over there." He waggled the fingers of his upturned palm at Sasha, and she handed over her keys. Everyone had to as soon as they arrived, receiving them back only after a good night's sleep and a big meal in the morning. If you weren't willing to surrender your keys, you weren't invited to stay.

Faryn hoisted herself up into the ATV as Sasha's car hot-rodded out of the driveway; then she pulled onto the well-worn dirt track leading behind their property.

"So what's the theme this year?" I asked as we bumped along in the grass behind their salmon-colored stucco house.

A corner of Faryn's mouth tipped up and she shook her head. "You gotta see it. You wouldn't buy it if I told you."

We hit a rut and the ATV bounced. Sasha craned around to check our gear on the trailer as Faryn rounded the tree line and said, "Welcome to winter wonderland."

I could hardly believe my eyes. It was snowing. In southwest Florida. In almost ninety-degree weather.

"Holy moly," Sasha said, her eyes as big as eggs.

Snow fell from the sky in flurries, in blizzards, collecting on the St. Augustine grass in drifts as high as a dachshund—which I knew because Jan and Faryn's wiener dog, Chili, was happily trotting through the accumulated snowfall, only his dark whip-like tail and beady little black eyes clearly visible. In the midst of the three-hundred-or-so-foot radius where the "snow" was being shot out of a huge machine was what appeared to be a ski jump, and scattered nearby were a couple of sleds, snow skis, and a snowboard.

"Jan's seriously proud of this," Faryn said. "One of his A/C clients is a commercial refrigeration company. These machines are designed to blow crushed ice over produce, but Jan had this idea."

A few dozen partygoers were already amid the drifts, making snowmen, having snowball fights, or sliding down the ski jump. Sasha grinned like a little kid who'd never seen snow before. Because actually, as far as I knew, Sasha had never seen snow before. Not a lot of us native Floridians ever had. She was practically bouncing in the seat.

Faryn dropped us off at our usual campsite—a prime one, shaded by rusty-trunked gumbo-limbo trees with their peeling, papery bark; weeping bottlebrush that dripped with fuzzy scarlet blooms; and sweet-smelling ylang ylang—and Sasha and I pitched our tent. While I unrolled my sleeping bag and got out my toothbrush and a flashlight for later, she dived right into unloading her supplies.

The thing that looked like a bed frame was, in fact, a bed frame. She set it up inside the tent, then slapped an air mattress on top of it that she inflated with a battery-powered pump. The Rubbermaids contained a comforter and sheets, two king-size pillows, throw rugs, camp lanterns, a magnetic overhead light, and the fan. She set an empty container beside the bed as a table, on which she lined up a box of tissues, Ziploc bags, Wet Wipes, and a host of medications: Pepto Bismol, Immodium, aspirin, Tylenol, a packet of vitamin B complex—and a bottle of Scope and a Water Pik.

Despite the anvil in my stomach, I couldn't help a laugh. "You idiot."

"Hey, it's not just the Boy Scouts who know a little something about being prepared."

By now the sun was starting to head toward the horizon, staining the sky first crimson, then flame, then finally violet and indigo. We headed back toward the clearing, where the snow machine could still be heard cranking out the powder as fast as the warm tropical evening melted it down.

"Fore!"

The shout came from Jan, who was lit by the glow of tiki torches placed around the clearing's perimeter, hunkered down over his skis in his tank top and cargo shorts at the top of the ski jump, his shades dropped down over his eyes as makeshift goggles. A dozen or more people stood watching as he launched himself down the slope.

He careened down flawlessly and slid upright to the bottom. But then apparently one of his skis caught on something under the snow, and Jan fell forward and slammed down face-first. I saw Faryn wince, off to the side.

"I'm good!" he said, popping back up like a carnival duck, to assorted catcalls and applause.

Sasha and I followed a trail that led around the clearing through a stand of bamboo that sounded like tongues of flame as they rustled in the breeze. We came out into another, smaller clearing, where a throng of people surrounded a thatched-roof tiki hut covering a bottle-lined bar.

Behind which, serving drinks, stood Chip Santana.

I stopped cold, staring.

Chip had a shaved head, a goatee, and a mad-at-the-world glare. Blue-green eyes and a devil's smile turned the whole assemblage into a dangerous, volatile ball of explosive just waiting to lure some hapless female close enough to go up in the inevitable blast.

I was not hapless. But it had taken all my concentration with Chip to remain in full possession of my hap.

I'd started seeing Chip Santana just a few weeks after I met Kendall. Not at all the self-aware, introspective type, Chip was the least likely patient I'd ever had. He'd started coming to therapy sessions at the insistence of his boss at the beach bar where he worked. After one too many bar fights, his manager said that Chip either got a handle on his temper, or he was out. It took every ounce of patience and tact I had in our weekly therapy sessions to help drain his brimming vitriol every week, but we had finally begun to do some constructive work together.

And then he started flirting with me.

It was no big deal at first—patients develop crushes on their therapists so often, it's practically industry-standard. It would be in the tone of his voice as he made some innocent statement sound suggestive, or a smile that seemed loaded with meaning, or an up-and-down raking of those ocean-colored eyes the length of my body that had nothing to do with doctor-patient privilege. Right before my practice had literally disintegrated, I had been just about to terminate treatment with Chip, because he was making me uncomfortable.

Which wasn't really his fault. Hostile and vitriolic as he could be, there was something primal and seductive about Chip Santana, and I'd begun to admit to myself that I was uncomfortably attracted to him.

I wasn't just concerned about the potential compromise my feelings posed to the patient-counselor relationship—our version of the Hippocratic oath. I held myself to an even higher standard, a principle of professional conduct I'd devised for myself years ago: the Evanston Code.

Dr. Janette Evanston, the best professor I ever studied with and still the best therapist I've ever seen. And in my senior year she tried to kill her husband with a Henckels carving knife. When she was led off the UF campus by the police, head tucked, hands cuffed behind her back, I stood on the sidewalk outside the psych building with my mouth hanging open like my jaw had come unhinged, rather than my professor.

But Dr. Evanston had set the bar for me. Whatever was going on in her homicidal mind, I'd never gotten even a whiff of it in all the time she served as my thesis adviser. She was a master at separating her personal and professional lives, and I tried to live up to her example. Right before she started serving her twenty-to-life.

I hadn't exactly thought through what reason to give Chip for wanting to terminate our work together. *I'm sorry, but as your therapist, Chip, I find you far too sexually attractive.* Big hit with the American Psychological Association. But luckily, once the practice was closed down, he'd had to find another therapist, rather than wait for me to reinstate my own practice somewhere else, or he'd be fired.

Sasha had stopped when she realized I wasn't beside her, and she turned around to look at me. "What's the matter?"

"That," I said, nodding toward the bar. "That's Chip Santana. One of...one of my former patients."

"Whoa. He's hot...sort of scary-hot, but hot," she finally decreed, after giving him such a thorough going-over I expected her to slap a "grade-A" sticker on his ass. "Well," she said finally. "I can see where it would be awkward for his therapist to come up and ask for a cocktail—or several. Why don't I go grab us drinks?"

She was gone before I could reply that, at the moment, technically I wasn't Chip Santana's therapist anymore.

I settled down to wait on one of a line of chaise lounges set up in the clearing, watching as Sasha leaned over the bar and shouted an order to Chip, then laughed at something he said. Behind the bar he was all charm, his hands in motion, his eyes taking in everything, making sure no one was neglected. That smile—that dangerous, light-up-the-night smile—was quick to his lips.

God. Those lips.

Finally Sasha walked back toward me with a plastic cup in each hand. She gave one to me and then flopped down on the chaise beside me without even jostling her drink.

"What were you two talking about for all this time?" I said casually.

"Don't worry—not you. I didn't even tell him I knew you. He has no idea you're at this party."

I looked over at Sasha in her full-on Maryann-on-the-island camping getup—tight-fitting Capri jeans, halter top, and bandanna wrapped around her head—and thought that was truer than she knew. With Sasha in full charm mode, Chip probably had no idea *any* other women were at this party. I took a sip of the cocktail she'd brought me. It tasted watery, as though it had sat for a while.

"So...what *did* y'all talk about?"

Sasha took a giant gulp. "Well, let's see...boating—that is apparently the subject of dearest interest to him. Did you know he has a fishing boat? And what else...oh, chemistry, of all things."

"*Chemistry?*"

"Yeah—he was telling me about bartending. Chip said it was like mixing up lab experiments, and he said he'd majored in chemistry or something like that."

"Oh...that kind of chemistry."

"Hey, Chip says there's an ice luge in the next clearing!"

"A what?"

"You know—a big block of ice with a channel cut out of it. Someone pours in a shot at the top, and you wait at the bottom with your mouth open."

"Lovely."

"I thought it sounded fun. Chip said it makes whatever you're drinking super cold."

"*Did* Chip say that?"

Silence fell between us, drowned out by the chatter of people at the bar and the thump of music from the next clearing and the muted squeals and shouts coming from the ski jump. Even in the darkness I could feel Sasha staring at me.

"Hey...how are you doing?" she asked finally.

I rubbed my suddenly throbbing temples. "Fine."

"Let's go check out the ice luge!"

"No, I'm okay."

I heard her sigh, and then she leaned back in her chaise. "Okay."

"You can go if you want, Sash. I'm fine."

"No, I'll stay here with you."

"No, really." I could feel my mood darkening, and all I wanted right now was to be by myself. "Go ahead. I'll come find you later."

I heard the creak of her chair and saw her sit forward. I knew she'd been dying to check out the rest of the party ever since we got here. "Are you sure?"

I made myself chuckle—she wouldn't leave if she thought I was upset. "It's not like I'm scared of the dark."

She just kept looking at me, and then: "Well...okay. Don't be too long or I'll come stalk you."

"Okeydokey. That's your specialty." I said it singsong, like a joke, but even I could hear the mean undercurrent. What was the matter with me?

Sasha didn't say anything, just picked up her drink, shot me an uncertain smile that brought up a fresh current of shame, and walked away.

When you are overflowing with self-loathing, the last thing you want to do is inflict yourself on anyone else. So I couldn't have picked a worse place to be tonight: surrounded by people everywhere I turned.

I tried to find places to sit by myself, nursing the drink Sasha had brought me, but every time I stumbled upon a vacant seating area, it wasn't long before I was joined by more partygoers making cheerful, friendly, drunken conversation that I couldn't summon the energy or inclination to respond to.

Finally, I headed away from the clearings and into a forested part of the property, slashing my way through undergrowth in a way that reminded me—painfully—of creeping into Kendall's complex through the saw palmettos. I wished I had the car keys. I could leave a note in the tent, let Sasha know I'd come back tomorrow and help her load up.

In the darkness of the new moon, I almost stumbled into a small drainage pond when the trees and greenery ended abruptly. The sounds of the party were distant enough now that I felt pretty sure no one would follow me out here, and I dropped down to the grass, tucking my legs up under me and staring out over the dark ditch of the pond.

The sudden scrape of metal made me jump with a girly little yip of surprise, and I saw a flame pop up just a few yards away.

"Who's there?" I barked, my heart pounding.

"Sorry. Didn't know anyone else was here."

I knew that gravelly rasp. "Chip?" I said in disbelief.

"Who's that?" His tone was suspicious.

"It's Brook Ogden."

I heard the crunching of dry St. Augustine grass, and a silhouette came clearer out of the darkness. Now I could see a reflection of the scant light off his shiny shaved head.

"Doc?" His voice rose at the end, making him sound young, like a kid caught by the principal behind the gym during math class.

I stood up, brushing off my jeans. "Hi."

I could see him clearly now—plain T-shirt keeping close acquaintance with the muscles underneath; cargo pants that skimmed his athletic thighs; running shoes; the cigarette held, unlit and forgotten, in one large hand. He was on a slight incline, one leg bent and hiked up higher than the other, and the pose made him look like the Marlboro Man. I scrounged for my professional detachment.

"Nice to see you again, Chip."

"Yeah, you too, Doc." I didn't know if Chip always called me "Doc" because it made him feel he was in more capable hands, or if he was somehow having a secret jibe at me. "What are you doing here?"

I made a gesture back toward the party. "Friends of mine. I come every year. You?" I added belatedly, remembering he didn't know I'd already seen him.

"Work. I'm bartending." He retrieved the pack from his back pocket and held it toward me. "Smoke?"

"Nah. Stunts your growth."

He laughed, then lit his. The ember glowed bright at the end of his lips, silence stretching long enough to make me uncomfortable, punctuated only by the sound of his breath as he drew on the cigarette and exhaled. Why couldn't I think of anything to say? It was always a little awkward seeing clients outside of work. But with Chip it was downright unsettling. Out here in near-total darkness, on the edges of a forest of palm trees and scrub pine and oak, I felt unbalanced, unprotected, as if he were a half-wild animal.

"I guess I'd better head back," he said finally. "There's only one other guy working with me. Your friends are keeping us pretty busy."

I wheezed out a chuckle. "Most of us aren't usually quite this wild. This is sort of a special occasion."

"I figured." Chip twisted the butt between his fingers until the smoldering tobacco fell out. He ground it out with his shoe and put the filter in his pocket. An environmentally conscious smoker. "Well, see you."

"I hope so." I cringed in the dark as his chuckle drifted to me over his shoulder. "Chip."

He stopped and angled himself toward me, his features again blurred into shadows. I was very, very conscious of the fact that it was dark, we were alone, and the party was far behind us.

"How's..." I wanted to ask how his work with his new therapist was coming, but that was bad form. "How's everything?"

"No complaints." His tone sounded amused.

Silence fell between us again, and for some reason I was desperate to break it, to keep him here.

"I, uh... I'm sorry I had to terminate our work together."

"Don't worry about it. I get it. It's good to see you, Doc. Enjoy the party." He turned and walked back toward the lights and the music and the noise, skirting the overgrowth until he turned a corner and was out of sight.

I scrubbed my hands over my face, wishing I could wipe away the whole encounter. It was bad enough that I was sinking deeper and deeper into behavior people came to *me* to learn how to avoid. But if I couldn't keep my own issues separate from my patients', then I wasn't fit for the one thing I was still good at, the only area in which I felt competent.

I wished I'd taken Chip up on the offer of a cigarette. Or bought the whole pack from him. Right now, sitting in my sorrows with a pack of smokes and a bottle of booze sounded like the only way to escape my own head and get away from myself. I turned to go back to the party, knowing that if oblivion was what I wanted, I was heading toward the right place.

But halfway back to the crush of laughing, shouting, happy partygoers, I realized I couldn't even summon enough social interaction to ask for a drink, or something—anything—to smoke. I turned and plodded back to Sasha's and my tent, let myself in through the zippered front flap, and collapsed onto my sleeping bag on the ground, hoping to fall asleep despite the noise and get through the hours until daybreak.

And somehow, despite the incessant thumping of a bass line from the band, despite the occasional crack of fireworks and the frequent loud bursts of raucous laughter, the noise turned into a soporific hum of sound that did lull me into a restless drowse.

I realized I'd managed to lose myself in unconsciousness only later, when the scratching sound at my tent flap and a hoarse whisper of, "Hey, Doc...you in there?" brought me jolting back to awareness, along with the realization that Chip Santana was standing outside of the tent I was sharing with Sasha, calling for me to come outside.

twenty-five

I sat up and pushed the hair back out of my face, shooting a look over to Sasha's elevated bed. She lay sprawled across the top of it, arms and legs jutting at right angles. I was tempted to press two fingers to her neck to check for a pulse. How had I not heard her stumble in?

I had just decided I'd dreamed Chip's hoarse whisper calling to me when I heard it again.

"Hey, Doc!" There was a muffled thump and a short, raspy laugh, and then I heard him moving off.

Quickly I threw back my sleeping bag and scrambled into drawstring pants and a sweatshirt over the long-sleeved tee I'd worn to hide my bandaged shoulder, then let myself out of the tent flap.

Chip must have heard the zipper; he was standing a few feet away, waiting. I could smell the acrid smoke from the cigarette dangling between two fingers by his side. The music had stopped, even the tribal pulsing of the drum circle, and the hush of night hovered over the property.

"Your friends are going to hate me. I've probably knocked on a dozen tents." His lowered pitch gave his voice even more gravel, like coarse sandpaper.

"What time is it?"

"Little after four."

"Oh... Are you through working?"

"Just got cleaned up." He squeezed off the lit end of his cigarette, ground it out, and pocketed the filter, then looked back up at me with a rascal's smile, like a kid looking for a coconspirator. "Let's go get some ice cream."

I couldn't help it: I laughed. "It's the middle of the night! Where are we going to get ice cream?"

"I have a few pints at home. We can grab a couple and walk over to the beach. It'll be fun."

I looked back at my tent, then shook my head. "I'd better not."

One of his forked eyebrows lifted, his lips still tilting upward. "Come on, Doc. Bend a spoon with me. I could use some company."

I like to think it was that last statement that got me. Being needed, being reminded that my job was to help people when they asked for it—specifically, up until recently, to help *this* person—and he had just asked for it.

Although even as I agreed, I knew what it really was. Chip Santana was dangerous, sexy, and seductively appealing. He had hunted through the party to find me—the epitome of the alpha male come to fetch his woman. And I loved it. I loved feeling that this pulsing ball of testosterone had picked *me* out of all his options tonight, had worked to come find *me*, and wanted *me*—only me—to come back to his house with him. After the feeling of running after Kendall when he walked away, desperately wanting him to want me again just a little, tiny bit, this was like a tidal wave of acceptance and approval.

I hesitated for a much shorter moment than I probably should have before nodding my head yes. All I'd wanted earlier was to be able to leave here, and now the universe had answered my request.

I didn't want to risk waking Sasha, so I didn't go back for my wallet or cell phone or even a pair of shoes—feeling as if I were watching myself from a distance, I just fell into step beside Chip Santana's long stride and followed him out to his hulking maroon SUV in Faryn and Jan's driveway.

"Are you okay to drive?" I said as he opened my door and helped me up into the passenger seat.

"Yeah, I don't drink."

"You don't drink? You're a bartender."

"That's why I don't drink. You see enough drunken idiots at your bar night after night, you wouldn't drink either."

Ah, yes. The idiots he ranted about in every session we'd ever had—meaning everyone who was not Chip, apparently.

Okay. So we were both stone-cold sober.

Chip walked around to his side and got in, and when he shut the door and started the engine, my heart jumped into gear along with the truck. The cab suddenly felt very, very small. He pulled through the semicircular drive and out onto the side street. The few houses we passed were dark, and there were no streetlights, so when Chip flipped open his Zippo and lit up again—and this time I noticed it was a joint—the flare of light almost hurt my eyes.

"This is how I relax," he said. "Easier on the system—and no one ever got in a fight or broke into a liquor store or attacked someone from getting high."

No. Most people didn't much get off the sofa when they were high, but I didn't say anything. When he passed it over to me, I took a hit.

Chip's face shone faintly orange in the reflected light from the dash of his truck, making it glow like a jack-o'-lantern, his hands on the wheel illuminated at the knuckles. The dim light picked out the beginnings of stubble on his cheeks and chin, as if that tender-looking skin there were trying to protect itself with tiny porcupine quills.

"You ever seen Bowman's at night?" His voice rumbled up out of the dimness like far-off thunder.

I shook my head, then realized he might not see it. "No. We went farther down the beach when I was a kid. Fewer cops."

He laughed, short and choppy. "They're cool with the locals. I go there at night a lot. Schools of fish run through the channel after sunset—it's almost too easy to cast a line and pluck one out."

"You fish?"

His head turned toward me, and even in the gloaming of the car I knew one of those satyr eyebrows was raised. He neglected to answer, and something about the intimacy of that made my heart pound.

"Right," I said, my chuckle sounding oddly low and throaty in my own ears. "Clearly."

We crested the bridge, and the two beach-bound lanes that were the only way onto Estero Island narrowed to one. Once you got this far there were no other routes—if you changed your mind you couldn't turn around till you'd already gotten all the way to where you were headed.

Chip lived on the bottom level of a house that must have been grandfathered in before the hurricane building codes that stated you couldn't build a living area below twelve feet elevation. It was a windowless space with cinder-block walls, and it reminded me of an old elementary school classroom. Chip went inside, but I just leaned against the doorjamb, reluctant to take that next step over the threshold.

A breath I didn't know I was holding rushed out in a whoosh when all he did was set his backpack down, open the freezer door, and retrieve two pints of Ben & Jerry's. He opened a drawer, clattered around for two spoons, and then came back toward me. I'd been second-guessing myself since I got in the car for falling so easily into what could only be a thinly veiled seduction scheme, but apparently we really *were* just going to share some ice cream on the beach. It was almost...sweet.

"Come on," he said, his voice in my ear as I stepped aside so he could lock the door behind us. "We'll walk."

Estero Boulevard was silent at this hour, no traffic, no tourists stumbling and laughing along the sidewalks on both sides of the three-lane road, no souvenir shops and bars pumping out steel-drum beach music along with blasts of air-conditioning to lure customers inside. I hadn't seen it like this since my friends and I used to sneak down here in high school after our parents fell asleep. Chip and I walked across the street and onto a sandy beach access path.

Even though they flopped loosely on my feet and I had to clench my toes to keep them on, I was grateful for the Birkenstocks he'd offered me at his apartment.

"What flavors do we have?" I asked, trying to make out the label of the one I held.

"Magic Brownies and Karamel Sutra."

They both sounded dangerous.

Out on the beach the water was calm, the way the gulf almost always was in Fort Myers. The earthy, rich scent of salt water and sea life filled my sinuses, and I felt some of my tension let go. I shuffled through the shifting sand behind Chip, following him wordlessly up the shoreline until the curve of Bowman's Beach crept into view. He sat down near a tiny dune anchored by sea oats. Lowering myself beside him, I handed him the pint of ice cream and shook out my frozen hand to get the blood to return to it.

Chip peeled the lids back and then handed me a pint and one of the spoons. "It's a little soft."

"That's okay."

We dug in directly out of the containers. I had the Karamel Sutra, the thick ribbon of caramel sweet and heavy in my mouth against the cool ice cream. After a few bites Chip pushed his spoon into my pint, and I followed his lead and tried his, rich and chocolatey. Sharing felt both intimate and innocent.

When I'd eaten all I could I raised my spoon in surrender. "I'm out."

"Me too." He capped the pints, and then looked at them in his hands. "I think I'm going to call them a wash. We'll never get them back to the freezer in time." He plopped them into the sand beside him.

I laughed. I felt drunk on sugar, on the darkness, on the sheer incongruity of being on a deserted beach in the middle of the night with my patient.

Former patient. With whom I was not behaving as a professional counselor.

I was acutely conscious that beneath my cotton drawstring

pants I wore only a pair of panties, and under the sweatshirt and tee I had on nothing else at all. I wore no makeup—every inch of my usual therapist's armor was gone.

"Chip," I said. "I'm sorry about our sessions."

He shrugged. "It's no big deal."

"It is. I let you down. I'm sorry."

"Yeah, well, I'm not."

That sobered up my sugar high. "You're not? I thought we... I thought we were doing some good work together."

"Yeah. We were."

"But you're not sorry we won't be working together anymore?"

"Nah."

I searched his face, wishing there were at least a sliver of moon for me to decipher his expression. "Oh. Well... Okay."

He took my hand where it was resting on my knees, and started tracing light, barely-there paths along my fingers, down the back of my hand, in the tender webbing between each finger. I shivered, although it wasn't cold.

"I don't want to work with you, Doc. I haven't wanted to work with you for a while." He turned my hand over and teased gentle trails from the pads of my fingers to the crease where they met my palm.

"Why not?" I said. Even to me, my quaking voice was barely audible.

He swirled a finger in my palm, and I felt it all the way through my body. "Because as long as I was working with you, I couldn't do what I really wanted to do. Which was this."

He tugged gently on my hand to pull me near, and then Chip Santana was so close, smelling of chocolate and cigarettes and something clean and sharp, like deodorant soap, despite the fact that he'd been working all night long, and before I could find the right answer, there was no chance for one: his lips were on mine.

They were soft, softer even than they looked.

I don't know how long he kissed me; my head was now spinning like a funnel cloud. I registered the unfamiliar tickle of his goatee. He kissed nothing like Kendall. He was nothing at all like Kendall.

He ended it sooner than I would have, but he didn't pull back. His face was close to mine. "You're not going to analyze that, are you?" he asked softly, in a rumble that vibrated directly into my reproductive system.

"Chip..." I was having trouble breathing. "Do you even know my first name?"

He touched my face with a hand. "Sure I do. It's Doc."

A laugh born of nerves exploded out of me. Chip chuckled too, caressing my cheek as gently and sensually as he had been touching my hand.

"What's your first name, Doc?" he asked, low, his breath in my mouth.

"Brook..." I murmured. "Brook Lyn."

"Brook Lyn." He danced his fingers across my palm, up my arm, along the crook of my elbow as though it were an erogenous zone. Which I had never realized until that moment that it was. "Brook Lyn," he said again. It sounded rich and sensual in his mouth. He took my face in his hands and brought his lips down onto mine again.

This was bad. It was wrong on so many levels. Even if it weren't for the muddy charcoal gray area of our doctor-patient relationship, Chip had anger issues. He was a thirty-six-year-old pot smoker who lived in a basement and tended bar. We'd hardly exchanged twelve lines of conversation outside of therapy sessions—or this makeout session. As far as potential relationships went, he was the dictionary entry under "bad bet."

But that wasn't what I wanted from him. It wasn't what I needed right now. What I needed was to feel attractive again. To erase that awful feeling I'd had when Kendall had disappeared on me, when he'd texted me that he "just couldn't do it," when he hung up in my ear. I needed to remind myself I wasn't the crazy girl who sent histrionic emails and text messages, stalked her ex...had gotten a tumescent-donkey tattoo. I was sexy and desirable and wanted.

Chip Santana, as Sasha herself had put it, was the ideal re-bound guy.

I almost physically felt the last thread of my resistance snap and fly into the soft sea breeze like so much cattail fluff.

His lips—oh, God those lips—coaxed my mouth open again, his tongue running along my lips, inside, his hands on my neck now...my shoulders, down my arms until they landed on my sides and my whole body arched toward him. My hands wrapped them-selves behind his head, pulling him closer, pressing my body as close as I could to the long, hard length of his, like I'd never been touched before and was starving for the contact.

For once I didn't think everything out to its logical conclusion. I didn't weigh the pros and cons, balance my options, and analyze the safest, smartest course of action. I let go. Finally, I let go and stopped worrying and followed my instincts, my gut, my raw, ata-vistic urges that demanded, *Yes. This man. Right here...right now.*

And that was how I found myself at the Fort Myers police sta-tion in the middle of the night, with sand crusted around the damp ankles of my cotton pants and in other places even less desirable, clutching a filthy pay phone and praying to God that Sasha had brought her cell phone into our tent with her.

twenty-six

Deputy Walter Dodd had no patience for the likes of me. I would have thought when he shone his flashlight into our eyes just like in the movies, we'd have gotten some sympathy points for our age—it wasn't like Chip and I were irresponsible kids causing trouble down at the beach. We were grown people, consenting adults, keeping quietly to ourselves and doing no one any harm.

But Dodd had been strangely unmoved by my arguments to that end. When neither of us could produce any form of ID—Chip had left his wallet in his backpack at his apartment and mine was still in the tent with Sasha—Dodd hauled us in.

I had no idea what time it was, but the sky was starting to lighten, so I assumed it was sometime after six a.m. He gestured us out of the backseat when we got to the police precinct—a place I'd visited only once in my entire life, as an elementary schooler on a field trip. I remembered that as being a lot more fun.

This time I was frog-marched through the back door, where the criminals skulked in. Dodd waved at the woman behind the wire cage as he led us past her and through to a hallway lined with several steel doors. Chip went into one. I went into a separate one.

It was nothing like Mayberry RFD. This was a concrete-and-steel box containing a sink, a metal toilet I could barely make myself look at, let alone use, and a stained concrete bench along one wall.

"When do we get our phone call?" I asked as Dodd started to shut me in.

"Funny about that," he said, not looking at me. "Despite what you see on all those cop shows, that's not a constitutional right." The door slammed behind him.

I stood in the middle of the cell, as if none of this were real as long as I didn't touch anything. Looking down at my dirty, wrinkled clothes, I patted the sand away from the damp places. A glance in the square of polished steel that served as a mirror showed me how much of it clung to my hair. I ran my hands through it, hearing the soft patter as the sand snowed down onto the floor. I turned away from my reflection.

Dodd walked by my window a few minutes later, and I heard him stop next door and say, "You got someone to call?" Some rattling and a clink, and then he and Chip walked past going in the opposite direction.

"Hey," I called out, knocking on the window. "What about ladies first?"

Dodd eyeballed my disheveled state through the Plexiglas. "When you act like a lady, we'll treat you like one."

I felt as intimidated as I had in elementary school. And just about as mature.

They came back just a few minutes later, Chip catching my eye and shaking his head. We weren't getting sprung, I assumed. Dodd secured Chip back in his cell and came to stand in front of mine.

"I assume there's someone you want to call and wake up first thing on a Sunday morning?" he drawled.

Dodd was no more than mid-thirties—close to my age—but he did a hell of a job as the Shame Police. I wished he'd just let me go pick a switch and get my punishment over with.

"Yes, please. Thank you, Deputy." Kiss-ass Numbah One.

He shook his head as he fitted the old-fashioned-looking key into the door. "You know," he said, taking his sweet time with the lock, "I expect this from the kids. They don't know any better. But you two..." He shook his head again, managing to convey a weary, worldly disappointment.

"I bet you're a great dad," I muttered as he led me down the hall. My steps echoed down its length, bounced back and back and back to my own ears off the hard floor and bare cinder-block walls. This was not exactly the walk of shame I had been braced for tonight.

Dodd led me to a mostly bare, characterless desk with a phone and some papers on it. He picked up the receiver and pressed 9, then handed it to me.

Sasha picked up on the first ring.

"Brook?" she blurted. "Is that you?"

"It's me."

"Jesus. Are you okay? I've been a wreck."

"I'm sorry, Sash. I'm so sorry." I stopped to iron the tremble out of my voice. "I'm fine—nothing happened. We just got picked up by Deputy Dawg"—*oops*—"I mean Deputy Dodd," I amended quickly. I sneaked a look to where he stood pretending not to listen, but I could tell I hadn't helped my case with him.

"We? Who's 'we'? What happened?"

"It's... We were..." I eyed the deputy again, and now he was looking straight at me with eyebrows raised and a look that said, *Go on. Tell her, why don't you?*

"I'll give you the full story later. Meanwhile..." I swallowed hard, gearing up to say words I never thought I'd need to use. "Um, can you come bail me out of jail?"

"I'm already in the car."

I closed my eyes against a surge of relief and gratitude. "Thanks," was all I could get out past my suddenly constricted throat.

"I'll be there in ten minutes. Don't go anywhere."

I couldn't tell if she meant it as a joke, but I couldn't even muster a chuckle. I set the phone back in its cradle and turned to look at Dodd.

He pushed himself away from the wall where he'd been leaning and fixed me with that hairy stare. "Deputy Dawg? That's really original."

I held out my arms, wrists together.

"Go ahead," I said wearily.

He took my elbow instead and wordlessly led me back to the holding cell.

Deputy Dodd released us on what he called a "copy of charges," a citation. He'd hauled me back out of the cell thirty minutes after he'd stuck me in there again. "Really, Deputy, you're sending a girl such mixed messages," I muttered as he led me out, long past even trying to suck up. Sasha stood waiting when we came out into the main area, and her eyes filled when she saw me. I could see how hard she was fighting not to launch herself into a hug. Instead she put her hand on my shoulder and stood close behind me after Dodd gestured roughly for me to sit at that same featureless desk where I'd called her. He sat behind it, scribbling in silence for a while.

"Your court date is April eighteenth at nine a.m." He stood, arms crossed, and I gathered I had been dismissed. "It will be an undiluted joy to see you again then. Perhaps this time with all your clothes on."

Heat crept up my face, but I forced my head to stay high as I walked with Sasha toward the entrance. But my dignified exit was ruined when I remembered Chip. Sasha and I waited awkwardly by the front door while Dodd went over the whole rigmarole again with him, and then we all walked out to Sasha's Jetta in dead silence.

The trip over the Matanzas Bridge to drop him off at home was awkward beyond words. Literally, far beyond words, as we three sat in near total silence broken only when Chip directed her to his street off Estero Boulevard. I cringed, hating that Sasha would see the tumbledown beach shack where he lived in the basement.

Long gone was the flirtatious Chip I'd spent the evening with. This was the Chip I'd worked with in therapy to help him control his seething rage. I was glad he was in the backseat by himself—he was like a land mine waiting to be detonated at the slightest touch. When we pulled into the graveled drive of the house he lived in, he let himself out with only a terse, "Later." He slammed the door and we watched him stalk inside and slam his apartment door behind him too.

Sasha let out a long breath. "Sheesh. Lovely guy."

"He's had a tough night." I didn't know why I was defending him.

"Yeah. So have you, honey. Oh, Brook..." She leaned across the seat and finally hugged me, and I let myself cling to her for a few moments before I drew away from our embrace. She put the car into gear and pulled back out onto Estero. "What the hell happened?"

"What do you think? I'm holding a ticket for public indecency, and you just picked me up from jail."

"Did you...?"

"No. We didn't get quite that far."

Sasha blew out a long breath. "Thank God."

I looked over at her. "What does that mean?"

Sasha shook her head. "Bad news, that one. You need to stay away from him."

I didn't say anything. Everything was rubbing me the wrong way right now, and the last person I wanted to take my embarrassment and anger and frustration out on was the one person who always showed up when I needed her.

"Brook..." Sasha said after long moments where we listened to nothing but her tires regularly thumping on the expansion joints as we crossed back over the bridge. "I'm really worried about you."

I gritted my teeth. Why was everyone trying to parent me—first Deputy Dawg, and now my best friend? If my own mother couldn't be bothered with the job, I didn't see why everyone else felt they had to leap into the breach.

"You don't need to worry," I grated out. "I'm fine."

"Stop saying that."

"What?"

"'I'm fine.' It's like your little mantra, Brook—no matter what happens, no matter how bad things get, all you ever say is, 'I'm fine.' I used to think you were just trying to keep people from worrying about you. But you're even kidding yourself with it. You're *not* fine, Brook. You're messed up right now. There's nothing wrong with that—anyone would be, with...you know, everything that's been happening. Especially after what happened with Michael." She said it slowly and deliberately, as if to make sure I didn't miss her mention of his name.

I clenched my teeth hard, but didn't rise to her bait.

Sasha gusted out a sigh ripe with frustration. "You have to let yourself feel what you're feeling or you're going to just break down one day!"

I stared out the window at Hurricane Pass, named for the storm that created it in the twenties, which washed away the old swing bridge and tore out a new channel, severing what was now San Carlos Island from the mainland. My hands were clenched into fists, and I concentrated on releasing my tight fingers one by one.

"Okay, Dr. Phil. Thanks," I said in a monotone.

"I mean it. Talk to me. You never let on that anything's wrong. I talk your ear off when I'm hurting, Brook. I tell you everything I'm going through."

"That's you, Sasha. It's not me."

"That's *human*."

"No," I bit out, "it's not. It's one way of dealing with things. And it's not the way I choose to do it. I don't wallow, I don't feel sorry for myself, and I don't act like an idiot."

"Oh. Okay." Sasha was concentrating hard on the road, her hands clutching tight to the wheel. "And I do—is that what you're saying?"

"No. You're just more of...an id person than I am."

She gave an unamused laugh. "I'm not as stupid as you think, Brook."

"I don't think you're stupid."

"Yes, you do. 'Id person' is just a condescending way of saying I can't regulate my impulses. Like a toddler."

"That's not..." Actually, that was a pretty good description of how Sasha went through a breakup. I struggled for a tactful way to end the sentence.

"Oh, my God." Sasha looked at me, and I felt the car slow down. "It's true? That's what you really think?"

"No—"

"I pour my heart out to you when it's broken—because you're my best friend. Because no one else knows me so well or loves me better than you do. I vomit everything up on you, and that's what helps me get through it." She had pulled all the way over to the side of San Carlos now, in front of the battered Love Boat ice-cream shop that had been there as long as I could remember. She turned in the seat to face me. "Are you...are you judging me every time?"

I fidgeted, uncomfortable. Was I? I deflected: "You don't vomit *everything* up, now, do you?"

"What? What does that mean?"

"I don't have an exclusive contract on keeping things to myself, Sasha. Who's been dating all hot and heavy for the last two weeks, and decided to keep her little secret all to herself?"

"I... Brook, I'm just trying to keep my head on straight this time, like you've always said."

I should have been proud of her—Sasha was finally trying to come at a relationship in a more adult way. But selfishly, the timing only made me feel worse about myself. Why did she have to start getting herself together right when I was falling apart? My humiliation made me go on the offensive.

"Sure, Sasha—that's great. For the first time in your entire dating life you're playing it cool. So cool you don't even tell your so-called best friend anything about it. But you want *me* to confide all my deepest, darkest in *you*."

"Brook, that's not why I—"

"That's really fair, Sash. It gives me all kinds of warm fuzzies about telling you every stupid, insecure, ridiculous, embarrassing thing about me."

"Why would you be embarrassed with *me*?"

"Why would you be embarrassed to tell me about your new

boyfriend now that you're so healthy and mature about it?" I said meanly.

"It is too!"

"What?" I snapped. "What is *what* too?"

"No." Sasha was staring straight ahead out the windshield. "It's *Stu*."

"What are you talking about? What does Stu have to do with anything?" But I knew. As soon as she said his name I knew.

I saw her swallow, and then she pulled her eyes to mine. "I didn't tell you because...because I know how I am about dating. And I like him, Brook. I mean, in that way. I really do *like* him, and we're... I don't know...good together, so far. Easy. I don't want to spoil it, because I'm scared to death that I will, so I haven't said anything to anyone. Not even you. I knew what you'd say."

I sat silent, processing. *Trying* to process. "You...and my baby brother, Stu...are dating." I kept my voice utterly uninflected.

"We're seeing where it goes. We're not putting too much on it right now."

"Huh. You get those catchphrases out of one of your dating self-help books?"

She blanched, but I ruthlessly stifled the twinge of shame that flared up in me.

"So just to make sure I'm all caught up here," I said, my voice horribly cold, "you've been secretly dating my brother for who knows how long. And he's been avoiding me because of that so he doesn't have to actually lie to my face about it, like you have been. And meanwhile you're also pitching big feature stories to your newspaper about my mother, who has had nothing to do with me or my father or my brother since she walked out on my family, so you can run down to Naples to spend hours and hours talking to her about her heartfelt feelings and dreams. Have I got it? You want to bogart my dad too, since you've managed to hijack the rest of my family for yourself?"

I'd never seen anyone actually go dead pale before. Sasha's face had shuttered like a house battened down for a hurricane. She just stared at me, and for a moment I flashed back to my brother at age seven, holding his bleeding hand and looking at Mugsy, our German shepherd, the two of them together inside the circle of pillows on the floor that we'd dedicated as a gladiator arena while I cheered their wrestling play on from the top bunk. In the moment before his wails filled the bedroom and my mom came running, the expression on Stu's face had been one of bewildered betrayal.

"Right." Sasha threw the car in gear and pulled back onto San Carlos.

"Sasha..." I said after a long, uncomfortable minute. "I didn't mean that the way it came out." But she said nothing, not even registering that I'd spoken. "Sash... I'm sorry. Really. I had a bad... I didn't mean... Please."

Nothing. We made the rest of the trip to my house in total silence. Sasha didn't even answer my goodbye when I got out of the car in my driveway, and the car was already moving in reverse before the passenger door fully shut.

twenty-seven

Even with everything else that had happened, all I could think about as I showered at home was my brother and my best friend.

Once, when Sasha and I were younger—but much too old for dolls—Stu caught us playing Barbies in our room.

"What are you two doing?" he demanded, standing in the doorway of my pink bedroom, his skinny prepubescent body puffed up with triumph.

I shoved Barbie and Stu's GI Joe—both naked in compromising positions—under my bed with a foot. "Get out of here, Stu," I shouted at him. "You can't come into my room."

"GI Joe is missing again. You're playing with dolls!"

"Shut up."

"I'll be GI Joe, if you want."

"No. We don't want. Go away, Stu."

His face grew stormy. "I'm telling. I'm telling everyone you're playing with Barbie dolls."

"We are not!"

"You are too. I'm telling everyone at school."

"Shut up, you little shit!" I started toward him, not sure what I meant to do, intent only on forcing his silence. I could imagine no greater shame than being revealed as a fourteen-year-old player of Barbies.

But Sasha shot to her feet and beat me to Stu. She reached around his head and pushed the door closed behind him, shutting the three of us in.

"Hey, Stuvie, you wanna make a deal?"

He scowled. "No."

"Come on. It's a good one."

Stu looked wary, but couldn't resist anything Sasha suggested. He never could. "What."

Sasha wiggled her torso as she shimmied the bottom of her purple T-shirt like a cancan girl. "You leave me and Brook alone for the rest of the day and I'll show you part of a boob."

Stu tried hard to mask the eagerness that leaped into his expression, but failed miserably. "Whatever. I don't care." He shrugged, but he looked more like an uncertain turtle hunching into its shell. "How big a part?"

Sasha held her palm out flat at her chest, just below her nipple. "To here."

Stu crossed his arms and jutted out his jaw. "An inch higher."

Sasha shook her head. "Nope. No way."

Stu moved his eyes to look at me, then at the pile of dolls on the floor that we'd hastily covered with Sasha's sweater when he burst through the door. His calculating expression made me nervous.

"Just do it, Sash," I said uneasily.

"Brook!"

"That's the deal," Stu said stubbornly, sensing his advantage. "Nipple or nothing."

Sasha regarded him through narrowed eyes, and then her expression melted into a catlike satisfaction and she poked a finger into Stu's neck, startling him into a laugh before he pushed at her arm and fought to regain his hard line.

"No nipple, little man," she said indulgently, but before he could give voice to the protest he'd already opened his mouth to utter, she added, "but I'll throw in part of the other boob."

"And can I touch it?"

Sasha laughed. "Maybe next time."

Stu looked like he was considering it, but I could tell the battle was already won. Sasha could probably have talked him into doing what she wanted just by the attention she was already paying him.

"Okay." His tongue darted out and then retracted back inside his mouth and he bit his lip. "Do it."

Sasha grasped his shoulders and turned him around. "After you leave us alone for the rest of the afternoon. I'll come into your room and do it before I leave."

Stu just nodded, pale and speechless. Waiting a couple of hours with the bottom half of Sasha's breasts at the end of them would probably just about kill him with anticipation and nerves. But it guaranteed he'd live up to his bargain.

Was that how early it had started? I wondered as I washed off the grime of camping and the beach and jail. Even back then, Sasha a fourteen-year-old blooming with hormones, Stu nearly thirteen—was that when they'd first felt an attraction to each other? With me left stupidly on the outside, unaware of any other undercurrents beneath the manipulable annoyance that was my baby brother?

It wasn't that I had never wanted Sasha and Stu to look at each other that way. It was that it had never entered my mind as something that could happen—like getting a phone call from your dog.

The rational side of me knew that I had lashed out at Sasha out of my own self-loathing and embarrassment and helplessness and hurt. But I had a sick feeling that this time I'd stepped too far over the line for us to ever pull back.

I toweled off and collapsed into bed, not even bothering to dry my hair. I slept for six hours—not nearly long enough, I realized when I peeled my crusty eyes open at three in the afternoon and squinted against the sun glaring in even through the blinds. But if I didn't get up now, I'd sleep the day away, and then be awake all night.

Bad things happened in the lonely stillness of night.

I checked my phone to see if, somehow, I'd slept through Sasha's call. It hadn't rung—but I noticed the voicemail icon was blinking, and wondered how long it had been since I'd checked it.

But it wasn't Sasha—it was a number I didn't recognize, and when I checked my voicemail I was disappointed again, because it wasn't Kendall either, and it wasn't Chip. It took me a moment to figure out *who* it was, since I didn't know the voice, but finally I realized—Ben, my stunt date from the other night.

"Hey, Brook...just wanted to say thanks for a nice time Friday. Unexpected surprise." A throat clearing, and then, "Oh, this is Ben. Probably you already figured that out." He laughed, a little awkwardly. "Anyway, I'd like to do it again sometime. Give me a call and let's plan it." It was time-stamped from yesterday afternoon—the perfect amount of time for a thank-you after a date if you liked the person and wanted to see them again.

Why hadn't I listened to that message before traipsing off with Chip Santana to make out on a beach in the middle of the night? Why hadn't I heard it before I got arrested?

Not that it mattered. Ben Garrett was a nice man, but he couldn't compete when my heart and my hormones were shoving two altogether different men into the front of my conscience. I couldn't even make the call to tell him I wasn't interested—I didn't have the energy to be polite.

My father was coming tomorrow morning to drywall the guest bathroom, which meant that I needed to work on my column today so I could turn it in by deadline. Fresh from jail and a terrible fight with my best friend, I had little in life that I wanted to do less. Or felt less qualified for.

But I booted up the laptop anyway, because I had no choice; I'd committed to the column, to the *Tropic Times*, to Lisa Albrecht.

Speaking of Lisa... I hadn't spoken with her once since I'd mailed her letter to her ex-husband. He had to have received it by now—had he called her? The total radio silence on her end wasn't a good sign—knowing Lisa, it probably meant she'd slid back into her overbearing, controlling quasi-stalking of Theodore, and wanted no interference from me.

And I couldn't even make myself pick up the phone and find out.

I stared at the blinking cursor for what felt like hours, typing not so much as a "the." For the first time I understood the term "writer's block"—I had it in spades. Or therapist's block. Or human block. It was ridiculous for me to be writing this column—I had nothing at all of any value to impart to anyone else.

I finally scratched out nine hundred words about not letting feelings of rejection and hurt overwhelm you after a breakup. It was pap—in the same vein as the treacly self-help books I'd mocked Sasha for in the car. And it was crap—complete bullshit. But I had a deadline to meet and I had to turn in something. I hit send without even giving the article a final edit.

I called Sasha. Fourteen times. She didn't pick up on any of them.

On Monday morning at seven thirty, the doorbell dragged me out of bed, where I'd been lying staring at my yellowed popcorn ceiling since just before five. My dad stood on the front porch with deli bags in his hands and a rise-and-shine smile on his face. "Ya ready to get this house into shape, doll?"

No. I wasn't ready for that. The house was a dump, and trying to renovate it into something lovely was like slapping lipstick on a corpse. But I manufactured a smile that felt like a crevice in my face and pushed some inflection into my voice when I said, "Sure, Daddy! Let me change into my work clothes."

We worked all day, nailing in two-by-fours to reinforce the joists, fitting the sheets of drywall into place, screwing them to the studs, taping and floating. For the first time I could remember, I didn't chatter to my dad as he buried himself in a project. We worked smoothly, as a team, but in near total silence broken only by the occasional instruction from him. By the time we swiped the last trowelful of joint compound over it, the bathroom wall looked as smooth and pristine as new construction—and I felt no pleasure as we stood to admire our handiwork.

"How 'bout that, doll," my dad said, gazing proudly at the perfect job he'd done.

"It's like it never happened."

My father shrugged. "You can't undo the damage. But since it let us get inside the wall...the new plumbing, the reinforced joists...it's practically in better shape now than it was before," he said, smiling.

"That's great, Daddy. Thank you."

"Doll." He turned to face me. "What's wrong?"

As soon as he spoke, I felt my eyes turn prickly and hot, and my throat grew too tight for speech. I was in imminent danger of sobbing like a wounded child—which would throw my dad entirely for a loop, and was the last thing he needed right now. I turned away, pretending to rub at the waxy grime along the doorjamb from years of passing shoulders. Tears had filled my eyes so full that I was afraid to blink them away for fear of sending them spilling down my cheeks. I swallowed—hard, twice—and gathered myself. I had no intention of unloading on him about my fight with Sasha and my humiliation with Chip and my brush with Johnny Law. And I couldn't say anything about Stu and Sasha, because I had no idea whether Dad already knew—and once their hookup ran its course it would be better if he didn't. But I had to tell him *something*.

"Dad," I said, breathing deep and willing myself calm. "Kendall and I broke up."

"Oh..." His face seemed to lose its muscle support beneath the skin, and his eyes grew soft and sad. "Oh, doll. I'm... Gosh, I'm sorry. You liked him an awful lot, huh?"

I nodded. It felt like years ago now, but I thought I loved him. I wanted—needed—him to be the one. My eyes prickled again.

"Sweetheart..." He reached out a hand and rubbed awkwardly up and down my upper arm. And then he rested it on my shoulder, holding me with a firm grip. The Dad equivalent of a sloppy hug. I reached up and twined my fingers with his and we just stood there like that, staring at the work we'd done and not at each other, for a stretch of time that should have felt uncomfortable, but didn't.

After a little while he pulled his hand away and gestured back toward the wall with it. "You know, it's just one little thing, doll. But I think it looks pretty good. Ya gotta start somewhere, huh?"

I leaned into his shoulder as I followed his gaze. "Yeah," I said. "I guess so, Daddy."

My phone rang later that night, and I leaped for it. But it wasn't Sasha—or anyone else I hoped to hear from.

"What is *this*?" Lisa Albrecht's acerbic voice barked.

I gritted my teeth. I wasn't in the mood for an Albrecht Attack. "Hello, Lisa. I'm fine, thanks. How are you?"

"What the hell is this column, Miss '*Breakup Doctor*'? Did you take a Tony Robbins seminar? Are you plagiarizing Marianne Williamson?"

I stayed determinedly silent, letting Lisa marinate in her own abrasiveness. After a thick pause, I heard a hard, deliberate sigh, and then:

"I am fine, Brook. How are you?" She spit it out staccato, and I could tell each word was choking her.

"I'm okay, thanks," I said pleasantly. "Nice of you to ask."

"You realize these are just time-wasting platitudes. No one really gives a crap about the answers."

"*I* do, Lisa. I actually do." And I felt a rush of relief to realize it was true—despite everything that had happened lately, as soon as I heard Lisa's (admittedly shrill and sarcastic) voice, I *was* concerned about her. I really did want to know how she was doing. Helping people was what I did, even if I was too pathetic and stupid at the moment to help myself. "How are things going with you—have you heard back from Theodore about the letter?"

Another swampy pause, and then: "No. Well, yes, actually. Sort of."

"What do you mean?"

And then we were having an actual conversation, rather than the usual angry monologue Lisa treated me to. She'd waited days for the letter to find its way into Theodore's hands, she said, forcing herself per my instructions not to call him and grill him about it.

"I left the house without my phone one night and just went for a drive to keep myself from calling," she told me. Another night she watched a movie with the twins and literally sat on her hands so she wouldn't be tempted. "I kept hearing your voice telling me I was pushing him into a corner. And I know...well, I *hate* feeling trapped like that, so I figured he must too."

Empathy. From Lisa Albrecht. Wow.

Finally, when Lisa had been just about ready to drive over there and force him to talk to her, the boys came home from having dinner with their father, and Michael casually said, "Dad asked how you were doing. I told him how amazing you were being—really strong and centered about all of it."

"I was ready to tear into a list of all the ways he screwed up our lives," Lisa said to me. "And then I thought... Well, this sounds stupid, I guess, but I kind of heard what my son had said—that he thought I was handling it so well. And I liked that. I don't want the boys learning that if life lets you down, you fall apart."

Ugh. No. Terrible thing to teach them. Thank God *I* wasn't their parent.

I gave Lisa lots of praise for her behavior—I'd already learned she responded to it like an eager puppy. And by the time we got back to the reason for her call—my subpar, phoned-in column—she was calmer and more constructive. And, I realized as we talked, she *was* a damn good editor. She called me on every cliché, showed me where the rhythm of the article stalled, and batted around ideas with me until I hung up ready to overhaul the column into what I really wanted to say.

I worked late into the night, but I was hardly conscious of the hours passing. When I finally hit send and powered down my computer, it was nearly midnight. I went to bed and fell into the first dreamless sleep I'd had in weeks.

twenty-eight

Sometimes you don't realize just how largely someone figures in your life until they're totally out of it.

It wasn't just the empty time that used to be filled with conversation and company. Not simply being used to having someone to bounce ideas off of, share thoughts and observations with, to laugh with over nothing. Losing someone was more than losing their company. You lost your whole routine, the little daily events that became second nature to you. It was that change that made the transition so much more keenly felt. It wasn't just one element that was suddenly absent from your life. It was everything connected to it: the habits, the scheduling of your time.

I missed Sasha. Terribly.

During the week I called her at least once a day. I left messages every time. Said I was enormously sorry. Asked her to call. I sent her an apologetic email telling her my tongue had gotten away from me, that I wished I could take back what I said, that I was abjectly sorry. Finally I texted, "Sasha, I'm really, really sorry." But nothing.

I heard nothing from Chip, either—but I hadn't really expected to. Given the embarrassing and criminal end to our evening, he probably didn't want to be reminded of his behavior any more than I did. After crossing the professional line so completely and irrevocably, I would never be able to face him again, and my sole consolation for the entire episode was that at least I had formally ended treatment with him before breaking every boundary imposed between therapist and patient.

Despite the shambles of my personal life, the Breakup Doctor requests continued to stream in, and during the week I met with five new clients. By Friday, when my latest column ran, I'd gotten twenty-one more emails from potential clients, and I was starting to get my feet under me again. Regardless of what was going on in my personal life, my new professional life was indisputably taking off. And little by little, I felt better. Lonely...but better.

I felt so much more solid, in fact, that I realized it was time to deal directly with the Kendall situation, instead of letting myself be sucked blindly into his undertow.

Not that I had any intention of confronting him. Now that I was more rational, myself again, I knew that was fruitless. He'd made his decision while he was actively in a relationship with me, seeing me every day, to all intents and purposes living with me. Which evidently he'd realized he didn't want to do. There was nothing to be gained by "talking it out" with him, except to make myself feel worse. He was clearly no longer interested in being with me, and finding out why wasn't productive. The only thing that *was* at this point was to tie off loose ends: go get the rest of my things from his house, return the few things I had of his, and put the whole thing behind me. Move forward.

I'd been working at home all day, answering emails from clients and potential clients, and I was in jeans and a T-shirt. But I changed into one of my work outfits—a sleek tweed pencil skirt and purple silk blouse that I knew flattered my coloring and made my eyes look like big brown Bambi eyes—with my usual cardigan over it to hide the bandage on my shoulder. I put on makeup. I slipped on a pair of pumps—having one of Sasha's designer pairs would have given me an extra boost of confidence, but I still felt good enough—and I headed over to his condo, this time straightforwardly, not skulking inside like a criminal. I looked as completely different as possible from that poor, sad, bedraggled girl in the rain outside his condo.

It was Friday evening, so I knew he wouldn't be home. Fridays were when Kendall met with coworkers and friends downtown after work—"social networking," he called it, as if he had to justify doing anything that wasn't work-related at every free moment. I planned to simply let myself in—I still had my key, if he hadn't changed the locks—get the last of my meager things I'd had at his house, and leave.

Kendall's car wasn't in his spot, of course. I felt an odd mixture of relief and regret, and I had to admit to myself that part of me had hoped he'd be home, that he'd see me looking professional and pulled-together. That he'd have to face me like a man as I took my belongings and removed myself finally and completely from his life. That he'd wonder what on earth he'd done, wish he could take it all back.

I walked the path I'd taken so many times before: around the residents' parking area and along the pathway that ran along the tea-colored water in the drainage pond.

I knew the divot on his doorjamb from where we'd jarringly learned that his new dining room table didn't fit through it. We'd flipped the tabletop face down on the grass outside his unit, its legs in the air like a dying bug while we painstakingly unscrewed each one, then screwed them back in once we carted the pieces inside. I knew that the doorbell didn't work, and hadn't since Kendall had moved in, and how we always forgot to buy a new one, literally slapping ourselves on the foreheads every time we came home from running errands with everything we needed except that.

I knew that the key slid into the lock as though it had been lubed, but that it caught partway through the turn and wouldn't go any farther unless you lifted up on the knob. I remembered the feel of the knob in my hand, cool in my palm even on the hottest day.

As the door swung open in front of me, it was as though nothing had changed. I was coming back home after a day at work, a night out with Sasha, buying groceries, and Kendall would still be at his office, the house quiet and perfect as a movie set until I set down whatever I had in my hands, turned on the stereo, filled the space with mealtime scents of sautéing onion and garlic.

It occurred to me for the first time, as I walked up the stairs to the silent main living area, that I had always come home to a sterile, pristine environment I needed to fill with sensory input, and Kendall came home to scents and sounds and company. We each got what the other wanted.

My heart was pounding like a living creature in my chest as I topped the staircase. What if his car was in the shop, and Kendall was home, sitting in the living room, aghast at my unannounced invasion of his house? What if he was waiting for what he thought was an intruder, armed with a bat or a knife or the gun he'd always talked of getting? Worst of all—the thought I couldn't shake despite having unearthed no evidence of it—what if he wasn't alone?

Yes, I still had my key—but using it wasn't part of the contract anymore. Another thing that made breakups so hard—you were stripped of so many rights overnight. The home you once entered as easily as your own was now off-limits to you; you were relegated to knocking on the door like any other visitor. The body you could reach out and casually touch, anywhere, now bore the new boundaries of social convention. It wasn't yours to claim anymore.

I should just leave my key on the breakfast bar overlooking the living room, let myself out and latch the door behind me. Or I should turn around and go, put the key in an envelope with nothing else and mail it back to Kendall. *Here. I don't even want the ability to come back into your life.*

Instead I dropped my purse and the keys on the sofa table behind his leather couch, just as I'd done countless times before.

The house looked so identical to the way it had for every one of those nights that for a moment I was disoriented. It was as though nothing had happened, the last weeks a strange and unsettling dream, but now I was back from the rabbit hole and everything was normal again. The burgundy afghan knitted by Kendall's grandmother was neatly folded across the wide arm of the cream leather sofa, where Kendall always replaced it after I dragged it over me at night in front of the television. The remote lay in the wooden tray on the cocktail table that he had bought specifically for it, next to the cordless phone—the only other place it was supposed to go when not on the charger—and his PS3 controllers.

He must love the fact that he didn't have to trail after me anymore, putting things back where they went. As soon as I was out of his life, Kendall must have gone through the house and eradicated every messy trace of me, every cluttery bottle or jar or tube, every sloppily hung, non-color-coded article of clothing in the extra closet. Knowing Kendall, it would be easy for me to take all of my things—they would be neatly packed in a clearly labeled box, tucked away in a guest room closet, waiting the requisite time to be returned to me with the least amount of emotion or drama. It made me sad that nothing I'd left behind here was important enough for me to have missed in the weeks since I'd been gone—doubles of my toiletries, spare panties and bras, a couple of outfits.

As I headed toward the master bedroom, another thought inescapably assailed me: What if, when I opened the smaller spare closet, someone else's things were hung there now?

The idea stopped me halfway down the hall. This was the moment I ought to turn around and leave, stop invading Kendall's privacy, stop poking a hard finger into my own wounds, and walk out the door and to my car. Leave Kendall and his home behind, literally and metaphorically.

The logical side of my brain pelted me with questions: What was I going to feel if I opened the closet and saw another woman's clothes so quickly replacing mine? What would it tell me about why my relationship ended? How would it help me understand and work through it?

The answers: Crappy. Nothing. It wouldn't.

I took another two steps forward and twisted the knob to the master bedroom, breath held.

And then I stopped cold, forgetting even to breathe.

Like a museum display of my last day with Kendall, the room stood just as it always looked. Just *exactly* as it had always looked. Not just the bed made with military precision, the pillows fluffed and arranged symmetrically. Not just Kendall's atomic alarm clock tilted toward his side of the bed at a 45-degree angle.

Next to the clock was the same framed picture that was always there. I remembered the day it had been taken: Sasha had invited Kendall and me to a grand-opening party for Hurricane, a new (and unfortunately named) waterfront bar and restaurant on Sanibel. The official grand opening was the following night, but the "soft opening" was media only—fountains of free booze and unlimited piles of food. Sasha had scored extra invitations, and Kendall for once came home from work at a normal time so we could meet her there.

While the waiters and bar staff milled among the crowd sucking up on a level I'd imagined only celebrities got ("Ready for a refill? Try these horseradish-crusted prime rib bites. May I take that olive pit for you?"), and Sasha networked with local TV reporters and editors from area magazines, Kendall and I explored every inch of the restaurant, noticing details both elegant and odd.

"Five-inch crown molding. Nice," he pointed out.

I nodded. "Classy. Travertine tile."

"Good choice." Kendall stomped a heel of his Ferragamo on the floor of the cocktail lounge. "Pergo. Cheap."

"Humidity," I excused the faux pas. We peered behind the bar. "Copper," I said, indicating the sink.

"Swank."

Outside on the wide deck overlooking Tarpon Bay a breeze blew the heavy, pleasant scents of seaweed and fish and salt toward us as we leaned against the off-white railing.

"Plastic?" Kendall raised an eyebrow, disbelieving.

I rapped my knuckles against the rail. "Recycled milk jugs. Environmentally conscious."

"Tacky."

I laughed. "Green."

He laughed too, and we looked out over the bay together, watching the sun start to descend. Then I felt his eyes on me, and I turned to see him staring. He tucked a flyaway strand of hair back behind my ear.

"Beautiful," he said softly.

He was capable of those moments—the ones that always caught me off guard, a sudden outpouring of sweetness and naked connection that trapped the breath in my chest and warmed it like sunbaked sand. I brought my hand up to his cheek, and we kissed like that—soft and gentle, holding each other's faces.

A flash of light had pulled us apart, and I turned to see Sasha standing there with her phone.

"Awww. You two are like a postcard out here. They ought to put you in their brochure."

"Shut up," I said, embarrassed, and Kendall and I started past her back inside. "Where's the dessert bar?"

Later she'd emailed the picture to me, with the subject line, "Still life: Sanibel face-sucking at sunset." It did look like a cheesy picture-perfect ad for romantic beach getaways: the sky pink and indigo and orange behind us, our hands framing our faces, mouths fused. But in the body of the note Sasha had written, "I actually love this photo." I forwarded it to Kendall, and two days later saw with a flush of pleased surprise that he'd printed and framed it and set it by the bedside.

Why was it still there?

I turned abruptly and yanked open the closet door the way you'd rip the Band-Aid off a wound—and there were my clothes, four or five hangers' worth still dangling where I'd hung them. Two pairs of shoes lay underneath, black pumps and a pair of sneakers.

But looking closer, I realized my things weren't exactly as I'd left them. The shoes I'd kicked off my feet into the closet were now lined up neatly side by side. My clothes had been straightened, the hangers evenly spaced on the rod.

The bathroom offered up more of the same incongruities: my toothbrush, still in the holder next to Kendall's, but now standing at attention; my lotion and hair gel on the dark marble counter, lined up like waiting soldiers. In the shower, my razor was in the soap holder, spooned up against Kendall's.

My legs felt shaky and I lowered myself to the toilet lid. (Kendall never left the seat up.)

I didn't understand. Not only had he *not* gotten rid of my things as quickly as he'd gotten rid of me, but they were preserved like some kind of shrine—a memorial to me, or to the relationship we had. Everything was still here, just as it had been—everything except for me.

I wanted to lie down on his king-size bed and let my sudden exhaustion take over. I wanted to slip into sleep and quiet all the voices in my head trying to make sense of what I was seeing. I wanted to be waiting when he came home, to pick back up where we left off, to go on as if the last few miserable weeks had been just a fight, a misunderstanding, a cooling-off period.

Except that we hadn't really fought, we hadn't said anything to be misunderstood, and there was nothing to cool off from. Things had just...stopped.

Ten minutes ago was normally when I would have called Sasha. She would have understood. Hell, she would have come to help me make sense of things.

The memory made a sharp ache for her start in my chest as acute as the one I'd felt since Kendall had bugged out of my life.

What was wrong with me that everyone who said they loved me had left me? Kendall...Sasha...my own mom. My eyes grew stupidly wet, and I grabbed a wad of toilet paper and pressed it to my face.

I bit my tongue hard, blinked quickly, and carefully dabbed the tissue along my lash line. I needed to stay looking my best. I didn't know when I'd made the decision, but I was heading downtown to find Kendall. It was long past time we had a face-to-face talk about what the hell had happened between us.

That was how you handled relationships when you were an adult. That was what I could never make Sasha understand—what I'd forgotten in the blind shock of Kendall's disappearance—that the direct approach was always best. The games and tricks and sneaky little operations Sasha employed after a breakup twisted her up in pretzel knots and didn't give her any answers. I knew that firsthand, now. Worse, they made her look like a crazy person.

Which she wasn't. At least, not in any arena of her life other than dating. She was funny and talented and hardworking and strong and loyal.

I flutter-blinked again and forced my mind back to the mission at hand. Getting weepy over our broken friendship wasn't going to solve anything right now.

I balled up my tissue and stood to toss it under the toilet lid and flushed. No traces of my visit. In the mirror where I'd gotten ready so many mornings, I finger-fluffed my hair, wiped away the last traces of smeared mascara, pinched my cheeks to chase away the paleness that had washed out my face.

In the car I swiped on more lip gloss and felt strong again. *Nothing's ever so bad for a woman that a bit of lipstick can't make it a little better.* One of my mom's more ridiculous sayings, but suddenly I understood what she meant.

I backed out of visitors' parking and pulled out onto McGregor, watching the palm trees and stucco of Kendall's complex growing smaller in my rearview mirror.

twenty-nine

I whipped my Honda into a vacant spot in the lawyer lot—right next to Kendall's Mercedes. Seeing his sleek black sedan there brought up a welter of conflicting feelings—hurt that apparently I wasn't good enough for him, but my parking lot was; irritation that I'd insider-traded the valuable secret to him in misplaced trust; and, crazily, hope and tenderness—surely his parking here meant he still cared about me?

If anything else, Kendall was a creature of habit. He would be at one of three trendy hangouts: the Bar Belle, built along a cozy alley off Hendry Street; Andale's, where I'd had my date with Ben—poor Ben, who was far too nice for me in my present state; or Ship to Shore, tucked away by the river where Hendry met First Street.

I worked my way into downtown from the edges, starting at Ship to Shore with my fast-beating heart held in my suddenly dry mouth.

There is no such thing as stealth or anonymity in a town where, even though the population is around fifty thousand, only a small portion has lived here their whole lives, and that same ten percent or so can be found at some bar downtown on most any given night. The regulars sat outside, under the string lights, where it was quiet enough to talk and still legal to smoke. I was met on the patio by a hail of greetings before I even set foot inside.

"Hey, Brook—pull up a chair." Marti Greckle, who came home from college as the wife of a high-profile real estate developer who never seemed to be with her at her nightly happy hours.

"Hey, Marti...guys," I called back.

"Brook! So glad to see you! You look great! Grab a drink and join us!" Barbra "spelled like Streisand" Adams, cheerleader in high school, cheerleader now.

"Maybe later," I said vaguely as my eyes scanned the patio.

"Where you been, girl?" Terry Tillmore, my lab partner in biology, who now ran a hair salon and day spa downtown.

"Oh, busy, busy." Kendall wasn't here.

"You look...different, Brook. Did you finally lose that extra weight?" Melissa Overton, in every single one of my homerooms from first grade to twelfth, by virtue of our last names. For years we had wiped a patina of civility over our mutual hatred for each other, which started in tenth grade when she slept with my boyfriend Jack Andrews while I was busy deciding if I was ready to go "all the way" with him, and continued as she spread her attentions throughout town like the Typhoid Mary of sexual favors.

"I'll catch up to you guys another time," I said, ignoring her as I turned to go.

"Looking for Kendall, sweetie?" Melissa's voice was like syrup dripping into the sudden cracks of stillness on the patio. So it was common knowledge, then.

I turned around and fixed a bright smile on my face. "Actually, I'm meeting someone. Hey—how's the TV biz these days?"

I wanted to bite my tongue as soon as I'd said it—Melissa had been fired from her on-air job at KSUN after a very public drinking-and-driving accident. I hadn't meant to sink to the level of trading barbs with her.

"Oh, I've got a great new job now, hon. I've moved on—like a lot of people we know." Her smile was smug and mean.

My heart tripped in my chest and I felt my cheeks heat. Had all of them heard that Kendall had walked out on our relationship? Did everyone know what had happened between us except me? All my friends that I'd introduced to him, giving him an instant social life in a town where he knew literally no one the day he met me?

"Well, good for you, Melissa." I forced the words past a tight throat. Engaging with her only threw gasoline on her fire. *Dignity*, Dr. Evanston whispered in my mind. *Hold on to your dignity.* Even with her hands cuffed behind her back, I remembered, Dr. Evanston had held her head high. "See you guys."

Andale's was next. I hoped Jeffrey would be there—he would know if Kendall had been in, and if so, where he was now. But the same girl from my date with Ben was behind the bar, a stranger to me. I glanced over at the table where I had sat with Ben that night, empty now. I had never returned his call. Shame shot through me, and something else...an unsettled twist of regret.

The small bar area was packed with the suits and dresses of the after-hours business crowd, milling about like a school of sharks fighting over the same chewed-up chum. The spice of life was at a sad premium in the Fort Myers dating world.

No Kendall—thank God. I didn't think I could handle seeing him chatting up someone new in the same restaurant where we'd gone so many times.

It had to be the Bar Belle.

I took a deep breath, trying to steady my jumpy nerves. *Cowgirl up.* They were my mother's words. *All you want is a rational, adult discussion. That's the very least you're entitled to.*

I felt myself relax minutely. That was true. I wasn't here for some dramatic, emotional confrontation. All I wanted was answers. Some closure—a hackneyed word, but still valid. I was ready for this. I *was* entitled to it.

The Bar Belle was packed—it was always packed, by virtue of being about the size of a bowling lane: long and skinny, so narrow that two-deep at the bar meant barely any room to walk behind. It was an uncomfortable place to try to be heard or to talk to more than just the person on either side of you, but the owners were longtime Fort Myers residents, heavily involved in the community, and as welcoming to every patron as though they were family. And if you were a regular, your drink was waiting for you on the bar before you made it from the front door to a stool, rounds of shots were often provided, and musical selections were at your whims.

Kendall had hated the place the first time we went. "Too loud." "Awkward layout." "Limited menu." But I introduced him to Peter and David—the same way I'd introduced him to almost everyone he knew in Fort Myers—and they immediately created a special drink for him called the Kendalltini, and asked about his business, and complimented his shoes, and he was won over.

I should have been prepared to find him standing in the same spot where I'd met him after work a dozen times, an amber Kendalltini in one hand, the other gesturing in the air as he regaled his friend Ricky—and not some woman, thank God—with some fascinating tale of arbitrage or penny stocks or odd lots. I *was* prepared. But it still didn't keep my heart from slamming inside my chest at the sight of him.

His golden brown hair carried a curl he hated and I loved. It was longer—not much, probably no more than it ever got between haircuts, but I hadn't noticed it so much when I saw him every day. Now it made him look a little bit different. Softer, younger. He wore a suit—he almost always wore a suit—and a tie I didn't recognize.

He didn't see me, and for one quick beat of time I had him to myself. Until the moment when he would look up, catch my eye, and whatever would happen after that would happen, he was only mine for this one second—mine to look at, mine to love.

That hit me like a fist. I'd expected to see him and hate him. To be filled with rage, with hurt, with fury. Not to feel this wave of love for him crash over me, suck me under. For this frozen space of time he was simply mine again, and I ate him with my eyes.

And then he did look up, and I saw the exact moment when he realized the woman he'd been idly checking out down the length of the bar was me. His eyes grew wide; his whole body seemed to contract; he plunked his drink down on the bar and miscalculated the distance, Kendalltini sloshing over the sides.

Then it was like a domino effect. Ricky saw Kendall seize like an epileptic and turned around to see what caused it. Behind the bar David snapped to attention at the spilled drink, heading Kendall's way to clean it up; his gaze followed Kendall's and he saw me too. His expression was more gratifying: He managed to convey greeting and welcome all at once. Peter saw David looking and his head turned toward me, and suddenly I felt spotlighted at the end of the bar, the old gunslinger come to chase the new kid outta town.

It was my imagination that things grew silent as I forced my feet to carry me forward, a factor of the roaring in my ears, drowning out the buzz of the bar that logic told me still carried on around me. The drama building up like a cloudbank was confined to one tiny segment of the room's population; the rest of the clientele drank on, unaware of the storm brewing.

As if it were a close-up in a movie, I saw Ricky reach up to Kendall's sleeve and tug—*Let's get out of here, man*—saw Kendall's arm flop toward him and then back, as if he had no muscle control. And then all I could see was Kendall's eyes, glued to me as he watched me approach. They were shadowed into dark pools from here in the dim light, but I could see them perfectly in my head: light blue, a tiny center of gold rimming the pupil. I'd lost myself in those eyes and their unusual golden centers—evidence that Kendall was special, different, extraordinary.

I moved through the press of people in the narrow space as if I were covered in oil, bodies seeming to just glide off to the side, out of my way, as I moved like a barracuda toward a flash of metal glinting in sunlight.

And then we were in front of each other, only inches away because of the packed bar, and Ricky's panicky face fell out of my peripheral vision, and all that filled it was Kendall.

"Hi." I mouthed it, tried to speak it, but my voice had dried in my throat.

"Brook." He didn't say it like I was anathema. He didn't say it like I was someone who'd finally caught up to him when he'd been studiously trying to avoid her. He said it like water after a long hike, like rain after a drought. "Brook..."

It would have been so natural to lean forward and sink my lips into his. The same way we had done hundreds of times, almost instinctively. And I wasn't blind to his reaction—Kendall would have kissed me back. Would have welcomed it.

But Dr. Evanston and my mother and my own rationality "ahemed" in my head, and I remembered why I was here. What answers I needed. I'd gotten the first one—did Kendall still care about me? "Yes" was evident in every line of his body that strained toward mine. But that didn't address the list of other questions about his withdrawal that I had to have answers to before I gave in to the pull I felt even now to fall into him, let his arms wrap around me, bury my face in his neck and forget all the pain and bewilderment and hurt of the last few weeks.

"Let's get out of here," he said, and it was hard to tell in the loud Bar Belle, but it sounded like his voice was hoarse.

"Kendall." It was Ricky.

"Man, not now." He reached into his jacket pocket, pulled out a wallet, threw money on the bar. Reached for my arm, and I felt floaty and light.

"Ken!" Ricky's voice was loud, even in the noise of the crowd. A few people nearby stopped talking to look our way. Ricky had leaned in to Kendall and had hold of his arm, tight, and was furiously saying something close into his ear. He looked like a jilted girlfriend.

Ricky, who probably loved having Kendall to himself every night now, who'd probably whispered in his ear just like this a hundred times while we were dating, I realized with dawning anger: *Get rid of her. She's cramping your style, man. You don't want to be tied down.* Ricky, who had his playmate back now and didn't want to lose him. Ricky...the enemy. I waited, still and inert, to see which life Kendall would choose.

Kendall had stopped pulling away from Ricky's tentacled grasp and was listening. The look on his face was con- fused...torn...rebellious. I latched on to the latter and staked all my hopes to it.

Ricky made one last plea, and finally Kendall yanked away, shrugged his shoulders angrily, straightening his suit jacket. He picked up the bills he'd flung to the bar, and my heart sank. But as he tucked them into his jacket pocket he leaned to me and touched my arm, and the contact swept through me like a riptide.

"Outside. Where we can talk." His voice in my ear made me shiver.

We'd be under the watchful eye of mother-hen Ricky, in the safe environment of a bar populated with people we both knew, instead of alone together at Kendall's condo, where I knew we'd been headed minutes before. It was only a partial victory—but it was a victory. He'd chosen me...at least for now.

I nodded and turned to the rear door for the patio, where wrought-iron patio furniture created an outdoor sitting area made inviting with string lights and swags of fabric. The temperature was probably in the sixties, but Floridians' have thin blood, and the tables sat empty in the slight coolness of the March night.

Kendall lagged behind, turning to Peter behind the bar, who'd watched our whole exchange with avid eyes. Ricky kept up his stream of poison the whole time—I turned to see him grow animated as Kendall determinedly faced forward. Soaking it in? Tuning him out? I couldn't tell.

I pushed out the door and picked the rearmost table, in case anyone else came outside. The breeze blew the rich, clean smell of the Caloosahatchee over me as I settled into the hard seat, my head curiously light, my body numb, my heart racing and aching and full.

He pushed open the door with a hip after a couple of minutes that felt like hours, both hands full with a drink for each of us. A gimlet for me—he hadn't had to ask. He set them down, sat, and finally we were alone.

And I had no idea what to say. There had been so many versions of this moment in my head over the last weeks that now they all blended together in an unintelligible cacophony, and with Kendall finally here, in front of me, attentive and listening and *present*, I couldn't think of what more it was that I possibly needed to know.

Kendall was never good with awkward silences. He finally had to fill it. "I...I am so, so sorry."

It spread over my heart like ointment on a wound. *More. More.*

"I screwed this up."

Yes. Maybe there was nothing I needed to say. Maybe I could simply sit here, just make myself an audience so that Kendall could say it all, everything I had dreamed of hearing. *I messed up. I made a huge mistake. I love you. I want you back.*

But the script stopped too soon. Kendall lapsed into silence and contemplated his Kendalltini as though mermaids might breach from its surface.

I leaned toward him, moving my hand but stopping just short of resting it on top of his where it lay on the table. Too soon.

"Kendall." God, it was good to let his name fill my mouth again. "Kendall... What happened?"

He slumped forward as if someone had replaced his spine with rubber, elbows on the table, looking down through the wrought-iron waffling of the table to the dingy bricks below it. "I don't know."

I had to resist the urge to slap him. My reaction caught me by surprise; all I had been feeling since I saw him was melted. But I kept my voice modulated, calm, neutral.

"I'm not sure what you mean by that."

He fingered the base of his glass, and I wondered if he'd answer.

"I...guess I got scared," he said, almost inaudibly.

"Scared of what?"

"I don't know."

"I need more than that, Kendall."

"Yeah. I know. Okay...scared of... We moved so fast. Everything all of a sudden started happening so fast. And the next thing I knew you were about to move in."

I must have looked as incredulous as I felt, but Kendall wouldn't have seen it. He hadn't looked up at me once since he'd started talking.

"Kendall...*you're* the one who asked me to move in."

"I know!" he exploded. "I know! Why do you think this has been so hard for me?"

No, Brook—don't follow that path. If you get sidetracked on that comment, you'll never get back on the road to where you want to go.

Dr. Evanston? My mom? Sasha? I couldn't tell whose voice that was, but I didn't care—it was good advice. I literally bit my tongue and clenched my jaw against the retort I wanted to swing at him like an anvil.

"Can you explain what you mean by that?" I was therapizing him—Sasha would have caught it in a second, but Kendall was too involved in whatever was happening inside his head. And there was a reason therapists used this stuff—it worked.

"Brook... I loved you. I still love you. I thought... Well, I wanted us to spend our lives together."

Flowers opened in my heart. Dried rivers flowed. Arias were sung.

"But I didn't know if I was...was ready for that again."

Locusts invaded. The earth grew fallow. Dirges sounded.

I carefully reminded myself not to get off task. And couldn't help myself.

"'Again'?"

The silence after my one word weighed about fifty tons. Kendall looked up for the first time and searched my face, and I could actually see him calculating, watched potential tactics flit across his face and be discarded in the space of a few seconds.

"Yeah. After, you know. Teresa."

Let it go. Move on. But I couldn't. Nothing in his words specifically told me there was more here, but I could see it in his face. Sensed it.

"You mean...after you moved to Chicago for her? To live together?"

He nodded, jerkily.

"Yeah. We were...more than just living together." The words were muttered, quiet.

I bit the inside of my cheek and nodded stiffly. "Engaged?" Even in my own state, I could see that Kendall was miserable, and I felt a vague twinge of sympathy for him.

He cleared his throat. "Married."

I'd misheard. I had to have misheard.

"You were... You had... What?"

"We were married. Not long." He said it like a palliative, quick, desperate. "Or not long working at it, anyway. But it's over now, Brook. It's been final for months."

Months was slowed down, dragged out in my ears like the presidential assassination scene in a cheesy old movie. *Months* was how you marked the passage of short-term, recent things...tax periods...pregnancies... *Months* was how you spoke of a baby's age. *Months* might have been less long than we'd been together.

"When was it actually final?" The voice coming out of my mouth was Wise Therapist's voice: reasoned, objective, unemotional. The hysteric in my head marveled at the calm, level sound of it.

Kendall was too far gone into his own play to register that he ought to tread carefully. Too relieved, maybe, at my steady reaction. It made him incautious.

"End of January. I took you out to celebrate that night— remember? We went to Caravelli's, stayed the night in Naples...?"

Oh, I did remember. It was the most excruciatingly romantic thing Kendall had ever done for me—that almost any boyfriend had ever done. He instructed me to dress up and pack an overnight bag, and told me nothing else. Picked me up at my house, had me wait in the lobby while he checked us into the Bay Inn on Fifth Avenue. Dinner at swanky Caravelli's, and back upstairs to our room—a suite—where there were white roses and chocolate-covered strawberries and champagne.

I was so surprised that my no-nonsense, business-focused beau had a hidden and ornate romantic side. So moved that all of this was spontaneous, no occasion, no reason. So overwhelmed that all of it was just...for me.

But Kendall had been having his own private celebration, a secret commemoration of his freedom. For me the night had been a turning point for us—when I began to realize we were more than just casual, that I meant more to him than a fling. For him, it had been his own personal marking of a milestone. I was just along for the ride.

And it was also the night he'd asked me to move in.

"So that was when your"—I made myself say the word—"divorce was final."

He nodded pathetically.

"Were you going to tell me? Ever?"

"Brook... Of course—of course I would have. I was just waiting until the time was right."

The right time might have been when we met, I reflected. The right time might have been on one of our early dates, when it was clear things were heating up between us, or when we started to get serious. I wanted to ask Kendall what he deemed "the right time" would have been—pictured him down on a knee, avowing his love and asking me to spend the rest of my life with him: *And oh, before I forget, I've done this once before.*

But I kept my tone modulated—I knew from experience that as soon as you got emotional, most men tuned out. And, I reminded myself, I had kept something from him too.

"Kendall." I breathed deeply. "I can understand why you wouldn't have told me this early in." I couldn't. "But how could you have asked me to move in with you without telling me?"

He looked down into his fascinating drink again, then flicked a glance toward the door to the Bar Belle. He shifted in his chair. Fingered the stem of his martini glass. Cleared his throat and smoothed the sharp crease of his pants.

"I didn't... I didn't...know."

"You didn't know *what*? That you were married?"

"I didn't know..." He muttered something else that sounded vaguely English.

"What? I didn't hear you."

His face contracted like a fist. "I didn't know that I was going to ask you to move in. I hadn't exactly planned it."

My fingers and face felt suddenly cold, and I sat staring at him. "What do you mean?"

"I...I just... I was feeling happy Brook, and we had such a good time that night, and...so I..."

"So you asked me to *live* with you?"

"It just popped out."

"It popped *out*?" I yelled in disbelief.

"Brook... shhh-shhh." I didn't know if he was trying to soothe me or silence me, but it set me even further off.

"Were you just asking out of *relief*, Kendall? Was it even about me?"

"Brook!" He glanced quickly around the patio.

"*What*, Kendall? What was it?"

He pushed back his chair and stood. "Look, we're not doing this here. Wait while I pay my tab and we can go—"

"No!" I grabbed his arm and shot to my feet. "You're not running away from this. Turn around. Goddammit, Kendall, turn around and be a man!"

He yanked his arm away and stepped back. "Jesus! What the hell has gotten into you?"

"What's gotten into me? What's gotten *into me*, Kendall"—my voice dripped with a nasty sarcasm that made me shrill—"is that in the last five minutes I've found out you were having a completely different relationship than I was. What's gotten 'into me' is the realization that most of our relationship was a lie."

"Brook, calm down," he hissed.

"No, I don't think so." The pitch of my voice rose along with my volume. "We're not going to 'calm down' and 'talk about this rationally' this time. Here's a radical idea, Kendall—instead let's be honest for once. Let's actually say things we mean. Oh, and hey— another nutty thought—what if we actually have a real fucking emotion for a change?"

He raised his hands as though I were holding him at gunpoint and started backing away, toward the door to the bar. "You're not rational. You need to calm down and call me when we can talk like adults."

"I *am* talking like an adult. Why don't you *act* like an adult, Kendall, instead of like a recalcitrant child who's afraid of getting in trouble."

"I'm out of here."

But I was too far gone for a retreat. I lunged forward and grabbed an edge of his suit, yanking him back. Some part of me registered that we'd drawn the attention, even through the glass, of everyone at the Bar Belle. But I couldn't stop myself; I was out of control.

"What are you doing? Quit it, Brook." The harder he pulled away, the more I jerked the expensive tropical wool toward me.

"You don't mess with someone's emotions like that. You don't tell them things just to make them feel better. You don't just up and *leave*! You don't say you love someone and then leave them!" I didn't think I was talking just about Kendall anymore.

"Back off! Let go of me!"

Looking back, I think he probably did the only thing he could do in that position to get himself out of my death grasp on his lapels: he set his hands on my chest and pushed me away.

But Kendall was a big man, and strong, and charged up with emotion (for maybe the very first time—or at least, the first time with me).

His hands hit my breasts hard and the push hurt. I stumbled back a step and my heel caught in the brickwork. I felt myself losing my balance, flailed wildly trying to catch it, but plowed backward, my tailbone cracking against the edge of the wrought-iron table as I went down, bringing it tilting over on top of me. Our glasses slid off and over, Kendalltini and gimlet splashing over my chest and lap and the martini glass shattering on the patio beside me. My highball glass landed in my lap.

"Brook! Oh, my God." Kendall started forward.

"Stay away from me!"

The doors behind him crashed open and people swelled out as

if propelled through them. Wet and sticky, I started to scramble furiously to my feet.

"Brook, the glass!" Kendall was still coming, a hand out to help me up.

"Do not touch me!" I was screaming. I reached down to lever myself off the brick and instantly realized what he'd meant as broken glass cut into my palm. I cried out and lifted my hand, glittering with glass and red with blood.

Peter and David were heading over, their faces alarmed, Ricky's face bobbing amid the onlookers, looking at me with a fierce pity. I thought I saw Melissa Overton's smug, gloating face in the crowd that was still swelling outside on the patio, everyone staring at me, but rage and shame were blinding me, blending all the faces together.

"You need a doctor." To Kendall's credit he was still there, still trying to help, but his expression was distant, his tone flat and removed, as if he were a passerby who'd witnessed an accident.

"You need a soul." I couldn't stop my mouth. It was like I'd sprung a toxic leak.

By this time Peter had come to one side of me, David on the other—"You okay, honey?" "Careful now..."—and they were hoisting me up under my armpits.

Kendall threw his hands in the air, washing his hands of me, of us, and turned to go inside. Leaving me there on the patio, sopping, bleeding, humiliated in front of a crowd of mostly strangers.

"That's right. Walk away. That's what you do, isn't it? That's all your infantile little emotions are capable of." I was shouting it after him, a fishwife, a harpy, a Jerry Springer special.

Kendall didn't even slow down.

And because I hadn't hit actual rock bottom yet, I had one last encore, my aria, the big denouement of our scene. The gimlet glass was still clutched in my hand from where I'd picked it off my lap as Peter and David had taken my arms. I jerked out of David's grip on my right and cocked my arm back, let the glass fly with all my strength toward the back of Kendall's head. He started to turn at the collective gasp and a couple of shouts from the erstwhile audience, and I had a satisfying image of it smacking his pretty face.

But my aim was off, and it sailed harmlessly past him, exploding like a bomb against the concrete wall of the bar beside the door.

Kendall flinched, but didn't turn around, just looked back over his shoulder, and even in profile I could see his disgusted expression.

"Jesus, Brook. You're fucking insane. Get some help."

thirty

I sat in my car. My hands trembled—it took three tries to get the key into the ignition. Some part of me registered that I was in no shape to drive, but it was drowned out by the urge to get away, to put as much distance between myself and what had just happened, as soon as possible. I wished I could do the same thing with my life—just drive off, pull away, stare back in the rearview mirror at the pathetic creature I was leaving behind.

But she was still with me when I pulled into my driveway at the house. Still there when I let myself in past the ruined living room, the hateful kitchen, into the barren master bedroom, disinterestedly cleaned and bandaged my hand, and fell into my bed still wearing my clothes. She curled up with me under the covers, and even shutting my eyes I couldn't escape her.

I couldn't sleep for a long time. I lay there, eyes wide and dry and scratchy, straining fruitlessly to hear the ringing of my phone. But it didn't ring. I couldn't think who might call.

In the screaming silence I heard, over and over, the replay in my head of Kendall's words, accompanied by the slide show of my own behavior in the bar. But gradually it all blurred into a white noise of self-hatred, and I drifted off. When I woke up sometime later it was still dark, but I didn't bother looking at the clock beside the bed. I blinked at the ceiling, feeling the crust in my eyes, my lashes caked together with clumped mascara. I hadn't eaten since sometime in the afternoon, but filling my belly didn't seem a compelling enough reason to drag myself from the bed. I was hot, and that did motivate me—but only enough to unbutton my cardigan and pull it out from beneath the covers, then slip out of my skirt and discard it the same way.

I rolled back onto my side and shut my eyes, and waited for oblivion to claim me again.

When I woke the next time, it was light, and it was Gloria Gaynor who called me out of sleep—the "I Will Survive" melody Sasha had programmed in after Kendall's disappearance. I turned over and fumbled my phone out of my purse, not knowing who I was hoping for, just realizing that my heart leaped when I heard it ringing.

"Doll!" My dad always greeted me as if I were the world's best surprise. "You wanna finish up that bathroom today?"

I sank back, deflated. "What time is it?"

"Ah, a little late—almost nine—but a perfect time to get started. Whattaya think?"

"I don't think so, Daddy..."

"Come on, now, sweetheart. Soonest begun, soonest done."

I rubbed my crusty eyes, my fingers coming away with black smears of makeup. "Maybe not today."

"No time like the present. I'm on my way—you eat yet?"

I sat up reluctantly, pushing tangled hair away from my face. It wasn't at all like him to be this insistent. Had something happened? Had he heard something from my mom...something bad? Maybe he needed to talk. I didn't know if I had any rally left in me, but I couldn't let my father down.

"Yeah, Daddy. Okay. Give me a few minutes?" I needed to at least take a shower. It wouldn't do him any good to see me looking like scrambled death.

"I'm gonna treat us to something from Merritt's Bakery. By the time I get through that line on a Saturday morning it'll be at least a half hour, doll. Up and at 'em." Besides having suddenly sprung a cliché leak, my dad had become uncharacteristically dogged and persistent.

We hung up and I sat shaking my head, wondering what on earth could have happened that turned my dad into my mother.

Dad showed up with a bulging bag full of the best baked goods in Fort Myers—chocolate croissants and puffy cream-filled pastries and mini cinnamon rolls so tender and fragrant you could eat half a dozen before you realized it. I tried hard to scarf them with my usual gusto, but just the thought of all that rich butter and sugar made my stomach turn. I pulled apart a cinnamon roll on my plate—it was still steaming inside—and hoped my father wouldn't notice how little made it into my mouth.

I don't know what I was expecting—for him to show up a wreck, dark circles under his eyes, a distant expression, face slack and pale. But he was just the same old Daddy, with that big, happy-to-see-you smile he'd always greeted me with.

Of course, we weren't a confessional kind of family. If he had something on his mind, maybe it would work its way to the surface.

As always, my father was efficient and focused. We screwed the Backerboard to the fresh new wall to ready it for the tile, and then created an efficient assembly line where I buttered the back of each tile with Mastik and he spaced-and-placed them against the wall.

ICAN had had boxes and boxes of leftover tiles, and I had chosen a six-inch earthy slate-look porcelain, along with bronze and gold glass accent tiles I could never have afforded anywhere else. As we laid tile after tile in place, for the first time my house actually started to resemble the elegant vision Sasha and I had invoked the day I'd bought it. I wished she could see it.

I thought he might start talking as we worked, within the safe remove of concentrating on a project, instead of having to face me. But Daddy stayed mum, our conversation limited to instructions and requests strictly about the job at hand. So after a while, with the only sounds the soft scrape of my trowel against porcelain, I filled in the silences, hoping that if I opened the conversational floodgates, whatever was on his mind would come pouring out. Hoping it would drown out the ocean of shame and regret I was floundering in.

I asked about his cabinets. I asked about fishing. I asked about other projects he was working on. I didn't realize until I was trying to draw my dad out, instead of spouting my usual stream of free association about my own life that I so easily slipped into with him, how little I actually knew of him.

The cabinets, he said, were coming along. Of course, they had been "coming along" for nearly a year now, so that could mean anything from total disarray to close to finished. He hadn't been fishing lately—he didn't hear much from Stu in the past couple of weeks.

Yeah. No wonder. Stu had had his hands full of Sasha, I thought with a sharp flash of hurt.

His next project would be countertops. He got the idea when we were at ICAN, looking at their slabs of beautiful granite. "Can't have such pretty new cabinets and put that awful old stuff back in for your mom," Dad said.

I wanted to snap out my knee-jerk retort that my mom didn't deserve his effort, his consideration. I wanted to ask him why he was being such a patsy for her. I wanted to shake some spine into him, some self-worth, enough ego so that he stopped lying down and waiting patiently for her to grace him once again with her presence, and instead realize he deserved better, confront her, demand she get her act together or she would lose him.

Instead, I bit back all my venom and focused on what Dad needed. He loved my mom, and for whatever reason he was letting her steer the course of his life. If I attacked her again he'd only get defensive of her, as he did every time.

It was time to come clean with my father. If he thought he was helping me with a problem, in the process, my smart, wonderful, loving dad would have to see the parallels to his own life and come to his own realizations about how he was being treated.

"Dad…" I handed him a tile and reached for another as he laid it carefully into place. "I could use some advice."

He glanced over, his fingertips pressed gently to the tile, holding it steady. "Of course, doll. What about?"

And, haltingly, through my own shame, I told him about what I had done last night—how I had confronted Kendall, how I'd thought for just a few minutes that everything was going to be all right, and how I'd humiliated myself when I realized that it wasn't. My dad didn't watch me while I spoke—and I was grateful. Just as I'd done when I was younger, I talked to his back and shoulders and the back of his head, his reassuringly capable, constant motions calming my soul and loosening my tongue.

When I finished my story I stopped talking, and we worked for a few minutes in a quiet that felt soothing rather than awkward. I'd told my dad about my behavior as a way to help him find some relief from *his* pain, but in the process I'd lightened something in my own chest.

"Ah, doll," he said finally, carefully taping down a completed row of tiles to keep them from sliding out of place as the Mastik dried. "It's amazing the awful things you can do that you don't think you're capable of doing to someone you love."

I didn't know if he meant me or Kendall. "Can you forgive them?" I asked my dad. And I wasn't sure if I was asking whether I could forgive Kendall, or whether Kendall could ever forgive me. Or whether it was even Kendall I was talking about at all.

I'd gotten sidetracked with my own problems, and I'd forgotten I was trying to guide my dad onto a path. I pushed my thoughts back to my mother. "When someone does something...awful like that...even though they love you...when they've crossed a certain line, can that be forgiven?" Dad didn't speak for a moment, and I hoped he was considering the question for himself. I buttered the back of another tile. "And should it be? It seems to me that if you love someone, it means *not* doing something on purpose to hurt them. It means thinking things through before you do or say things you can't take back. That's what love is." I handed my dad the tile. "Isn't it?"

Dad fixed the tile to the top of the next row, square and perfect. He tapped it to remove air bubbles underneath, and he didn't look back at me. I waited.

Finally he spoke. "I'm gonna tell you something, Brook Lyn." Dad never used my whole name. "And then we aren't ever going to discuss it again. This isn't something anyone else knows, except your mother, and if I share it with you, I'm asking you not to share it with anyone else—ever. Not your brother. Not Sasha. And not your mother. If she ever finds out I'm telling you this, I would have a hard time forgiving you for that. Can you agree to this?"

His tone had gone flat and dead serious, and all I could do was nod, the sudden dread burgeoning in my gut swallowing any words. But my father was looking directly at me now, not working, and one look at his expression told me he needed something more formal and binding than a nod. I swallowed hard and mustered, "Okay, Dad. I promise."

He bobbed his head once, sharply, as if making a resolve. "All right. All right, then." He carefully placed the small rubber mallet he was holding on the side of the tub and then stared down at it as if it held the secrets of life. His lips stayed closed, but they moved as if he were tasting something bitter, something unpleasant he was too polite to spit out.

And then his words came out short and sharp and clear and impossible to misunderstand: "I had an affair."

Of all the things I had expected my father to tell me, that was nowhere on the list. Not my father, who loved my mother so much that sometimes, growing up, Stu and I had felt jealous, left out of their circle of two.

"N-no..." I stammered nonsensically. "No, you didn't."

"Stop it, Brook Lyn. Some things are true whether you want them to be or not." His tone shut me up, and he looked down at his hands, as if their idleness were a mystery to him.

"It was a long time ago. You were so young... Stu was just a baby. Your mother... Your mother was—she is—the best mother in the world, whether you see that or not. Everything she does, she does for you kids. And at the time..." He choked on a breath. "At the time I didn't understand that. I wanted back that part of her I had when we met... But that energy went into you kids, and I..."

My father lifted his head and wiped his face, though his cheeks were dry. "I don't need to go into that with you. Who it was and how it happened doesn't matter—it didn't matter then, either. It was stupid—the stupidest thing I ever did. I almost lost your mom over it. But I didn't. She forgave me—finally. It took a long time, but your mother tried to understand, and she forgave me, and she stayed with me. She didn't leave."

He looked at me for the first time since he'd started his terrible story. "I don't know what's going on with your mother right now. I don't know...what she needs, I guess. But I'll be waiting for her to figure out what that is. I'm not going anywhere, and if she decides, after she figures things out, that I'm what she wants...I'll be right here. No matter what. Because I love her. Because I will always love her. You understand what I'm telling you?"

I felt inexplicably angry. Angry at my dad for being no better than any other man. Angry at my mom for leaving so long after she'd forgiven his transgression. Angry at Kendall, who bailed out not at the first sign of trouble, but without *any* sign of trouble. Angry at the world because nothing and no one was as it seemed, and you could never fully trust anyone, and in the end maybe love didn't mean much after all.

"It's not fair," was what tumbled out of my mouth.

My father put his hand on mine, just for a moment, before leaning down to pick up another tile and handing it to me. "Whoever promised life was fair, doll?"

We worked the rest of the job without speaking any more of what my father had said. I wasn't sure of *his* reasons—whether he was sorry to have confessed, or didn't want to talk about it further, or that he'd simply said all he intended to say on the subject. I only knew my own—that I needed to process it, to figure out what it meant, whether it changed my family or my history or my relationship with my dad—or my mom.

By the time he left the bathroom tile was in place, and even without grout it looked polished and beautiful and elegant—but it didn't matter to me anymore. I saw my father out the door and stripped off my stained work clothes and showered, and then tumbled into bed before seven o'clock without even walking back into the bathroom to admire the results of all our hard work.

I lay there for a long time, just thinking—about my dad, what he'd told me. How it must have felt to my mom when she found out what he'd done. How lost and betrayed and hurt she must have been...and, with two small kids at home and no job to support them, how helpless and scared. I thought about how that might shape a person.

And I thought about Michael. For the first time since the last time I'd seen him—when I'd gathered up all the notebooks and clippings and ads I'd brought over to talk about the wedding and let myself out of his apartment, saying, "So I'll meet you at the bakery at four for the tasting—please don't be late this time"—I let myself think about the man I'd loved so much it actually ached in my chest. The man who'd left me just a few short weeks before our wedding.

If we knew that the last time we'd see someone was the last time, it would change everything—the way we looked at them, took them in, made a connection. We wouldn't be so blithely caught up in our own problems and concerns and stupid to-do lists that we'd miss making eye contact, sharing a smile. That we'd overlook the fact that they might be having problems and concerns of their own—life-shaking ones—that could affect the path you thought you had charted together.

That was what happened to me and Michael, I guess. We had dated for two years, and I'd never known anything like it. I literally could not get enough of him when I was with him—I wanted to touch him, be next to him, be reassured that yes, this tall, good-looking, talented, smart, funny man had chosen *me*, wanted to be with *me*. And yet I battled those insecure impulses, and was so proud that I managed to keep my independence, that I didn't get clingy, or even let him realize how desperately I wanted to, how heavily my fear of losing him pressed in on me.

Whenever he walked into my apartment after work and bee-lined over to me, as if I were the thing he'd been looking forward to all day, I reveled in it. Every time *he* initiated the contact I had been holding myself back from making—a touch, a caress, sometimes taking my hand—it felt like a personal victory. I wasn't needy. I wasn't a pathetic, clingy woman who defined herself through a man. I was holding on to my*self*, in the healthy way I advised all my patients—and tried to tell Sasha.

When Michael and I made love was the only time I could let all my craving, my passion for him loose. I wanted to touch every inch of him, drink in his smell—there wasn't one thing on his body that I found distasteful or unappealing. I consumed him with my hands, my mouth, able only in bed to let myself touch him and hold him and run my hands over every millimeter of his skin, under the safe umbrella of sex. He was my drug. When we were apart for long, or I hadn't heard from him, I felt an actual pain in my chest, my heart fluttering like a trapped bird with the fear that all of it could dis-solve in an instant. Even after we got engaged, that breathtaking fear remained. I was terrified that it could all go wrong, that I could lose everything.

But I never let on. I was *not* Sasha—I wouldn't let my self-worth be that tied in with whether the man in my life stuck around. Or at least, I wouldn't show it.

When Michael actually did walk out of my life...nothing hap-pened. I didn't fall apart the way I'd been terrified I would. He called just before the cake tasting I'd scheduled, and said, "Brook, I'm sorry—I can't do this."

He'd left almost all the wedding planning to me, and I was overwhelmed. That was my explanation for why, instead of asking him what was wrong, being concerned about his feelings, I snapped out, "Oh, for god's sake, Michael—it's cake. Surely you can do cake, at least?"

There was a long silence that filled me with nothing but impatience at the time. And then he'd said in a fractured voice, "No, not the cake. All of it. Any of it. I can't go through with this."

A fist had squeezed my heart as I realized what he meant, but all I said, my tone wooden, was, "Okay. That's fine." And I hung up.

I went on to the tasting as though nothing had happened. A few days later I went and got my few things from his apartment, and left my key on the kitchen counter. We didn't talk it out, or try to work on things. Michael left Fort Myers not long after that, and I never asked him why he'd changed his mind. I told myself it didn't matter.

But it did matter. Maybe it was just a radar blip—momentary cold feet. Maybe we could have worked things out. At least if I'd asked why, I might have been able to work past my pain and let it go. It wouldn't have undone what had happened, might not have saved me and Michael. But it would have let me *feel*, and that was the part I'd simply skipped over.

Kendall's disappearance was the chink in the dam that held back everything I'd pushed down since then. All the crazy that had washed out behind it...some of it was for Kendall, but a lot of it was for Michael.

Tears welled in my eyes at that realization, and I just let them run down my temples and into my pillow. I lay there for a long time like that, and when I finally felt myself beginning to drift off, my face was still wet.

Sleep is a palliative unmatched by anything in medical science, and mine was thick and dreamless. I slept nearly eleven hours and woke up early, and I knew, clear as the day dawning outside my window, what I had to do next.

After I'd confronted Kendall Friday night, looking for the answers I needed, he had sat opposite me and looked into my face and told me he was sorry. It was everything I had needed to hear, and it had started to heal the angry wound left when he'd walked out on me.

But in the end it wasn't enough for me, and the moment I'd realized that was when I'd snapped.

If you screwed up and hurt someone you genuinely, deeply loved, you did everything in your power to make it right again, the way my dad had tried for who knew how long to gain my mother's forgiveness and, with his constant, steady love, to regain her trust.

I had made plenty of mistakes of my own. Love wasn't always enough to keep you from making bad choices, from messing things up...from being human. But with the people who mattered most to you, if it was important, you fixed it—or did everything in your power to try. You had to get back on your horse and cowgirl up.

I waited out the early-morning hours until the sounds of lawn mowers and passing cars and playing children told me most of the world was awake. And then I got in my car and headed over to try to make things right again, if I could, with the one person who mattered to me more than anyone.

thirty-one

My heart was pounding as I levered my elbow awkwardly over the doorbell and pressed until I heard it chiming inside. It felt jarring to ring the doorbell like a visitor, and even more disconcerting to be breathless with nerves standing outside a threshold I'd crossed with complete confidence in my welcome hundreds of times before.

Sasha opened the door with dark smudges under her eyes and a sheet crease across one cheek, and I almost felt the urge to smile: It was the first time I'd ever seen her looking as haphazard as the rest of the world when she woke up.

I had carrot cake from Merritt's Bakery in a plastic container in one hand—her favorite, that she rarely let herself eat—and a cup of hot chai tea in the other. As peace offerings went they were meager, but I hadn't bought them just to soften my friend toward me. I also wanted something in my hands.

"I didn't know if this was a good time to talk," I said uncertainly when she didn't offer any kind of greeting. "But if it isn't or if you aren't alone..." I swallowed hard and made myself go on. "If Stu's here and you don't want to talk in front of him, I'll come back later. Anytime you say." Her expression remained utterly blank, but she wasn't closing the door in my face, so I plowed ahead, wanting to get out whatever I could before she stopped me.

"Sasha, I'm sorry. I know I said that before, but I should've been standing here last week saying it right after you dropped me off. I should have been here saying it a hundred times since. I should have never let you pull out of my driveway without telling it to your face. I said stupid things that aren't true because I was... I was ashamed of myself, and angry, and hurt, and I took it out on the one person...the only person who's never let me down or given me any reason—ever—to doubt you or your intentions. I've said a *lot* of stupid things to you over the years, because it made me feel like I had my life together if I treated you like yours was always falling apart. I am so sorry, and I will do anything I have to do—for however long it takes—to make things right between us again. To earn your trust back, and to...to deserve you."

She was still standing in the open doorway, just staring at me in a disconcertingly penetrating way that made me squirm. But I was literally at her disposal. I would stand there until she slammed the door, or told me to get the hell out of her life, or slapped me, or whatever she chose to do.

Which ended up being none of the things I'd braced myself for.

"How the hell are we supposed to hug this out with all that crap in your hands, you idiot?" Sasha reached over and plucked the cake and cup from me, set them on the ground, and wrapped her arms around me. I held on to her so tightly I knew it had to be hard for her to breathe, but I couldn't make myself ease up, and Sasha didn't ask me to.

Sitting on Sasha's living room floor, sharing the carrot cake with her right from the container, I told her everything about Kendall, from his asking me to move in with him to how I'd been behaving since he broke up with me. I even took off my shirt and lifted the bandage on my tattoo to show it to her.

To Sasha's credit, she tried hard to keep her expression neutral as she gazed upon the well-endowed donkey, but finally it was too much for her, and she dissolved into helpless laughter that soon had tears running down her face. It was strange—instead of the fresh wave of shame I'd braced for, or hostile defensiveness at her amusement, confessing my awful behavior to Sasha let me start to see the wonderfully silly ridiculousness of it—just a little—and my laughter joined hers. For the first time in weeks, I felt better.

I had a lot more penance I wanted to do for how I'd treated her, but Sasha kept waving off my apologies.

"You've punished yourself enough," she said between a bout of giggles. "Forgiven."

"No, I need to tell you this, Sash—I treat you like you can't handle your own relationships without me, like I'm some kind of guru about it."

"That's because I *can't* handle my own relationships, you moron. I know I act like a crazy person. I fall apart. And I don't *want* to get through them without you, Brook, because you *help*."

I gaped at her. "How can you still say that? Look at me—I've committed every breakup screw-up there is."

Sasha shrugged, finally swallowing a hunk of cake I'd worried would choke her. "Who cares? You're through it now. That's what matters."

"I didn't want to go *through* it. I just wanted to get *past* it."

"Honey, I think the only way past it *is* through it."

"Sasha, I humiliated myself."

Her fork lay limp in her hand for a moment while she looked at me, her eyebrows drawn together. "Really? That's how you see what happened?"

I gave a dry laugh. "Seriously? You see some other spin?"

Sasha put her fork down—I thought at first so she could give me her full attention, but it was only so she could pick up the now empty plastic container and use her finger to swipe up the cream-cheese icing stuck to the side.

"Well—and this is only from my perspective, you understand—but it seems to me like you just finally handled a breakup like a normal person. You loved someone; he rejected you; you wanted that love back. So you got a little emotional about it—big whoop. Looks like you're just a human, not a perfect machine. Like every other human in the entire world throughout history. Upward, onward, bam, end of story."

She was still concentrating hard on cleaning out the plastic container, though there was little left but PVC coating. I made a note in the back of my mind to treat Sasha to more dessert—she was clearly deprived.

My best friend—the one I had always regarded as an emotional train wreck where relationships were concerned—had just casually spouted out more Zen wisdom than anything I'd ever achieved in years of therapy with a patient. How had I never seen that her craziness after a breakup was her way of venting her feelings instead of bottling them up till they blew? How had I never understood until this moment that Sasha was the healthy one emotionally, and I was the one repressing and denying any human emotion that didn't fit within my strict parameters for acceptable behavior? She'd had it all figured out all along. Sasha was freaking Rain Man.

"That's...that's just genius," I said slowly. "Six years of schooling, years of therapy practice, and now an advice column, and I still didn't know what you've just instinctively known all along."

"Oh, no, no, no, missy." Sasha finally finished with the plastic and tossed it to the floor before she started chewing it like a rawhide as I'd feared. "This does not get to be yet another reason to beat yourself up. Let's not forget that my brilliant coping devices include breaking and entering, destruction of property, and the occasional minor felony." She shrugged. "I'm a mess sometimes, Brook. I know that. I'm just okay with it. I have you—my sane voice of reason when I need one. That's the only reason I get through stuff. And it's most of the reason I have anything constructive to tell you right now." She laughed. "And you know when *everyone* gives great breakup advice? When they're not in the middle of one—which I, for once, am not."

And then there we were, staring right in the face of my best friend and my brother and their new relationship I had no idea how to handle.

But thinking I'd lost Sasha had made me look at *our* relationship a lot closer, and see where I'd tried to jam her into the mold I'd created: where I wanted her to act the way I wanted her to, the way I decided was best. Instead of letting her be who she was, and loving her for exactly that. The way she always—*always*—loved me.

I took a deep, fortifying breath, looked my best friend right in her beautiful aqua eyes, and said, "Tell me about you and Stu. I'd love to hear."

thirty-two

I left Sasha's around four o'clock that afternoon with a heart lighter than it had been in weeks, a head full of complicated emotions about her and Stu, and in my purse, a compact disc containing the interview she'd conducted with my mother.

"Just listen," she told me, pressing it into my hand when I'd finally left. "It's interesting."

At home I wandered into the guest bathroom and looked again at the gleaming tile that Dad and I had put in. I hadn't talked to my dad since his revelation to me. I didn't know what he was feeling—was he sorry he'd told me, worried how I was taking it, remorseful that he'd betrayed my mom—once by cheating on her, and again my confessing it to me? I needed to call him, to tell him how I felt—except I didn't know yet. In the space of a few hours my entire idea of my father had changed, the whole dynamic of my family I always thought I understood, and I didn't know what to do with that.

It was still early, so I hauled all the supplies my dad and I had bought inside from the garage and started working, mixing up a bucket of grout to finish off the bathroom tub. I carried in my laptop, too, and even set the CD into it to listen while I worked, but in the end I never pushed play, and I finished the job to only the scraping sounds of my trowel and the gentle drip of water from my sponge.

On Monday morning I wrote my column, and this time it flowed like floodwater:

What happens if, despite all your efforts, your determination, your calm, rational thoughts in the light of day, you still just can't handle your bad breakup?

No matter how much we wish relationships could be broken down like scientific formulae, separated into their constituent parts that always react in predictable ways, they aren't, and they don't. Because they're between human beings, and we are all messy and illogical and flawed.

Rejection touches a nerve so deep and primordial, sometimes we can't stop ourselves from acting instinctively—for our survival. From our earliest societies, if your tribe rejected you—and ejected you—you were literally, utterly vulnerable to destruction: from starvation, from exposure, from saber-toothed tigers and bears. As children, we knew that without our parents' love and care, we would die. Somewhere inside, we are still hard-wired to panic at rejection, to desperately cling to the people who love us. Our atavistic instincts make us fight to hold on to the safety and protection of love.

It's hard to override instincts. The logical human mind is a wondrous and powerful thing, but it's got nothing on ingrained unconscious drives.

So despite knowing better, you find yourself standing out in front of your ex's house in the rain, staring into the windows and contemplating breaking in. You write the sappy letters; you make the ill-advised late-night drunken phone calls; you cry and scream and throw things and behave in ways you never—not once in your whole rational life—would have predicted yourself doing.

This may hurt, and it may be frightening, and you may not think you can live through the welter of pain and fear that has overcome your usual rational mind. But you can, and you will. This too, truly, will pass.

And in the meantime, if you are overwhelmed by your basic instincts, if you fight too hard and too fiercely to hold on to the love you think you will die without, if you make stupid, embarrassing mistakes—in other words, if you are human—forgive yourself: over and over and over again.

You messed up. You will probably mess up again. We can't help it—that's what we do. Don't let those occasional lapses into irrational behavior define you or become who you are. Stand up, dust off, get back on your horse and ride.

Remember that romantic love—wonderful, intense, life-altering though it can be—isn't the sum total of the love in your life. Your romantic partner isn't your entire "tribe"; he or she isn't the sole source of the acceptance and support that we all—to a person, without exception—need. Find all the rich veins of love running through your life and mine them: Family. Friends. Pets.

No, it isn't the same. In the first swamping wave of rejection it won't even feel like remotely enough. But it is there even when the person you think you can't live without decides not *to be there anymore. You are* not *alone. In the wise words of Gloria Gaynor, you will survive.*

Forgive yourself. Forgive the people you love—even the one who rejected you, because they are human too, and dealing with their own insecurities and pain and mistakes.

Then take a breath, calm down, and cowgirl— or -boy—up.

My dad was right about the bathroom—finishing just the one little thing made a huge difference in how I saw the whole house. It had been so easy just to ignore the work it needed when I could escape to Kendall's perfect condo every night. Now that I was literally faced with it every day, I had to deal with it. And suddenly, looking at how much we'd improved just that one little area, I *wanted* to. The vision in my head the night Sasha and I sat on my living room floor after my closing, dreaming of how we could make the house look—the one I'd carried with me until all the hidden little issues it had overwhelmed me and made me give up on ever making it into what I hoped—began to bloom in my mind again.

The Breakup Doctor was getting me—little by little, but finally close enough for me to get excited—back to my regular practice. I could be up and running within a couple of weeks, if I worked hard enough.

But regardless of how reluctant I might have been to tear myself away from what I wanted to be doing—working on the house—to what I needed to do—my new clients—the moment I sat down with anyone, everything else fell away and I was completely, totally involved in their problems.

Bristol MacGuire was currently in the on-again portion of the back-and-forth cycle she and her boyfriend James had perpetuated for years. "But I don't know...the last few times it hasn't been like I thought it would when we get back together," she told me over coffee at the Sunrise Café off Cypress. "It doesn't feel...healthy."

"That's because it's not, and you've been trying to tell yourself that for years every time you break up with him," I told her after listening to her entire story. "It's scary to be alone. You won't be forever—but you might be for a while. Do you have the courage to trust your instincts that are telling you that you want something better, someone different? Can you believe in yourself enough to make it through the hard part of ending it once and for all?"

She swore she wanted to try. I left her with my card, instructions to call me when her resolve faltered—no matter the time—and a bright, hopeful expression on her face that had erased the beaten one she'd shown up with.

I sneaked back to the house between all my appointments to get in as much work as I could—even if it was just painting a single wall with one of the random gallons of paint I'd bought half-price from the "oops" rack at Home Depot, along with a package of the cheapest brushes I could buy. ("They're only really good for one job," the paint clerk had warned me disapprovingly. "That's okay," I told him. "So am I.") Then I would head out again to meet with whoever was next in my calendar.

Frank Farqu—unfortunate name—fidgeted and squirmed as we talked about his ex-girlfriend Carole. Finally, after creative probing on my part, I got the whole story out of him—she'd broken up with him two months earlier, but he couldn't stand to let her go. He called her at all hours of the day and night, left notes on her car at her work, sent flowers every week, and was even in the process of closing on a house in her neighborhood—across the street from hers. "But I got it at foreclosure—really cheap," he assured me, as though that explained everything.

"Frank," I said gently, "you're stalking her." This time the memory of my own behavior brought up a flare of empathy, rather than shame.

He looked horrified. "No! It's not like that! I would never do anything to hurt her—I love her!"

There followed a careful discourse by me on the difference between dating and stalking (one was mutual, and the other was criminal). I managed to convince him not to close on the house—and I gave him the name of my friend Monique, a real estate attorney who could help him get out of the contract—but realized that Frank needed more intensive care than a brief Breakup Doctor consult could provide. We set up weekly appointments, with regular consults in the meantime, as I didn't think Frank should be left to his own devices that long. And I managed to extract a promise from him that he would leave Carole completely alone for twenty-four hours, when he and I would meet again. Baby steps.

Finally, when I found a block of time one evening to get one entire room painted—my future office—I set up my ladder, opened and stirred the can of paint—"Elysian Fields," a mossy green—then brought in my laptop and pressed play.

thirty-three

I heard the clearing of a throat, and then, "Okay," came Sasha's voice. "So let's start with just making sure I have your name spelled correctly. Is it –I-A-N or –I-E-N-N-E?"

That startled a laugh out of me at the same time I heard one from my mother. I'd thought Sasha knew.

"Oh, honey, neither. Vivien's just a nickname."

"It is? For what?"

"Ruth Edna."

I knew this story—the clunky, unmusical name she hated, legacy from each of her grandmothers. "You don't look like a Ruth Edna," my father told her when he met her, and he rechristened her Vivien because he said she reminded him of Vivien Leigh.

She didn't look like Vivien Leigh, either. Not at all. But my dad met her playing Leigh's most famous role—or at least a facsimile of it—and for all his other wonderful qualities, he was not a man of vast imagination.

As I stroked on the first line of paint along the top of the wall where it met the ceiling, I listened to Mom tell Sasha the story, and Sasha's delighted laughter. "It's perfect for you. It suits you much better than Ruth Edna."

"But history will out," my mom said. "Better print the real one."

There was a strange intimacy in listening to my mother talking like this, her voice devoid of the careful tones she used when talking to me. As if I were eavesdropping on her in a private moment.

"So this role..." Sasha prompted her.

"Eleanor. The queen."

"Yes. Katharine Hepburn played it first, didn't she?"

"Not first. But most famously, yes."

"Right...sorry." I heard a whisking sound, and pictured Sasha slashing through something in her notes.

"The first Eleanor on Broadway was the British actress Rosemary Harris, in 1966. You'd probably only know her from those *Spider-Man* movies—she played Peter Parker's aunt. Her Eleanor was opposite Robert Preston, an old Western actor. Did you ever see the film *The Music Man*?"

"No, ma'am."

"Mmmm. Well, it's a good one. That's probably his most famous role—Harold Hill. Rent it sometime."

"Okay, I will." I rolled my eyes, but Sasha sounded earnest.

"And in that same Broadway production there was an up-and-coming actor who played Philip, king of France. His name was Christopher Walken. I'm guessing you know him?"

I could tell my mom was teasing her now from Sasha's laugh.

"Yes, ma'am. Him I know."

"Well. It's not the history of the show you came to talk about. Why don't you ask the questions now."

"Okay." Another pause, and I heard the shuffling of some papers. I'd watched Sasha do interviews before, and been amazed by her technique: She charmed the socks off her subjects and got them talking, and pretty soon they were telling her things they'd probably never told their closest friends. This hesitant, rudderless interview wasn't her style, and I could tell it was making her nervous to talk to my mother like this, one on one.

Another throat clearing. "Okay. So...um...how about we start with how you got this role? I've heard every actress in town was vying for it."

"Oh, I don't know about that."

"Well, I talked to your director, Howard Rollins, and he said competition was pretty fierce."

"You talked to Howard?" My mom sounded surprised.

"Yes. And a couple of your costars. And your stage manager, Connie."

"You're a good girl, Sasha. Very thorough."

"Thanks, Mrs. O." She sounded so happy. How did I not realize how badly Sasha needed mothering, how much she had always craved it from my mom as much as I had tried to get out from under it?

"Well, the auditions were quite busy," my mom conceded. "I will say that."

"There were"—papers shuffled again—"eighty-one women who auditioned."

A silence; my mom made no reply.

"Howard Rollins—your director—said"—more flipping through her notes—"'I knew a number of local actresses who were well equipped to play this role, or I wouldn't have selected this particular play. But only Viv Ogden was born to play it.'"

"He's being hyperbolic." But the raw pleasure in my mother's tone was clear. I finished the first section of cutting in and stepped down to move the ladder. It wasn't a bad color—a soft, cool green. Soothing actually—probably why it was so often used in prisons.

"Did you know Rollins before this play?"

"*Of* him, certainly. Most of my favorite productions have been directed by him. I do follow the local theater scene fairly closely."

She did? I'd never heard her mention it once until the Mom Bomb.

"Tell me a little bit about your previous acting career."

Career. Please. The mechanical precision required to cut an even line along the ceiling demanded all of my focus, but not all of my attention.

I knew these stories, and I tuned partway out as my brush deposited paint along the wall. My mother's litany of her past theatrical triumphs formed a droning backdrop to the repetitive dip-wipe-stroke of the painting.

A green tongue of paint lapped over onto the ceiling in a sloppy stroke and I stepped down off the ladder and out to the garage for a rag. I didn't bother shutting off the recorder as I left, and by the time I'd gotten back into the room, the rag dampened at the kitchen sink, and started scrubbing the errant strip of paint, my mother was still reciting.

"...That was the role that won me 'Best Local Actress' by the *Tropic Times* for the first time—out of three years running. And the year I was offered a partial scholarship to school."

"Wow, I never knew that," Sasha bubbled. "What school?"

"Juilliard."

The one-word answer snapped my head around from cleaning my mess as if my mother were in the room. Juilliard? My mom had gone to Juilliard?

"Are you fucking kidding me?" Sasha's response echoed my own thoughts. "You went to Juilliard? Jesus, Mrs. O!" In her excitement she forgot that it was never, ever okay to curse around my mother.

But for the first time in my life, my mom didn't correct the language with a rebuke sharp as a slap. "I did not."

There was a lengthy silence, and I tried to picture what they were doing. I wished the interview were videotaped so I could see the expression on my mother's face.

"Why?" Sasha's voice was hesitant—my mother's tone was meant to put an end to the conversation. But even Sasha's obsequiousness around my mother was no match for her journalist's instinct for where the story was. "Why didn't you go if you had a scholarship?"

For a long moment my mother didn't answer, and I began to think she would simply stubbornly wait Sasha out—sit there in silence until my best friend went on to a new line of questioning. But then she spoke.

"A *partial* scholarship. I didn't have enough money for the rest of my tuition."

"But weren't your parents—"

"They did not support a career in the arts." My mother's staccato reply cut Sasha off, and there was another long silence. I felt for Sash—I could picture her sitting there, brimming with follow-up questions, biting them back because of my mother's rigid response. I waited, slumped against a rung of the ladder, the towel limp in my hands, for her to start a new line of questioning.

Instead I heard a rustling, as though something or someone were moving. "I'm so sorry, Mrs. O. That really sucks."

"Sasha...is there a need for the language?" My mother was obviously recovering herself.

"You know what?" Sasha's tone was righteous. "Sometimes there totally fucking is."

The laugh that burst out of my mother was like none I'd ever heard from her. Loose, loud, a guffaw almost. My mother did not guffaw.

Sasha's giggle echoed it, and I felt a quick spark of resentment all over again. She was sharing the kind of moment with my mom I'd never been offered. Seeing a side of her my mother had never— *would* never—show me.

I dropped the towel and picked up my brush again to resume painting. Dip, wipe, stroke.

Maybe she couldn't.

The interview had picked back up, that momentary lapse behind Sasha and my mom as they carried on with their question-and-answer session. All business again.

I thought about what my dad had told me, and tried to imagine my mother's face when she'd found out my father had betrayed her.

My mother was the engine of our family. My dad was a wonderful dreamer, happy noodling idly with his woodworking and his newspaper and his projects—happy amid his family.But it was my mom who guarded the budget and wiped the noses and drew the boundaries and then enforced them so that everything worked as it should. So we grew up with structure.

Maybe my mom got so used to fulfilling that role, she didn't know how to do what my dad did—to just relax and be herself.

Maybe she was afraid that if she let go of her firm hold of the reins, no one would be guiding the wagon.

Instead of replacing me in my mother's affections, the way I'd always felt...maybe Sasha just gave my mom what she needed—the chance to let down her guard and be herself with someone she didn't feel wholly, all-encompassingly responsible for.

I let the CD play out as I finished cutting in the room and then started rolling the paint onto the walls, listening only sporadically to their talk about the play amid the cacophony of thoughts teeming in my head.

That night I called my father.

He asked how things were going with me, and I knew he knew about Stu and Sasha. Of course—how had I not seen that before? The family grapevine.

We didn't talk about what he had told me that day in my guest bathroom, and I understood then that we never would again. I still wasn't sure exactly what I felt about the whole thing. But it didn't matter. My dad was still my dad.

I told him what I'd done in the house since he'd been over, and what I still needed to do, and I asked for his help, and for the rest of the week my dad spent his days at my house, working. I came home in every spare second between Breakup Doctor appointments to do whatever I could. Together we laid down the wood flooring I'd bought at ICAN, one plank at a time. We built a simple doorframe at the entrance to the back hallway and hung a door, shutting off the office space from my living space. I moved in the furniture I'd bought secondhand, and within a week and a half we were finished and I realized we had done it—I had my practice.

That night I called Sasha and asked her to come over. We stood in the back hallway, where we could see into both guest rooms and the bathroom, glasses of wine in our hands and the door to the rest of my house shut. She'd sat and dreamed with me of what my house could one day look like, and even though only a small part of it was finished, I wanted to share with her the beginnings of that vision.

"It's perfect," she said, looking at my waiting room with its cranberry walls and plush beige love seat and two sturdy chairs and secondhand end table with a fresh bunch of hibiscus flowers in a bowl on top of it.

We turned together to take in my office: a serviceable wood desk I'd found at a used-office-supply store, a plain rolling chair from Office Depot behind it, and a simple, clean leather sofa I'd found at a consignment store, its deep brown almost elegant against the Elysian Fields-green walls.

When I opened the door to the bathroom with all the fanfare of a circus barker, she gasped. Dad and I had realized we'd had enough leftover tile to do the counter as well, and I'd edged it in the same glass tiles that bordered the tub. With plush new towels—my one splurge—and some scented soaps and lotions, the bathroom looked almost like a magazine picture.

Sasha shook her head, amazed. "Brookie, you did it."

"Oh, there's still a ton to be done. Most of the house, actually. But at least I'm ready to start my practice back up. Finally."

Sasha took a sip of her wine, running her hand along the smooth glass tiles along the counter's overhang. "What do you mean? You already have a practice."

She walked back out of the bathroom and toward the waiting room to look closer at the rest of the renovations, while I stood rooted to the spot as if pole-axed.

She was right. I'd started up my practice weeks ago, the first day I'd met with Lisa Albrecht to talk about her breakup with her husband. I'd been running it ever since, right up to as recently as an hour ago, when I'd hung up with a giddy Duncan O'Neill, who'd taken my questions and had a long talk with his husband, and found out Wagner was horrified at the idea that Duncan thought he'd sleep with women.

"He only likes to *flirt* with them!" he'd crowed into the phone. "I think it makes him feel universally attractive—you know, not *just* to men. He'd never admit that, of course. But he was appalled at the idea of having sex with a woman. Appalled!" He sounded so happy I didn't trouble myself figuring out how their unusual dynamic worked for them as a couple, or why. It was enough that it did. And it felt great to help Duncan figure things out.

I leaned back against my freshly tiled counter, staring at the bathroom without seeing it. I'd been so caught up in defining my career a certain way, I'd completely overlooked that I was already doing what I was best at—helping people get through the hard parts of life.

Sasha wandered back in from her tour with a sigh. "I love it. Now I have to buy a house, too, you bitch."

I laughed and pushed myself away from the counter, picking up my wine from where I'd set it down. "I know where there's a nice one coming on the market, cheap," I said, thinking of Frank Farqu as I took her arm and we walked into the rest of my house together.

thirty-four

One week later on a Saturday night, I found myself standing exactly where I never thought I would be: in the lobby of the Neapolitan Theater, a bouquet of fresh purple irises in my arms, as I waited with Sasha and Stu—who were holding hands in a way that I hoped would eventually look less incongruous to me—for my mother to come out from backstage after her show.

Sasha's article about her had run this morning, timed to coincide with opening night, and I'd read it not knowing what to expect.

It was excellent—Sasha's writing always was. But she had done a particularly insightful job with my mom. It wasn't the sycophantic love-fest I'd half feared it might be, but a thoughtful, realistic portrait of a complex woman—practical and creative, an artist and a wife and mother. My mom had talked about our family a little—not much; she was private by nature, but with a gentle, proprietary pride. Even about my dad.

I looked over to where he stood by a pilaster, his plastic stem glass of wine forgotten on a table at his elbow and a spray of white lilies in his hand. They were her favorites.

I'd expected my father to look awkward in his suit, uncomfortable, fidgeting with the tie around his neck as though it were a too-tight leash. But he wore it like Cary Grant, the suit jacket filling out his chest and shoulders in a way that made him seem bigger, more solid. "Tall, slender men wear clothes better than anyone else," my mom had always said, and looking at my dad in his dapper charcoal gray suit I had to agree. He was lit up with pride for her, no hint in his expression that he was anything other than thrilled to be there, supporting his wife.

My heart was pounding strangely. I hadn't laid eyes on my mother in almost two months—since the day she'd dropped the Mom Bomb and I'd stormed away from the house. I'd spoken to her only once—the day I cut my foot. When she'd walked out tonight for her first entrance I felt as if I were in a vacuum, not so much distant from my own body as apart from it, lost from almost her first line in the story unraveling on the stage. I expected to feel disoriented watching my mother perform, but it didn't feel like I was seeing her at all. The regal, brilliantly scheming, emotionally aching woman on the stage was someone else entirely—a stranger to me. My dad was right—she was a star up there.

When a door at the back of the lobby opened and my mother stepped out of it, I felt tears rush inexplicably to my eyes. Queen Eleanor was gone now, and it was her again—just my mom.

She looked out over the crowd of friends and family milling around talking to their own loved ones in the cast and crew or waiting for someone to come out from backstage. Her gaze landed on my dad, and they just looked at each other for a long moment that felt slowed-down. I saw the uncertainty in her eyes, the hesitation, and then I saw the instant she got what she was looking for. I didn't know what it was—reassurance, validation?—because I couldn't see his face, only her reaction. But I didn't need to see it. She'd looked for him first—looked *to* him—and whatever happened, I knew that in some way everything would be okay.

Dad hung back while Stu and Sasha and I met Mom halfway down the expanse of the lobby. Sasha plunged into a hug; when she pulled back she touched Stu on the elbow in a gentle, familiar way, and he stepped forward and gave Mom his usual one-armed hug and said something I couldn't hear from where I was standing, but it made my mother smile.

And then I was in front of her with my irises. "Mom," I said, and I held them out. She took them and smelled them, even though she was the one who taught me irises had no scent and that was why they were always the perfect flower to bring to a hostess whose preferences and sensitivities you might not know.

"How did you like the show?" she asked me, her face half-hidden amid the purple-and-yellow blooms.

I told her the truth: "You were great, Mom. You are amazing."

She lifted her head up and she was smiling at me with the Mom smile, her camera smile, the one that didn't let her gums show.

"Thank you, Brook Lyn."

I stepped closer to her and wrapped my arms low around her waist, the way I had when I was a little girl, before I had outgrown her and started curling an arm around her shoulders instead.

As I felt her arms come around me, heard the crinkle of the plastic around the flowers brushing my back, smelled her Sung perfume, I hoped she'd heard everything I meant, and that I wasn't just talking about the play.

We had all ridden separately—Sasha and Stu because they were staying at a hotel down in Naples tonight and spending tomorrow at the beach, and my father because, to my surprise, my mother had asked him to come to the cast party with her, as her date.

I drove back home alone, and on the darkened, quiet late-night stretch of Tamiami Trail that led back to Fort Myers I thought about Kendall. About what had gone wrong between us, and how much of it was inevitable because of how raw we'd both been when we started the relationship, and how much I would never understand. I wondered how much of the way I handled our breakup might not have been about Kendall at all, but about the wounded places I'd sectioned off after Michael.

And then, as if evoking his name pried open the compartment I'd shoved him into and slammed shut so tightly, all the memories of our two years together flooded over me like storm surge crashing over a seawall. Finally, I let myself think about Michael. About the way his green eyes had crinkled up at the corners when he smiled.

About his laugh—a loud bark of a thing that made me laugh, too, every time I heard it, even if I didn't know what was funny. About his unbottled enthusiasm about everything he ever took on, whether it was working on a new song or learning to ride a motorcycle...or me.

I remembered the day I met him—we were in adjacent stalls at a self-serve car wash on Gladiolus, and he popped his head around the concrete-block corner to ask—not if I could loan him some quarters, or had change for a bill—but whether I could trade him a dollar for a hundred pennies.

I had smiled as I gave him the dollar and waved off the coins. "Why do you have a hundred pennies?" I asked.

And he shrugged and said, "My dad's a coin collector. He's been trying to find a 1943 copper penny—only forty were ever struck—so I sometimes buy a few rolls just to help him look."

I thought about how little kindnesses like that, those small thoughtful gestures, were so much a part of who he was: taking my car to a gas station every month to check the oil and the wiper fluid and the air in my tires; warming my side of the bed on nights when it got below sixty, because he knew I hated cold sheets; bringing me small gifts for no reason—my favorite candy bar, a CD from an artist I'd mentioned liking, a spray of gladiolus because he noticed them while he was standing in line at the grocery store and knew they were my favorites.

I was happy with Michael—happier than I had ever been in a relationship. But more than that, I was proud. I'd spent my whole adult life helping other people make smart choices, helping them learn not to be self-destructive, how to be rational, to hold high standards for themselves and stick to them. I had never let myself lose my head over a man; never let myself get too deep into a relationship once I realized someone wasn't worth it—never pulled a Sasha. I practiced what I preached to my patients and my friends, I stayed true to my beliefs, and I waited for a man who was everything I said a partner should be. When Michael and I got engaged, I felt like a walking banner for a life well lived, as if I were the perfect embodiment of everything I professed in my practice and among my friends and family, a shining example of how to do it *right*.

I loved Michael. I really did—it was hard not to, with his relish of everyday life, and his energy and sincerity, and his unalterable optimism. But for whatever reason, we hadn't worked out—he had gotten spooked, or changed his mind, or panicked, or who knew what. As with Kendall, I would probably never know all of the reasons it wasn't enough. Why I wasn't enough for him.

But his abrupt departure from my life left me with more than just a broken heart and a head full of confusion. It took away the thing I was most proud of—my judgment—and left me feeling no smarter than anyone else where relationships were concerned. I could see now how much that had hurt me, beyond the pain of losing him. I wasn't just rejected—I'd been invalidated.

Maybe Kendall had simply been a reaction to all of that. He was the exact opposite of Michael—buttoned-up, careful, traditional. Maybe, more than anything, he was an overcorrection.

I thought I'd loved Kendall too...but had I just been proving something to myself? Trying to undo what had happened with Michael, to show myself—and Sasha...and my mother—that I hadn't made a mistake. That I knew what I was doing. That I was still doing it right.

Maybe I'd been so busy judging Kendall as a broken person when I met him, someone to stay far away from where a relationship was concerned, I hadn't seen that *I* was broken too. Broken and not ready to pursue something new with anyone else.

The same way I had been the night I called poor Ben Garrett and used him to palliate my own wounded feelings after Kendall walked out on me.

My mind shifted to Ben. To the way he'd shown up for our date with an open smile on his face; how he drove me home because I wasn't in any shape to drive, and let me take over his car stereo, never complaining even when I was maniacally changing stations like a deejay with ADD; and the way he threw back his head and laughed when I'd turned his ICAN joke around on him.

I'd made every mistake in the book with him—asking him out at the last minute, using him to get back at Kendall, never returning his call after what was actually, for me, a really good date. And he was a good guy. Not perfect. Not the exact "right" type of man. But nice.

Nice was a start. For now, nice was enough.

But I'd never returned his call after our date, and that had been three weeks ago.

I flicked my eyes to the numbers glowing on the dashboard clock. Nearly eleven o'clock on a Saturday night.

Sasha's good advice played through my head as I took a deep breath—into my diaphragm—and let it slowly out. In. Out. *All* of Sasha's good advice played in my head—that I was only human, like everyone else. That mistakes were only stumbles, and you picked up and moved through them, and you did the best you could, and you hoped for the best, and if it didn't happen...you just reached for the people you loved, the ones you could count on, and then you tried again.

I picked up the phone and scrolled through my call history. When I found Ben's name I pressed it; the call connected, and the line rang. Rang. Rang again. Of course—it was Saturday night. What did I expect? Suddenly the ringing stopped and a voice I was surprised seemed so familiar said, "Brook...hi!"

One last breath, because with my suddenly racing heart, I needed it. And then:

"Hi, Ben. I hope it's not too late to call." I meant it in every way possible.

He laughed—the open, warm laugh I remembered from our lone date more than a week ago, and said, "It's a little late. But not too late."

An unexpected smile crawled over my face and I felt something loosen around my chest as I opened my mouth to talk, not sure whether something stupid was going to come out of it, but willing to take the chance.

phoebe fox

Phoebe Fox has been a contributor and regular columnist for a number of national, regional, and local publications; a movie, theater, and book reviewer; a screenwriter; and has even been known to help with homework revisions for nieces and nephews. She lives in Austin, Texas, with her husband and two excellent dogs.

Henery Press Books

And finally, before you go...
Here are a few lively chick lit mysteries
you might enjoy:

BOARD STIFF

Kendel Lynn

An Elliott Lisbon Mystery (#1)

As director of the Ballantyne Foundation on Sea Pine Island, SC, Elliott Lisbon scratches her detective itch by performing discreet inquiries for Foundation donors. Usually nothing more serious than retrieving a pilfered Pomeranian. Until Jane Hatting, Ballantyne board chair, is accused of murder. The Ballantyne's reputation tanks, Jane's headed to a jail cell, and Elliott's sexy ex is the new lieutenant in town.

Armed with moxie and her Mini Coop, Elliott uncovers a trail of blackmail schemes, gambling debts, illicit affairs, and investment scams. But the deeper she digs to clear Jane's name, the guiltier Jane looks. The closer she gets to the truth, the more treacherous her investigation becomes. With victims piling up faster than shells at a clambake, Elliott realizes she's next on the killer's list.

Available at booksellers nationwide and online

Visit www.henerypress.com for details

DINERS, DIVES & DEAD ENDS

Terri L. Austin

A Rose Strickland Mystery (#1)

As a struggling waitress and part-time college student, Rose Strickland's life is stalled in the slow lane. But when her close friend, Axton, disappears, Rose suddenly finds herself serving up more than hot coffee and flapjacks. Now she's hashing it out with sexy bad guys and scrambling to find clues in a race to save Axton before his time runs out.

With her anime-loving bestie, her septuagenarian boss, and a pair of IT wise men along for the ride, Rose discovers political corruption, illegal gambling, and shady corporations. She's gone from zero to sixty and quickly learns when you're speeding down the fast lane, it's easy to crash and burn.

Available at booksellers nationwide and online

Visit www.henerypress.com for details

PILLOW STALK

Diane Vallere

A Mad for Mod Mystery (#1)

Interior Decorator Madison Night has modeled her life after Doris Day's character in *Pillow Talk*, but when a killer targets women dressed like the bubbly actress, Madison's signature sixties style places her in the middle of a homicide investigation.

The local detective connects the new crimes to a twenty-year old cold case, and Madison's long-trusted contractor emerges as the leading suspect. As the body count piles up like a stack of plush pillows, Madison uncovers a Soviet spy, a campaign to destroy all Doris Day movies, and six minutes of film that will change her life forever.

Available at booksellers nationwide and online

Visit www.henerypress.com for details

DOUBLE WHAMMY

Gretchen Archer

A Davis Way Crime Caper (#1)

Davis Way thinks she's hit the jackpot when she lands a job as the fifth wheel on an elite security team at the fabulous Bellissimo Resort and Casino in Biloxi, Mississippi. But once there, she runs straight into her ex-ex husband, a rigged slot machine, her evil twin, and a trail of dead bodies. Davis learns the truth and it does not set her free—in fact, it lands her in the pokey.

Buried under a mistaken identity, unable to seek help from her family, her hot streak runs cold until her landlord Bradley Cole steps in. Make that her landlord, lawyer, and love interest. With his help, Davis must win this high stakes game before her luck runs out.

Available at booksellers nationwide and online

Visit www.henerypress.com for details

OTHER PEOPLE'S BAGGAGE

Kendel Lynn, Gigi Pandian, Diane Vallere

Three interconnected mystery novellas. Baggage claim can be terminal. These are the stories of what happened after three women with a knack for solving mysteries each grabbed the wrong bag.

MIDNIGHT ICE by Diane Vallere: When interior decorator Madison Night crosses the country to distance herself from a recent breakup, she learns it's harder to escape her past than she thought, and diamonds are rarely a girl's best friend.

SWITCH BACK by Kendel Lynn: Ballantyne Foundation director Elliott Lisbon travels to Texas after inheriting an entire town, but when she learns the benefactor was murdered, she must unlock the small town's big secrets or she'll never get out alive.

FOOL'S GOLD by Gigi Pandian: When a world-famous chess set is stolen from a locked room during the Edinburgh Fringe Festival, historian Jaya Jones and her magician best friend must outwit actresses and alchemists to solve the baffling crime.

Available at booksellers nationwide and online

Visit www.henerypress.com for details

FINDING SKY

Susan O'Brien

A Nicki Valentine Mystery

Suburban widow and P.I. in training Nicki Valentine can barely keep track of her two kids, never mind anyone else. But when her best friend's adoption plan is jeopardized by the young birth mother's disappearance, Nicki is persuaded to help. Nearly everyone else believes the teenager ran away, but Nicki trusts her BFF's judgment, and the feeling is mutual.

The case leads where few moms go (teen parties, gang shootings) and places they can't avoid (preschool parties, OB-GYNs' offices). Nicki has everything to lose and much to gain — including the attention of her unnervingly hot P.I. instructor. Thankfully, Nicki is armed with her pesky conscience, occasional babysitters, a fully stocked minivan, and nature's best defense system: women's intuition.

Available October 2014

Visit www.henerypress.com for details

CPSIA information can be obtained at www.ICGtesting.com
Printed in the USA
BVOW06s1950060616

450948BV00011B/94/P

9 781940 976150